Five Spice Street

Five Spice Street

CAN XUE

TRANSLATED BY KAREN GERNANT

AND CHEN ZEPING

YALE UNIVERSITY PRESS ■ NEW HAVEN & LONDON

A MARGELLOS
WORLD REPUBLIC OF LETTERS BOOK

The Margellos World Republic of Letters is dedicated to making literary works from around the globe available in English through translation. It brings to the English-speaking world the work of leading poets, novelists, essayists, philosophers, and playwrights from Europe, Latin America, Africa, Asia, and the Middle East to stimulate international discourse and creative exchange.

This novel was originally published in Chinese under the title *Wu Xiang Jie*. The line drawings, reproduced from the original book, are by Wei Ke.

Set in Electra type by Keystone Typesetting, Inc., Orwigsburg, Pennsylvania. Printed in the United States of America by Sheridan Books, Ann Arbor, Michigan.

Library of Congress Cataloging-in-Publication Data
Canxue, 1953–
[Wu xiang jie. English]
Five spice street / Can Xue ; translated by Karen Gernant and Chen Zeping.
    p. cm. — (Margellos world republic of letters)
ISBN 978-0-300-12227-5 (alk. paper)
I. Gernant, Karen. II. Chen, Zeping. III. Title.
PL2912.A5174W8213   2009
895.1′352—dc22   2008035054

A catalogue record for this book is available from the British Library.

This paper meets the requirements of ANSI/NISO Z39.48-1992 (Permanence of Paper).

10 9 8 7 6 5 4 3 2 1

To Jonathan Brent

CONTENTS

Preliminaries

 1 Madam X's Age and Mr. Q's Looks / 3

 2 Madam X's Occupations / 20

 3 Madam X's and the Widow's
Differing Opinions about "Sex" / 48

 4 Mr. Q and His Family / 68

5 The Failure of Reeducation / 77

 6 Madam X Talks Abstractly of Her Experiences with Men / 85

The Way Things Are Done

 1 A Few Opinions about the Story's Beginning / 99

 2 Some Implications / 151

 3 The Tails' Confessions / 187

 4 Mr. Q's Character / 196

5 Madam X Is Up a Creek / 211

 6 Who Made the First Move? / 216

 7 How to Wrap Up All the
Issues Left Hanging / 244

 8 The Rationality of the Widow's Historical
Contribution and Status / 270

 9 The Vague Positions of Mr. Q and
Madam X's Husband / 283

 10 How We Reversed the Negative
and Elected Madam X Our
Representative / 305

11 Madam X's Steps Are Buoyant; On Broad Five Spice Street, She Walks toward Tomorrow / 319

Preliminaries

1

MADAM X'S AGE AND MR. Q'S LOOKS

When it comes to Madam X's age, opinions differ here on Five Spice Street. One person's guess is as good as another's. There are at least twenty-eight points of view. At one extreme, she's about fifty (for now, let's fix it at fifty); at the other, she's twenty-two.

The one who says she's about fifty is a much-admired forty-five-year-old widow, plump and pretty. Her husband died years ago. It's said that she often sees Madam X making herself up in her room, applying "powder an inch thick" that "completely masks the wrinkles in her neck"—a neck "almost without flesh." What is the widow's vantage point for spying? She indignantly "refuses to divulge it." The writer would like to interject something about this lovely widow. She's classy, a cut above others, and plays a pivotal role in this story. She's influenced the writer his whole life, and he, in turn, has always paid her special respect.

The one who says Madam X is twenty-two is himself twenty-two. In his words, one foggy morning, he "chanced to meet" Madam X by a well; "unexpectedly, she gave him a winsome smile," "revealing a mouthful of white teeth." And from the "uninhibited melody" of her laughter, "the sturdiness" of her teeth, the "sexiness" of her appearance, and various other factors, he concluded that Madam X couldn't be a day over twenty-two. This guy works in a factory that produces coal briquettes, and that's what he said to a neighbor as he squatted in the public toilet after getting off work and washing away the coal dust. "Hmmm," the neighbor wondered. On closer examination, why did he say precisely twenty-two, and not twenty-one or twenty-three? Neighbors see each other all the time, so why hide behind this "chance meeting"? There must be something shameful. Not to mention words that always mean trouble, like "foggy" and "sexiness." Clearly, we must discount much of what he said.

And then there are the twenty-six other opinions, each with some validity. One respectable middle-aged man is worth mentioning. He's a good, loyal friend of Madam X's husband. Whenever someone mentions his good friend's wife, he pulls at the person's sleeve and solemnly proclaims that Madam X is thirty-five, because he's "seen her ID card with his own eyes" (X's family were outsiders on Five Spice Street). His voice would quaver. He would grow livid, but no one appreciated his chivalry. Instead, they thought he was "poking his nose into other people's business"; he was a "hypocrite"; maybe he had even "tasted the sugarplum as well." The man "grew thinner by the day" from this vilification. Dyspepsia gave him bad breath. The one who divulged this was the widow's good friend, a graceful and charming forty-eight-year-old woman.

Once at twilight, these longtime doubts and suspicions seemed to reach a resolution, but it was short-lived. In fact, there were two resolutions. The crowd was split into contending factions. No conclusion could be reached.

It was dusk on a sultry summer day. After dinner, everyone was sitting out on the street to enjoy the cool breeze when suddenly "two balls of white light," like meteors, streamed in the air and Madam X's white silk skirt that "shone all through with light" flashed in front of them. The little boy was also dressed in white, but no one could tell what the material was. When their astonishment subsided, people clamored. The faction of young and middle-aged men led by the young coal worker asserted that Madam X was about twenty-eight. And judging from her "graceful, slender" figure, the "smooth softness" of her arms and legs, and various other factors, they decided that indeed she was "even younger." But the crowd of young and middle-aged women led by the much-admired widow asserted that Madam X was "more than forty-five." Through close inspection, they discovered that her neck had been disguised. Indeed, in several places there were "pores as large as grains of rice" and "layer upon layer of flabby skin." They accused the men of "shamelessly peeking under the woman's skirt." Enlightened, the men inquired with great delight into the particulars of the women's "close inspection." The commotion went on for about two hours. Madam X's husband's good friend constituted a faction by himself: he took on the whole crowd, and several athletic young men knocked him to the ground. He "burst into tears." When it was over, the widow hopped onto a stone table and, thrusting out her full breasts, shouted that she wanted "to uphold the values of traditional aesthetics."

Madam X's age became a major issue on our street. When anyone left a group, he stood his own ground, and so at least twenty-eight different views flourished. No one wanted to argue continuously anymore. Madam X's husband, a thirty-eight-year-old stud, also—without rhyme or reason—simply accepted the young coal worker's view that his wife was twenty-two and not thirty-five, as his good friend had insisted on the basis of her ID card. Weighed down by habit and inertia, he was always tender and affectionate toward his wife. It's said that from the very beginning he "couldn't see a single blemish in her." Consequently, we judged his opinion the most unbelievable, because "it seemed that he didn't use his eyes to look at the truth; he let his imagination run wild. His head was filled with optimism." (These are the widow's words; the facts narrated later bear out the brilliance of her perception.)

The mystery of Madam X's age wasn't resolved, and later, more and more doubts arose. The day after hearing that Madam X and a certain Mr. Q, an office clerk, were involved in a furtive, sneaky way, the much-admired widow secretly entered her room and stole a look at her ID card. She noticed that the column with her age had been artfully altered, but the evidence left by the alteration not only confirmed the widow's estimate, it "proved it precisely." At the same time, another of X's husband's friends—a young man with sideburns —declared that Madam X wasn't thirty-five, but thirty-two, because he and Madam X had been born in the same year and had been childhood sweethearts. Their parents had even considered betrothing them. As for X, in her youth, she had always been shy and tender with him. It was only because he hadn't yet understood male-female relationships that he hadn't allowed their relationship to develop. How could X suddenly have become three years older than he? Several other guys also tried to muddy the waters. Apart from the twenty-eight opinions already noted, one said she was thirty-seven and a half, another said forty-six and a half, another said twenty-nine and a half, and the last claimed twenty-six and a half. With the addition of a half-year's difference, the issue became very profound and philosophical.

Though the matter remains unresolved, let's take her husband's good friend's investigation into her ID card and postulate that she's thirty-five. This is expedient for a number of reasons: we don't have to consider her a young girl (after all, her son is already six years old), nor do we have to consider her an older woman (even though some, like the widow, calculate she was about fifty, which didn't neces-sarily mean that she was an "older" woman—a subtle difference. The widow is precise and knows the nuances of language). As for her husband, he's free to think she's twenty-two if he likes. No one has the right to interfere. We can only wait for him to "wake up" on his own (the widow's words). The stream of drivel from the young coal worker and the guys who deliberately muddied the waters is worth even less. They were merely satisfying their own needs with-out offering an ounce of sincerity.

The controversy about her age was part of a generally vague and contradictory image of Madam X. She is a middle-aged woman, very thin, with white teeth, a neck that's either slender or flabby, skin that's either smooth or rough, a voice that's either melodious or wild, and a body that's either sexy or devoid of sex. When this obscure image takes us by surprise and "discloses its true face," everything unfathomable becomes clear, but only for an instant. Let's put it aside for now.

We can't approve of her husband's impression, because it raises the most questions. Although he's tall and sturdy, and knows how to handle himself around other people, when talk turns to his wife he acts in a feminine, even servile way. Indeed, when he talks, he suddenly becomes stupefied, as if having a seizure. He forgets the thread of the conversation and suggests that you play "hopscotch" with him. Right away he finds some chalk to draw a grid on the ground. If you refuse, he just forgets about you and throws himself into hopscotch.

The image of Madam X's adulterer (that's the way everyone referred to Mr. Q) was the most shocking of all. Out of a sense of duty, the much-admired widow had torn open a letter of his to Madam X. The letter revealed that the first time Mr. Q looked at X's face, he saw *only one* immense continuously flickering saffron-colored eyeball. Then he swooned and couldn't see a thing. To the very end of the scandal, he never *got a good look* at Madam X. He didn't because he *couldn't*. When Madam X was in front of him, all he could see was one saffron-colored eyeball, and when that eyeball flickered, hot tears welled up in his eyes. How could he see clearly? Perhaps his letter was deliberately mystifying, designed to win favor with Madam X's odd, shadowy mentality. Maybe it was code or double-talk.

The odd thing is that Madam X's confession echoed his, and it preceded their acquaintance. (This information is supplied by Madam X's colleague. Madam X loved unburdening herself in non-sensical ways and could hold nothing back. She was uninhibited with this woman, whose temperament was diametrically opposed to hers. If it had been possible, she would have "unburdened herself to the whole world.") Back then, she sat in her gloomy room, happily preening and boasting, "The reason my eyeballs are so exceptional is that I pay them close attention. I'm not kidding. I observe them constantly in a mirror—even when walking, I always carry a small round mirror and constantly take it out for a look. I'd really love to see what they're like when I'm sleeping. It's impossible, but I just wonder what they're up to. What is so hard at work behind these lenses? I've done research on their excretions. I have a microscope, which I bought especially for this purpose. I'm simply fascinated and have made a lot of headway. I've also collected some mirrors for my little darling Bao (note: her only son). When he gets a little older, I want to get him interested in his own eyeballs. Everyone says that eyes are windows to the soul, but no one thinks about this window. They forget this window and let it collect dust until it's changed beyond recognition." She blinked as she talked, and kept raising her eyebrows for emphasis.

Although she stressed this often, her colleague saw no proof of her supernatural ability, nor did anyone else on the whole of Five Spice Street—including her husband, who cherished his wife very much. Was Mr. Q the only person who recognized Madam X's supernatural power? Maybe this isn't exactly right, because the world is a lot larger than Five Spice Street. Moreover, judging by the coal worker's statement, didn't X have a certain indefinable "sex appeal"? Who could guarantee that men outside Five Spice Street wouldn't notice her supernatural sexual power when smitten by her? How could you dismiss this possibility just because her husband didn't see it?

Or—another take on it: we certainly aren't suggesting that Mr. Q's perception of Madam X's supernatural power amounts to understanding her completely and profoundly. Rather, he understands her only superficially, in a one-dimensional way. Q has one major failing: he doesn't like to inquire into another person's background and never asks about anyone's business. He prefers to be alone, where he can speak his thoughts out loud and fancy himself a passionate lover. Mr. Q and Madam X became acquainted by chance and later consorted with each other for six months, but he's never known her real age. In this respect, Mr. Q isn't like Madam X's husband, who assumes she's twenty-two, but probably is closer to the truth in postulating that she's twenty-eight or twenty-nine. Of course, this is partly out of selfishness and desire, but we won't go into this for the moment.

Speaking of Mr. Q's superficial understanding of Madam X and the absurdity of their relationship, we can illustrate this with a dialogue supplied by Madam X's colleague.

X: I don't have to look for you intentionally. You'll surely come. (X playfully affected a drowsy expression.)

Q: Through the crowds of people, I've always walked toward your eyes. I'm confused and muddled, seeing nothing, including you. (Q was acting like an idiot, like a dolt.)

X: We'll meet each other every Wednesday at a certain intersection. Even if we wanted to avoid this, we couldn't.

Q: Perhaps I'll turn into a long-tailed pheasant; then I'll be able to perch on a high tree limb.

The colleague reinforced this dialogue with the following information: every time they met, their talk seemed a continuation of their last conversation; it was also completely meaningless nonsense, always on the same topic. What's more, each time, neither greeted the other, as if they were continuing their previous encounter. But when they talked, it was as if—apart from crazy talk—anything else (for example, greetings, introductions, remarks about the things around them) was superfluous, discordant. At this point, the colleague covered half her mouth and said in a thin voice, "Is this a sort of 'concealed person'—'The Invisible'?" With that, her hair stood on end, and she didn't dare continue.

As for Mr. Q's looks, although there aren't as many opinions about it as about Madam X's age, opinions do differ here on Five Spice Street. We need to stress a little something: our people don't really like talking about a man's appearance, because they embrace the proverb: There's no such thing as an ugly man. So what does Mr. Q look like? All we have to rely on is the odd adjective and a few unintentional changes in the tone of people's conversations.

The first to produce an impression of Mr. Q's looks was the widow's forty-eight-year-old friend. She thought "there was nothing remarkable" about Mr. Q (she curled her lip and spat). She "couldn't even remember what he looked like," "he seemed to be a big dumb guy," "anyhow, he couldn't be more ordinary." After saying this, she felt she'd lost some dignity and immediately changed the subject. She began talking of the miraculous effects of *qigong.** As she spoke, she tossed her head, as if to rid her mind of "disturbing thoughts."

---

* In traditional Chinese medicine, the use of movement, meditation, and regulation of breathing to improve health.

On the surface, the women of Five Spice Street had no interest in Mr. Q's looks, never mind observing him in detail. If you put the question to them directly, they would answer in three words: he is ugly. Did the women of Five Spice Street never make eye contact with Mr. Q? Actually, that's not the case. After all, those adjectives and the strange tone of voice used to describe him were almost all produced by these women. Speaking of Q, they hedged and evaded, talking lightly and indirectly. Doesn't this show tremendous interest and sensitivity? Sometimes they affected indifference. One might raise the topic, circle all around it, and then return to sounding out a second person so that this second person would bring up what the first had wanted to say. Thus, they enjoyed a sense of satisfaction.

All of Five Spice Street's women were masters of this conversational art. For example, the widow's female friend, after talking at length about qigong, touched on ethnography, leading to a line from a folk song: "Southern Women and Northern Men." When the other person fully understood this line, she would shift the topic from northern men to a man of big stature. Then, both would come around to the issue of Q's looks. Through suggestive language they bounced this topic back and forth until dark, when each happily exclaimed, "I had a really good time today!"

The second to come up with an impression of Q was a lame woman who hadn't been able to get out of bed for years. She was twenty-eight, all bones. A kind of ray emanated from her sunken, jet-black eyes. That ray at any moment could force young men to "retreat thirty feet" (the widow's words). The first day that Q came to Five Spice Street, she saw him once. At the time, she was opening the curtains next to her bed (of course, her bed was next to the window). When Q walked by, their eyes met. Summoning all her strength, the woman fixed him with her gaze for a full twenty-five seconds (her estimate). At first, Mr. Q was flustered, and with one hand warded off the ray from her eyes, but then, instead of "retreating thirty feet," he reluctantly smiled and walked on. The woman opened her window with a *peng* and shouted shrilly at Mr. Q's receding figure, "A wolfhound! A wolfhound! Please look out for thunder!" Later, feeling sentimental, the lame woman said, Mr. Q certainly wasn't like a wolf, but rather like a catfish instead: he had a barbel-like mustache. When he shaved, he got rid of it, but if you looked carefully, you could still see it. The one who looked like a wolfhound was the scoundrel who had taken her virginity years earlier. Q merely resembled him in certain ways. Precisely because of this, as soon as she set eyes on him, she was incensed and launched an attack. That's the only way she could express her hatred.

Still, Q wasn't the first who looked like him. Over the years, she had cussed out countless people. That's the only way she could maintain her equanimity. She added that she hated the wolfhound most—well, not for taking her virginity, but for daring after just one night to "take off without a word of farewell." This was enough to torment a woman with regret for a lifetime. If only he would repent, she said, and then kneel before her and beg forgiveness, she could consider forgiving him for deflowering her. This, however, didn't mean that she wanted even a hint of a relationship, because after "having her heart broken" that night, she became "clear-headed and methodical." Had she with great difficulty vanquished external and internal pressures and become an iron woman who wanted to suffer all over again? No! All the guys harboring this illusion were wrong. The lame woman's description of Q certainly couldn't be taken as true, because she thought Q resembled her former lover, whose very existence was doubtful. Never mind that she hadn't gotten a good look at Q. No one had seen her lover either, and even she couldn't say for sure what he looked like. Was there any chance that she had pulled this out of thin air? Or was it possible that she was deliberately spreading misinformation and taking the opportunity to raise her own status? Why didn't she even have a photo or two of her lover? (If she had, wouldn't she have shown it around a long time ago?!) Even worse, perhaps there'd been no lover, and that's why she had stared at Q and picked a quarrel. Was this merely her way of flirting and vamping? (When foxes can't eat grapes, they say grapes are catfish.) If this was so, then we on Five Spice Street should congratulate Q for not falling into her trap. When all is said and done, it would have been ten thousand times worse to be seduced by her than by X.

The third to notice Q's looks was a woman who claimed she was X's younger sister and also that she herself was twenty-nine. (Nobody could prove this.) When Q first arrived on Five Spice Street, she and her older sister had been together the whole day "from beginning to end." She had "carefully taken stock of Q for a long time" and noticed that Q's appearance looked "very familiar." Even though "there was not the slightest similarity" to her sister's appearance, it seemed as if "there was a kind of invisible connection to it." But as to any special characteristics of Q's looks, she weaseled and said, "You'll know when you see him," "It's something you feel but can't describe," "Anyhow, there's something a little bizarre," "You can't judge him by traditional aesthetics," and so forth. You knew she was covering up for her sister. Her words revealed neither intelligence nor clear-headed analysis. She's muddle-headed and obstinate; her biased views are worthless.

We have one more piece of information for the readers: this younger sister, or anyhow the one who called herself a younger sister, abandoned her simple and tolerant husband later on to take up with another man. It was an "amicable settlement," and they are still on "good terms with each other." This made everyone realize: a person like X is certainly not an immortal set apart from the world. Careful analysis shows that she carries a malignant disease (affected people don't realize they're sick). She also can manipulate people behind their backs. Isn't she the one who sent the whole of Five Spice Street into foolish turmoil, making everyone wild with lust? Without setting foot outside her house, she stirred things up as if mustering an army, made it impossible for all the people the length of the street to defend themselves, and created bedlam. Where did her power come from? Why were people close to her (including her husband, younger sister, son, and Q) completely taken in and changed until they did odd and inexplicable things—and moreover did them brazenly without a thought? Was this all caused by X's supernatural ability? Doesn't this sound dubious? What kind of education had X received to grow up like this? It's a riddle. In any case, all it took was for her to move her eyeballs and people on Five Spice Street would break out in a rash. When she talked to herself in the middle of the night, everyone on the street listened intently in their dreams. According to the writer's tally, at least two persons wanted to sacrifice their lives for her under any circumstances. Eventually, they moved to roadside work sheds and lived tragic lives filled with hardship, *all* because of X.

The fourth person who noticed Mr. Q's appearance was a widow so old she looked like dry bamboo. She wore a little black felt hat on her little bald head, and she nodded all day long, like a chicken pecking rice. It was quite by chance that she noticed Mr. Q. At dusk on a winter day, a deliveryman was unable to pull his load of coal to her home because of the steep grade. The old dame looked all around for assistance. Only one person came to help: Q. Afterwards, she grabbed the front of Q's coat by the buttons to steady herself. She looked him all over and then finally exclaimed, "What a large face—broad enough to hold mountains and rivers!" A fleeting impulse caused her to make this remark. Before long, she forgot the incident, even Q. If someone mentioned Q, she confused Q with one of her cousins from long ago (whether this cousin actually existed was extremely doubtful) and thought of them as one and the same. She talked at length of how marvelous her cousin's "square face" was. All the while, she nodded, pecking rice. She was very old and began hallucinating easily. Later, she hallucinated almost continuously. Her eyes would cross and she'd swallow saliva while she talked. Once begun, there was no end to it—*gudong gudong.* It was distressing. Someone raised doubts: had the old woman hallucinated what happened at twilight on that winter day? She was so old and her vision so blurry, could she have been mistaken about who it was? Suppose that the one who helped lug the coal was in fact her nephew (she insisted that this nephew hadn't entered her house for more than twenty years), and that because of the grudge she'd felt toward him for more than twenty years, she had purposely concealed his benevolence and instead had given the credit to a certain

Q, who was then being talked about: this was entirely possible and reasonable. From her wild talk about his face being "roomy enough to hold mountains and rivers," you could spot the flaws in her statement. Her impression of Q's looks boiled down to one point: he had a very broad face. But "holding mountains and rivers," this shocking image—applied so impulsively—must have some other meaning.

Had the old woman been rejuvenated in a trance and hallucinated that she'd run into a sweetheart from the past, clung fast to him, and persisted in a passionate daydream? Did this have anything to do with "hallucinogens"? Someone raised another doubt: was she pretending to be crazy in order to monopolize Q? Q dominated everyone's conversations—everyone was interested in him—and now through chicanery this old woman had appropriated him for herself, and insisted that he was some old lover from thirty years ago, even though it was clear that Q was young. She brooked no disagreement. If this world conformed to her wishes, who knew what might happen?

The fifth who noticed Q's appearance was a man, the husband. As the saying goes, Beauty is in the eyes of the beholder. But in today's world, that isn't quite right, because even rivals in love see the beauty in each other. Madam X's husband is unusually handsome (the widow, the widow's female friend, and everyone living on Five Spice Street think so). Too bad he was completely in the dark about it: even if someone told him, he'd be surprised and then immediately forget it. He was uninterested in his own appearance and cared nothing about other people's opinions of him. Perhaps it can be said that he was "self-confident." His feelings were like a baby's—innocent and good, but a little stubborn. As a cuckold, he probably drew more attention than anyone else on Five Spice Street, but he acted just the same: letting well enough alone, calmly going about his business, as if nothing were happening. The women led by the widow had thoroughly researched his attitudes and finally produced a physiological explanation "inappropriate to explain" in front of others. (When she mentioned the "reason," the widow poked her female friend in the waist and flushed a deep red.) The husband had only one word for Q's appearance: handsome. Once he unintentionally mentioned this to his good friend (the one who had looked into Madam X's age), and after his friend's wife heard this, it spread fast. This was a great revelation for Five Spice Street residents, who had been speculating, but without much to show for it; now all their doubts vanished. They greatly admired the widow's genius for probing, especially when they went a step further and came up with the term "eunuch's psychology" to describe the husband. What joy they felt at having come up so spontaneously with this diagnosis.

Everything happened behind his back. Indifferent, Madam X's husband shut the door as usual and went on with his days, and as usual was haughty and cold toward other women. He walked with his head high and his chest thrust out, making it clear that he didn't look at any woman except X. It really drove the women of Five Spice Street crazy. True, they couldn't all be considered beautiful, but there were some who were sophisticated and elegant, and others who were warm and affectionate. The widow, for example. In no respect could Madam X—this skinny monkey—compare with her. And she herself said that although she was more than forty-five years old, she "had never been defeated by any man," "she wouldn't mind if as many as two hundred men showed up at once." She whispered all this to X's colleague, who broadcast it to all the residents of Five Spice Street. She made so much noise that all the middle-aged and young men (and even some of the old men) were squinting and itching to try. The widow also said (in a loud voice this time) that his haughtiness was a pose; she didn't think it was genuine but rather showed his desperate inner struggle to keep his lust under control. Whenever—with her full breasts thrust out—she encountered him, she "saw with a sidelong glance" that he was "shaking all over" and "twitching as if insane." Just "one look from her" would cause his line of defense to "collapse." But, as everybody knew, she had always been an honest, straightforward woman. Ever since her husband died, she had cultivated herself through meditation, so now she had few desires and no interest in this sort of game. Consequently, his longing for her was nothing more than a hopeless dream. She would "never be moved by it."

There were many other opinions about Q's appearance, but for reasons of space, we won't mention them. The opinions of these five people produce a blurred, mutually conflicting impression: Q is a large man, either ugly or handsome, or with nothing remarkable about him, with a broad square face and an odd expression—he looks a little like a catfish.

We still haven't mentioned the opinion of an extremely important person: X. How does X view Q? How could we forget her? Without her, there would be no story! Her image of Q was simple: *"I've never laid eyes on him."* Someone doubted this: wasn't X joking —playing with words? No, "what she said was sincere" (the female colleague's words). In truth, X *didn't look at people with her eyes.* (Here, she was much different from Q. Q wanted to look at people with his eyes, but some obstacle always prevented him. For example, when he looked at X, his tear glands turned into a major obstacle. Thus, Q's disposition wasn't nearly as clear-cut as X's, but was always hovering between seeing and not seeing, always ambiguous.) Someone else suggested: maybe X has never laid eyes on her husband—this handsome man—either, and so she has no idea that he's so handsome and therefore she mistakenly cast him off and got hung up on "the ugly" Q? Wasn't this the most regrettable thing she'd ever done in her whole life? Not necessarily. You have to realize that X hasn't always been like this. When she was young, she *chose* this handsome man only with her eyes; she reeled him in and they became husband and wife. X's personality grew ever more eccentric and inappropriate since she began her occult practices (about this, later). After she bought the mirrors and the microscope from the junk shop, she even announced that her eyes "had retired." That is, except for things in the mirror, she looked at nothing. Some people were unconvinced, for this presumed that X hadn't seen Q and didn't know what he looked like, and thus she didn't have any way of knowing if he even existed. How could she have a relationship with him? Here something is worth emphasizing: that is, X definitely knows what Q looks like, though without seeing Q with *her eyes*. Instead, she senses him by means of a supernatural ability. This is *ten thousand times truer* than seeing. (X's own words.) This only seems absurd. According to the colleague's report: on a certain fine morning, she saw X—as usual—walking along the crowded main street, looking in her mirror and taking bold strides, as if she had some sure plan in mind. The colleague swooped down. Scurrying up, she seized hold of X's shoulders and carefully took stock of her eyes. Her appraisal of X's eyeballs left her "speechless": "all the life had gone out of them, and they had lost any ability to see." The colleague sighed sympathetically. "It's self-glorification and a hair-splitting mentality that have poisoned her. If she were a little more objective, she would have noticed a long time ago another woman right next to her who was in fact much more remarkable than she, though she had never openly entered into a contest with her. X wouldn't have ended up this way if she'd been aware of it." (From this, we can also infer: in his letter, Q's strange description of X's eyeballs was probably something he imagined.)

Okay, since X did not see Q with her eyes but "sensed" him, we'll take a look at what this "Q" she sensed was all about. X's younger sister divulged that X had said that Q was the man she would meet at the intersection on Wednesdays: he wore a woolen overcoat (actually, Q didn't even have a woolen overcoat), his voice was deep (this was essentially true), and his eyes possessed at least five different colors. (How could this be?!) She had no interest in men with sonorous voices and monochromatic eyes. Now she had met Q, and his eyes were precisely the eyes she had "sought in her dreams." She didn't have to mention his deep voice. With Q it was "the second time she fell in love." When she said this, X lost control, ripping a sheet of white paper into scraps with her long, slender fingers and then tossing them into the air, where they flew up like butterflies. Such behavior suggests "hallucinatory drugs."

"Hallucinatory drugs" also suggests another of X's strange hobbies. Anyone who looks for X knows that X hides in the bedroom to engage in some kind of activity involving the sounds of jumping and other noises whose cause is unknown. At such times, through a crack in the door, she sometimes tells people, "Please wait a moment." The wait might be long or short, sometimes ten minutes and sometimes more than half an hour. While she engaged in this secret activity, it didn't matter who it was; no one—not even her husband or her darling son—could go in. Because of the curtains, no one knew what she was doing. It's to the widow's credit that Five Spice Street's residents aren't still fretting over this. It was a rainy night when the much-admired widow obtained first-hand information. (She announced that her method was a secret.) It was dark outside the window. Listening to the rain, the widow reported to several residents that what X was concealing inside the room was "downright dull" and she "couldn't figure out what possible pleasure lay in it." Her activity was nothing more than skipping naked back and forth in front of the mirror like a little child (she had a large full-length mirror, bought second-hand; the image was unusually clear and true). Then she kicked, bent over, and turned around and around to appraise her waist, her breasts, her rear end, her legs, and other spots. "She struck a flirtatious pose" and "was unbearably vulgar." In fact, you couldn't say her breasts were the least bit full; at most, they weren't any better than a teenage girl's. A mature woman naturally ought to have mature beauty—a lingering, winning charm in order to bewitch men. What did such childish breasts and a tiny wasp-like waist count for? Could this world be upside down? Why was Madam X so happy with herself, going so far as to look at her reflection for an hour or two every day? Did she behold a non-existent phantom? It's said that this is a symptom of hysteria. After finishing her report, the widow told the residents: Madam X's inner world is arrogant, narcissistic, and selfish. She attaches so much importance to her body: every day, she closes the door and looks at it, and yet to the people all around, she claims "not to use her eyes to see them," her eyes were "retired," she "didn't have any feelings" because she had "grown a plate of steel on her body." After hearing the widow's report, Five Spice Street's residents felt a load had been lifted from their shoulders.

The people of Five Spice Street had bitterly despised and feared

X's behavior behind closed doors, and they'd come up with a lot of strange ideas: one said that X was manufacturing dynamite in the house and getting ready to set it off in the public toilet; one said she was raising scorpions and planning to retaliate against the people who had talked about her; one said she was practicing certain "arts" and could force a person into the grave using only her idiodynamics; and still another, who thought himself clever, said that X was working on ways to make herself invisible, because he had once peeped inside, and no one was there, yet he had heard scuffling and kicking. Of course, the widow later refuted this. After learning what Madam X was doing inside, some gossips thought that people would want to drill holes in the wall of Madam X's home and wait to feast their eyes. What would they wait for? What would they get from it? Nothing. Not only did crowds of people not drill holes but they never brought this matter up again.

2

MADAM X'S OCCUPATIONS

Madam X and her husband manage a small snack shop located on the corner. They sell sautéed broad beans, fried broad beans, five spice melon seeds, plain melon seeds, sautéed peanuts, fried peanuts, and so on. They employ no workers. Every day the husband goes somewhere and hauls back fresh broad beans, peanuts, and melon seeds. Then they wash, cook, and sell them. Generally, they're extremely busy, and all year long, aromas waft from this corner. We've mentioned that Madam X and her family are outsiders. Before coming here, what kind of work did they do? They never want to talk about this. Only when forced will they reply, with a smile, "We made our living by searching garbage heaps for odds and ends." Finally, when there was a general survey of the residents, in the column on the form having to do with their prior work, they wrote "party cadres." The neighbors were greatly surprised: if they had been "government employees" before coming here, then how had they sunk so low as to be running a snack shop, totally unrelated to the government? From being government employees to selling broad beans was like dropping from heaven into hell: had they caused some trouble in their office and been driven out? The residents of Five Spice Street believed that something terribly shocking was being covered up. Day and night, they felt uneasy. For example: why couldn't these two ever just be like the others on Five Spice Street and become part of the community? Certainly no one had stopped them from doing this! Why did they always have to engage in secretive activity, causing others to be doubly wary and suspicious?

On the surface, they seemed urbane and ordinary, but the people of Five Spice Street sniffed out something not quite right—completely unusual—from their reserved manner and distracted demeanor. They intuitively sensed that they were dissidents, and on this basis excluded them from the Five Spice Street community. But these two not only continued their snack stand with a clear conscience, they gloried in it, as if this were some high-class livelihood worth flaunting. They also indoctrinated their son, Little Bao: if someone asked him what—ideally—he would choose to do when he grew up, he answered without hesitation, "Work in a snack shop."

The snack shop is Madam X and her husband's public occupation. Madam X also has a secret business that everyone knows about; she chose a complicated name for it: "diversion to dispel boredom—or mischief-making." Nobody can say for sure what this is: when others investigate, they learn nothing. If you question those who take part in it, it's even more tangled and unclear, for they explain things in double-talk: "If you close your eyes, you'll see the spectacle of spaceships and the Earth colliding," "a twig poked through a red heart and a blue heart and hanging in midair," "ten articles of clothing are hanging in the closet; if you take one out, you can sense the body heat in it."

From the first day that X came to Five Spice Street, she stealthily pursued this "diversion to dispel boredom." Most who seek her out are boys and girls in their early teens. Her activity continues smoothly when they are present, but she doesn't take any fee. (To tell the truth, Madam X's expression is unfathomable; it's still debatable whether she even sees these people who show up in her room.) Once, her activity was investigated by the authorities; then, because of insufficient evidence, she got away with paying a 100-yuan fine and spending a week being forced to study relevant regulations. After this incident, Madam X became even more aggressive and reckless. She didn't mind being degenerate. What kind of activity is Madam X engaged in? What does her activity lead to, and does it have any influence? Why—as if possessed—do young boys and girls go to her small room? What lures them? It isn't just the government's investigative unit but also the much-admired widow who can't answer these questions.

The widow broke into Madam X's inner room numerous times at night, using her admirable spirit of exploration, and spent several nights with Madam X and her young confederates. She left no stone unturned in her questioning. She even placed a stethoscope, cold, on the napes of their necks to listen from behind their backs. She took great pains but learned very little indeed.

The widow discovered they were in a kind of helpless state. They sat next to each other, propped against the wall, staring into little mirrors taken from Madam X's table, unmoving—like porcelain dolls. They kept this up all night long: it was deadly boring. The widow stood in the middle of the room, feeling an immaterial blast. Weird multi-colored flames seemed to leap from the mirrors into midair and broiled her until she perspired. She thought of leaving, but felt uneasy, so, gritting her teeth, she stood and stared: there wasn't any fire, and the porcelain figures sat leaning against the wall, unmoving, as always. Her expression tense and absorbed, Madam X was observing things on the glass plate with her microscope. At last, she said, "That's all." Then everyone's face glowed red. (Clear-eyed people could see that actually Madam X was talking to herself when she said "That's all.") On the way home, these kids were high as kites, chasing and teasing each other, all of a sudden climbing trees and leaping down, and at the same time loudly cursing Madam X as a "scoundrel," "making fun of people when she has nothing better to do," "experimenting with our nerves." "She thinks she's a fantastic genius, but in fact she's no better than dog shit." "What would happen if everyone played this kind of game?!" "Should the government restrict such activity?" And so on and on. It seemed difficult for them to supply any information, because they couldn't grasp what they had experienced. They were indifferent to its significance. Perhaps we can say that they went into Madam X's home because of a mysterious summons which often appeared on a starlit night. At the time, they didn't analyze it carefully and quickly forgot the intermittent disturbing sound. Now the strange sound is particularly intense, like bees singing. It comes from the demonic mirrors Madam X is fiddling with. Each mirror is a wonder that sends indescribable things into those numb eardrums, thus causing young people unwittingly to open their mouths wide as if inspired. We can also say that they go to Madam X's home because they mistakenly believe that she is one of them; they want to advance with her hand in hand. But after entering her room and seeing Madam X's numb expression and her deliberately superior act, they can't help but feel indignant. And then how can they still remember the original notion?

The widow was very disappointed. But she didn't believe in demons and had to get to the bottom of this. One after another, she took each by the scruff of the neck and shook the truth out. They were as if in a trance, all vague about the matter: "My body felt as if it wasn't my own—I was speechless with happiness." "I became confident of my lungs and heart." "Starlight blazed overhead; I was flying." "Secretly getting revenge, but abhorring the one who goaded me into it"—and other strange talk like this. They might as well have said nothing. So, did the widow draw a blank? Could she think of no other way to get to the essence of this business? Hardly. Our widow did not back away from difficulties. After several days of painful vacillation, she had a brainstorm. She made up her mind to find another way to break through. She gave chase for a long time. In a corner of a remote alley, she nabbed Madam X's husband—this strapping guy, this virginal and handsome man. Rubbing her breasts against his arms, she brought her face close to his arm and caught him completely off guard. Below is their conversation:

The widow: Which part of a woman's body is the most attractive? (She repeatedly hinted with her breasts and blushed with excitement.)

Madam X's husband: Why are you blocking my way?

The widow: I'm asking: What part of a woman's body does a man look at first? What causes his blood to boil until he can't control himself? Answer this question or I won't let you go.

Madam X's husband (looking embarrassed): It's complicated.

I'm not an expert. It depends on the man, and there are all kinds of men with different standards. . . . The most attractive? Hey, why won't you leave me alone? Do you take me for a fool?

The widow (despairing): There's no single criterion? Is there no justice in this world? If demons control men, what's the meaning of life? You guys really are pathetic!

Madam X's husband: Don't be unreasonable. You're asking for trouble.

The widow: What do you know? You mama's boy: have you ever experienced overwhelming joy? Have you ever been excited by a mature woman? You're afraid even to try, aren't you? You must be suffering from a disease! Is your wife's "dispelling boredom" connected to your illness? Answer me. Don't think I'm interested in you. All my life I've abhorred baby-like men, androgynous men like you! Can such a person kindle anyone's desire? I've always looked down on you. Sorry, what did I just ask? Oh yes, what does your wife do at night?

Madam X's husband: None of your business! You're crazy! (He withdrew from her ample breasts and left, swinging his arms.)

The widow (as if waking from a dream): Ah!

Our widow had been humiliated. Should she retreat and distance herself from Madam X's family? Of course not. Did she represent only her own bias? In fact, these blows only strengthened her belief, and consequently, she grew even more obdurate. Moreover, before long, the situation took a turn for the better. This time, the widow didn't act as usual: she didn't announce the results of her investigation. She didn't say even one word. The inside situation she understood was exclusively in her mind, and that world was rich and colorful. When someone impatiently asked about the inside situation, she narrowed the spidery lines around her eyes and squeezed out a significant sort of smile. Hands behind her back, she circled around that person a few times and then slapped him on the butt and laughed out loud. She laughed and laughed until the one who had asked the question flushed purple and didn't dare look up. Then she came up to him slowly and whispered in his ear, "Which do you prefer—a malnourished young girl or a healthy grown woman?" At the same time, she leered and pinched him until he was scared out of his wits. Finally, she shouted, "What do you take me for? Get out of here!"

At the same time, all the passersby saw a strange design on the whitewashed wall of Madam X's home. It was a charcoal drawing of a penis, a crude and childish work. Below it was a postscript: an illustration of a certain person's second occupation. Madam X gave no evidence she was angry; instead it was as if she'd found a treasure. She was excited for several days and recited these words to herself over and over: had she finally met a kindred soul in the darkness? Where was this person whose feelings struck a chord with her own? Why did he (she) contact her in this odd way? She thought and thought and finally had an inspiration: she decided to go ahead regardless. She placed a long table in the doorway and, light as a swallow, jumped onto the table and lectured to the air. The Five Spice Street crowds thronged there to watch the show. Everything she said seemed to be about sex, including "sexual intercourse" and other matters offensive to their ears. She sobbed as she lectured, and her throat quivered in a few key places. She said a friend would arrive soon; she thought about him or her day and night. She also said the thing she was involved in was the best, most wonderful, lofty thing: one day, it would all be clear. To make this happen, she had lived through her microscope for a long time. "This thing is so powerful!"

"Her speech made us want to try it; I think she's a great psychologist," the coal worker said earnestly, sighing with admiration.

"This kind of woman is so hot!" Old Meng, the fortune-teller from the pharmacy, was a little intoxicated as he narrowed his eyes. "I'm more than eighty years old—been with a lot of women in my time. Nowadays, some young people are quite unreasonable and don't have any respect for their elders, and even say we're just old rubbish. In fact, we might be better at it. One day, I'll prove it: sexual prowess isn't affected by aging. Not only isn't it affected, but it gets even better with age. I can go on forever, but they can't—these young sons-of-bitches!" He raised his skinny fist to show off his strength to the coal worker and the other young guys. "I'm much tougher than they are! If you don't believe it, just try me! Madam X's speech has made me feel young again. But her talking about this in public shows she has a problem. It's okay if a woman is horny, but flaunting it in public is too much! How can that be acceptable? Have we all gone crazy?"

"She meant these words for me," Madam X's first youthful love said. "She's been repressed a long time. I used to sympathize with her. Now she's a complete mess—talking nonsense all the time, no matter what the occasion. This has totally ruined my impression of her. What does she mean by this publicity stunt? When I saw her standing there, I felt only hatred in my heart: all at once, my wild love for her vanished without a trace. Although everything began because of me, from this point on, I swear I am her enemy: she's wounded my pride too much. How can a woman talk in public of her private affairs? Let's say a woman's lust is heating up and it's hard for her to control herself—still, she should do things in secret. This woman is just the opposite: ordinarily she pretends to be decent. If you proposition her, she turns you down cold, holds you at arm's length, and you would never imagine that she could pull something like this! I really can't stand it!"

The audience was growing larger: realizing that something was amiss, Madam X's husband worked his way anxiously through the crowd, intent on reaching Madam X's side. He was sweating profusely. At last, he shoved his way to a spot behind her and tugged at a corner of her clothing, trying to warn her of the growing danger. The other men thought he was going to monopolize Madam X and shouted angrily. They tripped him, and he fell over.

Madam X's emotions ran high, her daydreams came one on top of another, and she paid no attention to anything around her. She had no idea that someone was tugging at her, nor did she know who was in the audience. In fact, she hadn't expected anyone to listen to her lecture; she was talking to the people she only imagined. Flickering waves of light, radiated from her eyes and changed the people's faces into grotesque shapes. But from her own point of view, her shining eyes were blind—a sorry state of affairs indeed. If we could have chosen, we'd have preferred a pair of ordinary eyes to eyes shining with this strange light. Madam X herself wasn't sorrowful: she said she was accustomed to being blind; nothing suited her better. She also exulted over now being so "free and unfettered," "taking to the water like a duck"! She kept talking like this, bubbling over with sentiment and wit. As she talked, she sometimes interrupted herself to say, "I'm so moved by my own words, I could almost die." This was indeed a strange sort of consciousness: who could be so "moved"? Even "moved to death"?

Madam X was unaware that the crowd was squirming: things were coming to a head. Madam X's husband saw the danger signs and prepared to risk his life to protect his wife. He stopped trying to dissuade her, for he knew her nature and understood this wouldn't have the least effect. He watched tensely, waiting.

A crowd's emotions are always subtle, like the colored glass in a kaleidoscope. The audience had listened in a confusing mist to her nonsense for more than half an hour, straining to ponder the significance of her words. The men in the front row stretched out their arms, longing to pinch this young woman's cheeks or thighs; the men in the back were filled with indignation, wishing they could take the places of the ones in front. Suddenly, someone threw the first melon peel from the back (someone said it was from the widow's window). It scored a lucky hit and stuck to Madam X's left cheek. And then stones and tiles rained down on her. Her husband risked his life to protect her, and the two of them fled into their little house. They didn't even dare breathe. Yet their window was smashed, leaving a huge hole, and Madam X's calf was so badly hurt that "for two weeks, she couldn't work in the snack shop." It appeared that Madam X had lost: maybe she could pretend to be blind and not look at others, but the eyes of the public were fixed on her every movement. She was forced to recognize that the crowd's emotions were dangerous and volatile, and this left her even more dispirited. Her husband was so distressed that he sighed and groaned continuously and ran all over the city as if he were crazy, in search of "an herbal cure for the injury."

After two weeks, Madam X's leg wound was healed, but she hadn't recovered from the trauma to her soul. She had to work in the snack shop for her livelihood, but the rest of the time, Madam X was in a stupor: sometimes after she woke up, she didn't even recognize the people close to her (her husband and son) but called them "those people." The game of "dispelling boredom" naturally was also done away with. In her stupor, she ate almost nothing. She was on the way to becoming a transparent ghost, wandering back and forth in silence. Every day, when it was time to turn on the lights, the people of Five Spice Street saw the handsome husband leading his darling son, Little Bao, by the hand and supporting a pallid transparent shadow with the other hand for a leisurely walk along the crow-black river. They walked a few steps and then stopped, listening intently to the billowing river. Their son kept skipping along and throwing stones into the water: he was happy. People gathered together and remarked: "Look, 'the Invisible!'" "This is what trying to please the public leads to." "It's all over for her."

People were too optimistic: this situation didn't last long. Suddenly one day, the husband's second good friend (the one who said he'd been in love with Madam X as a teenager) saw him walking on the street in high spirits with a large cardboard box clutched to his chest. Curious, he went up to him and, despite resistance, brazenly opened the box: inside was a microscope. That night Madam X's room was brightly lit, as if it were a holiday. The widow goaded her good friend to go in and look around; she saw that she had "polished all the mirrors and placed them in a conspicuous spot." Her face was glowing "orange," her hair was "as black as lacquer," the husband was even more "jubilant," and "every other minute, he jumped up uneasily and hugged her around the shoulders," as if afraid that she was about to lose her human shape and change into something unfathomable, but also as if "giddy with good fortune." His sickening sweetness was enough to "make a person throw up." Once again, the demonic mirrors issued a summons, and at night teenage boys and girls tossed and turned anew and grew moody. For reasons yet unknown, a few stood naked at the side of the street, and each was fined five yuan by the police. The next day at dusk, one after another, they made their way into Madam X's small room and sat there for two hours like imbeciles. Then, as before, they cursed Madam X as "boring" and "dull" and taunted her mercilessly. One even vowed that the next time he would steal her shoes. (But the next time, as soon as he went in, despite himself, he calmed down and became just like a porcelain doll. Then, after he left, he once more vowed that the next time he would steal her shoes for sure.)

Apparently only one person knew what Madam X did at night: her husband. Under his first good friend's close questioning, he divulged a little. From what he said, you could tell that Madam X must have explained everything she was doing, but this stud—because of his perpetual innocence—always perceived his wife's deeds with a child's mind, even its imagination and logic, and added some sweet images and obfuscations. When asked about Madam X's nighttime activities, he answered, "Observing the stars." Blushing, he added, "Just imagine· all the mirrors fly out the window, *huhuhu*, and enter outer space, and then with another *huhuhu* they fly back —isn't this work absolutely noble? It's precisely because this work draws away all her energy that the microscope is her lifeblood."

Along with his own peculiar way of thinking, each person develops a few small hobbies. For example, the husband was really interested in hopscotch: indeed, he could hopscotch any time of the day or night. His wife's hobby was no different, and nobody should make a big fuss about it. His good friend was listening patiently to his drivel and thinking: this guy has gone mad. Then he reflected that everyone close to Madam X acted a little like a lunatic; even their son, Little Bao, had shown symptoms of "being addicted to looking in the mirror." Although he tried hard to pull father and son back to reality in order to restrain Madam X's extreme inclinations, it was always futile. The husband finally summed up his views: "My wife is a most ordinary person." His friend shook his head. He could do nothing about the husband's infantile feelings. He could only watch the developments and await a turn for the better. Was Madam X really involved in astronomy? Was everything as simple as this? The handsome husband's intellect was highly questionable. There was proof that his eyes were deceived, that he could never distinguish right from wrong. Imagine turning a blind eye to the widow's bewitching figure and missing his chance without knowing it! A good-for-nothing like this: could he figure out what those demonic mirrors were for? Could he see the things in the mirrors at a glance? By all appearances, his talk was nothing more than an attempt to muddle along. To gloss over everything laughable about him, he posed as a stalwart husband, fooling even himself, while remaining smugly ignorant of reality.

Outsiders had no way to resolve this question, so we could appeal only to the superior knowledge of others. Another with inside information is Madam X's younger sister, who claims she's twenty-eight or twenty-nine. It just takes someone asking about Madam X's nighttime occupation, and this sister becomes emotional for no reason, sniveling and sobbing until her eyes are tiny and swollen. Let's listen to her incoherent narrative: "My sister used to be a charming, gentle little girl. The peach blossoms were brilliantly red. Then, suddenly, she threw Mother's spectacles into the mountain stream. Afterwards, we ran and ran until she leapt into the air, and I heard only her footsteps—*tita, tita*—overhead. In private, Papa and Mama said she had two calcium carbide lamps for eyes. Sometimes, her slender fingers would turn into a hawk's talons—very sharp and truly frightening. Mama was always grabbing her and cutting her nails until her fingers bled." She told us her older sister was the first person she'd heard of who could leap into the air and fly. Consequently, everything she did was utterly correct and unquestionable. She frequently went several days without eating or drinking, and after becoming as light as a feather, she flew out the window. She flew so high that when her younger sister saw her solitary silhouette drifting to and fro, she couldn't hold back tears. As she spoke, this sister left reason further and further behind, and the more unreasonable she became, the more excited she was and the more blind was her faith and adoration. Her thoughts were a mess, a hodgepodge; she was completely spineless. (This also leads us to think of her divorce case many years later: you could see that this woman's sole motivation was to keep up with the fads—she was a clumsy copycat.)

Although we didn't get anywhere close to the nub of the issue with Madam X's sister, we did obtain bits and pieces about Madam X's youth that were helpful in analyzing her temperament. It seems that ever since childhood, Madam X had fostered a deep-seated hatred not unrelated to her parents' neglect, for which, in truth, she had to bear much responsibility. (Some fathers—well-intentioned old papas—have romantic views of their children; they have a relaxed attitude and don't take charge of anything. The old mamas merely remember little things like cutting their children's fingernails.) In later years, the toxin of this hatred must have penetrated every capillary and hardened her heart. She became strange and saw everyone as her enemy. She slipped down a muddy slope into an incurable condition. Not only was she very complacent, but she also kept trying to drag everyone else down with her. Her means of alluring and abetting were unique: in the end, those who had been affected appreciated her greatly, as if they'd won new leases on life. We may well ask: if a person has had a murderous bent since childhood (to a child, throwing her mother's spectacles into a stream would be the same as murder), what kind of destructive instincts would she have as an adult? If these destructive instincts were constrained by objective conditions (Madam X has unfortunately never been able to freely act out her exceptionally strong lust), what kind of bizarre transformation would occur?

The circumstances we've analyzed make us increasingly pessimistic about Madam X's gloomy future. We have to say that on the rainy night years ago, it would have been better if her mother hadn't given birth to this ball of flesh so incompatible with the natural environment, world order, and peace. Although Madam X's parents have already passed away and are silent inside their urns in a graveyard, we couldn't help but curse them whenever we discussed this. If they hadn't irresponsibly brought Madam X into this world and fostered her murderous inclination through their unrealistic, uto-pian worldview, how could she have caused such a series of events? (Here, the writer inserts a sentence: the writer is characterizing Madam X in much the same manner as the people of Five Spice Street at the beginning of the story. This description wasn't immuta-ble, as we'll see later.) There were reasons for the guarded mentality of the crowds on Five Spice Street. They were all sharp-eyed, sober, and capable people. Before anything occurred, they could instinc-tively sniff out any danger and take precautions. So we needn't worry too much about them: they have their own ways to deal with outside menaces. Although at present they haven't made any head-way in their investigation, they have perfect preventive measures in reserve: when the time comes, they will certainly bring them out in full force. And so we can rest easy and wait quietly for things to develop.

This is how the younger sister explained her sister's activity, each time so distressed that she wanted to die. Once, after finishing up, she entangled a listener and asked him to find a sharp knife to "dig out her heart and examine it." He broke into a cold sweat. This sort of woman loves to stir up the waters and find a theoretical basis for future scandals. Nothing such a shameless piece of work could do would surprise us. She was capable of anything, and afterwards would act crazy, diddling with the cheap sympathy of others. After hearing that her older sister's scandals had come to light, she rushed to her sister's home. Having comforted her grieving, despairing, infantile brother-in-law, she made off with their biggest mirror, took it home, and beamed sunlight on the earthen wall on the other side of the street while letting out a sharp and piercing scream. An ink-black tramp walking past identified the light on the wall and *stood stock-still.* He squatted down and didn't move. At nightfall, he lit a fire with wastepaper and firewood. Leaning against the wall, he entered into a deep stupor. After three days and three nights, she packed up her belongings to join the tramp, and the two of them "eloped"! Isn't this the most fantastic thing? What does it mean when people stare openmouthed? Before long, word came about this tramp: "one ink-black slap left her deaf in both ears." Thinking of the words "ink-black slap," the crowds on Five Spice Street vented their disgust. This woman deserved a slap—the more, the better. We couldn't do it but were glad someone else had. Whenever she came to Five Spice Street, everyone's palms grew sweaty in anticipation. Everyone was sure that she came simply to provoke and incite, to instigate evil winds and stir up trouble. She was confused, but lewd and stubborn by nature. She particularly enjoyed novelty and deviant ideas. No one could deal with her.

No one could produce reliable information; even the shortcuts we tried all failed. We could only "sit and wait" for Madam X to betray herself. From our experience on Five Spice Street, no matter how shady and crooked one's conduct, as soon as the right time came, the truth would see the light of day. One mild spring morning, Old Woman Jin, who sold used books for a living next to the grocery store, struggled to wake up from a whole winter's lethargy: shuffling in old cotton shoes, her hair disheveled as a lion's mane, she stood under the eaves, pounding her chest and cursing herself. She remembered that before the winter, her hair was really glossy: you could almost call it "beautiful." Sleep had made a mess of it. After she finished cursing, she gazed around and saw the young coal worker swaying toward her. She dragged him inside, pushed him down on a worn-out cane chair, and whispered to him quietly. Stockpiled for a winter, her words poured out like a river. Every time he wanted to get up, she pushed him down again. Her old hands were like iron clamps; even the vigorous young coal worker could do nothing about it. Didn't people say, "The older the ginger, the hotter"? This is the secret that she had stored away like a treasure:

"I've been strangely confident all along. Sometimes when I wake up, I can't avoid being annoyed for a moment, as if my brain is empty. But that doesn't amount to anything: all I have to do is look at my palms for a minute and my strength returns. I've had this confidence ever since I was a young girl; at the time, I vowed I would poke an opening in the wall with an iron drill. And, sure enough, I did this later. When I walked on the street, I never gave way to the people I encountered. I am a strong person. One time, an old fart rushed up at me head-on. I rammed him with my hipbone and he fell over. My fiancé (unfortunately, I had a fiancé; fortunately, though, I didn't get married) stood nervously next to the door and said, 'Don't do that.' I glanced at him and persisted. Later, I thought I would test his endurance, so I kicked him in his thin chest. The beautiful kick killed him. How joyfully everything ended. What spunk. This is my unique spiritual temperament. The people of Five Spice Street might think I'm broke and down-and-out with no meat to eat. They look at me as they would a power pole. But they're wrong! One day I'll control everything, and everyone's welfare will be in my hands. This day will come. Things will occur that they can't imagine.

"It isn't that I don't understand self-reflection. I've asked myself countless times: Is my faith a product of my imagination? If I persist, will I dream my life away? I've already experienced a lot of trials, but none was life-threatening. Just *this one time* was unique, a time of wondrous glory. Only after this did I feel a fresh and flowering vigor—all my abjectness was swept away—like an old tree in early spring. No, like bearing a child at the age of one hundred. I mean a great mind maturing slowly! All along, I had a premonition that this uncommon life of mine held an opportunity; I told my poor mother this three times. I said this under a pine tree on a hill in the suburbs. There were two birds' nests in the tree. Looking at the nests, I spat the words out one by one from the cracks between my teeth: *'There will always be an opportunity.'* That's how I said it! Everything that happened later proved this true. Even I was greatly surprised, and it's too late to analyze it! What striking potential I had! What a dazzling blossom came from the silent seed of my childhood! If I had talked of this with people in the past, who would have believed me? The opportunity finally arrived, arrived so swiftly and ferociously that it almost caused me to lose my head: I looked on helplessly as it rolled away, my response as futile as fetching water in a bamboo basket. Of course, this was only 'almost.' In fact, I reacted quickly and grasped my opportunity for all I was worth. I saw the new situation clearly, adjusted my pace, and took action. I grabbed as much as I could, and all at once changed the prejudices of the people of Five Spice Street and established a new image in their minds. Here's an example. Have you noticed Zhou Sanji at the grocery store next door? The same one who every day for several decades, after having a bowel movement, purposely blocked my doorway while he fastened his dirty trousers? He engaged in this indelicate behavior to keep emphasizing that he—Zhou Sanji—is thousands of times more brilliant than I; he thinks the whole world should know this, and if some people still don't know, then it's his responsibility to publicize it. I endured the humiliation and—like a mouse—drew back into the room. How many years went by like this? Years without justice. Not until *this one time* when the clouds parted and the fog vanished did this situation reverse itself. This one time was brilliant, epoch-making, pioneering work."

Having said this, Old Woman Jin held her tongue to keep the listener in suspense. Shaky, she hobbled to the stove, picked up a poker, and wildly stoked the fire until coal dust flew all around the room and choked them, all the while hanging on to the young coal worker with her other hand. By now, the coal worker had figured out what she was intending and was twisting back and forth on the worn-out cane chair, breathing heavily, and blushing. All at once, he was sexually aroused. Though he had no object for his arousal, he couldn't control himself: it was unbearable. Old Woman Jin seemed to want to dig a hole in his flesh with her long fingernails. Every few minutes, she chanted in a low voice the name that made people quake: "X?" She felt that the secret hopes of her life, the remote and beautiful or gorgeous illusions, would all be realized. This reality was a reaction to the stirring name X, so she repeated this name over and over. It was like a lunatic's game. While she stared hard at the coal worker, her old eyes gradually lost focus and then turned into two fluctuating blood-red orbs, all at once bulging out of her eye sockets and then all at once drawing back in. The young man felt an irresistible pressure. In the grip of self-contempt and a confusion of unreal emotions, he quickly reached the most astonishing decision of his life: he would "fool around" with this witch.

When they finished fooling around, the door of the house suddenly opened. The two bare-assed people on the bed saw the respectable Zhou Sanji. He stuck his head inside and then stood hesitating for some time next to the door, looking very excited. When he left, he said something hard to figure out: "A new era has begun. The worries of winter have been swept away."

Still bare-assed, Old Woman Jin left the bed (she didn't let the young coal worker put his pants on, either), spat at Zhou Sanji's receding figure, and cursed him for being "unbearably vulgar." Then she started strolling around the room, around and around. Suddenly she stopped and exclaimed, "X and I will fight to the death!" Naked from the waist down, the young coal worker stood nervously on the bed, unable to figure out what was happening; he felt used. He became dejected and full of remorse. Why was this witch exploiting him? What was her motivation? His poor brain could never get a handle on it. We can assume that after repeated hints and inducements, his train of thought led from the name X to the body of this person who had always been his idol, and eventually to a certain spot in that body. As a consequence, he instinctively felt a sexual urge, and—confusing one object with another—he began fooling around recklessly and became a victim. Throughout the process, Old Woman Jin was absolutely calm and collected; we can say it was premeditated, that she had a plan all along, and that she manipulated the proceedings and easily achieved her immoral goal. The strange thing was that she didn't want any pleasure from the young coal worker's body. To tell the truth, she had long since passed the age for enjoying sex. Maybe we should say she "had no interest in fooling around," or that she even felt it was rather "repulsive." This incident became really complicated. Can we say that Old Woman Jin's traps and schemes were merely to vanquish one or two imaginary enemies? What sort of realm did she and the coal worker seek in that muddled life of theirs? Could an intrepid person like her sometimes make mistakes in her predictions? We couldn't figure this out. On our Five Spice Street, there's a rule of thumb: don't worry about what you can't understand; just wait quietly and things will work out. And if they didn't, then something was clearly wrong with you. Maybe the flaw was in your head, maybe it was in your toes—anyhow, it was incurable.

After this, Old Woman Jin changed greatly. Sometimes when she got up in the morning, she felt a tremendous confidence in her body. She looked at herself in the mirror, assumed various winning poses, and then decided to get rid of the outer clothing that veiled her body. She wanted to achieve a "complete revelation of her soul." She felt that all the conditions for this were already in place. And so she started going naked above the waist in order to bring about this "revelation." It's too bad the aesthetic judgment of the people of Five Spice Street wasn't receptive to this kind of "revelation." Their reaction was completely cold; all did their best to avert their gaze and pretend not to see this old woman's naked body. There was another major change in Old Woman Jin's life: she made trouble during Madam X's nighttime activities. If anyone had the guts to ask about this, she would raise her fist toward the sky and say, "Bah! It was a great mistake! I've been contemptibly robbed of my achievement! X? Who's X? Isn't it simply me? Of course it is. Who besides me has her demonic power? But you all blindly believe the deception that has turned pretense into reality. I proclaim loudly, I am X and X is I!" At dusk, she always fidgeted; unable to sit still at home, she ran into Madam X's home and made off with one of her mirrors. She boasted she had mastered all the minutest details about Madam X and had long since "defeated" her, claiming Madam X was now on the point of "retiring" from Five Spice Street. When she said this, naturally she didn't forget to jiggle her breasts for the enjoyment of others and then call out the coal worker's name, asking him to "give evidence." Everyone on Five Spice Street surrendered to her awesome presence.

And how about our young coal worker? It was really sad and hopeless to talk about him. Why on earth had he been born in the first place? And, since he had been, why had he suffered so many trials? Would this young guy who had suffered so much ever be able to recover? But let's not worry about his future; let's return to the present. All of a sudden, he's become a schizophrenic: apart from going to Old Woman Jin's, he stays behind closed doors all day and doesn't go out. Sometimes he could produce a blurry image in his blank brain: the image had a lot of mist-like lace, in the center of which was something resembling Madam X's silhouette or something that led people to think of her silhouette. It was only when he stepped into Old Woman Jin's home and "fooled around" with her that this image was produced. At such times, he often trembled with joy and crowed like a rooster. So it was as if bewitched that he made his way into Old Woman Jin's home every day, as if addicted to opium. No one could have imagined that this half-dead old hag who sold used books would suddenly flourish! That she would stand above the people of Five Spice Street! And then there was Zhou Sanji. Every day he watched helplessly as the coal worker walked into the home next door. Sometimes he went outside bare-assed, peed, and then went back in. The pleasure he'd had for decades was completely gone. Would he lose his mind and act like a lunatic?

Madam X wasn't the least aware of Old Woman Jin's wild ambush. As usual, she took it easy, was unconcerned, and remained precise in her manner. A case in point was a conversation with her husband:

Husband: If the crazy old woman comes back for another heist, should I beat her up?

Madam X: For twenty minutes today, I once again experienced a feeling of supreme tranquility. I think we should buy some more mirrors and put them away in boxes to use later.

Husband: I'm a little perturbed by what that woman is doing. How come you're indifferent to it?

Madam X: Just listen carefully to your pulse. A cloud will pass slowly before your eyes and then everything that's bothering you will vanish. And the next time, your eyes will be cloudy and your teeth will sparkle like stars, and you won't even be aware of some old lady arriving. We can hide the mirrors.

It seems we said above that Madam X not only affected people intimately related to her but also could secretly control others. Although she had never been aware of this ability, and had not deliberately made use of it, it was effective. After their talk, her handsome husband was of course a little confused, and he had to blunt his annoyance whenever Old Woman Jin intruded. As time passed, he even forgot what the old woman looked like, and once when they ran into each other, he asked in surprise, "Who are you?" Then, as if nothing had happened, he went about his own business. He wasn't at all angry when he caught her turning things upside down in his home. This sort of thing happened often. When he was clear-headed, he still argued with the old woman, even striking her once. At those times, he grumbled that his wife turned a deaf ear, but soon he was on the same wave length with her again.

After "sitting and waiting" for some days, a chance opportunity allowed our likable widow to get hold of another letter from Mr. Q to Madam X. The letter referred to Madam X's nighttime occupation. Although it was filled with innuendo and secret codes, the widow—relying on her ample experience and her astonishing ability to ferret out sexual relationships—seemed to discover a little something. The letter was like all the others between Mr. Q and Madam X: there was neither salutation nor signature, nor even beginning or end. The whole letter was artificial—hypocritically friendly, enough to turn your stomach. (At this point, the widow again raised doubts she'd been harboring for a long time: were these letters plagiarized, paragraph by paragraph, from the classics? This would save a lot of trouble and at the same time it would be unconventional and cater to the other's vanity, something the two idiots were happy to do.) Below are some excerpts:

1. "I hear your eyes are inflamed. I'm so worried that I'm on pins and needles—really, really afraid. If you go blind, then what? Of course you have your reasons to be unconcerned. You don't think vision is any good for you. On nights when the cool wind gently blows, you gaze sedately into those mirrors, a slight smile on your face, mysterious and sexy. I can't do this. I've tried. Even if I close

my eyes tight, my vision still penetrates my eyelids and takes in the outside world, filled with dense fog. I become delirious and panicky, and when I walk, I bump along and stumble, acting like a buffoon. At such times, I can always see your sprite-like smile, and so I hate you, and struggle with all my might to resist something."

2. ". . . Last night, you once again flew from the mirror to the night sky. At the time, I was lost in thought when suddenly I heard a *hu* and knew it was you. I pricked up my ears and followed you with my imagination. Your bare feet stirred up a puff of cool wind that blew against my face. During the day, I heard that someone wanted to retaliate against you. (One of the teenage boys or girls?) He might lurk under the bed or behind the cupboard. You have to carefully check the places in the room where someone could hide, and sweep those spots with the broom I gave you. You'll ridicule me again for being nervous. I know you'll say, 'I can't sense that person. Generally it's hard for me to sense other people. How can he hurt me?' I can imagine how you'll look as you say this. No matter what, I'll patrol outside your room all night tonight. I'm afraid of that person—that desperado."

3. "You say you can 'see clearly with your sensory organs' for a long time: that's because you know how to use those mirrors. When you sit down, you can immediately 'enter a meditative state.' I can only occasionally experience that state (for example, when I see you in the morning). Most days, I'm utterly confused. . . ."

From this letter, the widow drew several important conclusions: (1) She realized that Madam X had been faking all along; she hadn't achieved anything at all. It was only a cheap trick played over and over again to fool people. She longed to monopolize all the world's men (and even some women) and was keenly aware of their interest in novelty as well as their fragile nature, so she pretended to be learned and profound in order to hoodwink them until they were confused. (2) She confirmed one fact: a lot of people in the world were just like Madam X's husband—a virgin with stunted sexual competence. For such people, the less reliable a woman was, and the more able she was to arouse their fleeting, misty daydreams, the more interested they were in her, and the easier it was for them to be "enchanted." They were utterly ignorant of sex, yet always obstinately considered themselves right. It was easy to cure this mental illness: if a *real* woman entered their lives and they had a sexual relationship with her, then their fragile connection with Madam X would fall apart at once. Of course, she didn't mean to say that this absurdity existed only because there was no *real* woman in the world. There were real women (the widow frowned), but they were few and far between and weren't interested in sinking their claws into the kinds of virgins or androgynous trash who "were inept" and "unspeakably awkward." Only because of these strange circumstances could our Madam X play her tricks; everyone could only watch helplessly as she carried out her deceptions.

Something else happened while we were waiting quietly: it was directly related to Madam X's speech about sex. At that time, during the bedlam created by watermelon and cantaloupe rinds flying all over, a pair of hawk-keen eyes followed Madam X from start to finish. Indeed, that person was prepared to throw himself into the breach and—along with Madam X's husband—protect her, but before it was his turn to do so, the event concluded. Was he the scoundrel who drew the picture on the wall? Or was he a stranger? Three months later, this "ardent" (the female friend's word) young man walked into Madam X's home, and without even stating his name, he "calmly but firmly" sat down and "covetously" looked Madam X up and down. Then he came straight to the point about Madam X's lecture. After two hours, of which about an hour was spent in the silence of tacit understanding, the young man stood up and asked, "Do you think I'm right for you?" Madam X woke with a start from her dream, her gaze as limpid as water, and shook her head slowly: "No. Your eyes aren't soft enough, and they are only tricolored; they can't change color. As for me, it's been a long time since I was a girl glowing with youth. We wouldn't be able to satisfy each other." The youth left, utterly discomfited. From the window, Madam X watched his solitary silhouette. She fell unhappily into bed and lay there a long time. It didn't end then. Starting from an inner fanaticism from which he couldn't disentangle himself, the young man still desired Madam X. He said this wasn't a "sexual" temptation, but something he "couldn't explain." As he saw it, Madam X didn't have enough "sex appeal"; he could find plenty of women with "sex appeal," but none of them could hold his interest for long. Was it possible that something was wrong with his body? Or was his very idea defective? He was never able to think this through. He frequently still went to Madam X's home and sat for an hour, continuing their "spiritual communication." Hot tears brimmed in their eyes. But when he raised more demands or expressed something with his body, he met with Madam X's firm, unambiguous resistance. Once, shaking her by her thin shoulders, he asked:

"Why?"

Sadly but calmly Madam X replied, "We aren't right for each other."

"What isn't right?"

"To have a sexual relationship with you."

"How can you know?"

"I can sense this with my body."

"Damn mirrors!!" Out of control, he smashed one of Madam X's mirrors with his fist and dashed out the door, dripping with blood. Because of this, Madam X felt unsettled for a long time. She wasn't unaffected by the youth's charms, nor was she constrained by ideas of chastity or abstinence; it's better to say she was willfully reckless, for if she felt something was right, nothing would stop her. This time, she really liked him, and was frequently moved by a certain charm of his, but in truth, in his presence she wasn't sexually aroused. Nor could she fake it. That's just the way it was. If he straightened out his thinking, she would even like to maintain a "subtle" relationship: such a relationship would make them both feel natural and sensible. Too bad he was stubborn, old-fashioned, and rigid, and so her only option was to break off their friendship.

We can also listen to her friend's account. On the day when the youth arrived, she happened to be at Madam X's home. After he sat down, she "purposely stayed to one side and didn't leave," so she saw the whole scene from start to finish. Overcome by desire, they completely forgot she was there: they paid attention only to exchanging debauched vulgarities and to faking a kind of false solemnity. In fact, they could hardly contain themselves and wished they could "hop into bed at once." The funniest thing was that their conversation went on intermittently for more than ten minutes. During this time, neither looked at the other, neither moved, and "there were tears in their eyes." This all made her wonder if they might be practicing some kind of qigong. She decided to tease them by laughing out loud, but they "didn't hear"! They actually didn't hear anything. At that moment, Madam X had been wandering in a peaceful wonderland filled with sunshine and was unaware of any worldly annoyances. The young man's ears, however, shook from the sound of his crazy heartbeat, and he temporarily lost his vision. So the friend's prank came to nothing. Finally, she stood up, "kicked the door ferociously," and, filled with scorn, left the house.

Was Madam X very solemn in sexual relationships? From this incident, it seems she was, but people who know her well know otherwise. For example, she not only "doesn't turn male visitors away," she welcomes them—the more, the merrier. Sometimes she also "tries to seduce them," even "dropping in on them." While she's consorting with those people, naturally she has to be furtive. In particular, she has to fool her husband (even if he's such a "good husband"). People would probably have trouble believing that none of those men had a sexual relationship with her. In addition, Madam X surely doesn't want people to believe this. It's better to say that "she doesn't give a damn." She just keeps her mouth shut, and so do all the men she consorts with. Someone actually saw a man (definitely not Mr. Q) kiss Madam X on the main street in broad daylight, but this onlooker—out of "disgust and bashfulness"—was unable to see the expression on Madam X's face. He could verify, though, that Madam X offered no resistance. Maybe she was already limp with joy! Or maybe she'd had sexual relations with him all along! One day, the first good friend of Madam X's husband had also seen Madam X holding hands with an extremely young guy and then go off to spend a night with him on a barren hillside in the suburbs. She didn't return home until nine the next morning. The two of them were "wan and sallow" and "in high spirits." With bitter hatred and a heavy heart, the good friend admonished Madam X. Madam X just giggled.

"Nothing happened," she said. "He wanted to, but I finally prevailed. We're still good friends."

"Didn't it occur to you that he might use force? Perhaps you secretly hoped he would?"

"Of course it occurred to me. If he had, I would have felt bad for him. But thank God, it didn't come to that. I persuaded him with my perception."

"Did he kiss you?"

"So what if he did?" Madam X was thoroughly exasperated. "So what if he did?! So what? So what!"

Step by step, she forced her husband's friend to the wall. Whenever he recalled his embarrassment, he felt like crawling into a hole. Could such a wanton woman ever be solemn? We can only say that since she has lost all credibility, she must be acting.

We can't help but think of her demonic instinct to control. Madam X had countless completely different faces. She would disguise her face and brilliantly keep people from seeing any trace of affectation. Around the young man who, as we've said, had listened respectfully to her lecture, Madam X surely was relying on her rich experience to sense that if she put on an unusually solemn face and maintained a certain distance, never taking the last step, she would finally be able to tame that crazy, wild, unbridled horse, thereby satisfying her abnormal sexuality. Objectively, this wasn't premeditated: it was only her nature. So: Madam X is instinctively a good actor—she is always acting. We can also say that she isn't acting, because it is her nature to be a witch—toying with men is the most enjoyable part of her life. She doesn't hesitate to hurt people, but she also seems to consider other people. By temperament, she's cold and severe, but she also seems ebullient. It's impossible to sum up Madam X's character. Consider the energy we expended determining her age, and finally, irresponsibly, we had nothing to show for it. It was just a blur. How can we be sure about "character"—this infinitely more complicated issue? If we can't be clear about it, we won't try. As always, let's "wait quietly." But we have confirmed something: she is prone to willful recklessness. Although the residents of our Five Spice Street aren't ascetics and make a lot of allowances for people, we're all rather disciplined and orderly. Madam X's unruliness set our teeth on edge and we wished she would die. Of course we don't forget the few sordid, vulgar ones among us who wanted to take advantage of the opportunity. At the same time as they cursed her, they also secretly sounded her out and were generally rebuffed. Thus, they abhorred her even more than we did, and cursed her even more. Naturally, this scum cannot be considered part of our community.

Two examples would illustrate Madam X's shameless ways, but they would provide too much of a digression, because what we want to talk of now is Madam X's nighttime occupation. We've said so much but haven't come close to the true picture. It's all a mist. Of course we can also assert that there isn't a true picture, because it's all merely smoke and mirrors. Putting it this way is expedient, saves trouble, and eliminates difficulties and annoyances. But the effect of Madam X's nighttime occupation is also *clearly present*. You can't see it, you can't touch it, but every resident of Five Spice Street can feel it. Sometimes it's like a radioactive substance or shock waves, and sometimes like insect bites. It's said that after one night of conditioning at Madam X's home, the son of Madam X's colleague suffered a sudden worsening of his temperament: he became an alcoholic and a tramp, loitering and sleeping in the street and imperiling public safety. He boasted to everybody: begging (in fact, it was plundering) was wonderful, as if "the whole body is alight." Before this, he had thought of suicide. But now he wanted "to live forever, walk everywhere, look around, fight with anyone he wanted to fight with, fall in love with and have sex with any young woman he happened to run into." Driven to distraction, Madam X's colleague chased after this "unworthy son" with a long bamboo pole; the result was that he hit her with it and broke her arm. It was too horrible to look at. This brat is now in a barbaric region to the north.

With nothing to eat, he "ate the raw flesh of birds and beasts" and even drank a dead man's brains. He was living "very comfortably" and planned "never to return." After he left, his mother fell ill for a short time and was taken care of by Madam X. Madam X not only didn't try to save this son but, on the contrary, advised her female colleague to "move on with her life," "just act as if she'd never had this son." She said "this would be best for him." After the colleague recovered, she fought this malicious woman like a mother tiger. If Madam X hadn't been light and agile, her colleague would have "broken her legs." Over time, however, though the colleague didn't acknowledge it publicly, inwardly she realized the advantages of her son's running away, because at home he had never been on good terms with the family. He had threatened to "kill them" over trifling incidents, and even when his parents were making love at night, he would kick the door open and barge in and make some teasing, cynical remarks. Because of him, the family lived in fear and trembling, always on the verge of a nervous breakdown. With him gone, they were "free of worries."

The colleague had reaped benefits, yet not only was she not grateful to Madam X, she also rushed to the police station to report that Madam X "corrupted the youth," engaged in "prostitution," and "had grown rich from this." The trouble she caused was the talk of the town for quite a while, but finally the investigation ended for lack of evidence. Our Five Spice Street's view was that "you had to catch adulterers with their pants down!" But no one had caught Madam X "with her pants down." And the so-called "prostitution" was merely private guesswork, an individual judgment. So, as you can see, in general our people were not as presumptuous and impulsive as the colleague. When all is said and done, people in general are quite even-tempered and defer to the facts. They would rather "wait and see."

They had some views about the colleague's impatience. Beginning in May of that year, after she used a microphone to air the widow's secrets on the street, everyone had some unfavorable things to say about her, especially the middle-aged and young men, who privately called her "a black-headed housefly." Now she had suddenly rushed to the police station to make an indiscreet report: she wanted to be the first to take the credit, to be in the limelight. Everyone was even more disgusted. She created the whole mess. Had anybody asked her to do so? No! She had to put her finger in the pie because she thought she was clever! Had she gone crazy? If it went on like this, maybe she'd even want to centralize power in her hands, ride roughshod over the crowd on Five Spice Street, and lord it over them! Since when was she given the right to speak for our crowd? You have to realize that "nobody had ever respected her" (the widow's words)! Just think of how much harm she caused our respected widow, whose reputation still hasn't recovered. What a painful lesson. Should we still refuse to come to our senses and tolerate her continued troublemaking?

3

MADAM X'S AND THE WIDOW'S DIFFERING
OPINIONS ABOUT "SEX"

It seems we've hinted that the much-admired widow was both frigid and chaste. However, don't think that just because of this, she was some sexless saint. In fact, we'd better state just the opposite. She herself thinks so. She's always been confident about this, and with good reason. First, there's her figure. In the eyes of male connoisseurs, it's "steamy hot." Her breasts and buttocks are "uncommonly ample" and "provocative." (These were a certain middle-aged man's words, which the widow had noted down.) She was so innately stunning that even a dry stick would sense its male lust. (Of course, those androgynous pieces of garbage aren't included.) The widow's sexual power puts her in an awkward position. That is to say, she attracts numerous men, but keeps her chastity and can't "go beyond friendship with anybody." Therefore, she has never fully displayed her charms. We'll illuminate this below with some excerpts from her speech.

1. "I've always been irresistible. Men from twenty to fifty are all crazy about me. Sometimes I'm awakened at midnight by these hungry ghosts rapping on the lattice: it sounds like thunder. Sometimes I feel it's all nonsense. Too much sex appeal is disastrous for a woman. I want to live quietly, but they won't let me. Some handsome men have beautiful, charming wives (not as hot as I am, of course), but if they see me even once, they start pining away, they actually fall ill from wanting me. I actually wish I weren't so sexy; it doesn't do me any good, and it causes other people great pain. But a

person can't choose. This is how I am, and there's something gratifying about it: I can lead admirers down the right path and thus cleanse society and improve people. So even if it's a calamity to be 'hot,' it's also a woman's good fortune: sex is powerful, and with it women can dominate society."

2. "Most men are brainless and indulge in fantasies. They need us strong women to lead them. Especially today, when traditional aesthetic sentiments are under fire, we can see their cowardly nature even more clearly. In the end, some deviants pursue a kind of nihilistic, monstrous stimulant that is profoundly toxic and incurable, similar to homosexuality: both are unhealthy and abnormal. I think one reason for this phenomenon is women's frailty. Because they lack confidence in their sexuality and are never active, they've lost control over men. They've surrendered to men's tyranny and ended up with nothing but self-pity. In fact, it could have been quite different. We should have understood the function of our own bodies and attracted and controlled men that way and then tamed them. Although weirdos like Madam X live in this world, she's certainly not omnipotent. This much I know. I could reel in every man she's had a relationship with whenever I want. Each of them would drool over me. If my nature were different, I might become another Scarlett O'Hara, but this is my nature, and it's only because of this that a misfit like X can prevail for so long—and carry on with her occult activities. It's because X knows my nature so well that she can act like this without worrying. She puts me in an untenable position. I look 'hot,' but decades of self-cultivation dissipated my lust a long time ago. The result is that I can't act to *prove* her deceit and weakness. Nor will I stoop to fight with her for affection. I can't degrade myself by doing that. . . ."

3. "Men's sexual power is useless; it has no impact on life. Yet, a woman's sex is her magic weapon for defeating the outside world and revealing the significance of her existence. I simply can't imagine men with sexual power. Maybe women see all men—ugly, handsome, old, young—as basically the same as long as their organs are functioning. They all exert themselves in action. Maybe some are

a little stronger than others, but there's no essential distinction among them. Sexual power is unique to women: it is a kind of self-consciousness about one's bodily functions. When this consciousness sharpens, a woman becomes like a goddess. At that moment, each of her movements—each frown, each smile—makes men weak: they are shaken to the depths. (From these few words, it's clear our widow has reached a high level of philosophical understanding. We can't but admire this: she has dug deeply into the science of sex, and has done so on her own.) Under such conditions, if a woman can control herself and abstain from sex, her mysterious sex appeal will become fuller and riper until it sweeps all before her. (These words outraged the young and middle-aged men on Five Spice Street; they were unanimous: 'If a woman exists just for the sake of this nutty idea, isn't she just a "flower vase"?' They also said if there were a woman like this in their family, they'd 'beat the shit out of her.') Society these days is so prurient, and all the blame lies with us women: we're too lax, too lethargic."

The widow had a lot more to say, but we can't go into it all here. It's worth mentioning that while she was researching the science of sex, she sometimes also engaged in fieldwork. Without a thought for the hard work and slanderous gossip about her, she formulated a unique method that enabled her to get hold of credible original materials without being noticed. The guilty had no idea how their secrets had leaked out. They all wondered if the walls had eyes. Ever since Madam X and her husband moved to Five Spice Street, the widow made their sex life an important part of her investigation and employed various approaches. Sure, she couldn't fly over walls and walk on cliffs, nor was she "an invisible person." She completed her investigation using rigorous logic alone. The result was: Madam X and her husband's sex life was "particularly anguished," and their relationship was "filled with hatred." You could say that "there was no sex life" between them, just a kind of "abnormal sexual psychology." She said, "You can see the problem just by looking at the huge difference in their physiques: one is so strong, the other so frail. How could their sex be any good? Of course, the man is impotent, but the more impotent he is, the more he hangs on to unrealistic daydreams: he thinks he's strong, but when he really starts doing it, he shows once more that he's sheer rubbish. As for the woman, she's a tease, tantalizing all the men, while in fact she never follows through. These two were made for each other: they're a couple of jokes. Normal people can't figure out what kind of sexual relationship they have." She continued, "Where sex is concerned, they're as cold as ice. Maybe they're still 'virgins'! Their son, Little Bao, bears no physical resemblance to them. Maybe they brought him home from an orphanage —we don't know. Let's have a look at Madam X's buttocks and breasts—I've always suspected that she's still a virgin. This is entirely possible. I think it's in order to cover up this shameful reality that she purposely projects a wild, lascivious image. All the men who consort with her suffer, yet—as if bones were stuck in their throats—they can't speak out. Otherwise, why wouldn't even one man say a word about X's private life? Isn't this strange?" Now, with a "brazen" person—Mr. Q—appearing in Madam X's private life, the situation is becoming even more significant. The widow decided to carry out a thorough investigation and finally expose Madam X's "unsavory background," so that people would recognize the danger at last and would voluntarily "maintain the traditional aesthetic consciousness."

At this point, doubts pop up again in the readers' minds. If we say that this widow has all along kept herself as pure as jade, then perhaps she was also like this with her deceased husband. Maybe it's she (and not X) who is still a virgin? Is she qualified to prattle on about "sexual power"? Could she have tricked us? Did she make monkeys of us? Let's listen to her explanation. She said that she had had sex with only *one* man—her husband. Although she was unquestionably open, vibrant, spirited, and extraordinarily charming, she always strictly adhered to our traditional virtues and kept herself pure. As for her years of living as a widow, they were a little lonely and humdrum, yet it was precisely this quiet life, this kind of conscious self-cultivation, that now and then allowed her to reach the highest plane. There, she was sometimes moved to tears. No other enjoyment in the world held the same magnetic appeal, so she never did it with other men. Even if those crazy men broke the glass, prized open the door, and charged in, they wouldn't get what they wanted.

But this isn't to say that she's this way by nature. When she and her husband lived together, she enjoyed worldly pleasures. She doesn't deny this: she had a singularly fierce sexuality, to the point that "even seven or eight times a night couldn't satisfy her," and at any moment she could "come up with countless variations." Her husband (back then, he was a virile young guy) was no match for her, nor was he as imaginative. And so not long after they were married, he became impotent and grew thinner by the day. Before long, he died. For years, whenever anyone mentioned this, she sobbed convulsively.

"You can't possibly imagine those marvelous moments. No, there's no way to describe them. You can't imagine. Even years later, I still get excited. Whenever I think of him, I wonder whether he was a real person or a god from heaven. Really. In my mind, I've deified him. Is there still anyone like him in the world? Just looking at these handsome men all around, these ordinary people, makes me sick to my stomach, and I throw up. How could I possibly be interested in any of them?!"

Something else occurred to her after she finished weeping. "Sometimes I've thought that maybe there wasn't anything wonderful about him, that he was mediocre, and that it was only when I had that kind of relationship with him and at the same time bestowed my physical charms on him that he overwhelmed me. If he hadn't met me, he would have been only an ordinary man, no different from any other. It's only through a woman that a man can realize his virtues—and the woman must be strong, filled with the charm of sex. Otherwise, because of their fragile nature, men are likely to be corrupted by depraved women and become degenerate trouble-makers disturbing the tranquility of the world."

We can be sure of this much: although the widow had had a sexual relationship with only one man, she'd had plenty of experience. She was almost a master of sexology. Her experience didn't come from sexual relationships with a variety of men, but from her clear-headed, precise understanding of this sort of thing. And so the further away she was from men, the more dispassionate she was and the clearer her experience: she had a complete grasp of it. In men's eyes, this made her even more potent: you could look, but you couldn't touch. It's no exaggeration to say: the widow is the ideal incarnation of sex. The men's conduct on Five Spice Street proves this. Whenever she walks slowly and regally down the street, almost all the men stop in their tracks and idiotically "look back and smile." They promptly undress her in their minds and keep their eyes on the private parts of her body. They're intoxicated, flushed, and panting, and it's a long while before they calm down. They're distracted all day and continually look for chances to make up erotic stories. They imagine they're big heroes. They keep it up until nightfall, when they wake up and become despondent. Then they're deflated, unable even to make it with their wives. They vent. They rage at their wives for "having no sex appeal," for "being like dried fish." "It would be better to screw a hospital mannequin." "What could you do with this kind of wife?" "If it weren't for the ball and chain of this family, I'd long ago have become somebody," and so on and on. They can't help spouting nonsense like this. Some even leap out from the quilts, rashly spend the night naked on the floor, and get so sick they can't recover for a long time. Our widow understood all of this as well as the palm of her hand: she just calmly observed it and drew these deranged followers to her even more. Never tiring, she hoped to change society by her "refined influence."

The widow's notions about relations between the sexes always made Five Spice Street's men angry and unhappy. Naturally, deep down inside, they didn't believe her lies, but after her pronouncements, they always felt "a little uneasy," "as if suspended in midair." This feeling also affected their sex life with their wives. So some of them felt a nameless anger toward the widow. Because of his rising anger, one "truthful" middle-aged man, A, screwed up his courage and charged into the widow's home one dark night "in an act of desperation." "He didn't reemerge." It was a week before people finally saw him again. By then, he was a cripple, all skin and bones. He spat blood and had night sweats. All day long, he lay in a corner, curled up like an old cat. He had suffered brain damage and thought everyone who approached was a "panther." He shook from fright. Some curious people wanted to ask him the details of his experience, but they didn't succeed. His expression left them all in fear and trembling. They felt inside their pockets, afraid they'd lost something. It was plain to see: after "a night that no one could imagine," the widow was even more "fresh and tender, radiant and vivacious," "appearing in all her glory," and even more "unattainable." This transformation hindered her self-cultivation a little: she was "a little ill at ease" for several days, and her "memory seemed to slip." After giving it some serious thought, she decided to burn her bridges, "disclose" the facts, and sweep away the people's doubts about her. She began working on this one day at dusk in the open area in front of Madam X's door. When the widow sat down on a pile of logs, the men of Five Spice Street rushed up one after another. Their eyes gleamed with evil as they surrounded the widow like stars around the moon. First, the widow gazed at the window with the shades drawn at Madam X's home, and yawned for a minute or two, making the men fidget, and then she finally cleared her throat and began talking in a mosquito-like voice. As she talked, she shielded her throat with her hands, saying that she'd "caught a cold and lost her voice." The only thing the men could do was tighten the circle and keep squeezing in toward her. Everyone became small and flat, and their heads became pointed. They were like bream swimming back and forth, filling every bit of space. Two gutsy guys with no place to stand actually perched on the widow's hair and the tip of her nose. Just then, the curtains moved, and the widow's spirits rose, but she soon realized it was only the wind. How disappointing! Finally she focused her narrative and came to the main point. Every few sentences, the bream-like men pushed back and forth to get closer to her chest: they rubbed her breasts with their pointed heads and responded to her speech with *aha, aha.* Those in the back couldn't take this and squeezed those in the front row to the back while they themselves pressed forward for their share of "enjoyment." The gist of the widow's mosquito-like narrative was: she felt she had to clarify what happened that night. She had been "absolutely innocent" in this matter. She definitely wasn't like "*certain people*" (when she said this, she raised her voice a little and stared hard at the curtains), teasing the men, pretending to be filled with ardor, but, once the real thing came around, acting as if it hadn't: she'd take the men by their ears and make them look small while she herself had fun with it. She was a plain, pure-hearted woman: all her behavior grew from her inner desires. She wasn't seducing anyone, nor was she purposely letting anyone down, nor was she using this to control anybody. Although she had rolled in the hay with A that one night, she hadn't let him prevail. She concluded that the experience was also good for A. After all, he'd been in contact with a mature woman's body all through the process; one couldn't estimate the impact this would have on his life in the future. At least, it profoundly branded him: it was enough to make him resist any future temptation, and maybe because of this he would become disillusioned with the mortal world and—like her—begin cultivating morality. Men are very malleable, as past experience had confirmed for her.

Her sex research made it possible for the widow to reach her own conclusions and form her own system. All of her inspiration comes from deep thought. People admire this. At the same time, Madam X has been exploring the same field, but her attitude is precisely the opposite: she speculates recklessly, resorts to trickery, makes a loud clamor, even lecturing to the crowds when she has nothing to contribute, and confuses people with her evil motivations. One is real gold; the other is rotten copper. The widow's analogy hits the nail on the head even better: she comes right out and says that Madam X is a "counterfeit." As to what kind of fake, she won't say. She just "giggles" constantly, embarrassed to open her mouth. We surmise that she probably has the evidence in hand: clearly it relates to "sex." In the past, the people on our Five Spice Street no doubt believed that X was a woman, but now even this certainty is gone. We must be prudent about everything having to do with Madam X:

we can't take anything on faith. Let's listen to the hints the widow dropped:

"Has any man tasted her sugarplum? No. Has any man reaped sensual pleasure from her body? No. Isn't it impossible for a true woman to be a cloudy, misty thing? As lewd and depraved as she is, she can't have been above doing the kind of things I did. There must have been some obstacles that prevented her from acting freely. Isn't this clear if we carefully analyze her behavior?"

It seems it isn't so simple. If Madam X isn't a "woman" and merely attracts throngs of men with witchcraft, then the widow's hard work in her prolonged fight against her will soon expose her cheap tricks. As for the men, they must also be on guard and won't easily take the bait. But up to now, there isn't the slightest evidence that Madam X will fail. Those who consort with her (including a large group of teenagers) not only don't guard against her, they depend on her more and more with each passing day and run over to her home for unknown reasons. As for the widow's well-intentioned reminders, it's as though they're deaf: they don't listen. Nor do they respect her. It's as if the one with a sex problem isn't Madam X but the widow. As for Madam X, most of them never approve of her conduct, and some spare no effort in tearing her down: they want to suppress her contagious evil influence. The widow evidently knows that only by employing her "real ability" can she achieve her goal. Yet she can't, for that would destroy the "selfhood" the widow has cultivated for years. It appears that this deadly combat between her and Madam X will end in lasting stalemate. The widow can't accept this result, because this would be tantamount to admitting that her research wasn't complete—that it had no real worth, it was all malarkey. Our widow was up against an incalculably perilous future, yet without wavering, she chose the path filled with brambles and snares and pushed ahead. She was essentially a fanatical idealist unable to appreciate the life of philistines. Yearning for a pure and lofty life, she pursued her own goal.

Everyone knows that when our Madam X talks of sex, she is truly eloquent and long-winded. Everything she says is filled with dubious ardor. She never tires. The fact that she made the bizarre speech on the street proves that sex has always been her consuming issue. To put it simply, all of her activities—her work in the snack shop, looking into mirrors, observation of others' eyes, relations with men—are motivated by this. To reach her goal requires superhuman energy and physical strength, so she lives her life systematically and rigorously. As others see it, except for her nighttime occupation and addiction to looking into mirrors, her daily life is identical to theirs. They don't know it is a lie. Her real life is in her nighttime occupation and her looking into mirrors, both of which are directly related to sex. These matters consume all her strength: she's continually high-strung and thin. It seems she can never put on weight.

People were shocked at hearing her opinions of sex: not only could the crowds on Five Spice Street not get it through their heads, but even her husband and her younger sister—even her lover Q—could understand only bits and pieces. What was she thinking? Did she have the same inborn self-confidence as the widow? The answer is definitely yes—and not only that: her self-confidence surpassed the widow's and became a kind of wild arrogance. But the foundation of her arrogance was exactly the opposite of the foundation of the widow's self-confidence: she completely ignored "physiological functions" and thought that her "sexual power" originated from the light waves in her sightless eyes. This was preposterous.

"This is sexual power." Blushing, she was drowning in narcissism. "My attention to my eyes gives me perpetual youth and preserves a high degree of acuity about novel things."

She also said that she hadn't always possessed this power: her sex appeal surfaced gradually after her "occult" activities. Before that, it had been latent, and she was no different from other women. All at once, she towered far above other women. She became singularly graceful, suffused with sexual charm. She was certain she was "much more alluring now than when she was twenty." "And would never be decrepit."

It's true that in her affair with Q, the light in her eyes was the determining factor. But whether this constituted sex appeal, even

Mr. Q wasn't sure: after all, he was not accustomed to such notions. Still, when they were together, under Madam X's spell, Mr. Q fell into a trance, and he stared tearfully at Madam X's eyes while certain parts of Madam X's body kept appearing in his mind. All at once, he was aroused and could think only of "hopping into bed right away" with X. He wished to "please her in every way" to "ensure simultaneous orgasms." Of course, in the beginning, he just kept these thoughts to himself. Mr. Q—it seems we said this above—wasn't nearly as straight as Madam X: he always wavered and was weak-minded. He couldn't bear to hurt anyone. So, although he was aroused, he made every effort to cover it up. He also found reasons to explain himself. Madam X didn't give a damn what Mr. Q thought of her: with her body, she accepted a certain kind of "response" from him. Although at first they didn't "screw," still, from the very beginning, she thought: As far as sex was concerned, she and Mr. Q would be ideal together. Up to now, Q was the only "sexually" attractive man she knew. She had dreamed of this kind of man. Although she was wanton, she knew instinctively: she wasn't likely to meet another man like Mr. Q. She certainly wouldn't lightly let him slip away.

What did she really think of men? What made a man attractive? She didn't deny male sex appeal as the widow did, but rather set a high standard—inconceivably high. It was also simple and absurd. She set two criteria. We've already divulged them: the color of his eyes and the sound of his speaking voice. Normal people thought this was crazy. How was it related to the exuberance and actuality of "sex"? They doubted she used her eyes and ears. But according to her, it was her body's response that had led her to this and caused her to cast aside most of the men who'd shown interest in her. A couple were exceptional, but not in a sexual way: this was also determined by her physical response. She couldn't help it, and she wouldn't compromise for those men, either—even those she was very fond of. It seemed there was more than one Mr. Q. Someone even said she was a "nymphomaniac," another that she was "frigid." Because of this, Mr. Q was sometimes distressed, jealous, and fearful of losing her. He was always yearning to "make it" with her.

Though he couldn't shake this feeling off, he didn't dare pursue it. Finally, he "lost all interest in living."

At noon one day in Madam X's gloomy little room, her colleague asked what she really meant by sex. Was it just a figment of her "imagination"? Was it unrelated to the reality of "going to bed"? If it was something she had concocted to fool people, then (at this point, she began whispering in Madam X's ear) she needn't keep it a secret from her loyal friend of many years: she was more trustworthy than a locked safe. Madam X was taken in and opened the door to her heart.

She confirmed that for her sex was closely related to going to bed. Going to bed was the whole goal and the pinnacle of sex. It was the moment of unparalleled sweetness: you could simply say that it was her ideal come true. It was precisely because it was like this that she was somewhat too serious about it: Even something as tiny as a sesame seed could destroy her mood; she would feel joyless and lose her sexual urge. Madam X said this was her greatest limitation, and because of this she couldn't behave; she set the standards so high that men could never reach them. Her emotions went up and down, wearying other people. But in the past she hadn't always thought "the grass was greener on the other side." It was her "occult" activities that changed her. They kindled her sexual prowess and summoned the demons within her, and from then on she was like a hungry wolf looking everywhere for food and provoking endless trouble. Her colleague noticed that a little girl's innocent expression appeared on Madam X's face as she spoke in her self-absorbed way. She despised her even more, and she wished she could kick her under the table and make her scream in pain.

Her interest in a man, she revealed, always derived from the color of his eyes and the tone of his voice, which she had "the ability to distinguish in detail and concerning which she had a wealth of experience." This wasn't to say that she preferred romantic love— no, she detested it and thought it contrived. However, any man who measured up to her standards would have overwhelming happiness with her in bed. At such times, she would be uninhibited. She would spare nothing, and her partner would reap satisfaction such as he had never known before. From this, you can also see that she had a high opinion of herself—so high it sounded like boasting. She also divulged that although her standards might change, she could always promptly find the right men. Once she found one, she would pursue him to the end: she wouldn't give up halfway—never!— unless irrefutable evidence proved her mistaken. Only then would she "turn back."

After all this blustering, her colleague tried every trick in the book to lead her to talk of her "illicit affair," hoping to experience it vicariously. "What do you think of men's physiques?" "Which is better—a big guy or a little one?" "What's the difference between a married man and a virgin?" "Which is more exciting—a gentle type or a wild one?" But Madam X became deadly serious. It was as though she refused to comment on specific individuals and wanted a purely scientific discussion. She remained silent and looked as though she pitied her colleague and wanted to give her a hand. Her attitude provoked her colleague to spring to her feet (taking the opportunity to kick her) and shout that she was "a whore pretending to be a saint." She was so wanton that, as soon as she was with a man, all she wanted from the first minute was "to go to bed." "Going to bed" was the only truth. There was not the least reason to believe her self-worship bullshit. Unless her organs were defective, only a fool would believe that she would let the opportunity for such joy slip away. God only knew how many men she'd been with over the years. Otherwise, how could she have "the ability to distinguish in detail, as well as a wealth of experience with men"?

Shrugging, Madam X patiently explained that she couldn't convey her perceptions with words. She was indeed a little different from other people. Something others thought impossible happened to her. She couldn't help it. Please don't think she had closed down: actually, the door to her heart was open, and she'd been looking forward to being with people (including "making it" with men), but she hadn't succeeded, and her experience had "calmed her" long ago.

After the colleague left, she dropped in on Old Woman Jin. As it happened, Old Woman Jin and the coal worker had just gotten it on and were bare-assed. Because the female colleague blew in like a gust of wind (Old Woman Jin never bolted her door), they instantly sat up under the quilt but didn't move. They chatted with Madam X's colleague and petted each other affectionately. The colleague brought explosive news: Madam X was going to get married. Old Woman Jin was astonished. After looking all over for her trousers, she covered herself with a chemise and jumped out of bed. Then, she fired off a string of questions: Madam X is already married—how can she "get married"? Is this legal? Since she's going to get married, why didn't she do it either sooner or later? Why did she have to do it at this point—at the very time when Old Woman Jin was on the brink of success in love and was about to overwhelm Madam X in this arena? If she got married, wouldn't all of Old Woman Jin's efforts be wasted and she'd be up a creek? What on earth was Madam X up to? Was it possible that this gossip wasn't true at all and was meant only to confuse people? The colleague was laughing, urging Old Woman Jin to calm down. She sat her bottom down on the bed and crushed the coal worker's foot. He pulled back with a grimace. "Madam X," the colleague said slowly, "Madam X is really an invincible and mighty person!" and Old Woman Jin trembled all over.

She told them that Madam X was her best friend and that she was the strongest woman she'd ever encountered. All she had to do was crook her finger and people would do her bidding. If anyone tried to take advantage of her or set himself against her, he ended up the worse for it. Without turning a hair, she could set a deathtrap for him. As for her, she felt fortunate to have made such a friend, and if she had to exhaust all of her energy to defend Madam X's reputation, she wouldn't hesitate in the least. As for Madam X's power over men, of course she—Old Woman Jin—couldn't dispute this. Madam X simply didn't give her a thought. Old Woman Jin might feel she'd triumphed over Madam X by getting into bed with the coal worker. But Madam X didn't notice this trivial thing at all: she simply wasn't aware of it, because she was a woman of great talent and bold vision how could she care about a guy like this? Even if he persisted in thinking he was important to Madam X, this was just unrequited love, and Old Woman Jin's tactics were based only on misconceptions—an immature game, an irrelevant plaything, better not even to deal with. If Madam X can be said to have any real rival, it can only be she—Madam X's best friend: she's the only one she's afraid of. For she's the one who knows all of Madam X's secrets, who best understands Madam X's strange nature, and who has at least as much power to charm men. Who else would Madam X be afraid of? And so, although she is Madam X's best friend, she's also the rival that Madam X worries about. After years of observing men falling for Madam X's charm, she has figured out her trump cards. The most useful is sexual innuendo. In this, Madam X is extremely vulgar: she always talks directly to her partner of her "desires" and then waits for the person to be aroused so she can control him. Of course, she isn't aroused—and even cruelly mocks her partner for his physiological response. This trump card has withstood the test of time, and it wins every time. This is merely because most men are good-for-nothings; their very birth was a mistake. After she had observed and understood Madam X's inner steeliness, Madam X was scared to death and sought her out numerous times to explain herself. She said she wasn't a bystander where men were concerned, that now and then she looked forward to a sexual relationship with an ideal man, but she "couldn't find her ideal" and so turned out to be the way she is today. The colleague saw through her. Madam X was afraid this weak spot would become public knowledge and she would lose her admirers. Of course the colleague would never stab Madam X in the back. She just wished to make Madam X less arrogant. She isn't the only woman in the world. Someone else is much better; someone else is calm and modest. Why can't Madam X be like this? She wasn't inclined toward riotous passion—why did she have to fake it? Although it satisfied her vanity, what a blow to the men of the world (even if they were just garbage).

The colleague stopped and looked out the door. Then she bolted it securely and turned around. "Not long ago," she whispered, "there was a guy—I'm not exaggerating—he used to be one of her admirers, but after discovering me, he finally saw the light: he real-ized what real feminine charm is. I certainly didn't intend to steal her business. Not me. Each time, I just stayed off to one side, but men noticed me. This wasn't my fault; it was the awakening of their inner maleness. Oh my God! The real thing is here! Oh my God! The shimmering pearl is right here! This happened lots of times, too many to count. If I revealed the numbers, she'd be too ashamed to show her face. She completely overlooked me, this crazy person." She suddenly felt empty inside. "Why don't you light the stove in your house?" she yelled. Then she kicked the stove until it fell over and red coals scattered on the floor. Then, swinging her arms, she took her leave.

Old Woman Jin and the young coal worker looked at each other in despair. "Should we put our pants on?" the coal worker asked hesitantly. "Fuck off!" Old Woman Jin shouted. He misunderstood and "made it" with her again. They rolled onto the coals and wailed like stuck pigs.

To return to Madam X: Had she been born with her notions of sex? Had she ever experienced true success and failure? If not, then we can say only that her idea of sex is nothing but a mannerism. According to Madam X's younger sister, however, her ideas "have gone from being blurry to being focused and have changed over time to what they are today." There's not much chance of getting anything from analyzing what the sister said: we've already tried that. We'd be better off reasoning for ourselves: we could scour our eyes and could also think it through logically. From the way Madam X behaves, we can be sure she used to be a desperate slut. She'd "gone to bed" countless times (the proof is in the way her eyes light up when she mentions "going to bed"). With such a frightening sexual appetite, she must have destroyed quite a few men's careers and even caused someone's death. Sure, some women are a little dissolute—others won't mind very much when they "ease up" a little now and then—but we've never seen a woman like Madam X, who takes people's lives. It wasn't until she became notorious and was dismissed from the government office and drifted over to Five Spice Street that she had to exercise a little self-restraint. After a few months, she felt robbed of good times and wanted to make it up to herself. Before long, she showed her true nature. She emphasized that she "knew herself thoroughly and was very discreet," that she had now entered a "phase of sober reckoning with herself," and that her "dispel boredom" activities allowed her to "eliminate all worldly interference." She "could see her desire directly." From the standpoint of Madam X's welfare, it would have been better if she'd been mixed up all her life and never had to be awakened. She became so aggressive that she scared men away—who would dare risk his life? At the same time, she indulged in hopeless self-admiration and couldn't get along with people. (She claimed that men no longer meant anything to her.) Who knows what was in her mind? What did it have to do with men? She shouldn't have had such a high opinion of herself, because it was all a misconception that counted for nothing. If men meant nothing to her, why did she seek them out? Wouldn't it have been much more impressive to "keep herself as pure as jade," as the widow did? Madam X had no answers and stressed that since she started her occult activities, her body had become fresher by the day. Every time the big bell in the city tolled and the first light of morning broke, she leapt lightly from the crook in her husband's arm to the window, where she stood for a long time, feeling—as she told her sister—that "her breasts were so full, her buttocks rounded, her thighs long and supple, her whole body like swaying willow branches." One morning, our widow witnessed the entire drama and reported that there was "no way to describe" her reaction. She also said that Madam X's husband actually "abetted this behavior." Maybe her precious husband had been "in cahoots" with her all along.

Once aroused, Madam X's body would stir up endless trouble. She could have displayed her magic power anywhere, but unfortunately chose Five Spice Street, where people had lived in an orderly fashion for generations. No one imagined that a woman like this would ever show up here—not even Old Meng, the eighty-three-year-old fortune-teller at the pharmacy. Madam X had dropped down like an alien from outer space, started a snack shop with her husband, and made it clear they were here to stay. Only after a long time did we become aware of their presence. The ordinary Five Spice Street people were realists: though at first confused, they narrowed their eyes and took the measure of this couple. They accepted the facts and quickly worked out countermeasures. This couple was tolerated as a "dissident element." All along, the Five Spice Street people had been good at tolerating different ideas and individuals. It wasn't unprincipled compromise but a gradual assimilation in which over the years others fused into a single unit with themselves. From ancient times onward, this method had generally produced the desirable result. But not with Madam X.

From the day she landed on Five Spice Street to the present (about two or three years), Madam X's cancer-like stubbornness endangered others. It was as if it wasn't she who should be assimilated, but everyone else. Wasn't this what she pursued with clenched teeth? Of course, this was no big deal to a community with such a long tradition. This healthy organism might even benefit from producing antibodies. But, when all is said and done, mosquitoes are loathsome: they buzz and suck people's blood. Madam X was just such a loathsome spotted mosquito. We just hoped she wouldn't annoy people too much with her buzzing so that our kind people wouldn't have to kill her. Her notions were deeply at odds with the traditions of Five Spice Street.

Let's talk first of cooling off outside: this was the most abhorrent thing this couple did. In the summer, we southerners sit outside to enjoy the cool evening breeze, and we do this next to the main street. Small groups congregate until midnight to talk over all the major events, imagine the future, or criticize society. People had to take part, for important decisions were made here. Beginning with the first summer after they arrived, Madam X and her family showed their lack of breeding. As the crowds were enjoying the breeze, they strolled down the main street, eyes straight ahead. Afterwards, they closed the door of their little house and did not reemerge. The woman fiddled with her microscope, and the man "did who knows what." The young coal worker once went over to Madam X and "tactfully broached the subject," inviting her "to take part in a bit of a social movement," but she "laughed grimly" and bent her head again to look into the microscope, as if afraid that the coal worker might delay her even a minute. It was also as though she didn't recognize him. The coal worker sat in silence for a while, his inferiority complex mounting. When he went home, "he couldn't even walk steadily."

"Well," he said, oddly embarrassed, "she was busy with her own work, which is certainly superior. I was almost moved to tears. Her work is unique; we mustn't importune her. . . ."

Before he'd finished, the widow spat in his face, and lambasted him: "You're shameless. What kind of sugarplum did you get from that monkey spirit?"

Year after year went by, and Madam X and her husband still didn't participate in the gatherings; they still closed their door tight. Not only this, they attempted in vain to use their occult activities to break down the Five Spice Street community. Because of her, the number of people who came out for the cool breeze decreased a little, and the number who engaged in occult activities with her increased. This delighted her stupid husband: when he ran into anyone, he would say how wonderful Madam X's "unique skill" was. Once it was put into practice, no traditional custom could withstand it: it simply swept away all obstacles. This husband boasted like a child. Even so, we could see Madam X's "pervasive power" that others had overlooked.

Besides enjoying the evening breeze, there was another great interest: photography. Our Five Spice Street people thought taking pictures was grand—like celebrating a festival. In addition to taking pictures at home, every year when spring came and the flowers were in bloom, large groups squeezed into the photography studio in the city center for group photos. Then, they took them home as rare keepsakes, placed them in the best frames, and hung them on their walls. No matter whose home you went into, photos covered the walls and filled people with pride. Madam X's family was an exception. It was okay not to take part in this collective movement, but why make such extremely negative comments against it? She and her husband said that "there wasn't any advantage" to taking photos, that it was all "a gloss"; "if a person wants to see the reality, a lifelike self, the best method is to look in the mirror," "if a person doesn't dare look in a mirror, what does he take photos for?—it's all self-deception," and so on. While playing, even their son, Little Bao, often offhandedly said, "Photos, photos, photos! I'm sick to death of this!" There were a lot of other weird things about Madam X's family—too many to enumerate. They can be summed up, though, in one line: Everything they did was done purposely to destroy Five Spice Street's social system. They desperately wanted to take this hostility to the grave.

4

MR. Q AND HIS FAMILY

Below a hill in the suburbs was a row of red brick bungalows: our Mr. Q and his wife and two sons lived in a small flat here. Mr. Q and his wife were both about thirty-eight or thirty-nine years old (in private, they adamantly considered themselves forty-five, having already seen everything there was to see in the world). They were affable and gentle—easy to be around. They both worked in government offices. After they returned home from an exhausting day, their tiredness was swept away by their lively sons (ages nine and eleven), who threw themselves at them.

Outsiders saw a touching family picture. In the front and back yards, they grew pumpkins, bitter melons, and beans and also raised some snow-white longhaired rabbits, a large tiger cat, and one handsome and heroic wolf dog. Husband and wife loved the country and disliked the urban hullabaloo. In the warm summer sun, the air was filled with sweet scents and the hum of bees. Under the melon rack, Mr. Q would kiss his wife—a long kiss, as if their lips were sticky with honey. Afterwards, they would sit and cuddle on the long stone bench under the melon rack. Hot tears brimmed in their eyes as they immersed themselves in a sort of ancient reverie and forgot all their worries. Only when a bird called would they come to. Then they would be inspired to kiss again. They had lived this quiet, affectionate life for fifteen years that seemed to have gone by in the blink of an eye. From the beginning, they got on very well, and their affection had grown deeper by the day. It seemed that the two had become an indivisible whole. Until Mr. Q met Madam X.

Of course, their temperaments were not at all the same. Mr. Q's wife was a gentle, cowardly, simple woman. From the first day, she had adored him, and from adoration had gone on to love him. Her love was bone-deep. She had never given any other man a serious glance, because she thought that apart from Mr. Q, men were frightening and incomprehensible. Meeting Mr. Q had been her greatest good fortune. Waiting on Mr. Q wholeheartedly and taking on all the heavy family responsibilities, she now and then felt a young wife's pride from the bottom of her heart. At times like this, she was no longer cowardly, and her cheeks took on the blush of a young wife; all at once, she became graceful and charming. It was hard to be sure about Mr. Q's temperament. It was multi-layered. We can also say that he had never fully unveiled his true temperament, so we've never come up with a precise assessment. But his two main characteristics—generosity and kindness—were always evident. Other aspects of his temperament that became apparent in the half year of his contact with Madam X never fully emerged. From what he said, his behavior had been repressed because of his sense of "original sin" since the day he was born. No one could figure out how great his potential was, or what kind of abnormal thing he was capable of doing.

Mr. Q was chivalrous and warm. He loved his wife: from the very beginning, he decided he would never hurt her. He would always be a big brother to her and a protective, loving husband. In the beginning, their sex life wasn't so great, but they worked on it, and with mutual affection as an accelerator, they eventually achieved a great deal of satisfaction. His wife developed from a passive virgin into a lover who could satisfy Mr. Q body and soul. Q appreciated his wife and felt indebted to her. Words like the following added spice to their lives: "If you ever love another woman, I'll kill myself on the spot so that the two of you can fulfill your desires." "It was simply unforeseen that you would fall into my life: it was God making up to me for my long life alone." (The wife's words.) "If there is life after death and I could choose another wife in the hereafter, I would still choose you." "You're my ideal. You thoroughly changed me and made me a good, pure man. Other women would have corrupted me." "Is there any joy I haven't experienced? Is there anything that can move me more than this?!" (Mr. Q's words.) Although nauseating, this illustrates the depth of their love.

Yet, can we say that no one had ever come between them, that their lives had always been calm, with the blue sky and white clouds above and the cat and rabbits below, bees flying around them and little birds and insects sharing their affection? No. This would be a little too ideal. It was at odds with Mr. Q's frame of reference. Unfortunately, Mr. Q was very sexy. Sensitive women could see from his face and his behavior the carnal desire he restrained. They could also see how crazy he was about sex. Now and then, a lusty vigor would surge up and contend with reason. This both annoyed and confused him. But each time he surmounted the difficulties the demons were stirring up, returned to his peaceful little kingdom, and once more became a good man, a good loving husband.

The year he turned thirty-five (a man's best time), a gorgeous woman took stock of him and lay in wait at the foot of some dark stairs. She "grabbed" his arm and urgently expressed her desire.

"You live for this." Without listening to his protests, she fixed her eyes on his and waited with half-open lips for his kiss.

He didn't move. After a long time (the woman felt it must have been ten thousand years), they finally found a way out of the stalemate. Mr. Q sighed and said, "What is this about? We don't even know each other!"

The woman left in a huff. Afterwards, he told his wife that he had felt a passing lightheadedness but had quickly regained his equilibrium and "had seen through" her.

"She's a common flirt," he said to his wife (in an unduly bland manner that seemed to be glossing over something). "How can she compare with you!"

He weaseled out of it, and the woman quickly turned to another man. He felt fortunate and proud: he hadn't fallen for her trick; the sequel would have been unimaginable. At first glance, a woman might seem special although she actually wasn't. Wasn't this proof?

If a man took a risk for this kind of woman, what could he achieve except his own destruction? In general, women were loathsome. If there was another kind, he certainly hadn't seen it, so how could he prove there was? Up to now, he hadn't seen any relationship more perfect than his with his wife. He believed there could be nothing better. His vision was so sharp he couldn't be fooled. He was already forty-five: was there anything he couldn't see through?

His wife celebrated their (she did not say his, but always said their) victory as if it were a holiday. She couldn't help but redouble her caresses. She called him "my poor boy. My poor, solitary little boy." And he redoubled his response to her, ashamed of his momentary, contemptible thoughts. He vowed he would never tell her about this and would always preserve their love's perfection and purity. Who could compare with his wife? This graceful, pure, virginal person! This soul fully loaded with love! Each time, he marveled and adored her. In their fifteen years together, they'd probably encountered that kind of "trouble" four or five times. Each time, Q dealt with it properly. He would never let such a vulgar thing disturb his angel-like wife's mood (that would be the same as deliberately hurting her). If he had to, he would tell her afterwards. He would turn it into a joke. He would never let her have uneasy suspicions.

From the bottom of her heart, Q's wife knew that Q was charming, knew the way he appeared to other women. But she wasn't the least bit jealous. There was no room in her heart for jealousy. She was just uneasy. She thought of her husband as a charming child, skipping through the world as naked as the day he was born. All around were thorns and unseen wild animals. He could be hurt at any moment. He was her husband, her big brother, but emotionally he was also her child—a gullible, hotheaded child. She needed to guide him in the dark to a safe place. Excited about her mission, she couldn't help smiling.

"What are you so happy about?"

"Female stuff. Not for you."

The clouds passed, and the sky was once again blue and pure. The bean blossoms gave off their faint intoxicating scent. With one child on his knee, Mr. Q would cuddle his frail little wife in his strong arms: he was steeped in his happiness as father and husband. If this witch X hadn't appeared, or if it had been another woman and not X, then Q and his wife could have been a model of affection, an example for everyone to emulate.

The disastrous incident took place one fair afternoon in May. It was a day off for Mr. Q and his wife. From the time they got up early in the morning (they never slept in), Mr. Q had felt an uneasy stirring that lasted until afternoon. He scrupulously hid it from his wife. After lunch, he stood up and told his wife he was going out to get his fortune told, and then—his mind unsettled—he left. (Here, we'll add a little: Mr. Q was a truly superstitious person. In this, he was much different from Madam X, who practiced the occult arts without being superstitious herself. In the marrow of her bones, she was unusually self-confident: that is to say, she had always believed only in herself— not the gods, and not fate, either. She challenged fate, jeered at it. Whenever possible, she would do any wild thing to oppose fate. She would never admit defeat. Mr. Q was the opposite: he lived in fear, believed in the gods and fate, and seldom had any improper ideas. He often had his fortune told, and the outcome affected his mood, either stimulating him too much or leaving him dispirited. Some-times, for several days in a row, he acted frivolously—like a child: he mumbled and was in a wonderful mood. Sometimes, he'd sit upright and silent like an old man, mind empty and eyes vacant. Whenever this occurred, his wife knew someone had told his fortune again. He would give up his day off to walk several miles to see a fortune-teller. He would save money to pay these guys who held his destiny in their hands. Having his fortune told was his only hobby. Two days earlier, a colleague had told him that a real psychic lived on Five Spice Street in the city: it was said that she had incredible abilities but hadn't told anyone's fortune yet. If he went, perhaps he could charm her into telling his fortune. Mr. Q immediately filed this information away in his mind. We have no record of the details of this fortune-telling, because no one provided reliable information and Mr. Q hasn't told anyone of it, either. His letters threw light only on her eyeballs. He didn't say a word about fortune-telling. Madam X's sister (present at the time) only sighed about some totally unrelated things that referred vaguely to Mr. Q's looks. We've dealt with this above. Anyhow, this was the first time Mr. Q and Madam X met. It was a vital meeting, for it changed the course of a lot of people's lives. It also led to an innocent person's death. We'll discuss this later.

Here, we want to talk of the weather that day, because the weather was a decisive link in the whole affair. It really was an unfathomable, weird day! Of course, if we weren't making a special point of looking into the details, it might have been no different from any other spring day. Years later, the lame woman on Five Spice Street recalled that the weather that day was very fair. Beginning in the morning, white clouds like flowers wandered in the sky. Later, "these flowers even hung from the treetops." She stuck her head out the window; it was "like a wonderland" outside. "In addition to the cloud flowers, there was another unusual thing: the scent of the grass." You need to know there'd never been any grass on Five Spice Street; only some stunted trees stood at the side of the road. But now a strong, refreshing smell of grass suffused the air with a little green color that intoxicated people and made them sentimental. It was in this kind of atmosphere that our Mr. Q walked toward Madam X's little house. What happened next, and what kind of turn occurred in his life, is also comprehensible. We don't know where the fault lay that day: even God acted as matchmaker for this pair of adulterers.

Mr. Q's wife was utterly ignorant of what happened. She never inquired about her husband's associates or his activities. She wasn't curious about anything her husband didn't care to tell her. After Q returned at twilight, he was in an especially good mood; his wife just thought that "he must have been told a good fortune today," and felt happy for him. When the stars came out, the two snuggled in the doorway and sang "The Brook Below the Mountain" in soft voices. They were intoxicated for a long time. Mr. Q heard hidden meanings in the song that made him stop abruptly at the last note. His wife didn't even notice. They snuggled even closer.

"The scent of grass." Mr. Q suddenly shed tears. "Has spring really come?"

"Finally," his wife responded, choking with sobs.

A puff of fog from a green meteor on the horizon startled the hill. It quivered a few times as a magical silence settled down again everywhere. In his dreams that night, Mr. Q pondered the same question: "Can batteries be loaded into people's eyes?" The entire night, he struggled in and out of dreams. An incandescent light blinded him. He turned his head and saw a colorless, deserted glass road that stretched to a certain corner.

The second day that Mr. Q and Madam X met, after the lame woman encountered Mr. Q from the window, a miracle occurred. At first, she felt that ants were biting her legs, and then, "without knowing where her strength came from," she actually began all at once to lean on both crutches and wobbled out the door. We don't know whether she had heard where Mr. Q lived or not—we aren't even sure whether she'd heard anything about Mr. Q. However, she immediately "recognized him." Now, calling upon a blurry memory, she headed toward Mr. Q's home. Soon, she arrived at the small house with the melon rack. Q's wife was sitting there, listening to the bees sing, with a little red flower in her hair, her head swaying back and forth. She didn't even notice the lame woman who had stopped in front of her. She never paid much attention to outsiders. She thought her no more than a passerby waiting for someone in the doorway. She opened her eyes a little, then closed them again, absorbed in the singing of the bees.

"Hellooooo," the lame woman dragged out the sound sullenly. Q's wife thought it was the wind calling uneasily in the open country, for the wind was always doing this.

"Are you deaf?" Extending a thin, bony hand, the lame woman tapped her on the shoulder. Only then did Q's wife turn around in surprise and look at her with a sulky, aggrieved expression.

"The shadow streaking across in front of us is a wild dog." She was staring hard at Mrs. Q. "I've had experience with this: that was ten years ago, one twilight when the peas blossomed."

The woman now made eye contact with her. Skimming over her small puppet-like face were inauspicious dark clouds, but they quickly vanished.

"Something troubling you?" She gave the lame woman a compassionate look, indicating she should take the chair in front of her. "Not everyone's in a good mood like me. I hear of troubled people everywhere—truly wretched. Who are you?"

"Me? How could you know about me? I've heard the story about you and the wild dog. It has only three legs—right? Me? You know, I've been paralyzed in both legs for ten years, and as I was lying there, I heard a lot of things—so many that my head nearly exploded. When I was confined to bed, I saw you and the dog. Today, all at once, I've walked over here: it's really weird. The doctors say it's dangerous for me to lose my temper; I have a pain in my chest."

"It's too bad. This morning, I was thinking of weaving a crown of willow twigs to wear on my head. Beside the pond in back there are some weeping willows."

"Go to hell!" The lame woman stood up and, pointing with a crutch at the melon rack, told her off. "What's this? These ragged things hanging in front of the door: aren't they counterfeit? You're all nothing but walking corpses. It makes me dizzy just thinking of it!" She left in a rage.

Mrs. Q couldn't understand her outrage; she thought the woman bizarre. She grew timid whenever a stranger appeared. She couldn't make friends with anyone, for people were always bad-tempered and she didn't dare get close. In truth, she shouldn't have been born in this world, for there were too many threats all around. Luckily she had Q, her husband, her reliable friend who did away with the world's dangers for her. And so, for the first time in her life, she grew worried: where was Q? Where was her passionate boy? She changed her shoes, went to the path, and looked around. She heard only the wind whimpering. She looked again and again, and suddenly was ashamed of herself: she felt she was being unfair to him. This was disgraceful. After she calmed down, she went back to the melon rack to listen to the bees. But the bees were no longer singing: they were just whirling around in a crazy circle. The woman's head felt a little heavy, and her eyes a little blurred. Who on earth was that person? It seemed she had frequently been confronted with those blazing black eyes. When she went to the well to draw water, a lynx was squatting there. The path was always littered with wild animals' footprints. Could it be a portent? No, so why was she pulling a long face? She remembered her trunk that held all kinds of treasures—including some the lame woman could never imagine! Well, then, sing some songs. She was hoarse.

The lame woman walked far away, her crutches still echoing. . . .

It was really a terrifying day.

The bees didn't sing again that day.

"A fortune-teller came." She braced herself to joke with her husband.

"Recently, I haven't been too interested in fortune-telling." In high spirits, Q was looking at his wife. He kissed her little ears and smiled absent-mindedly.

"You're wonderful!" Gasping in admiration, she threw herself into his arms. "How about paying a little more attention to our bees and getting them to sing all the time?"

5

THE FAILURE OF REEDUCATION

One noon in the second year of Madam X's "dispel boredom" movement, there was a small get-together at the lame woman's home. More than a dozen charming, graceful women attended. This meeting wasn't convened by anyone but was brought about by telepathy: it was a "coincidence." These women were forthright like "feminists." As soon as they sat down in the room, each began cursing someone. Because they were on the same wave length, they were doubly stimulated—they shared a bitter hatred of the enemy and fought in high spirits, all of them eager and determined to throw all their energy into this.

In this charged atmosphere, the widow suggested that they ask Old Woman Jin to go out and buy some fried dough sticks in order "to lift their spirits" for "working energetically on this." Naturally, this suggestion drew unanimous approval, and soon the whole room was filled with the sound of fried dough sticks being eaten. Some people surreptitiously wiped their greasy fingers on the lame woman's quilt. After finishing the dough sticks, they ate some fried dough twists and then played cards. In the midst of such a good time, they nearly forgot the main point. Only when the female colleague prompted them did they start cursing someone again. This time, it wasn't the one they had begun with—the woman they all knew—but instead an eighty-year-old "who should have been dead a long time ago." After half an hour, they finally realized they had "shifted the objective of the struggle," and resumed cursing the first woman.

"She's still coming up with ideas for your children!" The widow brought up this most sensitive and thrilling issue and then launched into a lengthy self-analysis. Her emotions were like a surging flood: "Although I have no children, I will join you in struggling against her to the end. In the first place, I had the ability to have children, but my deceased husband and I didn't think children were important. You could say we didn't even think about it—and so the outcome was inevitable. You must remember that in those years, the old folks said that I would have at least a dozen children; they all described me as 'a mother hen good at laying eggs.' Fifty-eight people said this, and some were so excited they said it repeatedly. As you all know, I was great at sex. No one could compare with me. I was like a plot of fertile land: it was only necessary to sow good seeds and I could have continually born fruit. I wasn't like a certain person, who, even if she had sturdy seeds, either couldn't bear fruit or just bore one monstrous one. Her soil isn't fertile enough. You can't figure out if she's even a woman. Later on, I didn't care whether or not I had children. Having children doesn't mean anything. The important thing is a person's moral character. This is a person's true value. Although it's fine to have children, if they aren't brought up well, they can harm society. What's the point of having a child at odds with society from the moment it's born? Now, a lot of these destructive children have appeared in our community, and they're directly related to a certain person's conspiracy. How should we deal with this? Is it conceivable that we can't think of countermeasures?"

At this point, the widow remembered something: "The reason I didn't have children is related to my years of keeping myself as pure as jade: I considered this to be of the utmost importance. After my husband died of his illness, have any of my relationships with men gone beyond friendship? One after another, strong young men—in the prime of life—were hot for me. But I had long ago transcended the worldly and given up the vulgar, and never again showed any interest in this kind of thing. Whether a person has children or not doesn't matter. I'm concerned only to actualize my lofty ideals."

These sincere words opened up the female colleague's sluice gate of sentimentality. Thinking of her "evil son," she couldn't keep from wailing until her face was wet with tears and snot. First she wiped her face with her sleeve and then with the lame woman's grease-spotted quilt—leaving her face blotchy. Choking with sobs, she said she wanted to "fight a duel with" Madam X (she mentioned her by name; it would have been much better to be beautifully indirect, as the widow was; this showed that she lacked breeding). If she didn't succeed, she'd kill herself and let the law punish her. Sure enough, as she talked, she rammed her skull against the side of the bed. Nobody stopped her: indeed, they all looked on with avid interest, as if they wanted to see how strong her skull was. The female colleague rammed her head more than twenty times before looking up and dashing outside with a "wild look in her eyes."

"This is precisely the calamity that children bring down on us." The widow summed up calmly, "What's worth flaunting about this kind of child? It's just exposing one's own inferiority to the public through one's child. When people see her son, they can't help but associate him with her. If she didn't have a son, she could still pretend to be classy."

As soon as the widow stopped talking, the room turned quiet. After a while, the sound of intermittent sobs came from two corners of the room. Old Woman Jin and the widow's forty-eight-year-old friend were crying. They were crying because they were in the same boat as the widow—neither had children, nor could they in the future. As they thought of Madam X's intrigue with Five Spice Street's young generation, they hated her guts—God knows how much. In their trance, they imagined they had no children because of this detestable Madam X. If it weren't for Madam X, they would have been happy round-faced grannies with dozens of children and grandchildren at their knees.

Old Woman Jin thought back to her unappealing "love life" with the young coal worker: it had made her sad and lonely. Sure, she'd had fleeting feelings of triumph and joy, but they were just a flash in the pan. It was this woman X who had kept her from reveling in her love. Now she "abhorred to death" this young coal worker: her relationship with him was no more than an "obligation" (she couldn't bear to destroy him by abandoning him). If it weren't for Madam X, she certainly wouldn't have chosen this half-grown baby of a coal worker (she could get as many babies like this as she wanted). You have to know that in the past, she was a winsome woman. It was just because of her bad luck that she started hating men from the bottom of her heart and kept her distance. If she'd had a little better luck, every man would have wanted to throw himself at her feet and she could have chosen anyone she wanted. Now, she'd actually sunk so low as to end up the mistress of the young coal worker (the poor guy), and this had certainly not elevated her position on Five Spice Street; probably she'd fallen even further in other people's opinions. The curse responsible for all this was precisely Madam X's. This Madam X was a skilled sorceress. Anyone who saw her would involuntarily hallucinate, involuntarily start making mistakes. Generally, people would regret those mistakes for a lifetime. At the beginning, she'd had so many exciting plans! She'd spent so many good days immersed in fascinating ideas. She'd already defeated Zhou Sanji. She thought this victory was unquestionable. But beginning in the morning the day before yesterday, that damn back of his appeared again at her door. As he pulled up his pants, he was humming for fear she wouldn't notice him. Now everything was upside down. She had no idea how it had started. She just knew that all her effort had been fruitless, and she'd become a laughingstock. She couldn't hold up her head again. Zhou Sanji had also walked into her house at noon and announced to her and the coal worker: When he stood in her doorway and pulled his pants up, he wasn't doing it for her. He wouldn't give her even a passing thought if it weren't that he'd heard her shout at him yesterday. He stated that he stood in her doorway just to "ponder things."

And why was the forty-eight-year-old good friend crying? Let's listen carefully to what she confided to the widow. (The widow listened attentively, her expression serious.) She said that more than twenty years ago, when she was still a bewitching young woman, a boy fell in love with her at first sight. She was touched, but because of the disparity in their ages and because she was a widow, she "reined in her feelings" and didn't let them show at all. Twenty years had gone by, and the boy had become a man with work and a family. She was still alone. Her pure feelings for him were her spiritual sustenance. They both realized that their inner yearning hadn't vanished but had strengthened by the day. (Of course, she didn't take the next step and destroy his family.) Just then, like a thunderclap on a fine day, her handsome boy suddenly took a fancy to someone else. He pursued the woman all day and "started inquiring into her background." He became abnormally sensitive. Whenever someone was talking about the person for whom he felt this one-sided love, he wedged himself into the conversation and loudly and unscrupulously defended her, pretending to be her knight in shining armor. "He really was shameless." How could a normal person feel such desperate passion? This was incomprehensible. For example, she herself felt intensely passionate about the boy of old and the young man of today—it wasn't what ordinary people might imagine, but for sure she "wasn't desperate" and for sure she "wasn't shameless." This didn't mean that she was feigning her feelings. Everyone would say that her feelings were natural and reasonable. Only "desperation" was phony and inane! She wouldn't blame the one she cared about. The ones she abhorred were the evil woman and man who had lured him to evil ways. The evil man was the evil woman's husband. The one she cared about had been simple and gullible all along. God knows how he'd become friends with that husband, such good friends that they were loath to part from each other. At the time, she'd warned him, but he had just laughed. We can see how good-hearted he was, filled with kindness for others, considerate of others, not begrudging going through fire and water for them. She'd known him twenty years, and thus she knew his character: it was only because of this that they'd maintained their affection so long. Now everything was over—and so suddenly! So unexpectedly!

The women promised to keep this to themselves. One evening a few days later, choosing a time before the youngsters arrived, they suddenly appeared at Madam X's home. Madam X's husband was in the front room playing Chinese checkers with his son. Staring at the chessboard and absorbed in their game, he did not appear to attach much importance to the arrival of these people: indeed, he didn't even think of them as women, though they were all graceful, charming ladies. He didn't give them even a sidelong glance. Only a hint of a disdainful smile hung at the corner of his mouth. Wearing a white wool sweater, Madam X sat at the window, making complicated gestures. A tiny mirror hung from a button on the front of her sweater. She kept her back turned and gave no hint that she would ever face them. The ladies exchanged knowing glances, whispering and speculating on the meaning of her gestures.

Finally, on behalf of everyone else, the widow walked forward and pulled Madam X around to face the crowd. She said sorrowfully that she represented "the mothers" in exhorting her not to inflict any more harm on their children. She'd thought all along that it would be better for her to undertake some decent work for the community —for example, to make some proposals or write blackboard newspapers, or perhaps help educate the people about the new laws. All this was both legal and promising (she acknowledged that in some ways Madam X was a little more nimble than others). Why bother going on alone with that occult stuff? Even if she continued for ten or twenty years, she wouldn't gain the crowd's recognition or improve her own position. Even if at certain times she thought she had achieved huge and wonderful success, and congratulated herself on it, excessively proud of herself, so what? No one understood her, so what practical significance would that kind of success have? Who would care about her success? Of course, they all understood her—knew that she was aloof and that right now she had no immediate hope of changing her position in society. She was probably most interested in pursuing a certain kind of fresh stimulation. But a person doesn't live in a vacuum: her behavior shouldn't harm others. When it does, serious consequences follow.

As the widow was speaking, the crowd noticed that Madam X's face wasn't at all the face they usually saw, but was that of some person they didn't recognize. On that different face were growing two hoary eyeballs without pupils. The eyeballs weren't moving, as if they were dead. Only her long, thin fingers were twiddling incessantly with the tiny mirror on her chest. Her fingers were very expressive, as if giving a mystical performance. She didn't say a word.

After the widow finished, the female colleague spoke; after her came Old Woman Jin, and after her, the forty-eight-year-old friend. After her came Ms. B, and after her, Ms. A. Finally, everyone shouted: "Give up your destructive ploys! The children are our lifeblood!" Some held their chins up, as if to make this stranger's face return to its original appearance.

Only then did Madam X finally twitch, and opening her pupilless eyes, she asked, "What children?"

"The ones you summon here every day." Tapping X's knee with a crutch, the lame woman said, "Don't play innocent!"

"There aren't any children," she said succinctly and definitely. "I don't know what you're talking about. Perhaps there were some shadows that came into this room." Everyone stared openmouthed.

"I absolutely don't care if some things enter while I'm experimenting. It is trivial, absolutely irrelevant. Maybe the shadows you mentioned just now were the children?" she added, her purehearted pose irreproachable.

There was just one thing: no one could find the pupils in her eyes. From the next room, Madam X's husband heard the noise and thought the women were making trouble. He thrust his way through the crowd and blocked his frail wife with his broad back. In a low voice, he bellowed at the women: "What are you up to?"

The women began backing off, looking at each other in despair. Though the gutsy widow yelled, she didn't have the courage, either, to take on this burly man. Finally, they left, and the husband slammed the door with a *peng*. He stuck his head out the window and yelled that if anyone came to make trouble for his wife in the future, he would "knock her teeth out." He also said that "no civic activities" had "anything" to do with them. On the way home, the women ran into a large crowd of teenagers. They tried to block their way, but the youngsters were as slippery as fish. You couldn't get hold of them. Laughing and joking, they broke away.

"We lost." They sat down dejectedly at the side of the road.

"Let's wait until summer," Ms. B said, "the time for discussing national political issues. People's feelings run high, and then perhaps the situation we saw during the lecture will be repeated. We mustn't lose our self-confidence."

6

MADAM X TALKS ABSTRACTLY OF HER EXPERIENCES
WITH MEN

In her gloomy room, Madam X frequently talked about her experiences with men, mainly to her younger sister and the female
colleague. It was her favorite topic. At such times, she looked as
hesitant as a little child. Her voice was uncertain and her gestures
feeble. She kept looking around, as if worried that someone would
sneak in like a shadow. Nevertheless, according to what the two
listeners leaked, what she said was shameless and crude. She could
talk for a long time about each part of her ideal man's body (of
course such a person didn't exist; according to Madam X, even the
listeners didn't exist). She talked of the significance of all sorts of
behaviors and actions: among them, of course, were eye color and
voice, which she said she blended into the body.

Here are two of her shocking examples: "The instinctive movements of the hands and lips coalesce into the feelings of a person's
entire life. We needn't waste time understanding a man. It's enough
to see how he moves. Indeed, it isn't even necessary to see. We can
wait and taste them." "Strength and duration are the clearest indica-
tors of his individuality, but this must also be realized through a
woman; otherwise, it's self-deceptive and unmasculine." She said
some even more devilish words that we don't feel comfortable repeating. When she talked of these things, she spoke like a slut. She
was absolutely shameless. If anyone mentioned this, she'd curl her
lip and say she wasn't the one who should feel shame and then
denounce the other for "being perverted." No one could understand

her aloof expression when she talked or the entrancing little smile at the corners of her mouth. If we don't think of this as a performance, then we have to deal with her sexual problem, and that gives us a headache. In the Five Spice Street community's recollections, the first person and also the last person who talked of men in such dirty language, observing no taboos, was Madam X. Even the female colleague who knew her well sometimes couldn't stand it.

This colleague was also greatly interested in men and had a lot of experience. Not only did she have intercourse frequently with her husband (after their son left, even more frequently), she also took great pleasure in talking about it—fantasizing all kinds of titillating details as she talked, reliving the experience and reviewing it. She was really expert, but she didn't like Madam X's vague way of talking about intimacies between men and women, which kindled her secret emotions and made her impatient for the sequel but provided no real stimulation. In the end, she just drew a blank, as if she'd been made a fool of—she was ashamed and embarrassed. It was damnable! Arbitrary! If they were talking about men, they must have names; they must have bodies and relationships, so that people could grasp them. Madam X's insubstantial remarks were idiotic nonsense, a hodgepodge. Using a child's tone of voice, she feigned a great deal of experience. She talked and talked, but it was nothing but nonsense—or, rather, a hoax. Her steamy language became insipid. She talked as if reading a document. It was boring and tiresome.

When the colleague left, she ran into her fat husband. She stamped her feet and shouted abuse. Her husband drew her into his arms and patted her rump, hoping to calm her down.

"I've been robbed! I've been fleeced!" She jumped up and slapped her husband's face. She still hadn't vented all her hatred and was shaking all over.

"By whom?"

"A thief!"

"Where?"

"Help!"

Although Madam X didn't quite sense the people around her, she learned from various channels of the wrath they felt for her, and logic, too, told her the whole world was hostile. She'd known for years that if she told people her true feelings she'd be laughed at, because everyone saw things precisely opposite from the way she did. Even if it was the most ordinary, imperceptible feeling, she was absolutely different. Yet she'd been herself for a long time, and there was no way to change. Who was at fault? Madam X stubbornly believed it was everyone else. To go her own way, she not only didn't look around her with her eyes, she also didn't talk with people. Sometimes it seemed that she was chatting with you earnestly with an attentive expression, and then you noticed that she wasn't talking to you at all, but talking over your head—or, even worse, talking to herself. She would be annoyed if you reminded her you were there. She was used to this kind of conversation. It was her weapon for dealing with the world. You couldn't see this weapon, but it was awesome. It always left the crowds on Five Spice Street unsure whether or not they wanted to talk with her again. They also wondered whether she secretly laughed at them. Were her empty generalities a kind of jeering? If they couldn't figure this out, weren't they fools? Time after time, they secretly made up their minds that they must figure out Madam X's ideas, but their efforts were always futile: it was always exhausting to talk with Madam X, and you ended up losing your self-confidence.

Someone asked Madam X about this, and she very simply told the person: she certainly didn't have any intrigues and wouldn't bother to laugh at anyone—that's the only way she could talk with people. Since she held "different views" from everyone else and was like this by nature, she had no choice but to deal with people this way lest both sides be "unbearably anguished." Let's bring up an example: she called the carnal relationship between men and women sexual intercourse. Everyone felt this was too "frankly revealing," too unpoetic. It should be called something like "recreation," but this term "nauseated" her. So, since the crowd stuck to its opinion and she didn't intend to change, if neither interfered with the other, perhaps they could live in peaceful coexistence.

Madam X acted this way toward the crowd but not with her younger sister. The two were birds of a feather. Their conversations always had to "exhaust" the subject. Sometimes, they closed the door and talked most of the day. Their passionate conversations generally were devoted to the composition of eyes, the differences between men and women, and astrology. Madam X always gave her opinions freely, and her sister respected her, believing that these matters consumed every minute of her day. Madam X told her that, on the contrary, she didn't consider them, and that it was precisely for this reason that she was able "to keep a clear head" from start to finish. As soon as someone took the evil path of "considering," he would become muddle-headed and lose his original appearance and "become a parrot." If no one "considered," if they were all as simple and pure as she, then everyone would be much more free and easy together. It was only because people learned from birth to "consider" that everything became so singularly complicated and she was thought "abnormal," able only to float like a balloon in midair. Of course, her sister didn't understand all this talk. She had always respected her big sister unconditionally and never tried to reason it through. She had just one comment: "She can fly!" Whether innate or influenced by her sister, her logic was just as weird. When they talked behind the closed door, now and then you could hear their husky voices drifting from the window, singing a duet, "The Little Lonely Boat." They always sang the same song, but each time the sentimental meaning seemed different. If people came to visit at times like this, the husband solemnly kept them outside and told them in hushed tones, "They're singing inside— shh!"

Madam X repeatedly described her ideal man in her usual style: vulgar, inane, and pretentious. She acted as if she were fascinated by the aftertaste of real things. "When the time comes, neither can stop fondling the other, neither can stop talking. Language is also a way of hinting at feelings, because try as hard as you can to communicate your ardor and your dreams to the other, you can't just show your feelings through action—that isn't enough. And so you use language. At such times, language has more than just everyday meaning—if only in some simple syllables, some little sounds that have sprouted wings. I can elicit that kind of special language."

Madam X also sometimes sighed with feeling, "I can't find a pair of good hands. Men's hands should be animated, filled with warm strength. The hands represent the whole person, with a tide of feelings surging through them." Almost all men's hands are "completely dry, pale, and lifeless," no better than "a tool for releasing one's own lust." She could tell those "poor, thin, neutered things at a glance." These things "had never experienced the pleasure of fondling: they weren't womanly, nor did they become real men. It's as though they're counterfeit goods." Overjoyed, her sister was only too eager for more details. She also foolishly confided that sometimes she "jumped up and down with desire and almost couldn't control" herself. Madam X, of course, wasn't as simple and impulsive as her younger sister. She was experienced and astute. Only in vulgarity were the two sisters alike.

Madam X gave an example. She said that one day years ago, she happened to see a pair of eyes flash past her, and all at once they turned into eyes with three colors. Inwardly happy, she approached that person. At the same time, she felt two young hands, which "seemed to have some stories." When she had just made contact, she realized her stupid mistake: "Those hands were shriveled, malnourished, and a little sickly. When they fondled you, they twitched." She shook her head, embarrassed, and said she certainly wouldn't make that mistake again. The world was full of these kinds of stunted hands. "With my eyes closed, I can sense this very clearly." "This is a place where decrepitude and asexuality reproduce. With hands like this, a man certainly can't create anything."

Sometimes, after Madam X finished, the two would just sit across from one another in silence and watch the rays of the setting sun pass across the window screen. They listened to the clock strike on the glass mantle, and the younger sister often exclaimed: "In the past, we were all as lively as wild deer!" Madam X would respond with an insipid, perplexed smile. Wallowing in sloppy sentiment, Madam X disclosed one of her secrets.

One noon, Madam X was lying alone on the beach at the riverside. Nobody else was there. "The sky was that kind of sentimental color, without a cloud to be seen, and the edge of the sun was filled with sharp triangles." The sun "shone hot and unrestrained" on her body, giving her a lot of colorful hallucinations. She said, "It was just like his kisses." She "felt the reality of carnal intimacy." She didn't know how it happened, but she was suddenly aroused and felt she "had to take off all her clothes." And sure enough, she did. She lay there nude for a long time, and then stood up and "flew in the burning heat, running around wantonly, wildly." (Luckily, at the time, no one passed by; otherwise who knows what farce would have ensued!) Afterwards, she went to the riverside a number of times, but didn't take her clothes off. She just walked on the beach, in her words, "waiting for miracles." If the weather was good, she said, "Perhaps he will walk toward me in the sunshine." If it was raining, she said, "He'll walk toward me through the rain; there will be row after row of white mushrooms on the ground." But no miracles came; it was just wishful thinking. Inwardly, Madam X knew this very well. Later, after she was more experienced, she no longer played this kind of game. "You can only meet someone by chance," she said. Madam X's sister told a good friend her older sister's secret. That good friend then told her husband, and the husband told his good friend. His good friend was a gossip. And so Madam X's secret went the rounds of Five Spice Street until everyone knew it. Did she lose face as a result of this? Was she ashamed to show her face? Hardly. She didn't give a damn: it seemed "an inner joy was revealed on her face."

After Madam X's husband's good friend heard this, he took the husband to his home, where they talked in whispers for two hours. He accused Madam X's husband "of spoiling his wife this way." Someday, "there would be a big problem." By then, it "would be too late." He pounded his knee; bitter remorse was on his face. At first, the sentimental husband was at a loss, but then he felt sorry for this friend and began consoling him. He told him not to be "too irascible," for this would "be harmful to him," and not knowing when to stop, he also gave an example. He said that, because of a trivial matter, a colleague in the past "had had his heart broken" and was left with a myocardial infarction that even now frequently caused unspeakable suffering. "You need to take it easy," he said. The friend jumped out of his seat. "Hey!" he shouted. "Whose wife are we talking about? Are you a sadist?" To avoid a scene, the husband patted his shoulder and pushed him back into his chair. "Never mind," he said. "Actually, there's no need to make such a big deal about someone taking her clothes off. In fact, everyone thinks of doing this; it's just that other people exercise self-restraint and consider forbearance glorious—just look at how much self-control I exercise, and how ascetic I am. If someone else did this, everyone would condemn it." Sometimes he too wanted to strip and dance around on a public occasion, for he thought this would be great fun. But he didn't dare: "I don't have the guts." Of course, his wife was much braver than he, although she could also actualize her idea only in a deserted place. He could only admire and respect this. He certainly wouldn't interfere with her personal enjoyment. He wasn't a fool! Nobody could force him to be a fool!

"Then am I a fool?!" The good friend was furious. The husband looked at him with remorse: he couldn't stand it. They parted on bad terms for the first time in years. As soon as he left, the good friend roared at his wife, "Throw the stool he sat on into the garbage! I have really fucking had it!" He sulked for several days.

The men of Five Spice Street—consumed with Madam X's secret—became more sentimental and affectionate. Quite a few dashed to the riverside to "take in the scenery," waiting to catch that "great nude scene" (the widow's words) and then play things by ear. Each did this on his own, fearful that others would see through their intentions. If acquaintances ran into each other, their faces flushed as they exchanged small talk: "It's a sunny day, isn't it? No? But don't you feel a little hot? Haha . . ." Then they would turn and walk away, but not too far; they would just make the rounds in the vicinity. Naturally, this scheming was all for nothing. They didn't glimpse even Madam X's shadow. Miffed, they would whisper to themselves: this was a hoax from the beginning—how could this kind of thing go on? If the woman had the guts to strip in a public place, wouldn't it be better to screw some guys at home? Although stripping sounded exciting and even romantic, it certainly wasn't the same as making it with some men: it wasn't even close to the real thing. Why bother running over to a deserted wasteland to do this? It was incomprehensible. Was this some kind of symbolic act? Perhaps just camouflage? Was the real thing behind it? What kind of scene was it when a woman jumped around naked in a deserted place like this? If she couldn't control herself, she should have done something quietly at home. What did this "naked act" count for? The crowds on our Five Spice Street always had to think everything through every which way: they never reached a verdict lightly and would never give up on a riddle just because they were temporarily stumped. They had to give it hard thought; if they couldn't solve it, they would keep their eyes open. Sometimes, a small matter could trigger thoughts for a long time, and another small matter could suddenly enlighten them.

Our Madam X might be the world's most volatile and unpredictable person, whose every action and word was an inexplicable riddle. No experience or common knowledge could help in dealing with her. You'd have to treat her like an extraterrestrial. We'd have to come up with some totally new, extraordinary, non-logical approach. No flippancy, no emotionalism. Maintain composure at all costs. Even if we accomplished nothing, this would be better than shouting and reckless action. Up to now, though there've been some small mistakes, and one or two people have disturbed the main process, in general, our people are still observing: they haven't been indiscreet, nor have they been swayed. This is sensible and shows their good breeding. After Madam X took off her clothes, Five Spice Street became lively for a while: everyone was talking about it, and the talk led to continuous profound analysis and a rich association of ideas. Everyone's surplus energy now had a place where it could be vented. This in itself was noble—a great opportunity for everyone to refine his or her soul until it was sanctified. But unfortunately, among the people on Five Spice Street there were a few uncouth degenerates who didn't behave. They charged around everywhere, upsetting the social order and turning good into bad. They messed up everything. They themselves were in the dark about what they hoped to achieve. They just loved showing up all of a sudden and catching you off guard, leaving everything a mess, and then taking their time walking away.

This time, the one who jumped onto the stage was a woman named B—the woman who, during the failed attempt at reeducation, wanted everyone to "wait for summer" to settle up with Madam X. This woman analyzed the situation in great detail and also consulted with Madam X's friend for an entire day. During the consultation, they were suddenly inspired. The two of them came to a speedy decision: they would have an improvisation on Five Spice Street, using "living theatre" to re-create Madam X's striptease. They discussed this until their faces were red and their hearts were pounding. They drew up a plan, having considered carefully all the details and possible scenarios. Their eyes heavy with sleep, they mumbled and fell into bed, where they dreamed ambitious dreams. While sleeping, they conserved their strength and stored up their energy, getting ready for tense battle the next day. As soon as it was light, they appeared naked on the two corners of the main street. One walked from east to west, the other from west to east. Except for people who were paralyzed and confined to bed, everyone crowded onto the street. Too timid to approach, they watched this "avant-garde" pastime from a distance. At first, the crowd just screamed wildly. The enthusiasm of those two women was rising to high pitch: they were twisting their arms and hips and shaking their bellies in all kinds of ways; it was an endless tour de force. They cupped their hands around their mouths and cried out to the crowd, "Ha! Ha! Haha!" This seemed to inspire the crowd: one by one, people involuntarily began twisting. Soon they too wanted to take their clothes off. They couldn't restrain themselves: why not go with it? Maybe not take everything off, but going topless was a great pleasure.

So on this three-mile-long street, everyone was excited. All the people were hugging and kissing everyone they saw, touching others all over their bodies. One or two even "got on with it" on the spot. It was a noisy, rollicking scene. Everyone was sweating profusely and breathing hot and heavy like oxen. At first, the two women's husbands were furious, but now, when fresh, lively, fleshy women threw themselves at them, they changed their minds and seized the day. As they gasped for breath, the two people said, "After all, there's another side to life. All along, we have been too parochial, too unable to enjoy life, as if we were living most of our lives for nothing. We didn't get anything: we could only be jealous. Jealousy is the worst emotion, indicating impotence. It appears that we should add some new things to our morality; otherwise, we'll be out of date."

The fling went on for a whole day and had an odious, indelible influence on Five Spice Street. The next morning, upon opening their eyes, most people had forgotten their performances of the day before, and when they saw each other, they didn't talk of it, either. But with stern expressions, everyone began talking of "moral cultivation." Their expressions revealed anxiety, pessimism, and depression, and also some latent indignation at being taken advantage of. Then, they looked all around, all of them knowing very well who the others were looking for. The two women disappeared. Only after two or three days did they steal back to Five Spice Street. Their sensitive noses detected that there'd been a sharp turn in the course of events: they'd better stay out of the storm tide. It's said that as they fled, the two of them were at odds again. In order to shift the blame, they assaulted each other ferociously, even "knocking out one another's teeth."

Sitting at her window, Madam X saw the street scene in her mirror. She feigned self-composure and gave all her attention to combing her hair. After that she polished her shoes, and after that she showed her son how to use the microscope. Then, striking an astonished pose, she said to her husband, "What the hell? Did I ever give a lecture to these guys? When did I ever do that?" Humoring her, her husband said no. He said that she had certainly not given any lecture to "these guys." It was "these guys" who wistfully thought her soliloquy had been for them; this was their excuse for attacking her. "This is the biggest joke in the world." (From this, we can also see how hard this husband tried to please Madam X every day; no one could understand how he could tolerate this kind of peculiar way of life. He must have been possessed.)

Madam X also asked, "At the time, did I give them a little attention?"

"You're mistaken." Her husband was still toadying to her. "You've always liked talking with a hypothetical other. That time, you supposed that they were some other people; you definitely didn't notice them."

"That seems right." She calmed down, and her customary slight smile floated up on her face.

Days later, Madam X made light of the time she had taken her clothes off, and laughed it off as "epilepsy," which was "inexplicable, that's all." She decided to "meet someone only by chance." She said she had now completely stabilized: indeed, her feelings "could penetrate the mountain ranges and reach the polar region." Her fingers were becoming more "velvety and delicate" by the day; her "anxiety wouldn't return." From then on, sure enough, she seldom went out. She spent the entire day at home and in the snack shop, in every action showing "refinement and ease" (the sister's words). She kept her eyes down and never looked at other people (even when she was waiting on customers, she was like this; sometimes, she looked at the air over a person's head or at the ground beneath his feet, but you definitely couldn't catch a glimpse of her eyes). When she talked with you, she did so in a drifting, hesitant tone which embarrassed you. She herself was unaware of this.

More time went by, and Madam X lived her life quietly. Quite a few men grew interested in her, and she looked them over one by one. Finally, she confirmed that she hadn't *recognized* that person from among them. As for them, of course they couldn't bear her rigorous, cold looks, which defeated them the first time they challenged her, and they gave up thoughts of overstepping their bounds. She said that she would recognize the person she was longing to find. No matter where she was, no matter what the occasion, she would know; there'd be no mistake. He had unique eyes and strong hands and "hot blood surging through his veins."

But sometimes her view was diametrically opposite. "Maybe that person is just in my imagination." As the sun was setting on a winter day, she sighed and said to her sister, "I'm not worried about this. Whatever will be, will be. Anyhow, I want to experiment—see how high I can reach. Even if there's nothing afterwards, I always have to experiment. This is predestined."

With that, she turned her face toward the sunlight and asked her sister whether she saw anything in her eyes. Uncomprehending, her sister said it seemed as if her eyes had a few little fish swimming back and forth in them. Madam X told her: certainly not fish, but "the rays of her very being." Only that person could see these rays of her being, for that person had the same kind of eyes. They would recognize each other by their eyes. Now she felt that her eyes were glowing more each day. "Their intensity can illuminate everything in the universe."

The Way Things Are Done

A FEW OPINIONS ABOUT THE STORY'S BEGINNING

If an outsider asked ordinary people on Five Spice Street for details about this story, he might be surprised to learn that they wouldn't even acknowledge there was any story. None would be willing to waste their breath on it. They're all too busy, too preoccupied. If an outsider persisted, they'd fly into a rage, deeply insulted.

"We all have a lot to do and can't be bothered with this trivia. If you want to discuss techniques like developing color film or the relationship between the Constitution and the people—that's something else: we have to get to the theorctical roots of these questions. Some people with ulterior motives try to attach the present issue of X and Q to things that are of the essence. This modus operandi makes us indignant. Nobody takes X or Q seriously. Ordinarily, we seldom pay them any attention, but as soon as they're dragged up, it's as though we attach a lot of importance to them. Whoever raises the issue is luring us down the path of evil. They stretch the net and wait for their quarry. In fact, we don't have any story." Then they scatter, leaving the visitor behind. They're all sophisticated, reliable people.

We can't find fault with such generous, kind, ordinary people. They were indifferent to the injuries to their souls. As for the future, they were filled with confidence, always humble and down-to-earth. They discussed the past as though all their memories were rosy and beautiful. Everyone knew that they were glossing over the fateful, calamitous attacks they had suffered. The past was still vivid, and everybody had had tearful experiences. Now it was over, and it wasn't in their character to belabor yesterday's sorrows. The road ahead was long and strewn with problems. You just had to brace yourself and continue: there was no other choice. It was undeniable: to this day, that spectacular, weird time remained shadowy in their minds. Whenever they mulled it over alone, their past misgivings and humiliation and their sense of being duped, along with their regrets and remorse, surged up like a flood: there was nothing good about this. Each of them suppressed it, determined to cast off the past and move ahead in high spirits. In order to put it thoroughly behind them, they established strict timetables for work and rest. The timetables accounted for every minute and every second of the day. Everyone had to abide by them; special supervisors were assigned to ensure compliance. The objective was to control the free flood of sloppy sentiments and guarantee the healthy development of ideology.

As for the beginning of the unfortunate incident, five persons had dictated reports. These were on file. Each report was vividly told from a different angle of vision. Each person's original view refuted the views of others. Reading them, you'll be astonished at how complicated and confusing they are. This also showed the diversity and independence of the ordinary people's psychology. They weren't easily swayed and were singularly repelled by those who were. Nobody could force his opinion on them. If you wanted to try to smooth things over and bring about unanimity, you'd be ridiculed.

The Report of the Old Widow in the Little Black Felt Hat

"Whenever I think of my beloved cousin, I recall the time when I kicked off the blanket at midnight. You all know that the only thing on my bed that's worth anything is that coarse blanket. My quilt is thirty years old and has been in rags for a long time. The mat under the sheet is only straw. But the blanket is really worth something: when the sun catches it, its golden wool shines as though burning up. Forty years ago, my father gave me this blanket (at the time, my handsome cousin was also on the scene) and said, 'This is a genuine pure wool blanket.' I can still remember his voice and can remember even more clearly my cousin's charming little smile. (She swallowed her saliva again and again for ten minutes, closed her eyes, and didn't move, as if she had forgotten she was speaking. Not until the other person shook her shoulders roughly did she gradually come to.) How could I have kicked the blanket off? It's a long story. It was spring then, very humid and very hot. When you use a quilt, you shouldn't need to add a blanket.

"It was my damn nephew who caused all the problems. In fact, he wasn't any nephew of mine. For twelve years, he had been pretending to be my nephew. Even now, everyone believes his pretense. This is really peculiar. This guy was a rootless bum—an orphan. He was also a hypocrite who had lost his humanity: he stole and robbed, and drank people's lifeblood. A huge carbuncle hung perennially from his cheek. I don't know what caused the misunderstanding (I curse the son-of-a-bitch who spread this rumor). A lot of people thought he was the right person to deliver my coal. I detest the ill-disposed suggestion. If this guy really did so, I would fight him to the death. Although I'm old and weak, I can still beat this guy up with no problem. Anyhow, I definitely didn't let him set foot in my home; he would have to wait a long time before he could prevail. I watched the house for a whole winter, which is also to say that for a whole winter, I didn't light a fire (I couldn't do two things at the same time). It was frightfully damp in the house, but I was in a good mood. Then it was spring, and inside it seemed to be drizzling. I put the blanket on top of the quilt, and because it got too hot at midnight, I kicked it off. When I got up in the morning and looked around, the blanket was on the floor. That's when the incident occurred. Of course, the one who came in was my cousin, he helped me by bringing coal.

"Please notice: forty years later, he quietly arrived. When I needed him most, he came to my side. All along, I'd had a premonition: my cousin would come. When I battled with my so-called nephew on those bone-chilling winter nights, it was precisely this faith that sustained me and kept me from collapsing. That damn vampire had always coveted my blanket; he thought I would die that winter and was truly impatient. My cousin really did come: not only did he help me by delivering coal, but he also stood in the middle of the room for seven or eight minutes, his eyes filled with affection— affection running just as deep as it had forty years before. He said softly, "*I really didn't imagine.*" When he said this, he just moved his lips but made no sound. Still, I had no trouble hearing him. Tears blurred my vision. What a hot-blooded man! What feeling and meaning! After he left, my legs all of a sudden were stronger, and I walked about three miles. I even skipped a little and didn't feel the least bit tired. I felt I could probably still do you-know-what: wasn't it a miracle? (Her head drooped; it was as if she were sleeping, but after five minutes, she suddenly looked up again.)

"I'd had a vague feeling for a long time that some invisible danger was hanging over my cousin. I've felt this for forty years now. At last, everything I anticipated has occurred! My cousin is a virgin through and through; I emphasize this because I want everyone to know his purity and innocence—that he's been kept in the dark about passion between men and women: he's utterly ignorant of it. Forty years of trials are enough to prove his character and morals. This was precisely why Lady Mirror (that's what she disdainfully called Madame X) set her sights on him: she got a grip on him and wouldn't let go. I am sure it didn't give him any pleasure: indeed, he wouldn't have known what Lady Mirror was doing with his body. During this whole thing, did I just look on quietly? Or did I gloat, as certain people guessed I would? Who knows what kind of frightening years I've lived through? Ever since Lady Mirror stopped her sorcery, put away her microscope and various costumes, and eloped with my poor cousin, all I've had has been night after night of loneliness, deathly stillness, emptiness, and terror. All at once, I became so decrepit I couldn't even walk; I could only watch them receding into the boundless night until they disappeared.

"How did this start? Why did this tragedy occur? Nobody knows this little secret—that it came from a very trivial matter: it came from that load of coal! I shouldn't have asked the coal worker to deliver coal that day. Until the day I die, I'll never forgive myself: I have to keep damning myself. As it happened, my entryway is on a slope, and as it happened, that guy wasn't willing to pull it up the slope. Also as it happened, my gallant cousin arrived and helped. He must have gotten confused from the excitement of seeing me: in any case, he forgot where he was going and absent-mindedly followed the coal worker into Lady Mirror's little courtyard. He fell in the doorway and lost consciousness. Only at dusk did he emerge; his expression was frightening.

"Wait a minute. Now I have to go back and talk about that blanket. I left out an important part. Forty years ago, my cousin walked me back and carried the blanket for me. The women on the street all craned their necks enviously as they looked at the blanket. They also looked at my cousin and me (because of certain happenings, some people were too late to see us, and they regretted this greatly). They privately thought that my cousin and I were a couple made in heaven, and so that blanket was almost like a pledge of love: it tied our hearts together. Don't think I pay any attention to X's behavior. No! I've basically forgotten her. I didn't come here today to talk about her, but to talk about the connection between my cousin and that blanket. What kind of garbage is she? This monster who emerged from underground—why on earth do we need to be concerned with what she does? I'm busy enough with my own life! Now it's all the vogue to stare at some peculiar people. If someone strips on the main street and creates a hullabaloo or gets involved with a few more lovers, does she suddenly become somebody? Our people become more and more confused. We just aimlessly sought connections: this is really a shame! My cousin wallows in the mud because he fell in the doorway. He became corrupted while he was actually unconscious, and he's still showing symptoms of insanity and delirium: he can't break away. Can we possibly want to hit a person when he's down and at this critical time attack him with deadly force, or should we be indifferent and go all out, go with the fads, and kick the dying one away and concentrate on those irrelevant things done by unrelated people?

"I'm exhausted from talking. The topic of my talk today has been the connection between the blanket and my cousin. I haven't expressed the gist of what I wanted to say very well. I've been distracted by this and that because that irrelevant issue kept interfering with my train of thought and mixed me up. Only by rousing my last little bit of energy to get hold of myself could I finally rid myself of outside interference and approach the essence of the matter. But the moments were fleeting, and the interference returns. It gets worse each time until it finally saps all my energy. The ideas I want to express are still misty. The end. You degenerates!" (She suddenly fell to the ground, her legs and arms twitching. After about twenty minutes, she came around and indignantly departed.)

The Lame Woman's Report

"You mustn't believe anything about mirrors: that's all make-believe, ladies and gentlemen, it's all a pretense—a sleight of hand to distract your attention. You walked into a certain person's home one day, saw mirrors of all sizes all over the tabletop, and saw the person gesture as if something real was occurring. You all clamored like a pot of boiling water: Wow! A miracle! Her supernatural ability is really incredible! After I unfold the real picture, you'll raise a hue and cry all over again. Your greatest failing is that you're gullible and impulsive. None of the comments has anything to do with the incident per se. The true picture is permanently buried deep. You talk as if you know a lot, but it's doubtful that you do. What you see is far from the essence: instead, it's a kind of lie, an artificial sport.

"Now let me tell you about the so-called origin of what happened that afternoon. It was an eerie afternoon; death was vaguely in the air, making people extremely nervous. People jumped at each little noise. You'd sit by the window, and the curtains might suddenly be lifted by something and you'd see a sheep's skull. I walked more than two hours along an endless gray wall and finally arrived at that manipulator's home. She was sitting with her back to me and giggling. When I approached her, she was poking at an anthill with a rusty dagger. She poked it repeatedly and also stomped on it. The ants fled in a panic.

" 'There's something wrong with your husband. Everybody's talking about it.' I patted her back, doing my best to appear casual.

"'Shhh! Nonsense!' She took stock of me with narrowed eyes. 'Everything is going according to the predestined plan.'

"With that, she hauled me forcibly into her little pitch-black room and asked me to take a seat on a worn-out iron bed. Then she moved over a huge wooden trunk, opened it, and told me to look inside. In it were men's socks of all sizes, more than a hundred pairs of them, arranged in apple-pie order.

"'Every pair he's worn from the time he was born until now is preserved here. This is one of my secrets. He doesn't know about it.' She eagerly told me to look. 'Look at this pair with a hole in it; he wore it when he was eight, and it was torn because his toenails were too long. It amuses me to think of this: where could he go? Do you want me to turn a light on? No, okay then, I won't. As soon as the light is turned on, the cutworms start moving around and our vegetables are ruined. Year in and year out, this trunk is locked tight. I don't care. Where could he go?' she reiterated, and shrugged.

"By the light coming in from the small window, I got a good look at that woman's face. She was like a thirteen-year-old girl, barefoot and wearing two bows in her hair, prancing around in the room like a locust. What rubbed me the wrong way was that she showed no respect: she just kept setting out her playthings in front of me (a wrap-around that she hadn't finished knitting, a glass-bead necklace, a cartoon, a little plaster dog, and so forth). She intended to affirm her being with these miscellaneous things and establish a certain self-confidence, even hubris. Think about it: even such a pitiable thing struggled to stand out and finally climbed into her husband's head and took control over him and staged this scene. You, with your petrified brains, wouldn't have expected this!

"There are several suspicious things about this man Q. First, among the women on Five Spice Street, he's as familiar as a family member. When you're talking with someone, you need only mention him (even if not directly, the conversation might lead you to think of him), and she will immediately become absorbed and avidly inquire about all the details. It seemed that everyone felt a vague attraction to him and wanted to confide this. But all they could do was bashfully strike a pose and put on a nonchalant air, while in private they pitifully offered him their romantic passions. How could he achieve this social status out of all proportion to what he was? Had anyone carefully taken stock of every part of his body, or tasted his sugarplum, and then finally ascertained where his charms lay? (Of course not!)

"We can speculate that the reason lay in his relationship with X, or more precisely in daydreams about such a relationship. Here is an analogy: no one had ever made any inquiries about tangerines, but now research has shown that tangerines can prevent cancer and so people rush to buy them and the prices skyrocket. This kind of cancer-prevention psychology is the same as our daydreams. Suppose one day we find that our daydreams are just a subjective mistake, and we finally discover that in a small dark room at the end of a long wall a psycho is seated, gripping a rusty dagger. Bending over and gritting her teeth, she's counting the socks in the trunk. Ugly, plump cutworms are climbing all over outside the room. It's finally she who is everything. Q is only a puppet whose strings are being pulled. Then what would Q's image be? We'll get the answer without any doubt. Nevertheless, we all survive in daydreams. At such times, people seem charming and bashful, with expectant eyes. Each action is suffused with childishness. If a man darts past the window, everyone is inwardly pleased and whispers excitedly: 'What a living Apollo Q is!' They're determined to think of this silhouette as Q for no other reason than that they've daydreamed about a certain bewitching 'relationship' between him and X. The less sense we found in this strange behavior, the more we endowed it with beautiful poetry and magical colors—accessorized it to become the spiritual sustenance for our existence. This was the root cause of our inferiority.

"After we visualized the bewitching relationship between Q and X, we also put ourselves in X's position and measured ourselves against her, crazily considering our strong points and marveling at how much better we were than X—and how overjoyed we'd feel if we entered that realm with Q. What a great mistake Q had made. We mulled it over this way until we were exhausted and lost the last bit of self-confidence we had about our worth. We were like a dog sniffing after a certain person: we didn't know that the hero we were chasing was simply a puppet manipulated by a bizarre woman sitting in a dark room.

"Second, each of us imagined this Q to be a young, intrepid, stalwart man, a handsome man without equal. He was not only brave but sweet. His words were like a light, gentle rain warming people's hearts. You believed that there couldn't be any other Mr. Right in this world. At home, you paced impatiently, thought aloud, couldn't sleep, and tossed and turned all night. You jumped up at daybreak and ran to the public toilet, where, as you squatted, you sleepily confided these baffling feelings to one another. It was so exciting. By comparison, you felt your own husbands were intolerable. You crazily put yourselves on a pedestal, as if all of a sudden you had become aristocratic ladies. You were unapproachable to your husbands. If they wanted to get close to you, they were reduced to begging, even kneeling. And then even if you broke down and consented, you did so disdainfully, as cold as ice water. You would all be disappointed if you knew the truth I'm about to tell you. Remember the other day when someone saw him fall in front of Madam X's door (and he was knocked unconscious from the fall)? Have you given this serious thought? Is it possible for a healthy man walking on level ground to fall and lose consciousness?

"Of course, I know what this was all about. You may think I'm making this up out of jealousy. Or you may think I'm elevating myself by degrading others. I don't care what you think. I'll still stick to the truth. I won't give in. I want to tell you that on that eerie afternoon, you can't imagine what he looked like when he appeared at my window: he was *leaning on two sticks*. We looked at each other for no fewer than twenty-three minutes—not until the sticks could no longer hold up his heavy body did he, not without regret, turn and leave. With each step, he looked back, reluctant to part: he recognized his own kind.

"Third, this Q: we've all concluded that the only one he's interested in is X. We have no doubts about this. From his actions that afternoon, I could see that he wasn't headed straight for X's home; first, he stopped at my window for a significant twenty-three minutes. This illuminates the issue. If I had the least little hope for all of you, I wouldn't have been so inactive and let the bird out of the cage. You've disappointed me too much: my heart has been like dead ashes for a long time. I am too tired to take any action. I don't think X is his only objective. (He hasn't put all his eggs in one basket, as the saying goes.) If only we change a little and aren't quite so contrary and start acting a little more open-minded, it's completely possible that he will become interested in each one of you. He isn't a great hero who's all that perfect: he's no different from your own husbands; he's not the least bit better. It's your impertinence and carelessness that pushed him into X's arms. Now you regret this and for no reason come up with all kinds of romantic sentiments, even making him into an idol and worshipping him. What you've done has wiped out all the possibilities. This is exactly what I figured: it's just because of this that I've lost hope and recognize that any efforts are all for nothing. I was the first woman Q was interested in. It wouldn't have taken the slightest effort for me to win him over. I could have made some introductions, too, and then none of you would be as lonesome, sentimental, and frustrated as you are now. In a word, the opportunities have all slipped away. Why? Because of your stupidity! Because of your sloth! You just lay in bed moaning and daydreamed of non-existent, impossible things. You would do that even if the sky was going to collapse. If you're awakened, you dash over and close the curtains, but go out of your way to leave the door wide open. You stare hard at the door as you inwardly beckon with all the longing you can muster. If your husband came home at this time, you'd be furious and drive him out, cursing him angrily: 'You've wrecked my mood!'

"Now I can tell you a story. After you've listened to it, perhaps you'll understand some truths. My story is long and complicated. You need a lot of perseverance and patience to understand all the relationships in it. And still it's very likely that you'll fail. At most, there's only one chance in a thousand that you'll succeed. If you don't change your lax attitudes, you'll have no way—not in a million years—to enter into my story. The story I'm telling is how a woman or a man (perhaps a person who is lame as I am) gets on in life when the social system is abnormal. This story isn't at all related to the person in the small dark room at the end of the gray wall, but it's directly related to each of us seated here. Indeed, you could have entered the story directly and served as the protagonists. At that time, this possibility would have been completely revealed: it only waited for you to bring it into play. But you didn't. Instead, you wielded your slack but boundless imaginations to link some isolated things together, busily wove the threads together, and then threw the whole thing aside and were content with superficial understanding. Each person would go her own way, crying and grieving for no reason. Up to now, you still haven't figured out what's happened. What happened? An earthquake! A flash flood! Demons visiting! Or perhaps nothing happened. It was nothing more than eating an extra dumpling at breakfast and crying later because of a stomachache.

"No, I won't tell you the story. There'd be no point. I want to keep the story to myself. These little treasures are the consolation of my life; they're also a kind of self-defense. When I get up in the middle of the night, outside my window the sky is as unyielding as steel. The gray wall on the hill heaves and wobbles. My teeth chatter. I burrow under the quilt and wrap myself in those stories. My story is warm, focused, and a little stimulating: it belongs just to me. I must tell you again: your imaginary experiences don't exist. They don't have even a foreword. All the beginnings you've imagined are subjectively trumped up: they've resulted from sloppy romantic sentiments spilling over. The real beginning is lost, never to return.

"Once upon a time, there was a day, an afternoon, when a cloud drooped and the fragrance of grass sizzled in the air—it was very likely the beginning of our story. I was almost ready. If it weren't for hard realities and if I hadn't been swept away by decadent emotions, everything would have been realized. Now it's completely over. You may go on making silly assumptions or—like children—put yourselves in the other's position and taste fiery romantic emotions. Be my guest. But I'm surer than anyone about everything. I'd stand behind you and sneer in despair. Until the day that you turn back penitently and change your ways completely, no one will be able to fish the real story out of my mouth. I want to preserve my moral integrity and keep a clear head in this world of disordered manners and morals. I just want to live out the rest of my ordinary life simply and quietly. I don't want to lose my pure essence by associating with certain people just to cut a fine figure."

The Report of X's Husband's Good Friend
(the One Who Looked at the ID Card)

"The beginning? My God! As soon as you mentioned the beginning, I fell back into complicated, confusing worries. Every one of Madam X's beginnings was also mine. Her innumerable affairs had formed innumerable nested boxes in my life. As soon as you mention some new beginning, I become incredibly tense: my whole body is like a tautly drawn bow. Ever since X moved to our street, I've been close friends with her husband, and her main guardian. It's been non-stop disaster. Every time it seemed the trouble had finally ended, you breathed a long sigh and sat down to rest your frazzled mind. Just then, she would create a new disturbance, and so you had to spring to your feet again, as if you'd had an electric shock. No one can imagine how much her energy can flower. Almost every minute, almost every second, she's plotting a new beginning. Her husband's been in deep shit because of her, and I'm on affectionate terms with him. Socializing with her has sapped every bit of my strength. I was beat. I suffered from dizziness and loss of appetite every day. My life became a living hell. For a few years now, not only have I not eaten meat, but I've even stopped the most important thing—making love with my wife. I've become as thin as a shadow. Has X been grateful for the pains I've taken? It hasn't turned out the way anyone could have expected!

"One day, she summoned me to her room. She stared hard at me for ten minutes with her pupil-less eyes and then fiercely shoved me away. Shaking all over, she pulled her hair hysterically with both hands and paced back and forth in the room. She'd behaved like this for half an hour (how astonishingly patient I was!) when, finally, I couldn't take it any longer. I cleared my throat and gingerly asked if she was feeling a little better. Listen to her reply: 'Did I call you over here? I remember there was some person who often came here without being asked. He was always around. Is it possible that I asked you here—what on earth is this all about? Are you mistaken? Did I really ask you to come? Don't you have your own business to attend to? It really isn't good for you to be so concerned with other people.' What inconsiderate manners! From that day on, whenever she ran into me on the street, she crossed her eyes and didn't look at me. If I blocked her way, she just charged across, as if I were a scarecrow. When I dropped in to reason with her, she said she simply hadn't seen me: blocking her way was really a big mistake because she wasn't likely to see me. It would have been better for me to stay at home and make little clay figurines: that's much better for both mind and body. Maybe it would lead to my being artistic! And maybe I would discover the meaning of my existence from it! Why did I have to bother myself with this crazy shit?

"She also told me a story of another friend of hers: This woman used to have the bad habit of always running to the public toilet and talking with people there. As soon as she started talking, she forgot the time: she stank from spending the whole day in the toilet. Her husband was absolutely disgusted with her and wouldn't let her get into the bed. She had to sleep in the corridor. The husband couldn't put up with her: he simply kicked her out and threatened that if she dared go into the house, he would chop her to pieces! One day, X ran into this woman on the street, squatting in a pile of garbage looking for something to eat. X went up and chatted with her and taught her how to plait locusts from palm leaves. The woman learned quickly, and in the blink of an eye she became addicted to this hobby. She gave up chatting at the public toilet. Her husband took the woman back, and the whole family enjoyed a wonderful reunion. Of course I understood why she told me this. But her husband, my woeful friend, didn't. He stood to one side with a big smile. He nodded at each word his wife said, and then walked over and patted me affectionately on the back and stupidly assured me that everything his wife said was true. A nitwit, even an idiot whose eyeballs can't move, needs only slight inspiration from her in order to gradually become intelligent and normal. They echoed each other: the more they talked, the happier and more intimate they were. The husband was tightly encircling Madam X's waist with his hands, not letting go even a little. Later, X made an absurd suggestion: 'Why don't the two of us jump up onto the desk?' Sitting on top of the desk, holding hands and swinging their legs, they were even whistling at me!

"This shocked me greatly. For a long time, I couldn't figure out what had happened. I just felt ill and nauseated, and didn't want to go on living. Taking stock of this vast world with old, bleak eyes, I pondered: since people don't need you, and even your close friend treats you like a piece of shit—asking you to come and then driving you away whenever he wants—and behind your back makes fun of all your efforts, tramples all your good intentions underfoot, and blindly takes his wife's side, then what kind of role are you playing in a world like this? What good are all of your efforts, except to make you a laughingstock? I tossed the idea back and forth: it was really painful. I made up my mind to end my life in its prime with a knife on a fine moonlit night. I already had the knife ready and had also chosen the place—the patio behind my house.

"Just then, X and my friend came to my house, bringing their incomparably solicitous regards. They sat down clumsily and bashfully beside my bed and snuggled close together. After a while, my friend began taking an oath, saying that he would be my closest friend forever; he had no desire to betray me. He treasured every one of my favors and wouldn't forget them in a million years. If there was any small misunderstanding between the two of us, it must have been instigated by the villain who always tries to turn the world upside down. I should never change my opinion of him because of this. He gestured as he talked. Leaning against his shoulder, his wife swayed violently with his movements and closed her eyes tight as if hypnotized. He mentioned again the story from last time. He said they certainly weren't insinuating anything. If I lost my life because of this misunderstanding, they would be terribly grief-stricken. They had never doubted my intelligence and wisdom. Not long ago, his wife had also said that I was the most intelligent man in the world. He could vouch for her really having said this. Thinking they doubted my intelligence and wisdom was truly a huge injustice. He also often thought: if they lost such an intelligent and capable friend as I, how could they go on living? Who else would be as trustworthy? By the time he finished talking, his wife was sound asleep. She didn't even wake up when he shook her. He had to carry her home.

"Once again, friendship had awakened me in time to avert the danger. People who haven't experienced the joys and hardships of friendship are so pitiable! So empty! I had always placed friendship before everything else. Friendship is my life. To help my friends out of trouble, I could climb a mountain of daggers and enter a sea of fire, and wouldn't begrudge having my body smashed to smithereens. After they left, I got out of bed at once and washed my face, roused my energy, and made up my mind to repay my friends with redoubled loyalty and to my full ability. I wanted to drive out the sleeping demons (to do this, I put Tiger Balm on my temples). With wide open eyes, I watched out for my friend day and night. I also enlisted my wife for this work (although she was frail by nature and had limited ability, and had much less stamina than I). My wife ruined everything. I had never thought women could be so cranky, headstrong, and lacking in self-control. I learned a serious lesson that time.

"One day, when Madam X walked into the woods, my wife and I followed her. We saw her sit down on a rock. I could tell that there was another new beginning. I motioned to my wife, and we hid inside the hollow trunk of a large tree and watched her actions from a small hole. We just saw her stretch her legs out and lie down without moving. My wife and I were greatly agitated, and our faces were as red as if we'd been drinking. We were poking and teasing each other, making a great commotion inside the hollow tree. My wife kept shouting softly, 'Soon, we're going to see the best show we've seen in our whole lives! I can't hold on any longer! I'm going to faint!' She was shouting louder and louder. I gestured for her to calm down, fearing everything would go wrong. But she didn't listen and became even more agitated. She kept squirming and making *hua-hua* noises. It was unearthly. She threw a stone out of the hole toward Madam X's feet and then another. I tried to restrain her wild behavior. I clenched her hand and wouldn't let her fiddle with anything. I hadn't imagined that she would go nuts and bite me like a dog. 'This trick is just too much!' She said she'd been waiting for a long time to expose my secret. She'd come with me to the woods not to watch Madam X—she didn't care what other people did. Although she saw her every day, she had never said a word to her. Her object in coming to the woods was to watch me and expose my evil behavior. I was so asinine—I had never understood her inner secret. This really made her laugh her head off! Did I really think she was a fool? Was it possible that a man and a wife would stop having sex for no reason for almost half a year and she just wouldn't give a damn and would think it was normal?

"I had been glaringly wrong about her! One of these days she would bare her teeth and let me know just how shrewd she was. If she wanted to, she could take my life anytime. Her retaliation had nothing to do with having sex, for this had always disgusted her. She had always agreed to sex because she had no alternative, so—from her viewpoint—my calling off sex was the same as liberating her. If I changed my mind in the future and approached her for sex again, it would be a disaster. She had come with me in order to get a handle on me and put an end to my expectations. When we emerged, badly battered, from the hole in the tree, Madam X had already disappeared. All of a sudden, my wife realized the mistake she had made and began wailing with her head in her hands. I vowed that from then on, I would never bring her along for any action. Women ruin everything—especially fervent women without willpower. They're the worst. They do all kinds of terrible things and never give up until they've turned your plans into mush. They go crazy when they feel restricted and always give you a fatal blow at the moment of truth. After they've finished making trouble, they dissemble, feigning helplessness to evoke your sympathy and to hang on to the opportunity to make a scene next time. Women are generally like this, all very much the same with only minor differences. I was firmly determined to take action alone from now on, which also showed my complete sincerity toward my friend.

"On the path of your life, one false step might send you into hell. Not until I began acting alone did I realize in despair that—I don't know when this began—a tail was developing behind me. No matter how sharp I was, no matter how I changed my tactics, she always had ways to deal with me. And she didn't deal with me in a passive way: she was extremely aggressive. I couldn't get away from her. It made me dizzy. Did I guard Madam X every day and fulfill my responsibility to my friend, or did I play hide-and-seek with my wife? When I went out in the morning, my objective seemed clear, and so was my head, but as soon as I was halfway there, a dramatic transition often occurred. I felt dizzy: not only did I lose the object of my pursuit, but I became the object of other people's pursuit. I wanted to break loose. I dodged here and there—sometimes entering a bosk, sometimes hiding behind a pile of garbage, sometimes climbing to the roof from a certain attic. I almost turned into a monkey.

"My wife was enjoying this kind of game. But to me, it was really annoying, and the future seemed hopeless. Madam X's endless mutating tricks were hard enough for me to deal with, and now there were my wife's tricks, too! The more anxious I was to free myself of her entanglement, the more interested she became. She was also glowing with health, just as if she'd turned into a young girl in her prime. Every time I thought of a new way to break away, she immediately and feverishly redeployed all her shrewdness to deal with me, to compete with me for the advantage. I was really suffering. I said directly to her, if she went on like this, we would both end up being hurt. Was she aware of what she was doing? A person living in this world should have her own clear life tenets, should always pursue the same goals. To be a parasite or to hinder the actions of others was immoral. It was disgraceful. Also, if you foolishly and ignorantly idled away your time, you wouldn't have any memories when you were old, just some shadows of the life that you had lived. You would regret this. All my life, I've tried to attain the highest spiritual realm and abandoned all physical enjoyment. I've walked on a road filled with hardships and dangers. Too bad she couldn't become my most intimate friend, my helpmate. Instead, she left no stone unturned in destroying me. It's really been hard to endure.

"It's as if she isn't listening. She opens her eyes wide and looks astonished and then answers: 'You have to know that the objective of my pursuit is simply you. I've lived this long, and all along I've been submissive. Only because of the suggestion made by fortune-teller Meng from the pharmacy did I take a tumble: My whole life has been empty. For years, I've been blind to meaningful projects that would be worthwhile for me. It was the worst sort of stupor! Absolutely foolish!' She also said that I was the biggest riddle in the world: if she could understand me, she'd find her self-worth. Once she established this objective, she was completely refreshed—once more in the bloom of youth. For the first time, her ability was also fully displayed. Even I couldn't help acknowledging her strong challenge. All I could do was retreat to avoid conflict. Just think about it: the situation changed so much! Before, her life was so humiliating, dry as dust, absolutely without interest. She had been living like a maggot. No way could she go back to that. She'd rather die! It's been through her own hard struggles that she's attained her present promising life, which no one should destroy. No one can ever seduce her into turning back. No way! She's figured out every damn trick I played. She's no longer her old self. She is now much wiser, much smarter. No matter where I hid, even if I turned into an 'invisible man,' she'd still have ways to get hold of me. This absorbing work has made her feel so enriched, so happy. Her energy is inexhaustible. She is very sure that she has obtained the greatest happiness. Women who pursue sex exclusively all their lives gain very little and grow old fast. Some are even abused and abandoned by their husbands. As she sees it, they have lost much more. They are self-defeated. Women aren't inferior to men in anything: why can't they make their own decisions about what they will do, and contend with men? Why do they have to waste their youth and energy on men? Of course, a woman striving for independence will run into serious obstacles: there will be pressure from society and from men. There's nothing frightening about it. You just have to be determined and be strong-willed. No difficulty is insurmountable. She's made up her mind; I'd better give up. Can she possibly not know what I intended? She wouldn't give a shit what I said. Her work has picked up a lot now. She can't relent, because if she did, all her previous efforts would be wasted and people would laugh at her. No temptation could move her. I'd better give up and not talk with her anymore. With the kind of progress she's been making, how could she wash her hands of it? Someday, her work will achieve surprising results. Her success will be the end of me.

"So, do I now understand what my relationship with her is? I do what I have to do, and she also has to see her undertaking through to the end. Don't think I still have any control over her, and don't think, either, that she has the slightest interest in sex. The moment a woman wakes up, she can change into a tigress. I must have been living in a dream if I wasn't aware of even this. She—this tigress—doesn't enjoy saber rattling, nor does she like to snarl. She only wants to devour people. I just have to watch out for this, especially while sleeping, when any weird thing might happen. It would be better to worry about my own safety than to trick her with my bravado. She meant what she said. I couldn't blame anyone else: I had asked for all the bitter fruit; now I'd better quietly gulp it down. I could make allowances for my wife. All her weird transformations arose from a kind of subtle mindset for retaliation. I could do nothing about her mindset, because a person has limited energy.

"Let's imagine for a moment: a husband and wife have lived together for twenty years, very much in love. The faithful wife devoted her whole being to love. She had a boundless appetite for, and interest in, sex. But the husband, in addition to love, had other things he needed to do: he had a social circle, friends, and obligations. His best friend's wife caused his friend to sink into frightening circumstances. They couldn't extricate themselves. Everyone knew his character: he was always ready to help his friends; he was self-sacrificing. So he quickly got into the act and saw it through to the bitter end (his friend, of course, was endlessly grateful). Unfortunately, it was a knotty problem: he could get hold of it only by throwing all his strength and energy into it. The most important thing was that he had to be interested in it, enter into a mood that was foreign to him. Only if he was in the right mood could he understand that lady's whole world, understand the rules she lived by, and figure out all of her desires. Then, he couldn't relax: he had to play things by ear. If he didn't, he wouldn't get results. He was cautious and conscientious in his work, flinging aside all his miscellaneous thoughts. After a time, he developed a strong interest in that lady's world. He studied all her actions and appreciated them, analyzed them, and quickly became fascinated. At home, whether eating, working, or sleeping, he generally also thought about the lady. Her expressions and gestures were constantly in his mind. He was calculating all her possible moves and planning his next mission accordingly. He also unwittingly adopted the lady's peculiarities. Now and then, he ran over to the sink to take a look at his face (his family had never bought a mirror). Even more embarrassing was that with time, he was actually bashful when he saw the lady: he blushed and his heart leaped. This was really ridiculous. He hated himself for being this way, but he just couldn't help it. Of course, this didn't mean that he became romantically interested in her. He'd always embraced a saintly attitude toward women. This time, he was absolutely selfless in helping his friend: this was obvious to everyone. He was irreproachable. His restlessness was caused mostly by the fact that he was seldom in contact with any women but his wife. Some of it was just as people said: the lady had some evil ways. She tricked people with her sorcery and got her fun from making people crazy.

"Now you can understand what a difficult responsibility his friend had given him, what an enormous test it was for him. It was a miracle he had survived up to now and hadn't broken down either physically or mentally. He reckoned it up: to this point, thirty-six people had urged him to give this business up, spend time with his wife, and go home and enjoy his family. They said it wouldn't get him anywhere. He 'wouldn't have a chance to taste the sugarplum.' He would just 'hopelessly look forward to something, like a fool.' (What was he looking forward to? Money from heaven? Golden melons growing from the earth?) If things had gone on like this, he would have become impotent. You have to know that people can't for a minute be without the 'spare-time recreation.' Even in the face of all kinds of public pressure, he persevered. He dared to say that no one could be found who understood that lady's inner life as he did. No one knew her as well as he did, nor could anyone else truly guess her purpose (this prevented many frightening occurrences!). As he was absorbed in high-minded feelings about his friend and carrying out this very difficult work, a crisis befell his family. His wife was a loving person, but very hard-headed and monomaniacal about everything. She could not, nor did she want to, understand her husband's high-minded sentiments. She felt that she had been unreasonably deprived of the rights she should have had. Hadn't she enjoyed this continual 'spare-time recreation' for twenty years? Hadn't it all been beautiful and satisfying? It was the way she'd held on to her husband and her whole family. Now, suddenly, a witch had shown herself and taken control of her husband, and left her with an empty house and sleepless nights. How could she resign herself to this? She understood everything in the world with her narrow mind and denounced her husband's elaborate, lofty work as 'indecent behavior.' If her husband was a little late getting home, she said he was 'engaged in shameful activity.' If her husband didn't have the energy for sex, she said her family 'had become a nonentity'! 'A demon has taken my place.' She wrote posters all day long at home and pasted up words all over the place castigating her husband. This was a big joke in the neighborhood. Her husband became frightened and backed off, but when he reluctantly tried to have sex with her, she dodged away and cursed him: 'You're shameless,' you just want 'more women.' You 'want to screw every woman in the world.' Anyhow, it was bad language, not the least bit reasonable, and it became more and more contemptible, ominous, and crazy. Recently, their conjugal relationship had deteriorated to the point that it couldn't be remedied. For no reason, she concluded that she 'had found the value of her life.' This was to make things incessantly difficult for her husband—erect obstacles and set traps—and plot murder at an opportune time. She did all of these horrifying things. She was addicted to this. Her interest in sex, which had gradually dried up, now bloomed again and was revealed through a metamorphosis: she was as greedy as a wolf; it never stopped. There wasn't even a shadow left of the formerly gentle woman.

"After a period of antagonism between my wife and me, suddenly the worm turned and she had no more interest in me. For days on end, I was secretly happy and thought that the trouble-making demon had vanished and that everything would return to normal. When I went out in the morning, she patted my shoulder affectionately a few times and told me to 'just go on my way without worrying.' These good times didn't last long: an even greater blow landed on my head. My neighbor told me (as he talked, he stomped on my foot; he must have thought I was a moron) that my wife had had an affair with Old Meng the fortune-teller. They had openly gotten it on together upstairs in the pharmacy: everyone on the street knew this. My wife had also asserted: her husband had sanctioned her behavior. She and I each 'had found his and her own intimate friend.' This was like a bolt of lightning. I lost consciousness all at once. Later, I rushed to the second floor of the pharmacy and kicked open the door. I saw the two of them still rolling around in bed. Old Meng grabbed his glasses with his hook-like fingers, propped them on his nose, and looked all around. He didn't realize what had happened—he couldn't see me with his near-sighted eyes, which were almost blind.

" 'What has charged in here? Is it a dog or something?' he asked my wife as he hid behind her in fright.

"Seething, my wife slowly put her pants on, glanced at me with eyes like swords, and then said slowly, 'It's only a monkey. What else could it be?'

"Then she pointed straight at the door and stared at me until my face was half numb. I suddenly felt I should get out of there while there was still time. With that thought, I heaved a sigh of relief. When I turned around, I heard Old Meng tell my wife: 'Next time, we have to bolt the door. This kind of scene shouldn't be exposed to even a monkey. It's immoral.'

"As I was about to go downstairs, my wife blocked me. She hugged me tight and asked innocently, 'What do you think of him? Hunh? Isn't he unique? It's all because he enlightened me that I found my new life. Of course you remember what I used to be like: just recalling it, I'm terrified. I want to bring him home; we won't get in your way at all. He's noble. You haven't had the energy for "spare-time recreation" for a long time, have you? He's taught me the principles of conduct, and this is the only way I can pay him back. He's so pitiful. You just go about your business as usual. I get what I want, and you do, too.'

"I started trying to persuade her. I brought up more than a dozen examples to show her that this wasn't love, it was no more than a sense of indebtedness, and there were all kinds of ways to return favors, and sex was last on the list. This really was just too stupid. No one would understand it. She listened, inclining her head, then curled her lip and retorted that she did want to 'sacrifice herself.' It was the only right thing to do, and it was also quite fashionable.

"They drove me out of my home. I moved to a work shed next to the garbage dump. I was alone. Except for my work, there wasn't anything I was interested in. It was bleak at night. I looked at the starry sky through cracks in the shed's fir-bark roof, worrying minute by minute throughout that empty time. Sometimes, I would suddenly get up and wander all night outside my friend's home. Now, apart from the two people sound asleep in the small house, I have no family. More than any other time, I deeply realized that work, for me, was all there was. I'd already put all my eggs into one basket. As long as the friends in the small house were still here, my pursuit would eventually get me somewhere. There would come a day when I would prove everything I was trying to prove. I glued my ear to the window and listened to their breathing, confirming that they were still alive, still next to me, and then I felt reassured. I passed many lonely nights like this. My surreptitious struggles and sacrifices, the break-up of my family—these things, I scrupulously kept from my friends. The more down and out I was and the more I suffered, the richer I felt my life was. Embracing the secret of my self-sacrifice, I pretended to be happy and carefree as I talked with them. Deep in my heart, I felt great satisfaction.

"After a while, I grew accustomed to my new life—even began to be infatuated with it—because this life completely liberated my spirit. I consciously tortured my body. I moved the bed out of the work shed and also threw the quilt away. I made a den for myself by placing a few flagstones on the ground and a bundle of straw on the flagstones. Every night, I slept curled up in this nest; even if it was so cold that my skin turned pasty, I gritted my teeth and put up with it. When I caught a bad cold and lay shaking on the straw, I was still in good spirits. When my friend came to see me, I told him: 'I'm building myself up.' I told him that in the morning I still ate a good breakfast (actually, I hadn't eaten anything for two days), and asked him not to worry. I told him that my wife took meticulously good care of me and that I was in better health than ever. Looking doubtful, my friend took his leave, and tears almost spilled out of my eyes! This was so sublime! So grand! I was moved beyond words. My life was a delight! If a person gains true happiness from self-sacrifice, he'll savor all the enjoyment in earthly life. Someone like my wife is utterly worthless: although she's still alive, her soul died a long time ago and is wandering in the world like a ghost, getting in other people's way—a parasite on other people everywhere. This is the most tragic situation. How could she feel the subtlety of my spiritual life? She couldn't see any of this! Only now did I see that our marriage was a colossal mistake—how little she and I had in common. That I could break loose from that ball and chain was really my great good fortune. I hoped that she wouldn't change her views for the rest of her life and come back to entangle me.

"What is this one beginning of Madam X all about? Before the beginning, there was a long period of nothingness. She kept her door closed and didn't emerge, nor did she let anyone call on her. Every day, she stood woodenly alone in front of her window. Whoever talked with her, she was always smiling, turning a blind eye, making it difficult for the other person. During that time, there was also no evidence of anything that was going to happen. She seemed to have decided to live her life in silence. This really annoyed me. I redoubled my fasting and also tried to freeze myself, but none of this worked with them. They just indicated that my suffering was my own affair, an addiction. In a very short time, a huge emptiness was hanging over my head. I had lost my wits. Incredible demons were gnawing at my heart. Night after night, I risked running over to knock on the door of their small room. I wanted Madam X to show her true face: even if she raised the devil and went wild, it would still be better than this pretense, because this had to do with whether the three of us lived or died. The snare was right underfoot: I had to wake them up—tell them that sharp claws were hidden behind this external tranquility, and a lot of people had destroyed themselves just because of their indifferent attitude. I knocked on the door until my joints were swollen and I was dizzy, but they went on sleeping soundly. Not once did they answer.

"The next day I asked Madam X: had she heard anything during the night? Glaring at me, she said that she never heard anything, especially at night. Now, not only didn't she look at anything with her eyes, but she also didn't listen to anything with her ears. No matter what commotion occurred outside, she didn't hear a thing. Her world was a quiet one, an extensive plain, with little weeds growing shallowly in the mud, a scorching sun hanging high in the sky. She didn't even hear the cries of insects. If someone tried to disturb her with noise, this was a mistake. . . . Blah, blah, blah: all the nonsense gave me a headache. It appeared that she was dead set on getting rid of me—her protector. Just think how much I had suffered for her! Observing that I got thinner by the day for her sake, this frivolous woman not only just sat by and watched, she also told people I 'was odd,' and that she 'wouldn't give a dime for my protection,' or, rather, she 'abhorred' my protection, for she certainly hadn't encountered any danger, so why on earth would she need anyone to protect her? If I had a protection-mania, I should go home and protect my own wife.

"Of course, I wasn't surprised by what she said. Good medicine tastes bitter. Her reaction was absolutely normal. She had been harsh with me—fine, I didn't mind. I'm not a petty person who won't forgive a woman for impulsive behavior. Women were always impulsive and unself-conscious. Only with guidance would they stay away from evil ways. I wouldn't let my friend down, either, by ceasing to act as Madam X's protector. I can't become a frigid, worldly-wise person leading a stodgy life. I can't become utterly worthless like my wife. I saw that my poor friend needed my support more than ever: he was like a blind child walking into a dead end; he couldn't easily find the exit by himself. All his hopes lay with me. I was the only one who could rescue him. When driven to the wall, I launched a heroic solo movement. It flickered with sparks of brilliance, logic, and wisdom, lighting a long, dark passageway. What was it? What kind of outcome had been created? Was it directly related to Madam X's beginning? All of the secrets—you have to forgive me—will be my private treasure, stored forever in the bottom of my heart, because after enduring unspeakable suffering, I should have the prerogative of enjoying the pleasure alone. I don't want to share it with others, even if they're close friends. I'm going to greatly enjoy my monopoly over happiness. This happiness will go on until the day I leave this world. If you had my superhuman willpower and could suffer a long time, maybe one day you would also obtain it.

"I can divulge a little something to you: the beginning of Madam X's activity this time was guided and manipulated by me. No big deal—it just followed my will and evolved freely. My wife, as well as some other people, purposely exaggerated and added inflammatory details in order to disparage my ability. They have no idea about the great secrets. Their low-class insights prevented them from ever reaching any other conclusion. I'm the one who succeeded. I wasn't scared away by the situation or overwhelmed by the numerous difficulties. I rose up like a Titan!"

The Young Coal Worker's Report

"The special feelings that I have for this worthy lady are well known. All of you can see that for yourselves, so I won't go into detail. What I want to tell you about is my own spiritual life. Broadly speaking, this worthy lady directly triggered a succession of flowery, colorful actions by me: this proved I had had a great life. Previously, before the worthy lady moved to Five Spice Street, I hadn't had a spiritual life of my own. I was muddle-headed and ignorant, every day blindly following the crowd, eating like a horse, and sleeping like the dead—not even dreaming—and all unaware, I reached the age of twenty-two. I had been like this until one foggy morning when I ran into the incomparable worthy lady next to the well (I'm not using her name, because I know all too well that I'm not good enough to call her by name). She gave me a sweet, engaging smile. After that, I had a toothache for two weeks, and it was only after I had to have three teeth pulled that my beard started suddenly growing. And so it was that I became a real man.

"That day, my life underwent an earthshaking change. To celebrate my new life, and also to remind myself to be alert, I deliberately asked the dentist to pull all of my molars; I didn't want false teeth. And so, I have to eat in a special way and expend a lot more energy. Thus, I also realized even more completely how different I am from everyone else. Before I met the worthy lady, I was totally carefree. I wolfed my food down without any self-control, I was a philanderer, I talked at the public toilet in glib generalities, I was full of dirty words. My buddies and I flirted with all the women—young or old—whom we met on the street. We teased and joked and acted narcissistic, wearing so much cologne that we felt intoxicated. We did not know the difference between real love and our regular indulgences such as wearing cologne, flirting, and talking about women at the public toilet. We got excited talking about women and played around like this all year long, our heads crammed with absurdities.

"What on earth is the worthy lady all about? No way can I explain this to you. I remember that after encountering her next to the well,

I dreamed that night for the first time in my life. I dreamed of a porcupine that had plunged into a deep pond. The sequoias at the side of the pond toppled one after another. This dream was filled with threats. When I woke up the next morning, my mother asked me, 'Son, where's the other half of your face?' I felt my face and started howling. Then, with dazed eyes, I got out of bed and saw that bees were swarming all over the furniture. I shouted to Mother, 'Reality is so absurd!' Mother's hands were trembling, and she dropped a plate, which shattered. You mustn't pay much attention to Old Woman Jin: she doesn't represent anything; she's just one of my small props. In the midst of bitter, unrequited love, and because I was feeling so much ardor, I had to find a stand-in. Anyone would do. I probably chose her because she was the first woman I ever had, or maybe because she appreciated amorous feelings and was willing to get it on with me. But she had never appeared in any of my fantasies. I always saw the worthy lady every day at a certain place, but she certainly never saw me: I always hid. As soon as I left her, all sorts of fluids started seething in my body. I sprang to my feet like a frenzied lion and charged into Old Woman Jin's home, and as if drunk and crazy, I made it with her until my inner fire was extinguished.

"Ever since the worthy lady vanquished me, I haven't had the nerve to face her. Only when she's unaware of my presence can I admire her from a distance and then thoroughly bring into play my feelings of love and my limitless imagination. If I see her, even if I just see her back or hear her voice, my legs go weak and I can't say anything coherent. It's frightening. Luckily, she doesn't pay any attention to me: she's ruled by a crazy microscope. Her voice is only dimly discernible, her eyes have lost their sight, and she has no patience for people disturbing her. She always wishes they would soon vanish. Her disposition makes me respect and adore her all the more, and my feelings for her become all the more constant. When I lie in the dark, I sigh: if I hadn't met this worthy lady, if there hadn't been the misty fog and frost on the edge of the well, if she hadn't smiled, what would my life be like now? How long would that infantile behavior, neither male nor female (splashing cologne on myself, talking about women at the toilet, and so forth), have continued? When I was twenty-two, my destiny led me to a luminous turning point: a lady led me forward. No matter what twists and turns appear in life, and no matter how others censure the lady's character, my selfless love will remain the same.

"My relationship with Old Woman Jin comes from my affection for the worthy lady. As long as I still feel passion for the worthy lady, I can't leave Old Woman Jin. I very much like expressing my passion this way. (Although people reproach me for being absurd, I never waver.) I can't help it: every day, I repeatedly practice and become more skillful. I know that some people mention my passion and the vulgar 'spare-time recreation' in the same breath in order to detract from the value of my existence. How can you expect my former buddies to have any better opinions? They splash cologne all over themselves and swarm into the toilet and talk indiscreetly of relationships between men and women. They boast, and they're filled with self-satisfaction. Once someone goes beyond their limited notions, they crowd together to attack him. Looking scornful, they say, 'This is all there is to it. How can there be anything new?' I know how chilling this is. Really, my former friends can't evolve into civil people. It's too late. My verdict is completely pessimistic. Everything I've experienced has led me to this verdict. I can tell you about it.

"The first conflict occurred at noon that day. Winking and so delighted they couldn't contain themselves, my former buddies surrounded me at the toilet and kept making *sh-sh-sh* sounds. They pressed me to the wall, wanting me to make a clean breast of 'the inside story'—'c'mon, give your buddies some fun,' 'tell us all the juicy parts.' They also let me know: Since I had mentioned 'sex appeal'—no trivial matter—they had reason to conclude that I had a carnal relationship with the lady. Can you use this word offhandedly? Isn't it obvious what it refers to if you use it about someone other than your wife? On our Five Spice Street, 'sex appeal' means 'spare-time recreation.' Since long ago, these two expressions have meant the same thing, and the hidden meaning of 'spare-time recreation' is something everyone can understand. Both expressions are transparent and descriptive: they produce almost physiological pleasure. My buddies weren't interested in the semantics of the expression. They just wanted to understand what was going on, authenticate it, and learn something educational. They for sure didn't intend to try anything themselves with that lady: I didn't need to take precautions with them. In any case, not everyone was aroused just by seeing her. This lady had lived right under their noses for years. It's too bad that none of them had paid any attention to her, nor did they even know what she looked like. Only after I described her did they know that she had remarkable 'sex appeal.' Why wouldn't this make them look at her with new eyes?

"With a gloomy expression, I explained: 'There are some things in this world which can't be understood by the book. Sometimes, we have to change our way of thinking and look with brand-new eyes before we can enter into the essence of something.' This seems difficult and troublesome, but with hard struggle you can make it. Of course, if you want to reform, there will be sacrifices. For instance, I sacrificed all my molars. This partial loss, however, let me achieve total freedom. If you can't bear any loss, you'd better just blindly conform; you'll never be able to understand vital newfangled things.' My relationship with the worthy lady goes beyond the bounds of their ideas. This is a lofty relationship: it belongs to the future; it spans the present. There's been no physical contact in my relationship with the worthy lady. It was in my fantasies that I felt her sex appeal. This is real, not a bit abstract. Still, it isn't the same as 'spare-time recreation.' For the moment, I can't find the right word to express it, but anyhow, it's the momentum for my life development. They had to admit that beyond the notion they had, there was a huge space filled with novel things. I hoped they could all break through and try hard to expand their horizons and not be suffocated by parochial ideas.

"As soon as I finished saying all this, they were even more excited. They started clamoring and pulled at my pants, saying that they wanted to see if I was actually impotent. The young guy on the other side of the wall added fat to the fire by reminding everyone: 'People with this problem all talk a big line. They have one pack of dizzying reasons after another. They can talk the dead back to life. But they just want to distract you from their own invisible conditions. I know a guy who—after getting this condition—suddenly became very eloquent. Every day, in the scorching sun, he went to the street corner and clearly and logically analyzed old ideas and new ones and put forward an unlimited number of new scenarios. He also suggested that people all rub lard into their hair, and said that the more 'spare-time recreation,' the better, blah, blah, blah. . . . Everybody was really interested and asked him to demonstrate in public. He was sweating profusely, and fell to the ground and died.' When these guys were just about to pull down my pants, an old man (like Old Meng from the pharmacy) came stumbling into their midst, berated them, and held them back. Then he suggested 'giving me enough rope to hang myself.' He said this would bring out even more exciting scandals. Wouldn't this be much better?

"The second conflict occurred while we were cooling off outside. Those were days when my fortunes rose and fell. At the time, my buddies and I were discussing whether or not to put up advertisements for photographic equipment. Our discussion was lively, with a lot of views being presented. We also came up with the basic blueprint. Everyone was in a good mood. While all of us were absorbed in longing for the good life, we suddenly looked up and saw the worthy lady and her family stroll by in their leisurely way. They were talking loudly with their child about good birds and vermin. They were so rude that they didn't even look at us: it was as if they were walking through a pile of stakes. The man was also laughing foolishly, quite pleased with his high-pitched voice. And the woman cheered him on: 'Great! Go on! Talk a little louder!' Looking at each other in despair, we were terrified. We turned pale and fell silent. After they disappeared into the distance, an old woman thumped her chest and shouted, 'Aren't they just treating other people as if they were fools?!' Not until then did they become infuriated. After a quick brainstorming session, they looked around at me.

The spear was aimed at me: I was the cause of their arrogant bluster. Madam X used to be a sickly old woman whom no one respected; her husband always had to support her when they went for walks. Her hair was also very thin. After I started spouting nonsense about Madam X's 'sex appeal' and took some 'sweets' from her, she wasn't the same as before, although no one was sure exactly how she was different. In most people's eyes, she was still an old woman, but there was something about her attitude that told people she was no longer the same as usual. If she still wasn't a peerless beauty, she was at least a beautiful woman. The foundation for this view was hidden in the crowd. She could manipulate that person; she could master everyone via this person. He was the one who had elevated her position from that of a beggar so that everyone now paid attention to her, talked about her, looked up to her. In the meantime, so many of the charming, stylish women on the street were fading: no one was paying attention to them. It was as if her reality had vanished: wearing rose-colored glasses, everyone had discovered a goddess.

"I was being treated so unjustly it was hard to vindicate myself. I swore to them that this worthy lady and I were just 'soulmates.' Though I respected her greatly, she had no idea who I was. The more I said this, the less the crowd would relax its grip: they greatly distorted what I'd said in the past and forced me 'to come clean.' The old woman with the high-pitched voice suggested that the worthy lady and I 'perform again.' The crowd supported this proposal. They pushed me into the lady's house. (Two buddies watched from outside the window.) The lady was looking through her microscope, and because I blocked her light, she blew up. She didn't notice me in the middle of the room but charged into another room and told her husband that two oxen outside the window had wrecked her research. 'It's really damnable.' She wanted to find the hunting rifle and let the wild animals 'get a taste of her marksmanship.' The two buddies were so scared they took to their heels. Narrowing her eyes, she looked mockingly at the clowns outside the window and then turned around and noticed me. She was displeased. 'There's always something coming in. Damn it!' Her husband ran up to soothe her: he said that I wasn't a person but merely a rag drying on the clothesline. As he talked, he blocked me with his body and pushed me out of the house.

"After the second conflict, my despair reached new lows. My eyes were bloodshot. Like a caged wolf, I paced in the house and howled shrilly until I was exhausted. Then I sat down to think about my worries. When I thought of what that son-of-a-bitch neighbor guy said, I couldn't help feeling infuriated. It was impossible for these people to speak the same language as I did. They had stomped on all the feelings I'd stored up and on my selfless love. People are so alone in the world; it is so difficult for the light of ideals to penetrate the darkness. I was more sorrowful than at any other time, and my feelings for her ran even deeper. An invisible thread had linked the worthy lady and me together, to live or to die. I would go through purgatory for her. I was dominated by a self-denying fanaticism and a worshipful piety. I had a premonition that I would pull off a splendid feat. What would it be? You'd know it when you saw it.

"I stayed home every day and didn't go out again. I listened closely. I had reason to believe that the worthy lady would show up at my door. If she came unannounced and I wasn't home, I'd regret this for the rest of my life. I had to wait patiently and trustingly. I had to be neatly and freshly dressed to meet her. While she was here, I would ask her to sit on my only chair, which had a dogskin cushion, while I would stand to show her my heroic image and leave an indelible impression on her. I mustn't take this lightly and go to bed, because she might also come at midnight: this was the sticking point. I had a splendid idea: I would hang a rope from the window, tie a knot in it, and put my neck through the knot. Then if by any chance I fell asleep, the rope would wake me up. I also pounded a lot of bamboo tacks into the floor so that when I paced at night, I had to concentrate and circle scrupulously around these tacks. If I was careless, I'd be hurt. These ideas had a surprising effect: I was always in high spirits. I was highly alert twenty-four hours a day. I felt my life was fully enriched. As soon as I heard footsteps outside, I immediately smoothed my clothes and sat up straight. My heart throbbed. I didn't look out the window but at the ceiling—until the footsteps gradually went away. I kept up this pose, unable to extricate myself for a long time. And because Mother kept intruding on my feelings from time to time with vulgar things like food and sleep, I sprang to my feet and sternly warned her: if she kept doing this, I would prove my true feelings by committing suicide. Because of the elevated aesthetic realm I now occupied, she had to look at me with new eyes, and she understood a little better. Didn't she notice that I'd thrown out all my cologne? I'd bought a new toilet and planned not to use the public toilet any longer: why hadn't she noticed this?

"Did you ask about the beginning? See, this was it—such a long beginning that it's almost a section of history. I don't think it will have any conclusion. While I'm waiting, all the joy and anguish will quietly fade away. Only the perpetual rays of light are blazing ahead, and a new character is emerging. All of this was determined by the porcupine dream: it plunged into a deep pond, and one by one, the giant sequoias fell over beside the pond. From then on, the worthy lady and I made history together. But the clamor at the public toilet is so hard on the ears! Are my buddies splashing themselves with cologne again?"

The Writer's Report
"The writer knows well enough that we want to figure out how Madam X's love affair with Mr. Q began. Each person was burning to know, and each had pigheaded subjective biases; no one would give in, but they also hoped they would be unanimous in reaching an impartial solution so we could get a break from exhausting our brains on this. Of course, this was just a simple-minded wish. Although this looked simple, in fact it was very complicated. On our Five Spice Street, whenever a problem like this turned up, the answers were maddeningly endless. Where one person saw a wild boar, another saw a dove, and perhaps a third person saw a broom. We had to respect individuality and the facts: we had to accept all the various answers before we could rush across riptides and land on the radiant opposite shore. If you split hairs and got entangled in

non-essential details, and lacked flexibility, you would unwittingly become more and more confused, finally sinking to the bottom of the darkness. Magnanimity is humankind's noblest characteristic. In our diverse and confusing world, there are so many knots that can't be untied and so many bewildering doubts and suspicions that can only be melted and eliminated in a broad and generous heart.

"Perhaps this kind of thing had no fixed beginning: it was so unusual, so exciting, and so colorful that people speculated about it endlessly. So, in everyone's eyes, it rapidly evolved into some specific lenses that were directly interrelated with each individual. And then they affected each other and formed a sinuous net: this is also understandable. We ordinary people living on this three-mile-long street have always been closely linked. Superficially we looked cold and indifferent, but inwardly we were very enthusiastic, romantic, and humane. One person's business was everyone's business. Every day, we cared about nothing but other people's business and planned our actions accordingly. We might have looked narrow-minded and short-sighted, and as if we cared about nothing but our own small worlds. In fact, we were highly idealistic comrades in the same camp. Our little world was a microcosm of the outside world. Each individual pursuit was also a collective pursuit. Not only were we not disloyal to each other, we supported each other. 'All roads lead to heaven,' 'sublime in the rainbow.' In this place of ours, as soon as something big occurred, a series of chain reactions would immediately ensue and hundreds of individual lenses would appear, independent of each other and all mutually opposed. Sometimes a big mess managed to bring about a certain temporary, laughable unity, but this quickly collapsed of its own weight, and everyone took his own path, continuing to hold to his own opinion to the end. Each person's individuality had plenty of chances for practice and development. During this development, each person played God. We were pure-hearted and noble, filled with ardor and sincerity, one after another opening up a strange and beautiful new world, delighted with our achievements. Reality was reflected dramatically in our land. Fluky nature was tamed by the rules of our thought. This new world was fascinating. Here, the vines and trees that grew madly all year long, the birds that sang crankily, the ocean with its grand waves, the waterfalls that roared incessantly: behind all of this, the vital everlasting light was shining. This world was the original source of poetry and the eternal theme of art. In the scorching summer sun, when we opened our blurry, bloodshot eyes and gazed up at the sky, those calls that were everywhere—the low murmur—emerged, and the formations of the wild geese grew chaotic, the sun's rays turned purple, our flesh was divinely stirred, and our brains experienced the perfection of poetry. What appeared before us this time was merely a repetition of an ancient game that had been around for thousands of years. If one looked upon it with one's intellect, perhaps it was banal, even a little arid, and so perhaps it was also non-existent. The issue per se was not important. What was important was its artful reproduction in the people's minds, that magnificent creation, that powerful, untrammeled imagination, that rich, deep excavation toward essence, going into minute detail and not letting go. It's all of this that constitutes the priceless treasures of our boundless universe. Although we will one day be decrepit, the fantastic fruit on the tree of life will forever symbolize our wild, unruly passion.

"On this three-mile-long street of ours, Madam X and Mr. Q are bewildering and out of line. We don't want to admit this, for as soon as we do, it's as though we're making them the center of our lives, as though they created our history. Of course, this is nonsense. What kind of people are they? One is like an extraterrestrial who dropped down from who-knows-where and put down roots in the earth and doesn't plan to move again. The other is a masked, invisible man; even his features exist only in our guesswork: it's absolutely possible that he's headless or has a serpent's face and a human body. At first, we didn't have any extra energy to contemplate or be concerned with these two people who weren't much connected with us. In the beginning, we thought: let them live and die by themselves. They couldn't go on very long. Old Meng from the pharmacy reckoned that after five years, they would change into scaly anteaters and 'go through the wall and leave' Five Spice Street. Then the sun would shine everywhere, and there would be peace in the world. And so we would pass the time as we usually did, every day organizing our dust-covered albums, replacing them and hanging up large color photos, arranging for all kinds of large-scale and medium-scale group photos, and making rules for highway maintenance and the area for cooling off outside. We were so busy that we were almost about to forget these two. We were intoxicated with our heroism and merely gazed at the stretch of distant undulating mountains.

"We avoided talking about these two people for a long time and deliberately substituted 'H' and 'L' for their names. We almost got used to this, as if those two had disappeared from the street. The ones we talked of were two new people, much more worth noticing than X and Q. X and Q? No one could remember who they were; we had only 'H' and 'L.' Only this animated couple greatly interested us. They were special! But whether you pretended not to notice them, whether you used different names for them, these two low-down people were always secretly manufacturing a demagogic hullabaloo. Finally, 'the beginning' saw the light of day, and everyone on Five Spice Street began dashing madly here and there all day long—never able to get anything done. Everyone was suffering from serious worries and couldn't let anyone see how sick he was (that would hurt the struggle). All anyone could do was complain implicitly. For example:

"'We should have new laws to crack down on "H" and "L."' Unfortunately, our present laws are imperfect and have no provisions for dealing with people who have theoretically broken the law even though there's no evidence of it. Someone has been making use of this situation. Just think about it, it actually began, and with that, my "spare-time recreation" was destroyed. I'm not saying that I was impotent. This is just a kind of psychological reaction.'

"'I kept imagining that "H" and "L" had turned into two "mosquitoes." They were buzzing in the sky and disappeared without a trace. Peace and prosperity were coming back, flowers were blossoming, and life was beautiful again. Am I leading too befuddled a life? Yesterday, I unconsciously held out my hand and realized that my thumb had been numb for a long time.'

" 'Now we need to talk openly about sex as a scientific issue. Didn't those two people take advantage of our excessive seriousness, our virginal sense of shame, to set their defiance into motion? We have to cure our vegetative nervous disorder and boldly reveal our viewpoints. At the right time, we can also beat back their savage aggression with a public performance to show that we are totally open-minded.'

" 'This probably started a long time ago, and probably there has never been a real beginning, for what we thought was clear was actually covered by mist. It broke out at this point, no sooner and no later. Was it aimed right at us? How can my legs be as weak as they are? A voice is constantly whispering in my ear: "Two ears, three legs, two ears, three legs . . ." '

" 'The one who made this long speech was motivated by the expectation that his listeners would poke through the layer of tissue paper and reveal the vivid prototype. His adversary understood his intention well, but was sophisticated and astute enough to keep his own views veiled. That was the profundity of the game. If someone ignorantly shouted out his real views, he was just asking for scorn from the crowd.'

"This writer always wanted to take a fair-minded stand and write objectively about this incident's beginning. This doesn't mean that other people's vivid depictions were non-objective, inaccurate non-sense. The writer simply wants to try hard to string these diverse viewpoints together like pearls, bring them into focus, and achieve a static view, like the way the sun—before it sets—grasps the whole of the universe. 'Things will eventually get sorted out,' anyhow, and 'the whole thing will be obvious.' As the writer sat at home, eyes closed, pondering all of this, the uninvited crowd kept interrupting. These people were all swayed by their own emotions. They pulled the chair away while the writer was sitting on it, and brandishing clubs, they intimidated the writer by saying that while he was writing, he had to 'be practical and realistic,' 'be candid,' and then in a babel of voices, each person poured out his own views, which included a high-level sense of history and responsibility. They endlessly analyzed their superiority and inferiority, their achievements and their shortcomings, from the time of their birth until well into the future. As for the beginning of the incident between X and Q, they skimmed over this, dealing with it at one stroke—or not dealing with it at all. Totally forgot it. Yes, it was a minute, unimportant matter. They had come here to express their own passions. The matter of X and Q was nothing but an excuse that brought them together. In other words, the matter of X and Q was merely a fuse detonating individual passions that had been stored up a long time. After they finished expressing themselves, they started attacking each other.

"The much-admired widow said that Ms. B was 'a toad lusting after a swan.' She was 'an ugly woman who didn't know herself, who disgusted people with her crazy ideas. Would he (Mr. Q) bother to stare at you?' She stood up straight and pounded Ms. B's belly with her arms. 'You don't even know what color his eyes are. You just talk nonsense about his eyes being as big as an ox's. I'll tell you the truth: His eyes are triangular! You even made up the time of the beginning. It was midnight when he came, and gray piglets were running all over the streets. A hooligan was blowing a whistle. I left my house to go to the toilet and saw this with my own eyes. Even though no one saw me, I couldn't keep from blushing. Even now as I recall this, I still blush. You told us he came at noon, so your nonsense messed up such a good beginning. You and all egotistical demons ruin all the good things in the world. It's only because you're here that those two could take it easy and get along. One after another, you kept talking nonsense, and you've completely lost the last little bit of sober reason you might have had. You've dragged everyone into the dark abyss, and yet you think you're witty, you think you're brilliant, while those two took the advantage, got what they wanted, and were home free a long time ago. You guys have brought an end to the fineness of our generation.'

"Ms. B didn't chicken out, either. She kept trying to trip the widow with her foot and shouted 'Down with dictators!' She stressed that she 'was born in the spring, the productive season, and so she was diligent and great at logical reasoning.' She said the widow 'was unlikely to have any extraordinary sex appeal.' 'She's just jealous, that's all.' As she talked, she finally tripped the plump widow, who fell to the ground. The writer had to jump down from the table and intervene.

"Just then, the good friend of Madam X's husband started fighting with Old Meng. Old Meng groped for a stool with his wiry, withered hands and, shaking, held it high above his head, then fiercely smashed it down. As it happened, he hit his own feet. When the good friend heard the sound of bones breaking, he was scared out of his wits. He left Old Meng and hurried over to the writer, to whom he whispered: 'The day it all began was the birthday of my rebirth. Nobody can deny this. I realized this truth when I was in hell, where I suffered so many tribulations! How did I survive? Isn't the reality cruel in the extreme? Everything has confirmed my predictions. The ideal is coming true.'

"Then these two people suddenly began arguing again. Old Meng said he 'certainly didn't gain much.' That lady was a vampire, and the husband and wife were conspiring to frame him, and so he planned to 'keep his distance.' But before this, he 'had to be given a room in their house'—this would be 'just and reasonable.' If he didn't get a room, then he wouldn't stay away, but would 'wait for a lifetime' in their home. The good friend said that, as he saw it, 'money was like dirt.' He had long ago become like an itinerant monk: no temptation could corrupt him again. If Old Meng coveted that house, and just went ahead and dealt with his wife, he couldn't care less. Now the only things in his heart were big ones—nothing else. Didn't Old Meng see that he was sleeping on the street and begging? While he was talking, he grabbed the writer's hand again, insisting that the writer record the important thing in his heart—the 'good and glorious beginning' that he had memorized so that he could be 'a witness to history.' 'I've endured so many hardships!' He stressed again:

'Beautiful hair has fallen from my head like leaves blown down by the wind.' He had impatiently drawn a rather unsuitable analogy. The writer consoled him: he would write all of this down and string everything together like pearls. He wouldn't leave anything out, because he was talented. But he couldn't 'write it down on the spot,' for this superior, convoluted work must be pursued in circumstances in which he wouldn't be interrupted. He had to meditate with his eyes closed, let things ferment, and then let the inspiration flow, and write like a torrent of water that couldn't be held back.

"'Am I an ordinary bead on your string?' The good friend was unhappy. 'How dare you describe me with such an analogy? You insidious stenographer (he had always considered me a stenographer), I'm not a bead! It's you and your confederates who are beads! No, you're not even beads: you're merely a string of stinky tofu. The fine beginning belongs to me alone.'

"Just then, Old Meng grabbed the writer's other hand and began shouting that the writer ought, in good 'conscience,' to make a historical record of the housing issue, and mustn't 'forfeit his point of view' just because of a certain pressure. His foot was already broken: this was the sacrifice he'd made in championing the truth. Pushed and pulled between these two peremptory men, the writer was almost cut in two. They also tickled the writer in the ribs, so he giggled foolishly. In this hopeless state of affairs, the widow landed a fierce blow on his chest, and the writer fainted to the ground. He didn't know when the crowd dispersed.

"After the writer came to, he massaged his throbbing temples and, despite the pain he felt all over, went on with his work. He found that his chair was gone. He remembered that Old Meng had smashed his chair: maybe he'd only pretended his foot was hurt so that he could throw the chair out and come back later and steal it? Anyhow, there was no chair, so he'd better just sit on the floor. The writer put his notebook on the bed, sat on the floor, and began to write rapidly. He wrote day and night. Most of the righteous people approved of and admired the writer's work. Every night, they discussed the writer's drafts at meetings in the large hall, adding detailed explanatory notes, checking the records against their own experiences, broadmindedly weighing all the views in the document, and also making some suggestions, such as including photos on each page. But some did not approve of the writer's laborious work; instead, they demolished it. They broke in every day with unreasonable requests. They even became arrogant: they took the furniture out of the room and splashed ink over the manuscript. The hooligans' tricks were beyond imagination.

"The original text of part of the writer's manuscript read: 'In the early morning, suffused by fragrance and flower-like clouds, the scent of grass flowing from the faraway sky into the ancient three-mile-long street touched people's hearts and intoxicated every righteous, virtuous resident with the breath of spring. People's faces were like peach blossoms and filled with passion. A dark shadow appeared and made straight for the little door to Madam X's home. The sound of rapid knocking fell on each person's heart, just like Beethoven's Fifth. . . .' Later, this splendid section (exhibiting the writer's skill with words) had to be deleted, or the writer's life would have been endangered. Just as he was penning these words, a few ugly shrews charged in and looked on brazenly. They yelled and screamed, and kept brushing against the writer's face with their coarse, greasy hair, so there was no way the writer could continue with his work. They became even ruder, snatching his notebook and reading it aloud. After that, they glowered and flew into a rage, saying that the writer contradicted fact and toyed with words. If this flashy, false document wasn't changed, if the true history couldn't be restored, they wouldn't have the face to see people again. So they had to struggle to the death with the writer! The most poisonous sentence in the document was 'made straight for the little door to Madam X's home.' Who saw him 'make straight for'? Where's the evidence? As to the mystery of Mr. Q's arrival, they had at least a few hundred views, each with solid evidence, as well as historical proof. The writer, however, disregarded the crowd's wishes and went his own way. With a 'made straight for,' he peremptorily extinguished everyone's individuality. Who could put up with this? If he was going to persist in taking a cynical approach to historical documents, he'd better stop right now and avert a blood-letting incident. If he kept to one side and did nothing, well, the facts were still the facts, and everyone would remain confident that no one would be so pessimistic or desperate as to doubt the value of his existence. What he had done was no different from placing these women on a tightrope: any slight movement would cause them to fall and break their necks. It was extremely vicious! There was no point in keeping this document that distorted reality. In order to salvage his notebook, the writer could only endure the humiliation, publicly admit his wrongdoing, and delete the most exquisite part of his text. He also guaranteed that nothing like this would happen again and that he would always be honest and respect others.

"In the process of writing the document, the writer had run into another problem difficult to wriggle out of, an obstacle there was no way to get over: he had to track down the historical roots of the story. In this, he faced immense handicaps. He was isolated, with no one to help him. All he could lean on was his own talent: after days and nights of pondering, he was inspired in a dream and wrote down some very graceful words: '. . . On our flourishing, colorful street, each resident enjoys full freedom to the best of his ability. Like a duck taking to water, everyone is relaxed and happy. Vehicles full of wonderful foodstuffs roll past on the street, a photography studio with the best technology is open for us day and night, the green trees at the roadside are set off by the translucent blue sky—scenery that delights both the eye and the mind—and flocks of pigeons settle on the roofs of our temples. . . . The instant every person opens his eyes each morning, he takes a deep breath and shudders with joy from head to toe. Indeed, sometimes this beautiful rhythm moves us to tears and silent sobbing. In this worldly paradise, this Xanadu, people are peaceful and affectionate, caring for each other as for family members. There is no reason to be on guard. Everyone is magnanimous and passionate: everyone who comes here is given close attention. Everyone is sincere, and everyone displays chivalry. To draw a visual analogy: this ground is so fertile, the natural resources so abundant, that on this free land every seed that is sown has the chance to grow and mature and complete its life course. Peremptory actions and brutality have never been heard of here. It is like a large garden with a hundred flowers blooming at the same time, fragrant all day long, the scene alive with the joy of spring. Immortals sit with their eyes closed amid the flowers, and the mellow sound of stringed instruments resounds in the sky. . . . Could we guarantee that all the seeds would be strong and healthy? Could they all send forth exquisite flowers? Perhaps two seeds were sick and deformed, marinated in venom, and, after gestating in the spongy, fertile earth, then fanned in the warm spring wind, grew into weird shapes and occupied a plot of land among the hundred flowers. They were a flashy eyesore as they desperately dispersed their toxins everywhere. This has become the present reality. Is this way of putting it rather exaggerated? Well, then, say this is a tiny contaminant, such as a little boil on one's body: there's no need for surgery. One can let it run its natural course; that's a lot more practical. We certainly don't have to regard Madam X and Mr. Q as loathsome enemies or horned fiends. We won't consider this problem from the point of view of ignorant women. If the two of them are demons, how could our place still be called a Xanadu? Could we still enjoy our perpetual, serene paradise? We aren't looking at them this way (our magnanimous nature won't allow it), but we can come up with some reasonable, bold assumptions that will be authenticated in the future. For now, they can enlighten us and strengthen our confidence in exploring the truth. The writer has plenty of reason to assume that these two persons' ancestors must have included an endless succession of mentally ill people, even people suffering from hemophilia or gonorrhea. Naturally, their families had nothing to do with Five Spice Street. They had probably flourished in a remote little mountain village, a bare mountain where grass and trees didn't grow, a village filled with stupidity and barbarity, preserving shocking vices. A large fire consumed the village. This man and woman were the only two who survived: they left the village and came to our city and were mixed in with the residents of our city. They settled down here.

And thus we verified people's thinking of them as two deformed, sick seeds that had been steeped in poison. Thus, the historical roots of what happened on our street are plain as day.'

"All of a sudden, the writer grasped the truth: he was suddenly enlightened. After writing this section, his head was clear and his body relaxed. He was so pleased that he started humming a song, 'The Golden Sun Rises in the East.' That night, when the writer's document was read and discussed in the large hall, the writer was full of confidence as he sat beneath the stage and listened to some-one read it aloud. He began sobbing when he heard the best part, he was so amazed by his own talent. After the person finished reading aloud, the sound of furtive whispers immediately arose, and then became hushed—frighteningly quiet. Something was wrong: it was as though everyone was holding his breath. And then, at some point, these people scooted away from the meeting one by one. The writer finished crying, massaged his bloodshot eyes, and went up to the stage. In a hoarse voice he told the crowd how his opus was born. As he talked, he looked down and saw row after row of empty chairs, and so he sat down dejectedly on the floor. The crowd's emotions were hard to get hold of. This was a head-on blow! What was an artist if he lost his dear readers all at once? Wasn't he utterly worth-less? Hadn't he sunk to being a tramp? A flower bloomed beau-tifully, although without its stem and root, it was weird, ghostly. The artist could become sublime and his inspiration could flow uninter-ruptedly only when he was taken into the readers' warm and gen-erous embrace. But if the readers abandoned him, he became an orphan and his talent dried up. Art was also isolated from him. This is common sense; everyone knows it. Where on earth had the writer failed and made such an irreparable error? Why had a wall been erected between him and his readers? Could it be that, just as his writing had a period of growth, now it had been cut off at the waist by some demon, and everything was finished? Could his brilliant artistic career be ended like this for some unknown reason? What the hell kind of subtle relationship did the damn X and Q have with the crowds on Five Spice Street? The writer's freewheeling imagination, his inflated adjectives, and his artistic conceptions had evidently provoked the sensitive people, and so the document itself had to be abandoned. Why couldn't the writer understand this relationship by empathizing with others? Had his ideology begun to petrify? With great pain, the writer engaged repeatedly in self-criticism. With misty, tear-filled eyes, he also examined the part the readers had found offensive three times, and finally made up his mind that he would take the blame and go door to door, apologizing in person. The writer felt that taking this step wouldn't indicate inferiority, but rather would show his splendid individuality. Someday the crowds would understand genius and come to stand next to genius. Maybe they were looking out their windows and expecting his arrival. And maybe they were already feeling sorry for him and were opening their generous hearts, waiting for him to throw himself on their mercy! Maybe they already realized that they had simply overreacted.

"The first reader the writer called on was the widow who wore the little felt hat. The writer had weighed this matter several times and decided that he would make a good start at her place, because women, and especially old women, were all good, softhearted people who couldn't stand to see a young person's promising future ruined. When someone seeking help called on them, they would offer it warmly and give advice: some would even come out in the open on your behalf. Starting from their maternal instincts and also their women's intuition (upon coming into contact with young men, they always suddenly recaptured their passionate youth and would give the supplicant everything he hoped for), they were generous to a fault and didn't ask to be repaid. Embracing this hope, the writer walked that slippery slope and entered the old widow's home. It was midnight: there was no light on in the house, and the door was unlocked. To the right of the entry was a bed. The writer knew the widow wasn't asleep, because he heard groans and the sounds of tossing and turning. He felt his way to the bed, intending to sit on the side of it. Unexpectedly, the widow kicked him hard, and he almost fell. 'You can sit on the floor.' The widow said resolutely, 'It's as though a fire is burning in my heart. I am a very direct person.' The writer sat down gingerly on something that was like a pile of coal ashes. He didn't make a sound, intending to listen respectfully to what she had to teach him. The old woman was silent a long time and then finally let out an agonized sigh and began talking. 'Tonight, when I heard your document being read, my heart seemed to ignite. So many words written in a dirty notebook, and even a few inky fingerprints on the cover. You are too profligate, overindulging in trivia. I heard that while you're writing, you sit on the floor like this and never wash your hands. I can imagine that you also touch your saliva with your black fingers as you turn the pages. At first, I didn't care about whatever it was you wrote, because at the time I was dozing off. But when the one reading your document suddenly roared, I fell off my chair at once. After I got home, I couldn't get to sleep, because I kept wondering whether you were attacking through innuendo. Otherwise, how could that person shout so loud as to scare a person? I'm in a bad mood tonight. Maybe, because I'm downhearted, I won't want to help you. That shout was just too frightening. How can you reproduce that shout in your document? I planned to take part in the work of annotating your text along with everyone else. I think you are talented, but what was that shout all about? No, no. This contradicts my tastes and sentiments. Maybe you intended to show your superiority. You certainly make me seem very depraved. I'd rather stay away from doing the annotations. I'm so confused inside.' She made a few *gu-gu* sounds and then buried her head in the straw bedding.

"The writer humbly begged her to take his hand to show that she still wanted to be one of his readers, because otherwise 'he would go crazy.' No other gesture could have suited her fine character and grace more in revealing the beauty of her soul. The writer's hand was at the edge of the bed: did she feel it? She need only shift a little to touch it.

" 'It costs me nothing to do it, but I won't do it for nothing.' In the dark, she laughed vaguely and spat repeatedly. 'I'm the key person, aren't I? If I am persuaded, you can get everything you want. Both of us know this. I'm not a beauty, but I have enormous energy. My cousin knows this best. It's no exaggeration to say that he admires me greatly. Just think, after forty years, he's now an old man, and yet that incident remains fresh in his mind. Can ordinary people remember the past so well? I meditate on this subject from time to time, and I'm astonished at my ability. I see clearly that I can get anything I want. I was born with this omnipotence. Still, I always take the high road: I don't want to contend for fame and fortune. After I left the meeting tonight, I knew you'd come to see me. It wouldn't do any good for you to see others, but seeing me, you can get everything you want. What kind of person am I? Can anyone compare with me? Do you understand what I mean now? You're a stenographer who can at any time write about big events and about people who are characterized by individuality and charm. To you, the most important thing is to have the eyes to penetrate everything. You have to look upon the people around you with far-sighted eyes and analyze which people are worth recording and which are merely a flash in the pan who won't amount to anything. You shouldn't choose only the young and beautiful. More often than not, age is directly proportionate to charm. You'll learn this from experience. In this place, there are some persons of the hour who don't possess profound genius. They might attract a lot of attention because they're superficially active, but their hearts are absolute voids. These counterfeits can sometimes pull the wool over the eyes of young people like you, and—on an impulse—you might want to write them into history as heroes. If you do that, they would really start pushing society blindly, and so the entire course of history would slip—all because of your devil-may-care mistake. We can see from this the heavy responsibilities you stenographers must assume— how essential it is for a judicious person with abundant experience to guide you so that you'll make fewer mistakes. Is it possible that these nameless heroes who work in silence, these people who are humble and cautious on the surface and don't say much, don't go out much, and yet actually have astonishing abilities—is it possible that they aren't more worthy of being written into history than these phonies? Since you're engaged in this work, why haven't you noticed these worthy people all around you? Why haven't you shown great interest in them and pursued them? This is you young stenographers' biggest disadvantage. If a person doesn't notice his limitations when he's young and doesn't have a cultural forebear (sometimes this cultural forebear and the worthy person are identical) to provide prudent guidance, his latent genius will unconsciously slip away, and in the end, he will have wasted his life and accomplished nothing. Nothing in his entire life will be worth remembering. You don't run into worthy people all the time. Sometimes, in several centuries there's only one. The issue is whether you have keen enough eyesight to identify them at first glance. You also need luck. When they have just come to your side and modestly offered to guide you, you might not listen if you lack talent. You will probably think that's just boasting. But if you're a genius, you'll respond strongly, just like falling in love at first sight.'

"After the old widow finished, she went back to her usual reserved state, turned her back on the writer, and started gulping saliva repeatedly. She never touched the writer, whose hand was resting on her bed. It must be that she wouldn't excuse him for ignoring her in the past. She had to put on airs so that the writer would realize how impertinent and preposterous he had been all along. Since he was being treated like this, all kinds of feelings welled up in his heart. All along, he and everyone else had thought that the widow was a good-for-nothing old bag wearing a tattered old felt hat that was full of holes. She was dried up and had shrunk into the shape of a locust. She spent most of her time nodding her head and swallowing her saliva. All of the bodily fluids in her withered body must have turned into saliva. From far away you could hear the *gudong gudong* sound she made: the writer had always thought of this sound as a sign that she was still alive. Now it seemed that this metaphysical insight was problematic. The writer needed to cleanse himself from head to toe and then dissect himself with a scalpel before he could get to the root cause of his disease. Why did he always look up at the boundless sky every day and never see the people around him? These people were concealing intelligent and passionate hearts under their coarse and crude appearance: although the writer met up with them every day, he couldn't recognize them. This was because the writer was accustomed to praise and had become self-righteous. He didn't have time for contrary, idiosyncratic people: he thought they were beneath him. Every day, the writer was bent over his bed writing. He molded some gossamer-like figures that existed only in hallucinations. He adored them and described them as epic heroes. In his writing, all these figures were noble, elegant, and graceful. They were absolutely different from people like the old widow and others. They were like immortals, beyond ordinary life, and yet they were also like cardboard figures, without flesh and blood. Had the writer been developing a skill for years that had no foundation—a form that looked magnificent but was actually barren? Would this result in the collapse of the edifice the writer had created and trap him inside until he was smashed to pieces? He broke out in a cold sweat at the thought of this. Analyzing cause and effect, he realized how important it was for him to gain the widow's forgiveness. Winning her over was the same as winning over every reader. Otherwise, the writer might as well pronounce his artistic career at an end. And he might as well put the torch to all the notebooks he had labored over.

"'Maybe one day you'll wake up and see the rosy clouds filling the sky and you'll forgive me in spite of yourself.' Sobbing, the writer said miserably, 'Please promise me: *this is possible*. Then, with a thread of hope, I'll take my leave of you. This thread of hope will be my spiritual underpinning. I don't dare hope that you will tell me right now that you'll be my reader. I'm just begging you to give me that thread of hope. I promise you: I've made up my mind to do as you said. If you agree to give me this lifesaving hope, let's shake hands on it. Your hand holds the power of life and death over me.'

"The old bag thought for a long time and kicked the quilt fitfully. It seemed she couldn't decide what to say. Finally she answered slowly: 'Shake hands with you? Sure, that's easy enough to do, but I have another consideration. I've learned something in my lifetime.

People—these weird creatures—are very vainglorious. As soon as you give them a little appreciation, or even just forgiveness, they swell with pride. They boast everywhere, giddy all the time, never sure where they are or where they belong. Most people are like this by nature. As I see it, the world is going to collapse at the hands of those who take pleasure in doing charitable works. They distribute their cheap sympathy without hesitation. They comfort anyone, encourage anyone. Because of them, unscrupulous people stand up again right after being punished and continue their evildoing. Because they were supported, they would do even worse. No, I can't shake hands with you now. I don't sympathize with you at all. My beloved cousin doesn't sympathize with you, either. All our lives, the ones we've abhorred most are those who take pleasure in charitable works. If, after learning this painful lesson, you want to climb to a new beginning, if you take my advice, I can give you a thread of hope, but I am definitely not going to shake hands with you. If I did, you'd become even vainer and forget all the troubles you're facing. You'd sink into complacency again and you'd become flighty again. That's just the way people are. Go ahead and keep that thread of hope. I'll be watching you closely and hoping for your success. Please keep in mind: even if you succeed, you mustn't imagine that you can shake hands with me. I'll point out many of your other shortcomings, and I'll probably make you out to have no redeeming features. Only in this way will you improve. I loathe mediocrity. I have something else to declare: it's about swallowing saliva. I hear that people on the street criticize me a lot for this, just as if it's something indelicate they can't bear to see. They also allege that I have to swallow saliva three times for every sentence I speak. You just heard what it's really like. I talked for so long, and yet I didn't interrupt myself even once to swallow. My self-control is astonishing. As I said, there isn't anything I can't do. Inferior people sling mud at me in secret. They think if they mention a certain tiny shortcoming of a certain person, they can then exclude this person from the ranks of the worthies forever. Please. Who doesn't have shortcomings? The personages who made history often had short-comings that broke through, but that didn't affect their greatness. What matters is a person's essence and inherent ability. Some idio-syncratic shortcomings are perhaps signs of being worthy people. I loathe mediocrity. A mediocre person without any shortcomings has absolutely no excuse for living in this world.' "

2

SOME IMPLICATIONS

Now we are ready to enter the core of the story. We couldn't objectively narrate this in a routine way: Traditional styles wouldn't work; we had to innovate. Otherwise, people might start fighting for position. The walls might get damaged and the houses collapse. They might do anything. Or—who knows?—they might start quacking in unison like ducks, so no one could hear anyone else—quack from morning to night, and from night to morning, until you'd go crazy and give up. Over a long period, the furtive personal relationship between X and Q had become the spiritual sustenance for everyone on Five Spice Street. On the surface, we disavowed this, even scorned it, but in fact—night after night—everyone was caught up in dreams. Each one took part in the game, imagining himself the leading actor. During the day, whenever they heard of something happening, they would rush to the scene and inspect it closely. They were collecting traces to fuel their imaginations. Such actions were always taken alone. Frequent small-group discussions always took place in a certain person's house either with a dim light or with all the lights extinguished. It's said that talking about such things in the dark was "even more dramatic." The writer obtained his materials in just such a place.

After his big mistake, the writer was abandoned by his readers. Luckily the widow enlightened him, and once he won his readers over again, he regained his composure and became steadier. He no longer engaged in his art "by shutting himself in a small room," but lost no time reimmersing himself in the crowd, "bending over their chests to listen to them breathe." In this way, he promoted himself and became much more philosophical about himself and society, and much more confident.

In our discussions, we used to squeeze together, head against head, smelling each other's breath. Then, we lowered our voices, making them fainter than the buzzing of mosquitoes. It was as if we weren't talking at all, just moving our lips. We could only guess what others were saying from the movements of their lips. Certain ideas were communicated in a very subtle way. For example, "spare-time recreation" was not completely the same as sex, but neither was it completely the same as "platonic friendship." These are both extreme interpretations. We couldn't accept either; but arguing against one view wasn't the same as advocating the other. We had to distinguish the boundaries. And we distinguished on the basis of barely perceptible lip movements. Only the in-group could understand the profound meaning of these movements. If the lights weren't on, we reached our conclusions on the basis of buzzing sounds.

This kind of get-together was so interesting. Everyone was left with lasting memories. Today, years later, many still sigh and say they wish time could reverse itself—if only it could stop in that moment filled with mysterious conviviality, if only they could enjoy once more that grand throbbing of body and mind, they wouldn't mind having their lives cut short by a decade or two. That joy is gone forever. Only bleak melancholy remains. Those get-togethers in pitch-dark rooms, those swaying ghostly silhouettes on the walls, those voiceless furtive whispers, and the excitement of imagining oneself in the leading actor's role during long sleepless nights: where did all of these things go? Such sweet memories! If a person has the good fortune to reenter that realm once or twice when he is old, he can die without regrets. The writer lost no time joining in. Of course, he didn't go to hear them "say something." If he'd been motivated only by this, he would have run into a wall. The old ways were dead. You had to innovate because you couldn't "really hear" what anybody said. It was a thought movement, highly sentimental and inferential. Comprehending it depended on "intelligence."

The writer had quite a lot of talent and after hard practice gradually grasped certain main points that allowed him to enter that realm and obtain a lot. He transformed his old flamboyant, shallow writing style into one that stressed character and true feelings in a dignified way. He got rid of priggishness and turgid prose; he noted his feelings and embellished them imaginatively to represent reality.

The First Point: How Did X and Q's Adultery Begin?

Let's start our analysis with Mr. Q. As we said, he is a good husband and father with a devoted wife and two sons. They all love the rural life, growing melons and vegetables in their front and back gardens and raising cats, dogs, and rabbits. His only shortcomings are being superstitious and believing in fate. But it's precisely this that broke up his family. Ever since that lovely afternoon when he went calling and Madam X secretly told his fortune in that stifling room (we have no way of knowing the details), he changed into a person who had lost all reason and common sense. Sometimes, he unexpectedly even acted like a gangster: he was completely different from the simple, honest person he'd been before.

He announced to a friendly colleague: from now on, he would give up his self-restraint and be guided by destiny. This was providence, whose force was overwhelming. He had no way to resist it. All he could do was submit. If in the future this did him in, that was also providence. His eyes were wide open, his pupils unmoving, as he said this, and his teeth "chattered." His colleague asked what was going on, but he didn't hear and just spoke vaguely of some intersection, something about Wednesdays. He was agitated and his voice was shaking. Then he crowed like a rooster: his voice was magnificent. He kept crowing. His neck was puffy and his face reddened. His colleagues shouted for help, but he calmed down: "This is the way I am," he told them. "All of you can see this. I've been a little crazy all along, though I covered it up well. When I sit at my desk in the office, I'm often seized by an impulse to jump up on the desk and crow like a rooster, as you just saw. For years, I've kept myself from doing this in public."

After the adultery began, vague news of the scandal reached the office where he worked. His good colleague advised him to "end it" to avert trouble. He not only didn't feel grateful but blamed that person for not helping him. He castigated him for being a "timeserver," "a hypocrite," "hard as nails," and so forth. He also began shouting and smashed the window with a hammer. In short, he became someone else, doing all sorts of unimaginable things. His colleague had no choice but to forget his good intentions and resume his usual gloating manner. There's no evidence that Q wanted to "end this." Rather, he was like dry wood going up in a blaze. He paid attention to nothing else. He became irascible. "Just try that again," he'd say, grabbing your arm if he thought you said anything suggestive. Only after all kinds of sophistry and excuses by the other person would Q let go. One day, his superior handed him an assignment. He accused his superior of making things difficult for him, and a fist fight broke out. He actually "grabbed the superior's head and smashed it against the wall until it bled." He groaned and told people trying to intervene that he would "resign" and go off and "be a beggar." The others were speechless with fear. Madam X's sister said that Q had told her several times: he was predestined to have no way out, and so he had resolved to do something in desperation. His eyes were bright when he said this, and his face shone with a beatific luster. "There are still eyes like this in the world. Up to now, I still haven't figured out what makes your sister tick." Yet, his eyes told people that he knew very well what made her tick. Knew too well. He just didn't know what he himself was all about. If he did, God knows what might happen. How come a good man can change overnight into a gangster, a crook? There's got to be an explanation. The only conclusion we can reach is that the fortune-telling incident was the cause.

At one time, Mr. Q had embraced nihilism, and had been confused for thirty or forty years, and now suddenly he had started talking about waves in eyes and how some mysterious power had arrived. Of course, it was all nonsense: the sticking point was his superstitious thinking and passive attitude toward life. It's said that he has worried about calamities ever since he was eleven, worried that death would befall him before he had a chance to say good-bye to friends. He had always been frightened when walking on the street, and he also began to suffer from insomnia, "as if numerous rabbits were running out of my head." That's how he described it. What on earth was that instance of fortune-telling all about? Our Mr. Q had walked unsteadily onto Five Spice Street and helped the felt-hatted widow push the coal cart. Then he "stood for seven or eight minutes" in her home. After emerging, he "encountered" the lame woman, and finally he "passed out" and fell at the entrance of Madam X's home. No one saw how he got inside. Could it be that everything that happened later was only a matter of "flickering eyeballs"? (This also brings "hallucinogens" to mind. Was it possible that in the instant he was unconscious, he had been injected in a barbaric way? Wasn't "Phantoms in the Boarding House" playing then?) Waves were projected and the man's destiny was decided! Mr. Q has never divulged this detail, because "there's no way to recount this episode," "any language is a kind of blasphemy," "the moment I express this, I'll be dizzy," "this definitely can't be translated into words," and so forth. He simply spoke of "how bright" it was when he talked with the eyewitness, X's sister. Although that idiotic sister was there, she "couldn't see any of the evidence" and innocently told people, "I can vouch for this: it was love at first sight. Neither of them said a word, nor did they touch. They were just silent. That proved the strength of their sentiments and their morality." "As for telling his fortune, who says so? That didn't happen." On the surface, it seemed that "there wasn't any" fortune-telling. It's exactly this "nothing" that was the basis for everything that came later. Everything germinated in the midst of supposition. In this glaring light, Mr. Q completed his metamorphosis from a pupa to a butterfly. He bit off his shell and fatefully changed. (This was exactly what Madam X was so good at: using invisible idiodynamics.)

From that day forward, this man took an absolutely preposterous view of himself and felt that he was different from everyone else: not only was he different, he was also a cut above others. He shoved all of his responsibilities to the back of his mind, stuck his hands in his overcoat pockets, and, like a playboy, stood on the corner ogling women. He would pull at a woman's sleeve and unburden himself of his innermost thoughts. (The female colleague said he went on for nearly ten minutes.) This included words like "turkey" and "duck" and so on—words that clearly implied "going to bed." He seemed desperate and could "hardly stand still." Some thought he was "going to pounce." He also grew fond of looking in mirrors. Every day he would close the door and look at himself in the mirror at home (Q was very sensitive about his reputation). Passing a store window on the street, he would take stock of himself. He would stand in front of the window for a long time, until the shopkeepers became nervous. As for his wife—this woman as beautiful as a goddess—who loved him so much, he now just said "uh" to her soulful prattle and couldn't wait to get back to the mirror. One day, he said to his wife that he couldn't wear his coat any longer, because bugs were crawling on it. "I had a premonition a long time ago that this would happen. Have you heard it in the middle of the night—streams of them crawling over the coat? So many." He made a face, and his wife gave him a panic-stricken look. She was really frightened. Afterwards, he seemed sorry about this and quickly explained that he had intentionally talked of bugs. "A certain evil thought made me say that." Sometimes he was whimsical, but now he was okay again. His tone, however, was so melancholic and uncertain—as if he weren't "okay again." After a few days, his malady returned, and he mentioned bugs again, saying that his overcoat was "just threads"—no good at all anymore.

"As soon as I put it on, they start biting me." He poured this out painfully and picked the overcoat up with a pole to show his wife. He said, "They all fly in from the window in the middle of the night."

"What?"

"The bugs. Can't you see?" He insisted on burning the overcoat. His wife started crying.

"Please don't cry. What I said doesn't matter." He patted his wife's shoulder kindly to calm her down. "I've been hallucinating a lot recently; maybe it's because I'm getting older. Is there anything that we can't discredit?" His tone at the end was unsteady, almost as though he were asking himself a rhetorical question.

He no longer worked in his melon and vegetable gardens (and so the plants withered away quite soon), nor did he play with the cats and dogs. He just moved a cane chair outside and sat alone dozing in the sun. He smiled slightly and flexed his fingers over and over. No one knew what he was doing. If someone roused him, he answered brusquely, and then raised his hand and stared intently at the blazing sunlight for a long time before he turned around to face the visitor. It seemed as though he had just returned from another world.

"Behind everyone, there are at least two shadows. Some have even more." He said to his wife, "The shadows on the ground are like folding fans. Looking at them makes me dizzy. (I don't know when he began to talk like this, as if his voice were coming from a deep grotto.) It takes a lot of strength for me to focus my eyes enough to pull the doubled shadows into one. Of course, this isn't at all pleasurable. (His tone was now indignant and vehement.) All of you are so smug. It's ridiculous! If I tell the truth, you'll be furious again. You'll think I'm a mayfly. You'll agree with each other by exchanging understanding glances in order to set your minds at ease."

"The bees are still flying around outside. You must have heard them."

"Right, I did." He acknowledged this despondently, and then like a shadow, he contracted himself bit by bit back inside the room.

After Mr. Q completed his metamorphosis, he went to Five Spice Street in secret and began his adultery with Madam X on a certain day in a secret place that no one knew about. This occurred another four or five times, always without anyone's knowledge. If it hadn't been for that hapless cat, their adultery might have gone on forever. This isn't to say that all of us on Five Spice Street were numbskulls and didn't know what was going on under our noses. We just kept quiet, that's all. Our silence had far-reaching significance.

About the place and the facts of the adultery, those of us on Five Spice Street expressed ourselves in thoroughly abstract ways. This time, everyone kept a straight face. We didn't even move the corners of our mouths. Whether the lights were on or off, whether there were a lot of people or just a few, whether in our homes or on the main street, whenever the writer or any other outsider brought up this matter, all of us expressed ourselves with solemn, straight faces. Only if a person had a talent for abstract thought and had special training could he discover the instinctual understanding of those people. Otherwise, he would think them crass, unreasonable, and short-sighted. He would complain of their indifference to history. Many simple-minded scholars had arrived here cheerfully and believed that their passionate work would yield something. Inevitably, they would return to wherever they came from while blaming us for being uncooperative or even rocking the boat. They never examined the limitations of their concepts or were the least bit self-reflective. We have no use for this type of scholar and artist and wish they had stayed home. Why come here? We could plan our daily lives much more easily without them. Aside from disturbing people, is there anything they do? If a committed artist carefully considered the situation, he would realize that the straight faces on Five Spice Street did not indicate impoverished selves and empty heads. Instead, they implied infinitude, like a rainbow on the horizon or a mirage in the desert. We can easily offer five or six interpretations.

First, this is our privacy, which is like a precious treasure we don't want to share with outsiders. Our unique place is the only place that can produce such high-quality spiritual sustenance. Our own people all know how to view this matter. Each of us has his or her personal feelings about it, and it isn't necessary to talk it over with one another. And so we keep straight faces.

Second, are we sluggards? Are we idle and self-indulgent? Besides poking into a certain person's meaningless activities all day long, have we nothing else to do? Do you dare doubt that our people have any libido? Yes, some envious people like to insinuate that we do nothing but roam around all day long, spying, listening at the walls, and looking through cracks in the doors. We won't fall for this! And so we keep straight faces.

Third, what sort of person brings up such questions? Does he have the upbringing necessary to understand this sort of thing? Does he conduct himself in a serious manner? If he looks at the world with salacious, indecent eyes, we decent people on Five Spice Street won't have anything to do with him; he can just delve into his research by himself. Let reality give him a brutal lesson. Let him come to ridiculous conclusions. Who cares? We aren't obligated to let him pester us. And so we keep straight faces.

Fourth, when getting close to the essence of the matter, the highly cultured crowds on Five Spice Street always produce a single spontaneous response: something like this can't be explained in words, nor can it be conveyed with facial expressions. It can be sensed only with telepathy. This is very complicated and multi-layered. We wouldn't be a bit surprised if an outsider didn't possess this mental power. We are always very self-confident about this superiority of ours. If a rude outsider could become as wise as we after dashing around our street for a few days, that would be the saddest tragedy. No way! We don't care if they think we're not civil and don't care if they are furious with us. We persist in our old ways. We aren't going to swim with the tide. And so we keep straight faces.

Fifth, there may also be persons with ulterior motives: after ascertaining our true views, they then made unfair use of them with various kinds of guesswork. None of it was their business. They had nothing to do with it. But they tried to play the role of savior, as if we had to depend upon them—those rats who came out from the sewer to manage our community. And so we keep straight faces. We could give a lot of other reasons for keeping straight faces—almost everyone has at least two reasons, which might change several times a day.

If we want to understand this adultery from Q's side, we can raise the following possibilities: (1) That afternoon Q had the misfortune of falling at X's entrance, and while he was unconscious a person quick on his feet injected him with a hallucinogen. (2) Since childhood, Q had had a virus similar to rabies lying dormant in his body: when it surfaced, he became manic about self-sacrifice. The writer had just noted these key points when the female colleague, who'd been hiding behind him and spying, scared him by hooting loudly.

This time, the writer reacted promptly: he stood up from the floor and bowed in a refined and humble way. He took the female colleague's soft hand, brought it to his nose and smelled it, and in a gentle voice asked her what she thought of him. Did she like what he had written? As he talked, he stroked her face with his other hand. This moved her greatly, and she gradually calmed down and told the writer that she liked what he wrote. She just wanted to add something important. This was of the utmost importance: without it, history would be an expanse of darkness. If she hadn't dashed over here with her strong sense of social responsibility, well, it would be impossible to imagine the losses. She very much believed in the writer's artistic talent. Ever since he had adjusted his attitude and become endearing, she'd furtively observed everything he did. She believed wholeheartedly that now, with a fine artist as stenographer for the people, everybody would feel that "life had become rosy." She cheered the writer on, hoping his talent would "blaze with brilliance." She would be eternally grateful for his success. Their chaste friendship was incomparably lofty: was there anything more beautiful than the pursuit of spiritual communion? Her good friend Madam X had never experienced this sublime ardor; she was interested only in "going to bed." Thinking back on it now, that kind of person was too pedestrian! Too infuriating! As the female colleague talked, she shed tears. The writer took out a handkerchief and gently wiped them away. He gave her a hand and helped her sit on the edge of the bed, where she rested for a long time. The two sank into a sorrow from which they couldn't extricate themselves. Finally, filled with melancholy, the writer sent her on her way.

Supplemental Material: Another of Mr. Q and Madam X's Conversations on the Street

X: It's bright out today—are you aware of that? Every time you and I stand and talk in such bright light, I feel dissatisfied with you. Sometimes I have wicked thoughts: I think you're shrinking day by day. This change was unconscious; it couldn't be helped. I yearn for the cobblestones in the sunlight (she stretches out her hands as if grasping something in the air). Come closer to me. I'm going to cry. (Pretending to wipe away tears, she took the opportunity to lean against Q.)

Q (gently): Ah, don't cry. I'm here. There are two guys—one loafing around on the main street, and the other in a dark house. The one on the street is black and supple. He's about to melt into air in the daylight. The one in the house is white—a solid glaring white light. He would be well groomed even in a coffin. Listen: *he's* coming. Every time, he stands on that corner and stares at me, I can't move. This has happened three times.

X (looking ecstatic): I didn't bring any mirrors today. I feel very stimulated by you today. Please repeat the last sentence: it was wonderful.

Q: *I can't move.* Ah! (He looked frustrated. After a while, he started smiling sweetly again, showing his teeth to the glass of the roadside shop window.)

X (talking to herself): Let the miracle come! Let the miracle come!

Hiding behind a power pole, the female colleague had recorded this conversation in a small notebook without missing a word, noting that it was "after the adultery occurred." She furnished this conversation to the writer and exhorted him to keep her role secret because she had always felt sisterly love for this adorable, charming Madam X. (In fact, she leaked it to the writer only because she felt that she and the writer were like Damon and Pythias.) Madam X had often sought guidance from her in dealing with relationships between men and women. And because they were always together, Madam X always relied on her charms to attract crowds of men, though some might have thought that Madam X herself was also very good at this. For this reason, Madam X idealized her and babbled all her innermost thoughts to her. She held nothing back and also dragged her into anything she did. Madam X didn't mind that she had heard this conversation; she knew the female colleague was standing behind the power pole. She even raised her voice to make sure that the wind would carry her words to her friend's ears, even if she didn't want to overhear.

There was reason to think that Madam X had deliberately allowed her female friend to record their conversation. Maybe she'd figured that it would become part of the history books! She knew her female friend was loyal and trustworthy and never suspected that she would distort the facts. And so why did the friend insist that the writer conceal her? Did she have some things to be ashamed of? Was this a trick to gain advantages? No, absolutely not. She was always aboveboard. Madam X hinted at what she wanted in a very delicate way, neither by a meaningful glance nor by any twitching of her facial muscles. If Madam X hadn't given her this hint and if she hadn't felt sisterly toward Madam X, she wouldn't have stupidly hidden behind a power pole on the dusty road and—sweating profusely—recorded this conversation! Unfortunately, she didn't have any natural gift for stenography. She wrote slowly and didn't hear very well, either. Furthermore, she was disgusted with those insane words. The work left her exhausted. If in the end she was vilified and got the reputation of being a blabbermouth, how could she go on living? Even if she could stand it herself, how hard it would be for her dear friend Madam X!

In that gloomy room of hers, Madam X told her several times: if anything happened to her dear colleague and friend—if she was plotted against and lost her reputation or even her life—she wouldn't want to go on living, either! Madam X was just like her—a very passionate person. Their relationship had stood the test of time. Anyone would be moved by their mutual affection, so she couldn't do whatever she wished. She had to consider X's feelings in everything she did, and wanted her to be eternally happy. If the writer leaked her name so that those narrow-minded persons accused her of being a blabbermouth and the whole thing was made known to Madam X, she would be terminally hurt! She knew Madam X well. How could she bear the pain? Those men had approached her first, and only because of her tactful management did they gradually turn their attention to Madam

X. If she'd selfishly shown off her own charms, those men would have stuck around, so Madam X would never have enjoyed her good fortune. Madam X deeply appreciated this.

After saying all of this, the female colleague turned her moony eyes to the writer and asked if he understood. Had her secret kindled new inspiration in him? Did he want to record their ideal relationship in his notebook using a different style? The writer thought it over and agreed. When he got inspired, he would reproduce this moving scene and enter their unconventional feelings vividly into the history. He had fallen in love with Madam X's female colleague at first sight, and now he'd fallen deeper and couldn't extricate himself. He'd never experienced such a strange feeling before. It wasn't a bit carnal. The writer had only great admiration and heartfelt respect for this *beautiful* (please forgive the word) female colleague. Any other ideas would be improper. He had to get rid of those improper ideas. If he couldn't do it right away, he still had to try to keep his mind pure and transparent with her. Only in this way could the writer become enlightened and inspired. Otherwise, he would slip and wallow in the mud of vulgarity, write something garish, and finally get nowhere.

After he sent the female colleague off, the writer's thoughts returned to Madam X. The protagonist of this long story—the most colorful and romantic witch on Five Spice Street: what was she like when the adultery was going on? She couldn't be as abstract as a symbol or a thread of steam, could she? Could we reach a fair and reasonable conclusion by relying on those petty clues? There must be a lot to discover. If the writer didn't persevere and painstakingly sort out the main threads from this mess, the riddle would never be solved.

The most reliable first-hand information came from a woman whose husband was a friend of Madam X's brother-in-law. She was an emaciated, dark-skinned woman. She angrily drove the mosquitoes away with a big fan. Shaking her knees, she casually told the writer, "It's embarrassing to talk about this kind of thing." Then she blushed and jumped up and down as if bitten by bedbugs. She glanced at the crowd cooling off outside. (People were staring at her and pricking up their ears. Some who'd been sitting a little farther away moved their chairs closer.)

"Let's find a place where we can talk!" She started to run, dragging the writer by the arm. People followed closely. They were shouting who-knows-what. The writer was sweating profusely, but the woman seemed tremendously strong and lifted him up onto her square, thin shoulders and rushed ahead. We don't know how far they went. Finally, the woman placed the writer on a bed in a dark little room and bolted the door. The crowd besieged the little room: some kicked the door and rapped on the window. Others hurled stones inside.

"Shhhh! They'll leave. It's just vulgar curiosity. They're just like gluttonous children—never satisfied," the woman whispered to the writer.

After a while, they heard someone say in a high voice, "Probably she doesn't have any interesting secrets. They're probably just using this as an excuse to make out inside. The stenographer is kind of cute!"

The people fell quiet, and then they began grumbling, complaining that they'd run over for nothing. They gradually dispersed and went far away. In the dark, the woman kept poking the writer in the ribs, and giggled as she snuggled up to his neck, so happy she couldn't contain herself. When the writer finally really responded intimately, she jumped away and sat at the other end of the room as if disgusted. Her knees bumped together like the beating of a drum.

"Impressive!" she said all of a sudden.

"Who?!"

"Who else?! She said he was impressive, that he was an impressive man! A man out of the ordinary! Do you understand? You idiot! What are your qualifications to be a stenographer? Who chose you to come here? How do you dare assert that you're a stenographer? As you sit here in the dark, I see that you're simply a pile of mud! A pile of useless mud! My God! What could I have been thinking to carry

this wooden pole and dash over here? How can this be? I'm finished!!" She sobbed, and her fists fell like hail on the writer's back.

She said that because his conduct had tainted her image with the
people, she wanted the writer to "make up for the damage." She also
said that she had never laid eyes on a stenographer: she had been
friends with a government official! People like artists weren't trusted
by the people: nobody could take them seriously. As for their considering themselves important, that was just fishing. Who would fall
for an artist? If you did, you'd better not count on holding your head
up. She didn't want to be swayed by emotions—that would just
make trouble for her. The writer patiently endured this beating, not
uttering a word until the woman's sobs subsided.

"X and Q also mentioned the leak in the boat," she added, and
then tweaked the writer's cheek to show that they were all right
again.

Eyes blurry with sleep, the writer left the little room with the dark
woman, who immediately disappeared. The writer had no choice
but to stagger ahead in the dark. He didn't see anyone anywhere. All
was quiet. The many houses at the side of the road were a frightening black color. What lay ahead? The writer was nervous, and beads
of sweat seeped slowly from his forehead.

"I can give you first-hand information." He didn't know where
Old Woman Jin had come from; she was blocking his way and
smacked his shoulder. "Haha," she laughed out loud.

"Where am I?" The writer was confused.

"On our street! Are you possessed? Why don't you recognize it?
Come, let's sit on the curb and chat. Listen, everyone's asleep. No
one will disturb us. I guarantee I'll give you first-hand information.
You mustn't believe other people; don't believe anyone. They're all
making things up, that's for sure. They want to toy with you. For
example, the dark woman just now: do you think she's still young?
She's sixty years old—ten years older than I am! She must have told
you she's only forty; that's what she always tells people. She wears
bright clothing to make herself look younger, figuring that she can

fool the men. What a joke! How can anyone lack self-understanding and want to play an inappropriate role! Isn't this crazy? There's nothing more frightening, more tragic in life, than a person going crazy. When a good person goes crazy, she's no longer worth anything. Yet, she isn't aware of this; she gives attention only to playing the role of a clown. It's macabre! When that crazy woman locked you up in her room, I smelled something wrong and watched out for you here. (I've always had a warm spot in my heart for you.) I did this just in case she tried to murder you in desperation when she couldn't get what she wanted. You know, she could have done this, since there weren't any eyewitnesses. I know this sort of person. I had to wait in the dark and protect your life. You know: a mixed-up woman can be much more dangerous than an ordinary gangster. She is capable of all kinds of brutal things. Just now, when I saw you leave there safely, a big load was taken off my shoulders. In the end, she didn't do it to you! Just now I mentioned supplemental information. I tell you, what is the very most important thing to a stenographer? Sources. This is a vital issue, for it determines success or failure. A lot of people slip up here. If I want to find good material, the first thing I have to do is find a person who can supply such material. For instance, just now you almost made an irreparable mistake. In your confusion, you actually made inquiries of a mentally unbalanced sixty-year-old floozy. You fell into the trap she set for you and stayed in her room for one hour and twenty-five minutes. I wanted to rush over to warn you, but I couldn't because when it happened, I was arguing with someone about whether we should insist on printing enlarged color photos in our blackboard newspaper. What material could that lunatic give you? If I hadn't been secretly watching over you, any kind of tragedy might have occurred. People who give material to artists must be tough, wise, and experienced. Perhaps they've experienced the vicissitudes of life but haven't been struck down by brutal realities: they have an innate ability to turn all the suffering into nourishment for life. . . ."

Old Woman Jin looked up at the vast night sky and seemed so intoxicated by her emotions that she forgot to go on talking. She was absorbed in humming a march. As she hummed, she beat out the rhythm by tapping her heels on the road.

After about ten minutes, the writer tugged at her sleeve and gently reminded her: "The material?"

"Right. This is of the first importance. You have to be strong-minded and sharp-sighted and be able to distinguish the true from the false with just one look, and then your work will evolve. Some people who used to have talent were unfortunately taken in by a certain pose and went astray. They worked hard for a lifetime but didn't get anywhere. Lessons like this are widespread. We can't keep these schemers from living in this world, nor can we annihilate them; we can only heighten our ability to discriminate, and prevent tragedy. Too bad there are so few people with sufficient life experience and wisdom. Otherwise, how many brilliant talents would they train?" Her attention wandered and she began humming the march again. She tapped *da, da, da* . . . , her chin moving along with the rhythm.

"But you haven't given me your material!"

"Bah! Men are always like this. Listen to him, never satisfied, bothering you all the time, as if you owed him something. A charming woman is doomed in this world. Once you weaken and do what they want, they'll soon want more! Within five minutes, they start in on you again, just like the hungry ghosts. They make all kinds of requests and say that's what you promised them. What did I promise? What can a woman do? She certainly can't get anything from men; all she can do is give all she has to them, but it still isn't enough. They want still more, still more."

"I didn't ask you for anything. I just mentioned the material. . . ."

"Just! As if this isn't much trouble! In my lifetime, how many men have said 'just once more' to me? And after once more, they want another once more. It never ends. Don't they have even a little self-control and spirit of sacrifice? No! They just seek their own satisfaction!"

"Then shall I go home?'

"Go home! You haven't gotten what you wanted, so you go

home! They're all like this, all stamped out of the same mold. They don't know what warmth is, what affection is, or what continuous longing is. They want just one thing, and if they don't get it, they immediately show how cold they are inside. They just tell you loud and clear: I want to go home! They even purposely show you how tired they are, to frustrate you from head to toe. How can one bear this kind of world?"

"Just now, we were talking about X," the writer nervously reminded her.

"What does that have to do with me? Bah! Bah! I can't even get a handle on my own situation—it drives me nuts—so why would I want to be concerned about X! Who is she? What's she to me? Don't change the subject—don't try to pull any tricks! Is she the main point, or am I? How dare you diminish me? I'll make you know who I am. Humph!"

In the end, the writer couldn't get any information from Old Woman Jin. She was really tight-mouthed. And more than that, she hurried to a meeting and made an appeal: she wanted "women to unite and fight off men's encroachments, which are all too clearly under way—we can't take them lightly." After she finished her speech, she took out a dagger. Terrifying everyone, she sent a "flying dagger" to a wooden post in the back row of the hall. Everyone screamed and bedlam ensued, lasting as long as thirteen minutes.

"I'm also a talented dancer," she turned and said to the writer. "I've never had a chance to perform for you. I don't cut a smart figure. Maybe now you want to take me seriously? Too bad it's too late! I am many-layered: no one can see through me. If anyone thinks he can get something from me, that's impossible—like a toad lusting after a swan. I don't have illusions about people who claim to be artistic. What can any of you do?"

To tie up all the threads, the writer finally described Madam X's adultery in a few words: "It was carefully planned and calmly performed." By the time he finished writing this, it was dawn. Gazing out the window, he saw the sky's brilliant red over the hotel building: it was a day suffused with hope! A woman in blue flashed past the window: it was Madam X, the person who had brought the writer immense anguish and immense joy. The writer hurriedly stuck his head out the window to get a closer look, but then he discovered no one was there: it was only a sort of blue shadow drifting in the air. When he looked more attentively, even the shadow was gone; only some footsteps that seemed both familiar and suspicious sounded on the road. Dispirited, the writer fell onto the bed, and then all at once, his face glowed: he understood everything! He had gotten to the core of the matter! Finally, the tangles and detours of so much time could be summed up! Hallelujah! I salute you, my dear female colleague! I salute you, dear Old Woman Jin! And the sweet dark-skinned lady, too! With a red pen, the writer decisively crossed out the words he had just written and wrote the following inspired words:

"Madam X—this person who is both corporeal and non-existent—has left our history numerous riddles. It seems that one can't reach a conclusion about any of her activities through logic and reason, because this person is an assumption that might not be true—like a tree with massive foliage but shaky roots which will fall to the ground if it is lightly pushed. The only true existence is the illusion, the foggy mist that aroused our enormous interest."

The Second Point: Big Changes in Madam X
after the Adultery Began

The adultery definitely occurred. Although no one can be sure about the place and time, everyone knows it happened. Late one night, the writer took part in a meeting in a small, unlit room. Emotions ran high even among the most intelligent during the two hours and twenty-five minutes of this meeting; afterwards, opinions about this reached a consensus. Once the fact was established, Madam X virtually lost her freedom. Why do we have to say "virtually"? Because, ostensibly, those of us on Five Spice Street did not stop her freedom of movement: we weren't brought up to be like this. If someone goes about corrupting public morals, we certainly wouldn't club her to death. We were well-mannered people. Our people just lowered their heads and didn't look at her when they met her. When she went past, we all stared at her thin, frail back and cast a lot of cryptic looks. The staring could last for a long time (an hour at most). We expected that she would eventually sense it and figure it out by herself. We expected to restrict her activities in this indirect way, because we were very patient people. But it didn't work for a long time. This woman remained callous. Even though groups of people were staring at her behind her back, her activities were still as un-bridled as those of a three-year-old, and she was even wilder in what she said. More often than not, she'd take a flying leap while walking, despite all the people watching.

Now everyone sees the big changes in Madam X since this affair began; they couldn't be any clearer. The writer didn't have to do any investigating.

One big change was that in a short time her vision was restored. Almost everyone on Five Spice Street can confirm this. There were, of course, still a few questions. For example: Why did she still look as if she were floating when she walked? Why didn't she look at any-thing while walking on the street? But her vision really was restored: especially when she talked with people, her eyes were almost "a pair of shining stars"!

About two or three days after the adultery began, Madam X was selling peanuts in the snack shop. As she weighed the peanuts, she struck up a conversation with the widow in the little felt hat. She wasn't looking either above the old woman's head or at the ground, but was looking right at the old woman's face. For some unknown reason, she insisted on calling the woman "Young Miss Chen," as if she were deliberately trying to please her or as if the woman she saw really was a young girl—or maybe it was a little of both. The old woman was very excited. She blushed, and sweat appeared in the folds of her skin. She kept shrugging her shoulders, as if trying to produce a certain pose. "Her eyes are really strange. After being blind, they are now even brighter. I bet that they're just like a micro-scope—truly incredible!" This old woman said this to everyone.

Among the others who verified that Madam X had regained her

sight were the young coal worker and the widow's forty-eight-year-old friend. The coal worker asserted that Madam X's treatment of him had progressed from friendship to "intimacy," and also that when they parted (they met at the snack shop), she had pounded him hard on the back three times and called him her "acrobatic boy." Because of these three slaps, the coal worker's back felt funny for several days. The forty-eight-year-old friend said, "Formerly, she acted so inconceivably superior as a result of her eye disease. She must have been secretly anguished and despairing. Yet, I could not forgive her for the disgraceful thing she's done. The fact was unfortunately a fact, and it was unrelated to her eyes. There's no way I can sympathize with her. Even if her eyes were never bad, even if from the very beginning she could see people, even if she hadn't ignored me when I went into her home, I still couldn't change my mind. I can't compromise my principles. How come her eyes weren't better either sooner or later? Why now? This can't help her one bit. Madam X miscalculated this time!"

Madam X herself was indifferent about having regained her sight. It also wasn't certain that she had recognized this change. The enraptured people on Five Spice Street thought this was exciting, much like the adultery itself. After meals, they stood next to the road across from the snack shop, waiting for Madam X to emerge, and then they dashed madly across in front of Madam X, shoving her until she almost fell down. They did this to see how much sight Madam X had recovered and thereby to take another step in figuring out the subtle link between this change and the "adultery." This work was very interesting. Once it started, it didn't stop. Everyone showed striking tenacity and desperation. Day after day, they indulged in this. Madam X had a rough time: she didn't dare go outside. Maybe when she was walking, some guy would rush at her like a bullet that she couldn't dodge. Who knows?

One day, as they were having dinner, she said spitefully to her husband, "There are some things that I've been seeing all the time. I just didn't look at them, that's all. Even if I looked at them, I put on a wide-eyed expression. This was beyond their expectations, so they became nervous. It's fun to make people nervous. I always wanted to joke with them. What do you think? Sometimes, I gravely put on a straight face, as if I were having a hard time. Have you noticed the way they look when they're walking? They strain to stick out their rear ends, don't they? Actually, there's no need for that. It doesn't explain anything."

Her husband listened to her nonsense as if entranced, and finally answered, not very appropriately, "They're just like ducks!"

"For example, today I talked with that Wang girl who fries dough twists (she probably meant the widow). I talked with her about ways to get rid of rats. Her face blanched and she shivered. These people —what's in their minds? I didn't have to talk with her, this Wang girl. It was just an impulse: I wanted to scare her by mentioning rats. I know that's what she's most afraid of. She's always shouting, even in the middle of the night. Haven't you noticed? I enjoyed taking her by surprise." The more nonsense she talked, the more entranced her husband was. He nodded.

Now, whenever the people on Five Spice Street talked with Madam X, they couldn't help but mention her eyesight. Some flattered her by saying that she had "keen eyesight." Others didn't bother with flattery but spoke directly of their own feelings. They all avoided speaking of "adultery": they felt it would be barbaric to do so. Even if a lady was so weird, they certainly couldn't use this word in front of her! Not talking about it didn't mean that they went along with it. They used roundabout, measured ways to teach her a lesson. Let's quote what a few people said:

The widow: "I heard that your eyesight came back. This doesn't need to be emphasized. This doesn't amount to anything. A person was blind and then recovered. No big deal! If you hadn't told us, probably no one would have known. Actually, having good eyes, even if they're clairvoyant—that's nothing to be arrogant about. If you think you can do whatever you want because of this, then you're out of your mind. That's what some people think—did you know that? As for people who've lost their self-awareness, it would be much easier to live in the dark. Then no one would pay attention to you, and it would be possible to excuse your absurd behavior. But now it's tit for tat. There's no advantage for someone in regaining her eyesight!" (When she spat out these words, she bared two protruding front teeth.)

Old Meng: "Since you've recovered your vision, you don't need those mirrors any longer. I think the first thing you should do is throw away those mirrors; you mustn't begrudge giving them up. As soon as a person looks in a mirror, she hallucinates, and devastating lust automatically results. Look at the people all around: who else looks in mirrors? Nobody! So everyone is fine, and no one else has done anything strange. Isn't this clear?"

The female colleague: "Although I'm your friend, I don't think your bright vision is good for you at all: it's just made you even more ridiculous. Who will believe that this makes you more charming? Your charm was attested to a long time ago: the verdict on that came in when you and I were still colleagues. Now you still want to take great pains to make a new name for yourself. Actually, this doesn't suit you. This would lead to big trouble."

The husband's good friend: "Now you can see me, and it makes me uneasy. I'm not used to other people seeing me too well: that's like having an X-ray taken. To tell you the truth, I don't think your image is nearly as brilliant as before. Before, although you were flawed in various ways, when all is said and done, I was touched by your naïveté and unconsciously acted as your guardian all along. Now, though, you've changed in a certain way (an indirect reference to the adultery), and you actually act as if nothing has happened and intimidate me with your eyes. I feel really ashamed and wish I could find a hole to hide in."

How did Madam X react to these rebukes? Let's listen to some of what she said:

1. "I can see whatever I want to see. No big deal. Eyesight per se is actually quite unimportant. The way I use it is what makes the difference. Previously I used it rather economically, but now I deliberately throw it around. In any case, it depends on my own situations. For so many years, I didn't change any of my original inten-

tions; the next few decades will be the same. Now is the period in my life when I am most exultant. I've experienced the advantage of being freewheeling, and hope that—like me—you will also have this good fortune." (She said this to her younger sister.)

2. "The affair? So what? It's really bizarre: how can it be that other people don't have 'that affair'? It's said that everyone is whispering in secret, losing sleep at night, and staying close to the main street in the daytime—all because of 'that affair' of mine! I've been so happy that I've wanted to pat a certain one of you on the shoulder and talk of my inner feelings so that we could share them! As soon as I open my mouth, I notice that person's eyes are nervous—like a thief's. Then I have to give up. Ah, about the affair! You all treat me like a monkey. Have I been a monkey all along?" (She said this to her husband's good friend.)

3. "When I say 'kite' to one person, he answers with 'Pay attention to your shoes.' I've been saying things like this for a few decades: why hasn't anyone noticed this? Can people be so numb? They say the problem lies with me; they say I have a certain disease. I take great pleasure in deliberately exaggerating my illness. This scares them into forgetting me. These people are bizarre. I finally know that. Recently, I've been using my eyesight too much, and as a result I've discovered endless weird things. For example, F came to my house today. I looked up at him for a moment, and he turned shy at once: he flushed and couldn't sit still. I cleared my throat loudly a few times and asked him hesitantly, 'Are the veins in the table's wood jumping around a little too frequently? Today, everything in this room is jumping around too vigorously. You'll see that if you look at the curtains. Is there some reason for this? I can never come up with a definite idea about this.' He was listening in surprise. Frenzied light flashed from his eyes. I really wanted to see him take a hard fall. There's no reason for these pieces of garbage to be watching me like this. I have to come up with some ways to deal with their rude highhandedness." (She said this to her husband.)

If we analyze these three quotations, we can understand X's attitude: (1) She's quite a lot more complacent than before. (2) She does as she pleases (this is the same as before the adultery began). (3) The adultery itself made her "incredibly happy"—so much so that she wanted to "share it with someone" (she hasn't pointed this out herself, but isn't it clear as daylight?). (4) She deliberately exaggerates her disease in order to confuse people.

The second change in Madam X was horrible, too. The first one to encounter this change was Ms. B—the one who had made up her mind to wait until summer to seek revenge. One noon, Ms. B "was overflowing with optimism." She was humming a march, and her steps were buoyant as she walked to the street to post a banner. (Written on all of the red banners was: "Photography is important to the national economy and the people's livelihood.") When she passed Madam X's house, she was flattened by a snow-white bolt of lightning. She went blind for half an hour at most. This immediately made the rounds of the whole street: after dinner, everyone was talking about it. Tense discussion in a dark meeting, and confirmation from Ms. B herself, caused highly intelligent people to think the same thing: Madam X's supernatural power had evolved into a flood tide and had become a clear and present danger to everyone. For, in that unforgettable half hour, not only had Ms. B lost her vision, but "her whole body was paralyzed" and "she couldn't move." After she came to, she saw "several hundred silver whirlybirds hovering in the sky," and from Madam X's window "the biggest demonic mirror was hanging impressively." But Madam X herself "was standing under the mirror with her lover and her husband, caught up in the moment, and they were talking to each other in a kind of secret language."

After the dark meeting of highly intelligent people, the writer worked out a mistaken prediction which caused him to wake up to the superficiality of his scholarship. Following the meeting, the writer walked along in the dark with the adorable widow, absorbed in the excitement of the meeting: his myriad thoughts actually seemed to take on wings. So he opened his mouth and described what had been brewing in his mind for some time: "From now on, everyone has to adopt certain measures for dealing with Madam X." The adorable widow's imperturbability startled the writer, and he blushed.

"Why?" she answered in a low voice. "Adopt what measures? Are we all jittery? What you just said made me wonder. You've been a stenographer for so long, and you're still so fickle. I can't understand you."

The writer walked on with her for a long time in silence. She didn't say anything and her expression was grim. Not until they parted did she suddenly scold him: "It is most unwise to substitute one's own fantasies for the objective laws of nature."

The widow's opinion was representative of the attitudes of the elite group in the Five Spice Street community. For a long time after the meeting held in the dark, there was no activity anywhere on Five Spice Street: even if Madam X hung a demonic mirror high up in front of the window, others led their disciplined lives as usual. Similar meetings were held several times, but this didn't mean that there would "be any action," because the gentlemen attending these meetings were "old sparrows who had weathered many storms." They wouldn't do anything premature. When there was a meeting, they went: they loved taking part. The elitist style intoxicated them. The mysterious dark atmosphere intrigued them. So they all got to the meetings on time. They all wore dark overcoats and sat up solemnly in the dark room. Their calm and steady manner taught the writer a lesson, causing him to move from admiring them to imitating them. After a while, he was like a duck taking to the water. In order to squeeze into the elite circle and get his artistic talent recognized, the writer purchased a dark overcoat and earnestly prinked from head to toe. He mingled with the crowd at the meeting and then, without saying a word, took a seat in a corner. That's when the writer began learning how to be quiet like a smart person and began to understand that silence is golden. In the dark, who could tell who was talking? And even if they could, what did that mean? Because of our silence and composure, even if we were talking about major issues such as everyone's safety on the street, we wouldn't be jittery. Otherwise, wouldn't we be acting prematurely? Wouldn't that show we were capable of nothing but biting our nails over this kind of issue, so that people would say that a certain insignificant person's supernatural power was making the Five

Spice Street elite eager to prepare for combat? Wouldn't that sound ridiculous? No matter what others supposed, we instinctively *took no action*. We achieved victory through our special tactic—by living our daily lives as usual and not changing at all. No one paid any attention to a certain person's supernatural power, but instead we *held regular meetings*. This was our mighty offensive. No matter how strong they were, all the forts would be breached. When we wore dark clothing and quietly slipped into the meeting room, any cunning enemies were scared out of their wits. How did the counter-measures of the Five Spice Street elite affect Madam X? Perhaps not everyone can be sufficiently aware of these high-level spiritual actions. Was it possible that Madam X was also unaware of the coun-termeasures they took in the dark? Ms. B painstakingly investigated this. She reported that the countermeasures had been notably effective: Madam X's supernatural power was rapidly declining, she looked "more sallow by the day," the frequency of her going out had "atrophied a lot," and "the symptom of attempting suicide" was revealed in her words. At this point, Ms. B sprang to her feet and drew her finger across her neck to illustrate "attempting suicide." "What other way out does she have? None. When the people have formed a mighty force, confronting it with her little trick was no different from 'throwing straws against the wind.' Committing adul-tery was bad enough, and now she's also been deploying her evil supernatural stuff. She's asking for trouble!" She also told everyone a piece of astonishing hot news: a black curtain was hanging at Madam X's window, and it had been twenty-seven hours since she had closed her door and not emerged.

To satisfy his burning curiosity, the writer impulsively charged into Madam X's bedroom. It was as dark as a vault, and he was assailed by strong puffs of a floral scent—enough to choke a person.

"Have a seat. There's no problem with that chair," a voice said from a corner of the room. "There used to be some things in this room that were problematic, but I've solved them all one by one. I don't like sloppiness. Can you see now?" She propped herself up on the recliner.

One by one, the thick curtains, table, chairs, and bed appeared before the writer's eyes. Large and small mirrors were flickering continuously with white light, making everything in the room seem phony and affected. There were quite a few pots of flowers in the corner where Madam X sat, and that's where the fragrance was coming from, bringing with it a certain exaggeration. In this artificial environment, Madam X became strangely talkative.

"There's nothing wrong with anything here. All the legs on the chairs are sturdy; this isn't so outside this room. Once I went out and saw people sitting on problematic chairs. I was so frightened that I had to shut my eyes and flee back here. I should go out less frequently. Don't worry: everything in this room is sturdy. I don't like being suspended in the air." She smiled. She held out one gloved hand to the writer. Steeling himself, the writer shook it: he felt that the thing inside this glove was very suspicious.

"I've decided not to take my gloves off. Don't you think this is a good idea? The curtains are freshly mounted. Aren't they quite special? I just recently had this idea."

"Could it be that you had an unrealistic expectation of this world that you fabricated for yourself?" the writer said, deeply worried.

"Are you talking about self-image? I've never been concerned about that. I just look at myself in the mirror, but I don't have my photo taken. All of you know my foibles well. I'd inadvertently plunged into a kind of interlinked trap that was set by your—oh— Miss Chen. It's hard to break away from it. I sit here and gain an increasingly unambiguous impression of the outside world. You, for example: you're the one mending the net. You wanted to catch a little mouse. I made up my mind and solved all the problems." She laughed softly again. "What have you come for? No one else has come: they aren't used to being in a problem-free place. Young Miss Chen said, 'It's like an empty, transparent zone' in which 'people begin to float.'"

The writer felt depressed. A shaft of light flashed out from a certain mirror and reflected his eyes. "Will you still go on with your research about eyeballs?"

"There's no question but that my research has entered a high-level stage. I'm in the midst of struggling to break away from the microscope. I sometimes think: why don't I *create* a miracle? Creation would be much more interesting than research! This curtain is my first step. But this isn't a big deal. I will create a miracle out of nothing." After saying all this, she suddenly held her head high and picked up a mirror next to the table. She threw it to the floor, and it broke into pieces. "I'll create a miracle in this space. You can go. When you go out, be sure you don't let any light in. That gives me a headache."

Truly, the writer had no way to make any connection—even one as fragile as a hair—between what Madam X was doing in her dark room and the mighty offensive of the crowds outside. She sat there, blocking out the light with heavy curtains, making rustling noises as she created "miracles." Even if people couldn't restrain their inner enthusiasm and rushed in and started attacking her, it would be hard to say whether she reacted or not. The people on Five Spice Street all happened coincidentally to act in refined ways. They definitely didn't intend to turn to action: they just blindly used an invisible spiritual weapon. Outsiders regarded that weapon as a certain kind of "qigong," and no one could ensure that Madam X would be harmed by it. Looking at her, it didn't seem that she sensed this "qigong" at all, so after leaving Madam X's home, the writer was deeply worried: had the elites been mistaken in their judgment? And could this cause trouble that would be difficult to mend?

The third big change in Madam X came about unconsciously. Some time or other, she gave up her nighttime "dispel boredom" activities and hid out in the dark room, "concentrating on creating miracles." And thus the female colleague noticed that her good friend had "completely lost her femininity" and "wouldn't be able to attract even the ugliest man's interest." Her best friend was "deeply mortified" by this and yearned for "the good old days," because "those days had been so enraptured." "Living in those days, she felt she would always be a young girl, always superior, and absolutely confident."

After embracing the bygone days, she angrily changed the subject: "What do all of you think about this hanky-panky behind closed doors? She wants to create a false image of being loyal and steadfast: this is clear enough. Isn't this a joke? As for adultery, it doesn't make any difference whether there's one lover or twenty. Doesn't she even know this much? If we can say that her past behavior embodied a certain innocence and was a kind of free indulgence, she certainly doesn't have that excuse anymore. She's actually a complete sham, a person with detestable behavior. And all of a sudden she closes the door and changes from a devil into an angel! And becomes extremely serious! What's she trying to prove? Does she think she can get a lock on her lover's heart this way? Right. I remember this is just the kind of person she is. If she stares at someone, then she immediately affects a certain attitude, as if she has reformed completely overnight. I hear that her lover is a weirdo who is incredibly jealous. Because of him, she doesn't look at any other men. She hides inside all the time. Although she has no other choice, I still have to say that this is the most scandalous behavior I've ever seen in her. She even calls this behavior 'creation'—her 'creation.' Rather, she has created herself into a disgusting weirdo. Those who used to appreciate her all want to cover their noses and flee! When she leaves her room, her whole body reeks of sulfur. Whenever she opens her window, the passersby see thick smoke billowing out from her room! Who could still remember the likable woman I used to work with? She's ruined her self-image. This is really depressing." The female colleague began shedding tears. The people listening to her felt touched by the women's friendship: they all looked downcast.

Was Madam X really "creating miracles" in her room? Could she purposely throw out this smoke bomb and actually tryst inside with her lover? Answer: No. You have to realize that she wasn't so simple-minded or so driven by passion that she would entice her lover to her home for a daytime tryst. We mustn't underestimate our adversary. As for the site of their tryst, no one up to now has come up with any reliable information. One said it was on the mountain nearby;

another said it was behind the garbage dump; another said it was in Old Meng's attic (the one who had this opinion was the good friend of X's husband); another said it was in the meeting room, and so on and on and on. Out of more than a thousand people, there were at least five hundred different views. So we can see only that the crowds were motivated by their inner passion to come up with some irresponsible guesses. But the adultery actually did occur very recently. Inwardly, everyone was sure of this. In the dark meeting, they verified this with their high-level telepathy. Each person had actually "seen" the adultery, and they could still see it clearly. If you asked about it, they were unanimous. As for the place and the time—those were minor issues. The important point was that they had "seen" it. And this "seeing" was ever-present: it richly embodied the artistic temperament and poetic grace among the people on Five Spice Street. Since Madam X could become "invisible" in her adultery with Mr. Q, others couldn't get a handle on it. Yet, the elites on Five Spice Street could re-create her adultery by employing a special method—called "the fox is smart, the hunter is smarter."

It didn't matter whether Madam X was phony or real—nothing mattered. Now she really was staying away from men. No longer did any dizzying fragrance come from her person. Nor did she any longer have that sort of "sex appeal." When her sister asked about this, Madam X laughed out loud and said that she "hadn't even thought about it." How would she know if other people were interested in her? She had never bothered to figure out whether she was "chaste or lewd." She was simply being herself. She liked men. Too bad that when she opened her eyes, all she saw was garbage. Since now she had found the one she truly loved, "she wouldn't lay an eye on those pieces of garbage." She couldn't be happier: she didn't care what other people thought! That day, she and her sister sat for a long time in the dark room. By the light that came from the mirrors, her sister saw tears in Madam X's eyes: in fact, she wasn't as happy as she'd said she was. At once, her sister empathetically began to take pity on this "beloved older sister." She arbitrarily thought that her sister must be cold and took a woolen coat out of the closet and draped it over her shoulders. Yet, it was a warm May day. Everyone else was wearing light clothing. She seemed to stop worrying a little only when she saw her put on the coat.

"When I'm here, I feel alone. There are a lot of people outside, but I don't know them—and haven't for a long time. I pretend that they're old friends, but in fact, I've never been able to tell them apart. I just call out any old name and tell some stories. Sometimes, it's really quiet here. I don't know whether this is good or not, and there's no way to anticipate it: you can only wait. Do you still remember that we used to sing? That was a long time ago, wasn't it? As for your brother-in-law, I'm going to leave him. I've had a premonition of that."

"Let's sing then," her sister said, choking with sobs. (Listening to her sister's sentimental words, she was already all tears. Anyhow, she was completely confused. She realized only that a catastrophe was about to befall them.)

"Don't sing!" Madam X curled her body into a ball. "Listen closely: he's walking back and forth on the hill over there. I can hear him. When he isn't here, I sit in this corner and listen: I hear everything. You know, he doubts his own existence. This is agonizing for me. There is a certain fateful thing in this. It's coming: can I accept it?"

The sister's emotions were on the verge of exploding. Crying her eyes out, she wept for about fifteen minutes.

"You didn't understand," Madam X finally said. "Everything happened as I wished, even much better than I wished. You can't imagine how good it is. At the time, how many rules I made for my eyes!"

"Did you bring it into effect?" her sister asked, close to tears.

"Not just that!! I have everything—everything. . . . Ah, I want to keep him, I want to do my best to keep him!" She stamped her foot and looked decisive.

One day not long after the crowds noticed the third big change in Madam X, an obtrusive guy forced his way into her home and stood bravely in the midst of the flickering demonic mirrors. He asked Madam X a lot of flirtatious questions, such as "Are you lonely at night?" "What kind of experience have you had with masculine charms?" "Is reddish-gold velour sexy?" and so on. After he finished asking these questions, he noticed that Madam X had climbed up to the windowsill. Only his voice was whirling crazily in the dark room: it was like playing a record over and over again. "Help me with this curtain," she said to him. "I was just noticing that there's a new problem here." At this, the man ran off.

"She isn't at all the way she used to be. (In the past, when Mr. F and I talked about this at the toilet, we were simply crazy about her.)" The man announced, "When I was with her, she climbed up to the windowsill like a monkey. That was like having a pail of icy water thrown over my feverish body."

At this, everyone began tsk-tsk-ing in unison.

"Why did she become like this?" they said. "Isn't it too much? She has too high an estimation of her significance. She certainly didn't need to change. It would have been better if she had stayed the way she was."

After Madam X's third major change occurred, someone intercepted her husband on the road and forced a conversation on him. Now we'll make the conversation public. (At the time the one who intercepted him had his face covered, and afterwards he still didn't want to reveal his name for fear of getting entangled in all of this. We'll call him Mr. X.)

Mr. X: Wait up! Let me ask you something: What do you think about your wife's third major change?

X's husband: What's "the third major change"? Sorry, I haven't taken part in your civic activities for a long time. I'm afraid you'd drag me off to have my picture taken. I think everyone goes through some changes during a lifetime. One can't be the same day after day, and it's even possible to change four or five times in a day. It's best if each person pays attention to whether or not his eyes are diseased or inflamed and doesn't butt into other people's business. If a person gets into other people's business too much and neglects himself, he might go blind. The concern all of you have for us touches us in our hearts, but don't neglect yourselves for the sake of this and come down with a fatal disease.

Mr. X: Why did she stop carrying on her occult activities?

X's husband (sternly): She's observing the stars. (Rhetorical question:) Have you paid attention to your eyeballs? You must be careful! Without your being aware of it, a viral infection can create a nasty crisis for a person. One person was still fine in the morning, but by noon he was completely blind. Now my wife has invented a better method (he was bursting with pride): she can create constellations out of thin air. (At once, he was on guard again:) What am I doing telling you about this? Leave me alone!!!

After this conversation became public, everyone understood what it was about. Containing their inner excitement, they strolled around under the eaves, poking each other and quickly exchanging knowing looks. They were smiling all day long. Ms. B shuttled back and forth under the eaves, exhorting everyone to "hush," "stop walking around, and sit up straight against the wall."

What was it that they knew?

During this time, Madam X was still going about her routine work in the snack shop with her husband. At dusk every day, they still went walking together. It's just that they walked for a much longer time—about half the time of her "dispel boredom" activities. Sometimes, they walked without talking at all. Their son, Little Bao, was asleep on his father's shoulders. Despite following along a number of times, the people on Five Spice Street didn't learn anything. Those two were just strolling blindly, like two silent souls. This made the people following them stamp their feet in fury.

When they were taking a walk, we frequently heard the woman sigh loudly. She deliberately acted afraid of the cold and leaned close to her husband as she said loudly, "I feel there's an evil wind blowing. Aren't you aware of this? It's blowing so hard that my bones ache. Should we go back?" Her husband was enjoying his moment of glory: all the people on the street were craning their necks to look at them. He kept placating his wife—there isn't any wind, she could look up and see that even the leaves weren't moving at all. If there'd been any wind, there wasn't any now. It felt so good to take a walk at dusk: if it were possible, he would only too happily walk with her for a lifetime. That would be wonderful! That would explain the problem so well! (God only knew what problem it would explain; anyhow, this husband was a little idiotic.—The writer.) Madam X looked at her husband affectionately and said, "Then let's walk a little farther. There's no one here; it's absolutely deserted." Madam X was good at this kind of show. Whenever everyone was paying more attention to her, she would surprise you by announcing that she didn't see any-one. She did this to show how special and how important she was to the crowds. But if other people actually weren't noticing her and each person was simply going about his own business, this was incredibly hard for her to bear. She couldn't endure loneliness: she would strike up conversations with people everywhere, lest others ignore her. Unfortunately, all of us had a bad habit: sometimes, we couldn't keep calm. We looked all around, and—in insignificant people and events—we looked forward to finding a little something that was exciting. It was as though we didn't have anything better to do but be drawn to those people and things. We were flushed and full of desire; it was just like falling in love. This was the worst failing that certain people among us had.

Sure, there were some exceptions to this. For example, the widow and her forty-eight-year-old friend. Their behavior was entirely dif-ferent. They sat erect, and *from beginning to end* they looked at the clouds on the horizon. They looked melancholy and refused to listen. That's to say that they didn't listen to any of the weird things Madam X said. They could hang on to their mature femininity. If everyone had the same fine character they did, there'd have been no market for Madam X's schemes. In the midst of boredom, she cer-tainly would also be dejected and would be thinking about ending this show. Unfortunately, this wasn't the reality, and unfortunately, a lot of us unwittingly catered to her abnormal desires and showed great interest in her baffling pretense at profundity, so she was able to make use of our moods to be so defiant. The more attention people gave her, the more anxious she was to show that she looked down on them. As time went on, this had become a Pavlovian response. And from this she reaped unimaginable joy. Our widow was the first to see through this. She had gone to great lengths to educate these guys who refused to come to their senses. She kept advising them on the basis of her own experience and even impatiently slapped a certain person several times. But these congenitally lazy men kept walking toward the corner: they seemed to be incurable. Anytime Madam X and her family appeared next to the road, they couldn't help craning their necks to watch and listen attentively. It was as if they were deluded.

The widow and others weren't strong enough to change reality. All they could do was stay out of this stream of people and sit there with straight faces to show they were different. Clear-sighted people could see the polarization in the ranks and the disagreement in strategy. Although everyone felt the same—that is, they were opposed to X and her family—because of theoretical differences and intellectual disputes, victory became less and less possible. Most of their energy went into the internal struggle. It seemed that this kind of situation wouldn't change in the near future. Thus, the enemy was able to take advantage of this opening and walk around freely, spouting evil and being very aggressive. Seeing the intrigues that went on day in and day out, the widow was anxious. Every day when it was time for cooling off outside, she was as jittery as an ant on a hot pot as she called together her faction and formed a close charmed circle of these people. They all whispered to one another. The radical faction suggested throwing stones to force those three people "to go home." The more conservative faction suggested "temporarily suspending the cooling-off-outside movement" so that everyone would be in his or her own home at that time and the street would be deserted. If Madam X and her family still went out walking, fine; if she shouted something like "there's not one person here," fine. Anyhow, no one would be able to hear her. After two or three times, they would decide this wasn't interesting, and they would naturally end their performances.

3

THE TAILS' CONFESSIONS

Tail A: I'm also highly intelligent and cultured. I'm not bad-tempered, and I'm very forbearing. In general, no matter the circumstances, I don't alter my opinions. But this was obscene (I say obscene, because something was covered up behind it). I was hit by a deathblow and I was duped; my self-confidence wavered. What kind of person am I? Am I a useless idler who's been following a decent couple every evening just to create rumors and then finally has gotten nothing? Are they really so decent? Could it be that I've tailed them night after night just to prove this little bit? Since I can't prove what I wanted to prove, is it the other way around? Has it proved that I'm a jerk? In the beginning, I considered it a contest of wills. I was confident of victory. Now, I am less and less sure exactly what the problem is. No matter how hard I try, I can't escape the circle of demons. Nothing is what it seems. I'm so utterly unnerved my shoes slipped off while I was running. Now I suspect I might have been deluded by a lie, that my talent might have been misused. What I've been doing is something like alchemy. Is tailing proper for one of my status?

Tail B: To begin with, I had no time to care about these two people's whereabouts. Think about it: I had always been a tower of strength on the street. All the work was heaped on my head, and I was dead tired every day. I didn't even have time for a noontime nap, for as soon as I closed my eyes, someone would come and yell at me to put up banners or wall newspapers or call the people together for a meeting. Sometimes, I wanted to sit down and have a cigarette, but I couldn't because jealous people were always coveting my leadership position. I am a proud person. I wanted to do well in everything so that people would respect me. So where did I have the time and energy to be concerned with side issues? I throw myself wholeheartedly into whatever I do.

Now I want to charge these two rotten eggs with evildoing. No, I can't stand it! It's just too damnable! Like robbery, like a calamity. It leaves you speechless. Think about it: now I still haven't made my mark in anything. I'm young and still single. I have a great future, but it's far off. I'm not established in a job yet. I'm just full of beautiful fantasies, and then all of a sudden—these two rotten eggs! Who sent them to disturb our peaceful lives on Five Spice Street? Why do they swagger on the streets? And then lots of people started tailing them! Has this had any effect? Who dares to give this problem careful thought? All along, we've pretended to be ignorant of it! This is because all of us know our plight. Some have become so exhausted by this exasperating surveillance that they've fallen ill, and their lives are in danger! Yet, this isn't the worst. The worst is that they persist in their old ways. You crumble in the face of such an attitude. Like a night owl, you scurry here and there, while they— absolutely unaware—saunter along at their leisure. Embarrassment and feelings of inferiority overwhelm you. You wobble, you see spots, you ache with fatigue, and you can never hope to get better— you just keep following them. You can't expect quick success; you must even recognize that your efforts are in vain. You must recognize that your destiny is in their hands. Don't imagine breaking free. Because I was tailing them, I asked Madam X what she thought about the wide-ranging efforts to tail her. "Early this morning," she said, "I turned on the light and found the room filled with people sitting against the wall. The light forced them to narrow their eyes. One of them told me that they had lived in this room for years, observing me every day. They saw how overbearing I was, and that I'm cranky, impudent, and phony. Then he jumped on the table and began cursing loudly. He rushed at me and forced me to answer his questions. When he finished, he told me to go to the meeting hall. He said the meeting would result in a 'new beginning.'"

Madam X said that the ordinary people "perceived the minutest details." She went out of her way to emphasize this. Wasn't it clear what she meant? When did we begin to turn into fools? Not only had we turned into fools, but we also had no hope of shaking off this condition. The situation was clear enough. Maybe, if we stopped tailing them and took a live-and-let-live attitude, they would undergo an earthshaking change someday. Maybe we didn't need to have so many people engaged in this activity. It might be all right if just one or two people handled it. But if everyone thought this way, no one would come. Also, if the two who did come thought this way, perhaps they would start making light of this whole matter. And in the instant we took such an attitude, a major problem would arise. That would really be too bad.

So, whether we wanted to or not, the only option was: we had to continue tailing them, like a pack of loyal dogs following their masters and secretly protecting them. Even if we were dead tired, we couldn't let up in the slightest. This was foreordained by fate. Although we weren't one bit happy about it, although we often grumbled that the road was bumpy, although we lost sleep over it, although we gained nothing from it, although it was uninteresting, we couldn't extricate ourselves. As long as they went out, we were tied behind them. Sometimes, I can't keep from asking myself: What on earth is this all about? How did these two characters become our masters? They're nothing, and we always looked down on them, but unfortunately God likes to play games with people: the more you scoff at something, the more he will inflate its status, until your head is muddled and you busy yourself blindly with it. You can't control yourself.

Tail C: I came up with a scheme once: I planned to take a certain action while Madam X was walking. Of course, I couldn't do this alone: I needed the community's agreement; otherwise, people would think I had evil intentions. I thought through the numerous difficulties in achieving a consensus: each person had his own notions, so if I tried too hard, others would hate me. They'd all drop what they were doing and run over to question me: What's wrong with you? Do you want the glory for yourself alone? Do you think you are a prophet? How dare you cast everyone else to the side? As soon as they doubted me, they wouldn't cooperate. Not only that, they would want to abandon everything and would leave no stone unturned in wrecking my scheme. I had originally intended to announce my ideal scheme to the people, but as soon as I realized what this might lead to, my spirits sagged. It would be better for me to bury the scheme deep inside myself and wait for the whole thing to wind down on its own. As I saw it, this was the only way. Nobody could even think about taking advantage of me.

Every night, I'd stretch out on the canvas lounge chair and reflect on my unpredictable fate, on my extraordinary self-control, and on my character, which ran deeper by the day. I couldn't help choking up. The crowds' emotions were the hardest thing to figure out: one misstep might put you at odds with them. When I was young, I made numerous such mistakes. Now, of course, the situation was quite the reverse. I had done my utmost to appear ordinary, dull, and undistinguished throughout the process. I had been extremely careful not to overstep the limit. I had gone with the flow. No one knew my true ideas, even though the one I harbored was ingenious! This is why I never doubted that my work was useful and why I could be so self-assured. Without a spiritual pillar sustaining him, a person might as well be a walking corpse. When I saw how anxiety-ridden and how indecisive the people were, I became aware of my good fortune. I easily saw their mistakes. Sometimes, I wanted to roar at them. Unfortunately, mortals are always so short-sighted and ignorant of life. For most, thinking straight is like roosters laying eggs.

I felt keenly that this world lacked people with ideals and aspirations. Mediocrity was everywhere. Every project was left unfinished. All the talent died before it could be born. The future was hopeless. What a frustrating world! I'm not a pessimist: I'm just a fighter constantly striving to become stronger in today's reality. Look at everything I do, and you'll agree.

Tail D: Last night, when I walked to the riverbank, the south wind carried Madam X's voice. She said: "I don't want to give everything away, but I can reveal a little privileged information. I understand why everyone has been driven to the last extremity. I understand it to the core. From now on, no one should be anxious."

Probably no one will believe me because I can't point to concrete facts, and nobody can know whether I'm lying—just amusing myself at everyone else's expense. But how could I make public what Madam X said earlier? That's my secret alone: it came from many sleepless nights, or perhaps from a decree of the gods! Wouldn't telling everybody mean I was making light of it? In a lifetime, you might never encounter it at all. I can't stand to see everyone tailing (these words are probably too vulgar), plodding through wind and rain and even sinking straight into the trap. So all I can do is to vow to heaven that what I'm telling is the truth. I know the inside story of the whole thing. My information came from Madam X herself, and it is absolutely true.

Don't think that I'm cocky. No. I don't think I'm all that wonderful just because of this. I'm still one of you, and I'll pretend nothing has happened to me, just as usual. Yesterday, my cousin asked why I eat pickled vegetable soup and dried turnips at every meal. I answered that I have to adhere to this way of life until I die—and this definitely wasn't boasting. Tonight, I can still go out with everyone else and rush around: no one can see that I'm any different. I dislike attention: that's self-glorification. I think people who wildly flaunt themselves are very funny. They become intoxicated grasping shadows and forget to keep striding forward. They're like babies without experience: they just want to enjoy themselves and are always eager for life to favor them with more. The moment they discover a little something new (sometimes, only an illusion), they start clamoring about their success in case others don't know of it. They want prizes for their discoveries. A life of reaping without sowing has spoiled them. I am quite the opposite. I've lived an industrious and frugal life since childhood, one not lacking in ideals. All my life, I've consciously disciplined myself. Only in this way have I nurtured the good habits of being calm and not cutting a fashionable figure.

One individual never joined in the extensive surveillance and also kept cool and collected. This was the much-admired widow. Let's hear her views:

"Listen, everyone, I can't stand your irrational, ignorant behavior! Each of you came with your own selfish intentions and impulsively took part in this collective activity, keeping busy day and night. But can you grasp the substance of this matter? It's a maze that opened up in front of you, but you can't get in. You just pretend to know it well to cover up your own foolishness.

"Let me come straight to the point: Madam X, affecting a certain vague genius, has stirred up so many storms on our three-mile-long street and disturbed so many people's minds that she has altered their individual destinies. Everybody knows this. Out of inertia, we're used to this fixed, unchanging perspective. As soon as something comes up, we go all out to join in. But if we think about this deeply, we'll discover a big problem. (We generally have no time to reflect because all day long we're fervently busy with our civic activities.) Let me give you a simple example: at present, this surveillance is grounded in our firm belief that Madam X is engaged in a certain kind of unusual adultery.

"From the revelations at the meetings in the dark room, you knew something explosive was about to occur. But the reality was not what you thought. And it is going to stay this way. There is no sign of any change. And so you felt tricked and you became tenacious and thought you'd use this tenacious antagonism to solve your problems and make history develop in accord with the trajectory you had set. What if someone pointed out (unfortunately, such bright people are rare) that your belief was vague and untrustworthy in the first place? With all of your reasoning built on it, your idea couldn't hold up, could it? As soon as we grew excited, we endowed a certain subject with all kinds of charm and let ourselves be dazzled. Such unusual adultery, such a mysterious, unfathomable paramour: we manufactured all of this from our hopes and emotions. Why did we have to hope for this? Because we were bored, and because we were afraid, and so we shifted the crisis and came up with this surveillance.

"I want to tell you now: Madam X couldn't be the way she is in your imaginations. That is an inconceivable joke. In this perfectly mature society of ours, behavior is governed by iron discipline. This has become second nature. It guarantees peace and harmony. If now someone—who knows whether she's come from outer space or has simply grown out of the earth—shows up who is not part of this society and manipulates our collective will and makes us into dolls for her to hold, how can people come to see this? Isn't this the same as saying that our society is merely a plaything that can be manipulated and changed at will? Wouldn't this embarrass our elite? Thinking of this makes me really indignant. Some of us have college degrees and strict social training; some have taken on important leadership roles in the meetings in the dark room. They're imperturbable and capable of analyzing facts. For some years, I have trusted them almost unconditionally and supported their work. Now it seems I've been glaringly wrong! My simplicity and sincerity have brought me to an awkward pass. I've been tossed aside and ignored. Current fads have swept through the entire street. Everyone competes to trample traditional taste, boisterously congratulating themselves on the so-called 'rebirth.' They also say they've discovered a new continent: this new continent is Madam X. She's an ingenious person, with an infinite number of sleights of hand. Everyone should pay attention to her! What happened to our earlier calm?

"Looking back, I still remember clearly how correctly everyone treated a certain stenographer when he came here with his fantasies to undertake an investigation. Really, the people changed greatly. How did this get started? How could it have reached this point? Trying to get to the bottom of it, I have to denounce myself. I feel incredibly remorseful. During a meeting in the dark room last month, all kinds of clues already pointed to today's crisis. Then, however, I sat behind the platform, looking on with a child's gullible eyes. I didn't suspect the dangerous trend in the crowd's mood. I looked on calmly as everyone slid into the mud hole and wallowed. After the meeting, while the crowd was ready to act and was plotting activities, I was up to my elbows with something else and didn't have time to warn and deter everyone. Thus, things went from bad to worse. How could I have been so careless? Was it merely because of objective conditions? Was it a chance mistake? Most people would avoid the blame this way, and would even depict themselves as suffering heroes. But this is not the way I operate. Not only must I accept responsibility for all the mistakes, but I must also examine the squalor in my soul and find out where the root of my mistake lies.

"I remember clearly that I've been gullible since childhood. I used to glorify everyone who was around me, and looked only at the bright side of people. If someone stole something of mine, I not only wouldn't ask for it back, but I would also give him some other things. Touched by this, he would become my friend for life. Later, as a young person, I married the right man and regarded my husband as my protector god. I trusted him completely and was docile and obedient. I turned away from all outside temptations. Maybe my husband wasn't as perfect as I had thought, and maybe he had already fallen ill with an unmentionable disease and hushed it up when we got married, but none of this could keep me from feeling great ardor. Even now, I feel this ardor and don't waste it on outsiders. I'm bringing this up not because I want to overthrow the past but because I want to explain where the weak part of my character came from. When my husband was alive, someone mentioned a certain instance of his being unfaithful. I was so outraged I let out a stream of abuse at that person! To outsiders I was a very sexy young woman as beautiful as flowers, tied down by a nearly disabled man who had actually duped me. What kind of lamentable joke was this? Why couldn't I get a little happiness by finding someone else?

Couldn't I accomplish this just by crooking my little finger? A person's nature sets the course of her whole life. I was doomed to stick up for the traditional morality. Today, I'm still proud of this.

"I don't deny my weaknesses, nor do I deny that my weaknesses have affected the course of history. If I were a little stronger, a little more vigilant, not so innocent and gullible, lots of things would now be different. This is the fatal weakness of 'being a good sort.' I want to take responsibility for the losses that came because of my weakness, and I also want to locate the reason deep in my soul, because I'm the key to everyone's mistakes. All of this could have been averted. I'm ashamed of myself when I face this depressing situation."

4

MR. Q'S CHARACTER

Preoccupied by the massive surveillance of Madam X and her family, we had ignored Mr. Q. His nerves showed signs of cracking. As time went on he became an invalid. A strong woman in our community who hadn't participated in the tailing launched her own creative initiative. After days and nights of observing and re-flecting, she told us: two snakes were scrambling for control of Mr. Q's body, which resulted in his becoming two completely different persons—one by day, one by night.

One day, she hid in the bushes beside the road and saw Mr. Q leave his home. He was unimaginably cheerful, dribbling a ball and running like a child. Watching this, the woman (she was the lame one) became indignant! Unbelievably annoyed! Supporting herself with her canes, she dashed up, blocked Mr. Q's way, and shouted, "Hey!" Then she began rolling around in the middle of the road, glaring at him through the mist. The surprising thing was that Mr. Q actually "broke through," leaving her rolling on the ground alone. In the blink of an eye, he "disappeared." A few hours later, she noticed him twice near a warehouse; both times, he was happily dribbling the ball. As soon as he saw her, he disappeared again without a trace.

The same day, she had gone to Mr. Q's work place to make inquiries. Some people wrapped from head to toe in heavy blankets told her Mr. Q even brings the ball to the office and bounces it from time to time, as if he were addicted. Everyone knows he's abnormal; and the ball doesn't sound right, either. No one dares talk to him. As soon as they see him coming, they run off, leaving him alone in the office, dribbling the ball all day long.

They grumble, "This menace will affect our sex life. The dust might give us tuberculosis. Now we all feel cold." They sigh in despair and weep.

Mr. Q's behavior stimulated this woman's imagination. She continued her work even more actively and bravely. One day near evening, leaning on her canes, she chiseled her way into Mr. Q's den. With blue-veined hands, she grabbed Mr. Q's collar, stared into his eyes, and ordered him "to come to her." People suppose that what she yearned for didn't occur. What on earth did she desire? What was gnawing at her? Afterwards, she told others, "I wanted to play ball with him. I yearned for this constantly. Now I've achieved my goal. We shut his wife outside and played all through the night." This was a certain woman's (she adamantly requested that her background and name not be divulged) investigation of Mr. Q's daytime activity. The facts in this report need further validation.

Maybe the stories that Madam X's sister spread can explain this even better. She reported that Mr. Q had told her that he'd added five more colors to his eyes and now has ten. This occurred because he "was addicted" to dribbling the ball, which let him "defy aging and become young again." He immersed himself in all kinds of child's play and "liked it too much to stop." Indirectly, he also told the sister that Madam X was "too wonderful for words," and he himself now had to look in mirrors "forty or fifty times a day." He had already "quite unconsciously hidden a mirror in his pocket." At this point, he asked the sister time after time, "Don't you think I'm now a real stud?" After the sister reassured him, he happily ran off to dribble the ball.

This isn't all. He made up stories about his past, claiming that he had no father or mother, that he'd been born from a leather skin hanging on a tree. The day he was born, he had seen lots of silkworms spinning golden-yellow cocoons. "They spun back and forth, back and forth." A silly smile hung on his face. "Everyone jumps down from cocoons on the tree. Just look at their feet and you'll know. Ahead was a dark wood that people would fall into, just like ants that had lost their sense of smell. What's that sound?" The sister told him it was the footsteps of people on their street: they were tailing her sister and her family. "They were scattered in the dense woods, those bugs." He nodded, and his ears pricked up like a cat's.

Our widow, who hadn't participated in the crowd's activity either, expressed another opinion of Mr. Q's daytime character. This derived from personal experience for which she had paid a high price. She had concentrated a long time on her research and had long ago stopped thinking of Mr. Q. She could hardly even remember what he looked like. One day, the widow and Mr. Q ran into each other at a fence. Mr. Q "leered at her with a dirty smile hanging from his fleshy lips" and stared at her urgently with "erotic eyes." He was evidently scheming "something evil." The widow screamed and ran off. After almost a mile, she was still so afraid that "her face had turned pale." "He clearly wanted to rob me of my virtue," she said furiously. You have to realize that in the widow's eyes, Mr. Q had been no more than androgynous, "a eunuch." Whenever Mr. Q was mentioned, she'd held her head high and laughed and then asked, "Is it the guy picking up chicken bones to eat?" No one could imagine how she had dreamed up this description. A hypocrite or a horse thief or something of the sort would have made sense, but a guy picking up chicken bones to eat! How wonderful the widow was! Now, when everyone had forgotten him, and thought he was insignificant and unimportant, he suddenly appeared like a jackal— an incredibly oversexed and aggressive jackal.

"I was scared half to death." Her hand on her chest, the widow asked, "Under what circumstances can a sexless man—one who picks up chicken bones to eat—change into a sex maniac? Isn't this fascinating? What I said about what he did to me wasn't at all exaggerated: it was the absolute embodiment of libido. We can easily conclude that in their relationship, Madam X hasn't inspired any sexual consciousness in Mr. Q. Their infantile friendship could never reach the point of sexual contact. Why? Because after meeting a real woman, with that crazed, violent expression, in a split second he became a real man."

Since the encounter at the fence, the widow felt low and despondent all day long. Before bed, she saw rats and bare feet. She started using language from the meetings in the dark room to hint of a certain thing deep in her heart. She couldn't talk about that thing out loud, for if she did, it would no longer exist. She made comparisons and suggestions. If she hadn't been the one Mr. Q ran into at the fence, but had been, for example, the old woman with the felt hat, she could say for sure that Mr. Q would have had a much different expression. There was no need to test this. She had figured it out intuitively. And if Mr. Q had been playing with a puppet and hadn't seen this woman who was every inch a woman, she could just imagine the "sex appeal" Mr. Q's mouth and eyes would have had.

In general, other people were inclined to think that ever since Mr. Q and Madam X started their illicit affair, Mr. Q's appearance had changed greatly: it had become "filled with lust." Actually, this was nonsensical speculation— a conclusion based on prior beliefs without rigorous authentication or independent analysis. What happened at the fence had overturned these simple-minded fancies. Let's suppose something else: when Mr. Q rushed at her, the widow wasn't able to ward him off and was tarnished by him. Though lamentable, at the same time she could tell that after contact with the flesh of a real woman who released his libido, the sex appeal in his face would have vanished. Every day and all day long, the widow was entangled by these hypotheses and deductions. Her eyes grew dull, and her face withered. It's said that not long afterwards, Mr. Q repeated his sex attacks. Several beautiful women on Five Spice Street were ambushed in broad daylight—always near the warehouse. They said he launched his offensive with the ball and then rushed up wanting to "do it." Because the women ran off, there "was no doing it." But if they hadn't run off, very likely there would have been "doing it."

After learning that the adorable widow had been so traumatized by Mr. Q that she fell ill, the writer—filled with sympathy—went to see her. When he arrived she was in bad shape, wrapped in a heavy quilt and with perspiration falling like rain. That frightening scream had caused her to lose her hearing, and she couldn't converse. But when he sat by the bed, she seemed excited and talked without stopping. She spoke about the ideals of her youth and the pursuits, fears, agonies, and wreckage that had come from those ideals.

"How do the people see me?" Covering her mouth with the quilt, she spoke with great effort. "This is already clear. For decades, I've preserved the integrity of this visualization. Tell me whether what I say is true."

The writer nodded his head so vigorously that his chin hit his chest. After this, the widow cried her eyes out. Her tears soaked the quilt. Shaking her shoulders and wishing to calm her, the writer made *wuwuwuwu* sounds like a mother nursing a baby. He didn't imagine she'd start crying even harder. Now and then, she also gave him bitter, tear-filled looks. She curled her lip. Haggard and thin, pure and innocent as a child, she filled the writer with tenderness. She was wholly trusting. The writer couldn't keep tears from his eyes. Who took the initiative isn't known, but the writer burrowed into the widow's warm quilts and they cuddled.

And so it was that the writer was fortunate enough to experience the widow's ample body. Of course, not completely, because that would have been violating principles, and the widow herself had always detested that sort of thing. The writer supposed that she was looking only for comfort and pity, nothing more. She was so fragile! Illness had flattened her like a steam-roller. This time, after completely collapsing, she felt a few steps closer to the abyss. She urgently needed a real man to give her a helping hand. As for the writer, he was honored to play a knight's role. It was the first time in his life that he felt filled with honor and obligation. Although he was only an artist, this made him a hero.

From the moment the writer came in contact with the widow's body, she miraculously recovered her hearing, and they began talking with one another. Under the quilt, the writer and the widow solemnly vowed that after this they would support each other forever, would help each other forever. After this vow, the widow wrapped her legs tightly around the writer's legs and said, "Now, pull yourself together: aren't you aware of a certain dangerous kind of temptation?"

The writer was bewildered. She hinted again: "For example, things having to do with sex?"

All of a sudden, the writer understood. He sat up and began

quoting various proverbs and sayings, such as "serve one's country with absolute loyalty," "die for a just cause," "spiritual companions," "symbols of eternity," and so forth. Others might have seen this as hyperbole, but the writer thought it was just right. This speech roused him, and his blood boiled. It was as though he had arrived in an uncorrupted, relaxed, and happy wonderland.

The strange thing was that the widow didn't seem to enjoy the writer's speech. The more stimulated he was, the cloudier her face grew. Finally, she paid almost no attention to what he was saying. She rudely interrupted him, asking if bugs were biting him under the quilt. When he finished, the widow looked somber and said, "Doesn't it feel too warm for two of us to be under the quilt? I was really surprised just now when you crawled in."

Then, turning her back on him, she murmured, "If I'd known it would be like this, it would have been better. . . . Where did the crow crawl out from? I can't take its cawing anymore!"

At the height of his success, the writer felt doused with cold water and chilled from head to toe. He pitifully asked the widow for guidance. He didn't imagine she would flare up and call him a "rat" and order him "to get out now." She kicked him hard in the back—kicked him to the floor. The writer could do nothing but leave. This was a tragic, irreversible finale.

What was Mr. Q's completely different nighttime character? Let's return to the observations of the iron-willed woman we mentioned above. On a certain night, she heard weeping and wailing coming from Mr. Q's home. To find out for sure what was going on, she skillfully entered the house and listened closely for several hours. She discovered that the couple and their two sons were asleep, yet the man kept weeping. Mr. Q's uncontrollable grief seemed to come from his dream. Though sleeping, it seemed from his appearance that he was "struggling" hard. The woman stayed there until daylight; she waited until Mr. Q left the house. In the daylight, she saw Mr. Q change into a thin, shriveled old man. His gaze was unfocused. His eyes were swollen to the size of garlic bulbs. He also became paranoid, always fearful that his wife would trip and fall. Whenever he saw even a small stone on the road, he rushed ahead of his wife, kicked away the stone, and then, as if taking care of an infant, helped her walk on. As always, he did this with reverence and awe.

Another night, the woman noticed Mr. Q in the woods nearby. She considered approaching, but she heard two people's voices and shrewdly hid behind a large tree. She listened intently until she realized the conversation was between Mr. Q and himself. It seemed he had a special skill: he faked a voice completely different from his own and created, one might say, "a conversation partner." Mr. Q seemed intoxicated and crazy. He struck his head against the trunk of a tree so hard that blood trickled to his feet. Clearly determined to let himself go, he hit his temples with a stone until he saw stars and then stuck his head into a narrow hole in the tree. He kept it there until dawn. Among other things, he gulped down leaves and buried himself in mud, all the while whimpering like a dying person. It was enough to make your hair stand on end.

Finally, Mr. Q became two bodies: "in the daytime, he was a person; at night, a ghost." He appeared exhausted, near death. As for Madam X, who had long suspected this sort of malady, she—hard as nails—determined that they should part company. We'll talk of this later. For the moment, we'll listen to some comments from Madam X to gain a more thorough understanding of Mr. Q's malady.

When her sister asked "about his future," Madam X changed her usual manner. Her face clouded over, and after a long silence, two tears rolled slowly from her eyes. "He's going to be finished," she said, choking. "The scene is gradually unfolding. You have to know that during my nights of insomnia, I couldn't find him. I ran around crazily on the rooftop and searched every corner. But I never turned anything up. At sunrise, I sometimes was surprised to see him groaning in clumps of dried weeds. He was emaciated and frail, his bones like slender grasses, his eyes unseeing, his eyeballs showing a lifeless white. I knew that in the afternoon, I would run into him at the intersection, this stud with the peculiar voice. But the things that happened at night were more and more mysterious, and I was less and less able to endure it. It made my whole body sway lightly. I couldn't stand still."

In speaking of the "cause of this illness," she said: "Murder is committed at night when the winds of hell break bones and muscles. When I ran around on the rooftop—Oh! Why did it turn out this way? Why couldn't it have been the other way around?"

In despair, she said, "He entered my dream only once, but as a person with a totally different appearance. But I knew it was he who stood at the head of my bed. *Tick-tock, tick-tock, tick-tock* . . . 'Oh!!' I shouted at him. 'In the afternoon, at the intersection, in the sunshine, you showed up again in front of the window!' I shouted like this as a substitute for courage."

Despite all these depraved notions, Madam X and Mr. Q's adultery continued. How did they accomplish this in locations no one knew about? And how did they "enjoy themselves to the full"? Also, how can she substantiate her views of men? God only knows. As for details, she revealed nothing even to her sister. She seemed too wary. Maybe what went on between them wasn't as empty as the widow guessed. Even the widow wasn't really convinced.

Yet, it brought about a kind of reverse psychology on Five Spice Street. No one knows when people started being enthusiastic about painting murals, but all of a sudden murals began appearing on the walls along the street. All of them depicted sexual positions. Clear-eyed people knew at once that these were realistic depictions of "the adultery." Those bold, bare means of expression doubtless alluded to the fallacy in the widow's story. Everyone demonstrated a fierce appetite for invention. They didn't eat, they didn't sleep: they painted day and night. In his excitement, one spilled a bucket of oil paint on himself and turned into an oil-paint person. Another shouted crazily, tore a painted nude to bits, and then pasted the pieces on the wall and called it an "abstract." Sighing with feeling, people said: "Art can give people such sublime happiness! Aside from rationalists like the widow, who isn't moved by its power? Life withers if it's separated from imagination."

Madam X was unaware of all of this. Immersed in the adultery, she seized the pleasures of the moment without any thought for the future. Actually, she correctly sized up her situation: she knew her fantasies could not last. Calamity already loomed overhead, but in the eyes of others, she was still like someone without a care in the world: every day, there were two things she couldn't forget. One was the date at the intersection. She was always impatient: like a young girl, she ran until she was gasping for breath. She couldn't see anyone else; she couldn't hear anything. As soon as she reached the shop window, she grabbed the man with the beautiful eyes, as though clutching at a reef in the midst of surging waves, or as though burning with fiery lust. The second was the adultery which occurred in an unknown place. Although no one had any way to break this case and although this wantonness in broad daylight had become the shame of the community, Madam X and Mr. Q flaunted their adultery by holding hands in broad daylight as they crossed the street, ignoring everyone else. They grew younger and more sexually radiant by the day. The people on Five Spice Street did nothing but watch. What else could have better demonstrated our breeding? To move a step forward: Madam X and Mr. Q were sexually experienced adults (one can even say that Madam X had "abundant" sexual experience). Being in the prime of life, they took keen pleasure in their rapture. Is it possible that when they were in the unknown place, they did not remove their clothes right away and carry on in all kinds of ways? Is it possible that they carried on just as the widow had described— dumbstruck, bored, or reciting poetry, singing to each other, and murmuring sweet nothings to each other while sitting far apart? This was illogical. All the more so, since Mr. Q was not sexually defective (his two children are proof of that; at a glance, you can tell whose children they are). Madam X was even less sexually defective: the crowds on Five Spice Street blush for her, this woman to whom no standards could be applied. She had actually never acknowledged any of society's restrictions.

After being enlightened by such analysis, as well as by the depictions of the street murals, we found in the granary a likely solution (for the moment, we hypothesized that the adultery was being carried on there). Never mind whether Mr. Q had "an unmentionable disease" or whether his body had "broken into two" or whether Madam X had a premonition that there would be a day when they would "part company," right now they were like dry kindling, burning until they were possessed. In Madam X's words, it was "her sexual dream come true," "this life was not in vain," she was "thawing in multi-colored eyes," and so forth. Of course, this was all just beautiful words, perhaps used to conceal something. (Deep down, she should have been embarrassed by her abnormal lust.) After mulling her words over carefully, we finally understood that the words were hiding her thirst for sex, the number of times she had had sex, time after time of satisfaction and dissatisfaction, and so forth. Madam X herself understood what it was that she wanted to express, and so did Mr. Q. No matter how it was covered up or what pretexts were concocted (conversation at the intersection, the mirrors, the waves in the eyes, and so forth), sex was the only reason they met. For years, they had yearned for sex day and night, earnestly longed for it. (In this, Mr. Q lagged far behind Madam X. It was only after she teased him that his lust burst out.)

As the saying goes, "One who eats well doesn't understand another person's hunger." Because of their unusual appetite for sex, Madam X and Mr. Q were always hungry. Ordinary people couldn't understand this, either. We all liked a disciplined sex life (for example, two or three times a week, or up to ten times for some people) and were disgusted with lust that knew no bounds and harmed one's health. With healthy sex, one could think straight and be active in life. It filled us with appreciation for life. Now two perverted persons had suddenly appeared among us. Not only did they engage in unlimited sex and not only were they shamefully lewd, but they probably were spreading this disease, making people uneasy. Their thoughts always wandered to this possibility. Acne had recently appeared on the faces of some young and middle-aged men. Blushing, their wives complained, "This is just too much." Some others transformed bodily desire into spiritual desire and started painting. They also made up their minds "to devote themselves all their lives to artistic endeavors."

Mr. Q still dribbled balls, and in the daytime he was still a handsome, robust man. Even the widow often told people, "The instant his libido bursts forth, this guy is dazzling." As for who caused his "libido to burst forth," she had her own opinion. At this time, Madam X's appearance also underwent a great change. The most notable change was in her eyes. Her pupils were darker than before, and her eye sockets were not as dry, but were shimmering with tears that flooded her pupils. Maybe she had caught this from Mr. Q. Her tear ducts were actually exceedingly developed. She couldn't control them. When she blinked, liquid spilled out, blurring her vision. She had to carry three or four handkerchiefs and now and then pretended she had "caught a cold." Frequent creative and exciting sex transformed Madam X's internal secretions, as well as her breasts, which had been flat but now began to "grow higher and softer by the day." Even the widow, who had "observed close up for a long time," had "nothing to say." She now "scorned talking of this matter."

The widow had gradually formed a new viewpoint, which represented something latent in the annals of history. As a result of her own transformation, she gradually felt the solitude of an outrunner and became even more superior and aloof. Sometimes she didn't participate in the people's activities. One day, the writer respectfully listened to her new thoughts: "To tell the truth, the ass, tits, or whatever aren't the crux of the matter. The most important thing is a woman's inner spirit. Without this, a woman is no different from an empty shell, a pillowcase, an ashtray, a pair of slippers—that sort of thing. A person's appearance fades with the years, but the spirit blooms forever. Of the women I've known in my life, very few were enchanting. Excuse my honesty. Now my vision has changed a lot. I hardly see a person's appearance. When I look someone over, my eyes perforate his (her) body and go straight to his soul."

At her last words, the writer shivered uncontrollably and felt ashamed. Glancing at the writer for two seconds, she lost interest. She swallowed, and closed her eyes.

"Do you think I've finished talking?" She abruptly opened her eyes. "Hunh."

The writer had wanted to leave, but now he was too startled to move. He just stood there. He waited, but she didn't go on. When the writer was again on the point of leaving, she once more said abruptly, "Do you think I've finished talking? Don't get any ideas!"

This was repeated four or five times. A thread of a sneer hung from her face.

Madam X had now become a full-figured woman, although her tear ducts were a little overdeveloped, so she often looked as if she had a cold. Though small, this flaw disgusted people. There are now fresh opinions of her looks. Here are some we've collected:

"Even if she's icy cold toward me, with a severe expression that has nothing to do with sex, I still maintain that she is now more sexually attractive than before, with more lasting appeal, too. 'She gives off the scent of a mature female.' A full-bodied woman is more attractive than a skinny chick, especially at about age thirty. She certainly shouldn't be so cold to me. Don't I understand life?"

"I still think she looked much prettier before. Her appearance now hints at danger. She can't stand still. Whenever I run into her, I feel dizzy. A thin woman gives an impression of purity; my mother, for example, is that kind of woman. We always take her as the standard. She wears a white apron the year round."

"Formerly, although X scorned others, we could still see her pupils, and so we felt we knew her fairly well. Her image today is simply too dreadful. Even if you look straight at her, you can't see her pupils. There are just two flashes of turbid liquid that make you uneasy. It's as though you're going to do something evil. As if you've committed a certain crime. You feel disgraced. It's diabolical."

"A lewd sex life brands you. Isn't it monstrous when a woman who's always been sickly pale suddenly turns so seductive? There's nothing good about this kind of flash in the pan. She must have suffered greatly at night from the turbulence of her inner secretions. You can prove this just by looking at the precipitous increase in her tears. I am not a bit impressed by the superficial changes in this person. I pity her from the bottom of my heart."

"I had already lost the hope I had for her, and had decided to let go of her problems, but the dazzling change in her has rekindled my former feelings, and I feel stirred again in my innermost being. After all, this woman is the most troublesome woman I've ever known. You couldn't break away from her. I can't help but connect my lot with hers. Every change in her elicits a physiological echo from me. I'm going to suffer from insomnia again. My character contains a little too much of the tragic."

In all of this confusing chatter, Madam X's husband's good friend's opinion was unique. Sticking his long, emaciated head out of his window that faced the street, he told us a story:

"There's a street where a transparently pure youth and a transparently pure woman are living. They have silently loved each other for years, but because of a certain reason they've been unable to take the next step in their relationship. They've only admired each other from a distance. They both transcend the ordinary. Today, this type is scarcer and scarcer. They communicated with each other in a way that didn't require speaking directly. (They used various ways of expressing things: for example, talking of the weather, health, other people's sexual problems, and so on). Each knew the other's longing and encouraged each other in the dark. Several eventless years passed. All along, the young man took this friendship (or love) as a spiritual trust, and he lived happily. Like him, the woman was intoxicated by everything that existed between them. A thunderbolt struck the young man in the head and interrupted the fine day. Overnight, a beautiful woman became a poisonous snake, a pure and noble goddess became a depraved, demonic fox, and ideals became a ragged dishcloth! How did this happen? The young man was unable to respond. He grew so depressed and decadent that his health deteriorated. His life was destroyed. What a dreadful fate, such cruel irony. I can't bear imagining how he endured. He felt disgusted. Nothing about her body could arouse him, and he just wanted to shake off these worldly entanglements and attain a genuine, independent selfhood. Indeed, what did the changes in certain parts of the woman's body have to do with him? Hadn't she played enough tricks on him? Did he want to sink into that shameful muddy hole once more? He had been wasting his life for many years; he had forfeited his self-esteem and hadn't held fast to his ideals. Wasn't this lesson painful enough? Being young is beautiful, but at last a person has to grow up. He can't indulge in dreams and unreal idealism for a lifetime. He has to march on. He must acknowledge his past and become a new person. And so the young man did not join in the talk of the crowds; instead, he surveyed the world of his inner heart and forgot everything around him. In a kind of transparent state, he entered maturity."

Someone asked: since Mr. Q becomes a eunuch as soon as night falls, is it possible that this disease doesn't affect his sexual function at all? During the day he is not only not impotent, but he's even more vigorous and irresistible. The ways of the world are so strange! They truly are just this strange. Ever since the mysterious Madam X arrived on Five Spice Street, strange things have occurred one after the other, violating common practice. You must believe this, even if you don't want to. You could see how strong Q's sexual power was just by looking at the changes in Madam X's body, because she—according to the young coal worker—was actually "like a flower in blossom." Wherever she went, unless you were blind, you'd see desire written on her face. No man could keep from turning around and looking at her with a sweet smile, or keep from itching from head to toe. Indeed, no one had a handle on her. No one knew where and when she did it. It seemed that the whole day, she was busy with her husband at the snack shop. People merely presumed that the granary amour existed; they didn't have any first-hand proof. Certainly they were seen rendezvousing at the intersection, and their conversation was recorded by someone hidden behind the power pole, but this isn't the same as adultery.

And so there was a new perspective: Mr. Q's dual personality was a rumor that Madam X had deliberately spread in order to cover up her unspeakable deeds. She deliberately said that Mr. Q was a eunuch at night, a defective, in order to distract people from paying attention to him. Then people would let up on their spying. Thus, the two could catch people off guard and go into the granary, where they could indulge their passion. Their adultery had never gone on at any time during the day but happened only at midnight, at the very moment when Madam X proclaimed that she "couldn't find him" and that she could only "run crazily around on the rooftop." That so-called iron woman (iron? who are you kidding?) had been "bought" by this couple and had become the mouthpiece for their proclamations. Her so-called surveillance was simply nonsense trumped up to confuse people. A traitor had emerged within our community. All along, we had taken sentry duty and had followed her in the daytime. The discussion also focused on the daytime. Now it appeared that we had done all this in vain; we had been taken in by Madam X's plot. Whenever we heard her talk of such things as "bones like tender blades of grass" and "blindness in both eyes," we immediately felt compassion and threw away both principles and common sense. As the saying has it, "Age thirty is like a wolf, age forty like a tiger." At midnight, it was quiet everywhere. Nobody was around. Wasn't it obvious yet what was going on inside the ink-black granary? We should have placed the time at midnight! How many detours we had taken! As soon as this new perspective emerged, it was supported by most of the people and became the guiding thought of the entire community.

The people of Five Spice Street reacted in no time. They immediately altered their daily schedule, sleeping in the daytime and working intensely at night. Nonetheless, the results were very slight. Those two persons didn't even leave their own homes at night—nobody could deny the fact—unless they morphed into "invisible persons." And this change in work and rest times harmed everyone's health. In the daytime they couldn't sleep. They were listening to Mr. Q dribbling the ball at a certain spot for all he was worth. Its earthshaking sounds completely dispelled their drowsiness. Were the colleagues wrapped up in blankets in their offices able to doze off? How long would this uncertain situation continue?

5

MADAM X IS UP A CREEK

Madam X sat in her gloomy room, carefully analyzing future developments and possibilities. She concluded that she was standing on a huge, creaking sheet of thin ice. A crack was widening. She was finished. Her sister said she could fly. If so, why didn't she brush all of this off and leap into the air?

"Ah, I can't. You have no idea how much I've been drawn to all these things. I cared about nothing else." As she said this, she pointed at her toes, indicating that her feet were stuck to the ice. "There's nothing I can do."

It appeared that she had only herself to thank for the spot she was in. She'd asked for this. Now, stuck firmly to the ice, her feet were immobilized. If the ice cracked, she would sink. That was predictable. In any case, she was determined to act out the drama to the end.

As she was obstinately clinging to that thin sheet of ice, her sister's confidence in her abruptly wavered. She carefully stepped to the water's edge quite far from the ice. She didn't dare walk any farther. The sunshine was cold. The two sisters looked at each other and made megaphones of their hands and shouted. Madam X's face was livid, and she looked stern and impatient. She stamped her feet, widening the crack even more. Her sister's eyes were fervent and imploring, brimming with tears. She was all but kneeling. Their conversation lasted an hour and a half. Both were shouting themselves hoarse. Later, heedless of her own safety, the sister wanted to dash out onto the ice to save Madam X. But Madam X wasn't grateful and reproached her sternly. The sister went back, depressed.

The sister: Let's come up with a scheme that will satisfy both sides. Lift your toes lightly and run quickly across the ice. I'll meet you on this side. If we just make up our minds, we'll succeed.

Madam X: Before I pick up my toes, I must have the will to do so. But I prefer to stay where I am, wait for the crack to blast open, and then play it by ear. Do you think I've stayed too long? I've just begun! Ha, in every moment it begins! There is the fuchsia-colored glow of the weak sunset! Do I still have time to sort it out? I will decide. There is always a possible scheme. It emerges suddenly from chaos, like the lurking shark.

The sister: You have no choice. Look at that crack, look at that crack: it has already stretched from your feet to the edge of the ice. The shark has opened its mouth and is waiting on the reef over there. This water is so frighteningly black! It's so cold I'll soon freeze to death.

Madam X: I hear there isn't much time. Must this drama end? Finally, do I—this woman who sells peanuts—have to grit my teeth and hold out until the end, and flip my body—wounded all over by arrows—into the sea? Wait, I still want to do something whimsical: I want to dance on this sheet of ice. It's so bright! So bright!

The sister: Let's go, let's go. It's getting dark. Who's shouting? I'm scared to death.

Madam X: Who's there? Who are you? How can you stay there? Go away! I don't like spectators, not even friends or relatives: all of you hinder me. That time in the mountain gully, they acknowledged my steely heart. Go away! You gossipy woman! I never believed there could be any scheme that would be satisfactory to both sides. I have always been capricious, contemptible, and abnormal. Just go away! Don't exaggerate: it has nothing to do with winning or losing. I've done no more than find a different place to observe the stars. Heaven is so bright, the stars have passed by. Go!!

After her sister left, Madam X picked up a flashing sliver of ice and kept reflecting heaven's dim light in it. Sometimes she squatted, sometimes she stood. Then she struck the ice beneath her feet with an ice brick, freeing her feet. Perhaps someone thought she would get away, but she didn't. She sat down at the edge of the floating ice and thrust her feet into the black water. In a flash, she dreamed of the southern jungle and also of the swamps. She went on dreaming this way as she sat there elegantly with her eyes open. She was humming some song, and at the same time, the crack kept widening and breaking up the ice. The next day at dawn, her sister returned and saw that Madam X's face had grown rosy, and that she was more "radiant and beautiful" than she'd ever been, and was so "amiable" that the sister felt "a great load had been lifted from her shoulders." She finally made up her mind not to interfere.

But there was another question: Would the people on Five Spice Street be indifferent to Madam X's predicament? Was it possible that they were too busy to notice? Or would they be uninterested and look on with one eye closed? In fact, they didn't know where Madam X was, nor had they heard about the floating ice. This was Madam X's secret. You could say it was a fairyland. We had known for a long time that Madam X was a sort of sorceress. She could fabricate miracles—couldn't she also fabricate a fairyland? So she made up her mind to stay away from the crowds and to dwell on a floating sheet of ice. This was no more than a whim, a fairyland that ordinary people couldn't enter. Even her own sister could reach only the side of the enclosure and encounter her "meditation." With it, she could be a stranger to her own sister. Her ability had actually become more and more mighty. She could enter "a meditative state" at any time and at any place. When speaking with her, a certain person would sometimes notice that her sight was fixed, while her expression was roving. How would this person know that in this instant she had probably gone beyond the highest heavens! It was a big joke. We kicked up a fuss, followed her, and held meetings—in short, we took it quite seriously. She, however, was fine: she was sound asleep on the floating ice! We didn't know her secret, yet we were confident and persistent, blindly following the set path to the end.

Only years later did the younger sister reveal Madam X's magical ability. Word spread until everyone knew. Only then, feeling lost, did we remember a little something. Then someone shouted, "All our efforts gave full consideration to her intrigue. We were really canny!"

The little sister retorted: how did he know her older sister's ability? That wasn't possible. He was just talking. It didn't affect Madam X in the least. She never let anyone see her deploy her magic. She didn't use props. Her ability now was much loftier than when she'd been doing research with mirrors and microscopes. That research could be called low-level by comparison. Only now was she truly inventing and creating. No one else, including her followers, could attain this level. Not even she—her younger sister. As for the ordinary people, they were completely out of reach of Madam X's realm. If one kept probing, one might see some unusual expression on Madam X's face, but nothing more. She performed a special magic. Although her soul was wandering, she appeared no different from anyone else. She had never paraded her newly attained ability, nor did she think she was above others. Quite the opposite. She was a little diffident. She didn't want others to be aware of her new magical ability. The little sister—who had lived with Madam X and been influenced by her—approached the border of her older sister's fairyland several times, but though she had some sense of it, she couldn't completely understand it.

"It makes the heart quake," she said with a silly solemnity that elicited amused guffaws from the crowd.

"Who needs her to advertise this?" someone sneered. "You can't believe a word she says—like in a quack medicine show. Does she think we can't see through it? Magic ability? My ass! A person's brilliance has to be demonstrated at some point or it's just rubbish, words, a silver tongue. Special ability has to be shown. People have to see it. Are we blind? We've observed her closely for a long time. Where have we seen any fairyland? It must have been stage fright that made her pretend to be in a trance in order to fool people. Perhaps it's simply that she was sleepy and some muddle-headed persons among us mistook her sleepiness for a magic trick and started spreading nonsense. People can sense magic. If they can't perceive it, then it doesn't exist. We can't believe a certain foolish girl's boasting."

The crowd's indifference wasn't groundless. The floating ice or the region beyond the highest heavens was a private concern, with no connection to the outside world or influence over them. Why should we want to trouble ourselves with thinking about this? Didn't we have enough to do in a day? If Madam X enjoyed it and was infatuated with it, fine. But if she wanted to attract our sedate, serious attention with it—no way!

6

WHO MADE THE FIRST MOVE?

After Madam X and Mr. Q snuck undetected into the dark granary, we imagined what happened next. There's just one major unanswered question: who took the offensive—that is, who made the first move?

At the meeting in the dark room, our elites approached this sensitive subject from three different perspectives. After vehement debate, the group finally agreed with the first speaker. They reached their conclusion through a systematic analysis based on comparative studies in the context of a grand historical vision. Several major scholars and sociologists, with important roles in Five Spice Street's ideological realm, took part. The third speaker (Dr. C) impatiently asserted his viewpoint, never imagining that this would lead to a fiasco: the elites of our community shouldn't be underestimated!

The first speaker's (Dr. A) opinion was that the one who took the initiative was Mr. Q, although on the surface, Madam X was a lot more active (for the moment, let's hypothesize that the two persons were two factors) and also seemed constitutionally to be an aggressor, and it appeared that Mr. Q was very passive, as if he were an idiot who had fallen into her trap. Mr. Q—this factor—appeared to be so simple and innocent that it was absolutely plausible that Madam X—this factor—accosted him and tore his clothes off, toying with him as if with a puppet and treating him in a way he didn't deserve. But this scenario describes the way average people would think. It could not delude our Five Spice Street's elites. They've read widely and think profoundly. They don't jump to a superficial conclusion. The debate matured us. We applied the scientific method to history and made strict distinctions and deductions before confirming our agreement with Dr. A. The writer presents excerpts from the three speakers' comments:

Dr. A: From the standpoint of physiology, it is categorically impossible for a woman to have taken the initiative. Even less can it be said that she took the offensive. Despite being aggressive, combative, and energetic on the surface, Madam X couldn't have contravened natural law. Unless she is physiologically abnormal or isn't a woman at all, she is essentially passive. If that's so, who made the first move is even less of a question. Only inexperienced boys and impotent men welcome the myth of the aggressive female. No normal male can accept this kind of sexual experience. Even thinking about it makes them uneasy. Some find it monstrous and frightening.

No, we needn't waste more time on it. The problem is nonexistent. Only because this woman has an abnormal character do we vacillate and abandon common sense. Our premise is that she is a woman. Therefore, we can look at her only as a woman. If, however, she is a monster, then our premise is false. I've seen a lot of women who are aggressive and powerful, but once they're in bed, don't they act the same? Can they turn the world upside down? In fact, they themselves don't wish to. They realize that only by making themselves more feminine can they achieve the joy they seek. Their behavior during the day is intended simply to raise their status in the eyes of the crowd, to create a good self-image, as if they were above men. Men understand their psychology and smile a little with tolerance and understanding. Men don't puncture this little drama, because it's a trivial matter—irrelevant and insignificant. The only thing that matters is what occurs at night. A man might even allow his beloved to show off a little in public, because this expresses the woman's "character." Men are vain: they want their women to have character. They welcome it. The finer a figure a woman cuts, the prouder her spouse feels.

Women have been like this through the ages. They need to be

cherished and also pampered. Men know this. Madam X was unusual in actually challenging men, but how could she escape the destiny of being a woman? I assure you that in the first second in the dark granary, she was panicky and weak, as any other woman would have been, and felt compelled to submit. It goes without saying that the one who took the initiative was Mr. Q. In considering problems, one must not look at the surface, but must pierce to the essence with blade-like eyes. Regrettably, most people can't do this: all they know is blind belief and surveillance. They create bizarre stories. Our people's inertia is too strong and deficient in conscious activity! Yesterday, a simpleton ran up to tell me that Madam X's supernatural ability had a bewitching power that would make our Five Spice Street women the dominant gender. This fatuous ignorance is laughable. Unfortunately, many people support it.

I want to illuminate the issue with an example. Let me talk about my wife. Everyone knows "what she's like," quite an individual sort of woman. Once, during the day, she smashed a chamber pot on my head. I'm not particularly strong in sex; my sex life is disciplined. Was everything simply turned upside down? Did I become cynical and impotent just because my wife had character? Certain people might wish this, but we can deal with women. This is innate. We don't need to contend with them over position: who is superior and who is subordinate is determined by physiology. It can never be changed. A real man should be calm, steady, and properly modest. Women are often impatient and conceited. They aren't comfortable with their passivity and always have to rebel a little. There's certainly nothing wrong with this. Their liveliness increases male libido and makes our sex life even happier, more animated, and so we appreciate life even more. I have to say that marrying a woman with character (as long as it isn't someone like Madam X, who goes to extremes and is involved with magic) is a lifelong blessing for a man. Every quarrel enhances mutual feelings. After the dark clouds have passed, the sky is lucid and blue, and the golden sun shines brightly. I am precisely this sort of lucky man. After twelve years of this fortunate life, I'm still in good health. I have a ruddy face and am in good spirits. Practice has given me a profound understanding of a woman's essence, and I never have any doubts. I'm an expert on this subject. At this point, I must also talk about abstinence. In general, men have limitations in sex. It directly affects our constitution. We are weak in comparison with certain "know-how-to-do-it" women. Thus, abstinence becomes essential. Every happy relationship depends on it. Not only is abstinence good for one's body and mind, but it can also control one's partner, thus letting one reap an even greater pleasure. An overfed person won't appreciate food. A man should always keep his partner half starved so that she'll continue to be interested in sex and will be grateful for what she gets. This is the key to a quality sex life. My wife, for example, often beseeches me with tears. At such times I feel so manly, while she becomes nothing more than a ball of feminine flesh.

Perhaps when Madam X first met him in that large gloomy room, she took the initiative by shooting light waves from her eyes at Mr. Q, scaring him out of his wits. She had the upper hand. But so what? It wasn't a matter of being in bed. It was nothing but a game. At best, we can say, Madam X loves exhibiting herself. After all, women are women: they can't turn themselves into men, no matter how hard they try. But some people love spreading rumors. They talk of a tigress jumping out of some granary and peeling the clothes off the man, and so forth. It seems that they are greatly dissatisfied with their own sex lives and have to manufacture these kinds of monstrous fantasies. They wish their own wives would turn into tigresses so they could enjoy something abnormal. Actually, everyone knows that this tigress-like woman is a figment of their imagination. If a tiger really appeared, they would wet their pants—is anyone brave enough to enjoy this? The more impossible a thing is, the more people daydream about it. People are despicable. Fatuous. I am a teacher. My "spare-time recreation" is level-headed and reasonable. I feel a personal responsibility to fight blindness. I don't want to argue with ignorant persons over non-existent problems. I fulfill my responsibility by preserving moral integrity and my healthy, harmonious sex life with my wife.

I'm not interested in subjective assumptions about Mr. Q's initiative, what actions he performed, and so forth. Artists can provide detailed descriptions, but I work in the realm of theory based on strict scientific foundations. Thus, I've already exploded one myth. Artists need our guidance to construct the big picture, without which they can't create work of high quality. The line drawings on the walls, for instance, present numerous problems. The future is not at all rosy. Few of those artists followed the right guide. They doodled blindly, producing rough works that catered to some people's vulgar and abnormal tastes while debasing serious art. Such novelty elicits cheap applause but also involves ethical problems. Some who are contaminated are reluctant to fulfill their husband-wife obligations. They complain their wives are too tame to satisfy them, so they imagine doing it with a monster like the tigress. This is shocking!

I have an audacious idea. I thought of it after the most recent meeting in the dark room: I suggest mobilizing a campaign among our Five Spice Street men to promote manliness. There are various things we can do. For example, photography can be a significant part of the movement. We can take some group pictures just of men with meaningful facial expressions. At present, we lack such photos. Those hanging in people's homes are all too feminine-looking. Where has our masculinity gone? When did we change into womanly types, losing our gender's superiority to prostrate ourselves in worshipping an imaginary woman? How far we have gone in degrading ourselves! I propose that, beginning tomorrow, our Five Spice Street men go every day to the mountain to train their voices. We want to roar incessantly, show our power, and revive our latent masculine consciousness. We've sunk much too low. We've been sleeping in the swamp, creating a myth of a woman, thinking that with this we would control the spread of impotence. The result was just the opposite. More and more, we became thin-voiced men with wanton, feminized eyes. It was a painful experience. Revenge isn't at all impossible. If we continue being inert, we will be rotten from our very roots and punishment will surely ensue. When that day comes, female demons will emerge on earth. They will roar at the dark heavens, and men's trunks will snap and fall to the ground. Soft fibers will grow in their bodies. It is precisely this that is revenge! This shocking vision has never left my mind. Wake up, men! The tricks that a woman like X deploys naturally don't work with me. If every man were like me, women like X wouldn't exist. The despicable thing is that, unluckily, here we have the soil for her to exist and develop. This kind of poisonous thing grows and flourishes and becomes a menace. Everyone unwittingly talks about it. As it is talked about, the fantasy becomes reality and shackles our brains.

This morning, my wife glared at me with a strange expression. She lifted her chin in a weird way, too. I'm a sensitive man: I immediately felt this change was significant. This was an unprecedented challenge. Compared with this, every fight that had come before—even having the chamber pot smashed on my head—was trivial. Society's pestilence has infected our family life. Marital sex life is about to be wrecked or to change in essence. The man is no longer a man, the woman no longer a woman: they are unimaginable apparitions. I suspect that the day when we men are forced to fight for our very existence is upon us. It isn't a fight with weapons, and the enemy doesn't come from outside. Our enemy is simply ourselves. This unwieldy, indolent body, this rusty brain, our four frozen limbs, these inanimate eyes that indulge in fantasy: let's rebound! Let's preserve our moral integrity! Let's go to the mountain and train our voices! When we're walking, let's lift our feet high! Let's hang our fully masculine photos on our four walls!

Ms. B: Who says women don't have any initiative? This is a colossal misunderstanding. I can assert that more than ninety percent of all women possess initiative. Their libido is much stronger than men's. Their behavior and actions are also much more straightforward. You need only open your eyes and look all around, and you will notice that in nearly all husband-wife relationships, it's the woman who dominates. What are men? Stone, that's all. You have to place this stone on your chest and warm it up and bring it to life. This is the melancholy of women at night. Men are destroyed by their careers: they can never again see how coquettish and charming women are. The world is full of vivacious women and decrepit men. Not only are women superior in sex, but they determine society's historical development!

What does Madam X count for? She took the offensive against one good-for-nothing inside a certain granary. This certainly isn't her invention: everyone can do this; she merely followed convention. Is it possible to imagine that a vivacious woman can squat in a dark corner and simply wait forever, hoping that the stone will become a tiger and at a certain moment pounce on her? Why did she work her way into such a dark place? Because she couldn't control her lust any longer. Could she turn suddenly bashful and wait for the good-for-nothing man to take the initiative? In the dark, no one could see anything. It would have been strange only if she hadn't pounced and bitten that blockhead, and rebuked him: "You son-of-a-bitch—you made me wait so long." Not until the sun rises in the west will a woman wait for the man to take the initiative.

Men sometimes make the first move, but this doesn't mean they take the initiative. They are capricious and nonchalant about what they do. Halfway there, they might suddenly start whistling, or get up for a drink and forget what they're doing. If the woman isn't patient, or if she indulges in wishful thinking, she might go to pieces. You mustn't count on men: what are they good for? Let's just talk of my man. Everyone knows that he's dignified in appearance. He always initiates our "spare-time recreation." When he pounces, he sometimes gives the impression that he's full of energy, but I swear that nine times out of ten he falls asleep on top of me before we actually start doing it. Even if he succeeds once, it's halfhearted. He always complains that there's someone peeping outside the door, so both of us lose interest. It's left unfinished, and yet he seems relieved. Who makes the first move? Men. To whom? Definitely not their women, but a certain illusion. After their fantasy is over, they fall asleep, while women are ignored. They grieve and sigh all night. Decades of experience have made me understand. I haven't counted on men for a long time. I use them and tease them, confuse and disorient them, so they hang around me all day. Yet, I don't give a shit for them. They're all just big-time illusionists. They don't give their wives the time of day. They hate their wives. They call all of us "stumbling blocks," "disasters," and "monsters." In order to cover up their nighttime inability, they whine that they feel bored because we're "frigid." Their sexual energy regresses more by the day. They complain that we can't arouse them and if the situation doesn't change, they'll become impotent. With such nonsensical excuses, they go philandering. They purposely assume a dejected look and refuse to do their work. They sit under the eaves all day and gawk with lusting eyes at the women passing by. They leer and ogle and even make some moves. Naturally, the women welcome this, although at first they pretend to be shy. Then suddenly with quick eye contact, they dodge into a certain dark room to have some fun. But doesn't the quality of the thing change a little? After one or two bouts of illicit sex, does the man become imposing and gallant? Just look around and you'll find the answer.

For example, from these dark-room encounters, men attain a certain kind of "unexpected stimulation," "fresh sentiments," and so forth. Do they then become vigorous? They seem to, making some women think they have become a little too much for them. But they relapse. They're absent-minded, drowsy, and muddled. Just when you're about to come, he suddenly gets up to close the door, sings incessantly, curses people, and so forth. In any case, he relapses and makes a bad showing. A record of men's sexual failures would make an extremely amusing book! There are also those serious men whose facial muscles are strained in the whole process as if it were torture. They're sweaty as though about to faint. You can't help but feel great sympathy, and so you forget about getting pleasure and just hope he feels at peace. You act like this, and yet you get nothing in return. As he is about to leave, he stands there heroically (this kind of man sometimes is very athletic), flings a scornful glance at you, and utters a "hunh" through his nose. He decides that you're dysfunctional, while he is a defeated hero. Other men can't hold up for even a couple of minutes before they're paralyzed like a dead dog, but they don't acknowledge defeat and keep pestering you. They want you to confirm that their couple of minutes were wonderful. In this pestering, they seem to have fabulous stamina. If they had the same in real action, that would be wonderful. Exhausted by hours of this, you have no choice but to tell him "you're wonderful," "it's so great," "you are every inch a man," blah, blah, blah. Only then is he satisfied: he stands up and scampers out happily, leaving you alone and furious in the dark room. This is pretty much the same for all women. The upshot is that women get a raw deal and have to clear away the mess. They are tortured by hunger, too, and are uneasy both day and night. They are left with a good many illnesses that last a lifetime, as well as eternal regret. All serious, pure women die young. Yet, those men who are innately undeveloped can live a very long time. Women create everything and with difficulty sustain all of society. Men reap what they haven't sown and still complain all day long. They say we hamper their careers and don't let them achieve any satisfaction (as if they had big appetites). They've become so weak because of women. They claim we drag them down.

Let's get back to Madam X. What kind of man can Mr. Q be? These two flirted with each other for a long time, yet actually hadn't gone to bed until Madam X racked her brains to come up with a scheme. She dragged this good-for-nothing man into the granary, and only then did she get what she desired. Before that man entered the granary, he must have been irresolute and nervous. It's eighty or ninety percent certain that Madam X kicked him so hard in the butt that he tumbled inside. He got up from the mud, covered in dirt like a drowned mouse. What kind of initiative could he have taken? He was so alarmed that he couldn't figure out what was happening. It's likely that he simply sat on the ground and wailed. Can you expect him to be the one who took the initiative? If Madam X hadn't done her best to comfort him, and hadn't changed her ploy and teased him, he would have wanted to escape from the granary! From the beginning he undoubtedly had the idea of escaping. He wasn't thinking of actually doing this thing. The one who was thinking of doing it was Madam X. Someone may ask: Why did he go to the granary? Did he not want to, did Madam X force him? I can answer: on the way to the granary, he was harboring an illusion—he thought he was going there to observe his beloved's eyes! Hadn't he always been greatly interested in the light in the eyes? When Madam X asked him to go, he was overjoyed. We can imagine that he dribbled the ball as he ran. He thought it was a great opportunity to study the interesting subject in detail. He would never have dreamed that as soon as they went in, Madam X would close her eyes. What she wanted to do was the real thing. In fact, the so-called wavy light in Madam X's eyes was merely an artifice. She first deployed this trick to disarm him and then arranged everything to her heart's desire. This wasn't her invention. It had been around since ancient times, and Madam X was merely very practiced at performing it. As Mr. Q was walking behind her, dizzy from thinking about the wavy light, the clouds, and the butterflies, they reached the granary and he was kicked in the butt and fell. This was a good kick, very educational. He was kicked back to reality and began to fulfill a male's responsibilities. Weeping and wailing were useless, as was any thought of escape. He was in Madam X's clutches: did he dare not perform? So, he did. No matter how, it was done: this was acknowledged at our meeting in the dark room.

How unfair this world is to women! What is there that we don't have to plan, work hard on, and initiate, and what do we get for our efforts? Nothing! In sex, we women take the initiative, but it's the men who reap the pleasure. What a mockery! No matter how hard we try, the world always jokes with us and ridicules our desires. Men are not only poor in bed, but unfortunately they also command public opinion and never acknowledge that they are good-for-nothings. Each one says he's a hero and boasts everywhere that he's made it with lots and lots of women and in one night can perform many times in a row. They thrust out their chests as they walk down the street with their heads high, singing martial songs in loud voices. They leave us crestfallen. Really, anywhere except in bed, they dominate the world and lord it over us. They also say that their careers demand this, and tolerate no opposition. They all talk in a decisive tone. This is sick! It doesn't add up! Since ancient times, women have acquiesced in this. It's really miraculous.

Why do we accept it? Because we're lazy. When men manipulate the world, our eyes remain half closed. We're too lazy to reflect, but just happily parrot men's words. We do so simply to please men, and thereby make things easy for ourselves. Sometimes men really go too far and smear us, even lying about things in the bedroom. We feel wronged and become furious all over again. We want to fight back, but our brains are so rusty that we can't think of any words sharp enough. I've lain in the dark so many times thinking of our sorry condition. I've wanted to cry my eyes out and rid myself of my depression. Sometimes I jump out of bed, intending to wake my husband to interrogate him. I never succeed. After being satisfied, the man immediately falls asleep, dead to the world. There's no way to wake him. By daybreak, he has long since forgotten what happened the night before. He insists he performed like a hero. As he talks, his saliva runs out his mouth and his eyes are bright. Even if we say that it was Madam X who made the first move, so what? I want something more substantial than this kind of victory, which merely follows an ancient convention. The convention harms us, making us satisfied with present circumstances, and we overrate ourselves. So I say that we must not consider the question of initiative or victory. I loathe this initiative. It harms us and probably we'll never be able to get over it. We can't extricate ourselves from the mire, and yet we're still complacent and proud. As it happens, men are quite the opposite. When women are foolishly intoxicated, men figure out ways to strengthen this psychology; they understand profoundly that this is a kind of anesthetic that benefits them greatly. On suitable occasions, they sing our praises—"mother," "goddess," and so forth—but they're quietly laughing their heads off. And so, after being praised like this, our foolish sisters redouble their efforts to curry favor at night and take even more initiative. They take care of these good-for-nothings as if taking care of infants, doing all kinds of things that make people blush. The women are confused and don't even know whether they're satisfied or not.

Sisters, I've had an idea for a long time, and now I've made up my mind to unveil it. I propose that the women of every family establish a blackboard newspaper at the front door and post the men's nighttime performances. Hints and metaphors should be used. As a weekly newspaper it would act as a fire alarm for the whole society, showing our strength. I've thought it over: the reason men are successful is that they dominate public opinion. In any society, the realm of ideology is the most important of all. For years, women did not know this little secret. We've blindly accepted our fate and blindly worshipped those good-for-nothing men. We treat their public statements like decrees and never have our own. Just look at the present situation: Rain or shine, whenever men's blackboard newspapers are posted, women pour onto the street to read them. They scrutinize them and make foolish comments, such as:

"It's just what we are thinking; we need this kind of public voice!"

"Without this sophisticated theory to guide us, how would we ignorant people live?"

"Men have always been saviors. Their heroic spirit moves people. What can we do? Nothing. All we can do is subvert things. We should recognize our fate and our place and wait on men wholeheartedly."

After they read the blackboard newspaper, their silly beliefs grow even stronger. They rack their brains to identify women's weaknesses and redouble their efforts to "make good." Instead of sleeping, some watch over their husbands and repent that they haven't taken good enough care of them or been sufficiently submissive, and so forth. I'm convinced that a slave mentality is not inherent. It is spread through public opinion, and we are unwittingly taken in. We must fight fire with fire and use this weapon ourselves. Then we can turn the world upside down. Men cultivate their shining image in this damn blackboard newspaper and become unbearably haughty and self-absorbed as a result. If we vanquish them in public opinion, the situation will be reversed. When that time comes, our long night of suffering will be over and women will find pleasure, while sleepless men will suffer through the night. We women will be the authentic heroes: not only will we control sex, but we will also dominate society. When that time comes, we won't be hard. We'll be merciful and to the best of our ability let the men, too, achieve their share of satisfaction and happiness.

What is the essence of Madam X's actions? She has nothing to do with the argument I've presented. She will never attain so high a realm. In a dark place, she pounced, or he pounced. It makes no difference: it's meaningless. It has no spiritual value; it has nothing to do with independent consciousness. Nothing's new. I vote for the opinion that Madam X took the initiative, but there's nothing wonderful here. All of us women must work for the blackboard newspaper, for it will inaugurate a new era.

Dr. C: I have a unique opinion. I think they scuffled inside the granary because both wanted to be the first to take the offensive. They struggled for the initiative. The result was that they both got what they wanted: they were enraptured.

Wouldn't any man or woman want to show his or her lust and power? At first, each saw the other as a lion, and himself or herself as an agile hunter. They conceived all kinds of techniques and imagined various difficulties and dangers; then, on a dark cloudy morning, they set out with determination. The whole day, they alternately chased and waited until they were dead tired. Finally, when they were about to run out of patience, they began feeling lightheaded, and the granary was suddenly before them.

Each wanted to be first to occupy this blockhouse, this strategic place for victory. Thus, the lithe, slim-legged Madam X dashed to the front and was the first to enter. The strapping, clumsy Q had a technique, too: he hid outside the granary door and commenced a tactic of attrition. In the dark, they gazed at each other warily with green eyes, neither daring to relax. This standoff must have lasted about three hours. Suddenly, coincidentally, both of them pounced. In the first round, they simply pounced on air. They slipped and fell on their faces, and perhaps Q also lost a tooth. They desisted for about half an hour and then began the second round.

X outflanked him and kept circling inside the granary, planning to make Q faint. Q's tactic was to remain still. He relied on his sturdy constitution and strength. He guessed that X wouldn't be able to topple him. He rested for a while and even smoked a cigarette! The moment he finished his cigarette, X tripped him with her slim leg and Q fell. She also slipped into the mud. Q fell on top of her. X had originally wanted to bite him until he bled. God knows why she didn't, but the two stood up in the same instant and with quivering voices said, "Let's take our clothes off!" They then hurriedly undressed. The moment of rapture had arrived. They embraced. They were biting and pulling each other's hair. X pulled out at least five hundred strands of Q's hair, but I don't know if they really went all the way or not. That was least important, for they had already fully reaped their joy.

Then, they sat on a sack of grain and began singing a song from their childhood—"The Good Times When School Lets Out." With each line, they gave the other a sharp slap in the face, evidently to beat the time. Beating the time made X's tender face swell. Q's face didn't swell, because it was rough and as rigid as wood. Slapping it actually hurt the joints in X's hand. In high spirits, they said, "This is the only way to reach satisfaction. We are the first to experience real, harmonious sex. How pitiful other people are! What do they get from that animal-like intercourse? We really have courage!" Then they kissed. While they were kissing, each also tried to bite off the other's tongue. If it weren't that both were very agile and pulled back, something unbearably tragic might have occurred.

Dear ones, I'd like to make an argument below about the pleasant sensation of sex. For years, this subject has been steeped in endless fallacies and has become almost completely lost. Even with exceptional efforts, we have discovered only a few of its features. But in the end, it turned out to be nothing but a big joke life has played on us. Sexual joy is something miraculous high in the clouds. Indeed, in the meetings in the dark room, the elites have hinted about it with their lip movements. But that's irrelevant! This joy is something you can hardly attain; you certainly can't experience it merely from intercourse. It's a kind of game: when you almost reach it, it glides away from your body. And so you're dejected and blame your partner. You're so angry you jump up and roar: "Why do we want this damn thing? It's even harder to catch than the wind or shadows. To catch it you inevitably fall into your own trap and thrash inside it blindly.

Becoming an ascetic would be a lot easier and simpler. This longing makes me suffer to death! Suffer to death! Within six months, I'll be finished! Fuck the joy—someone has made it up to trick people!" Although you've stated this decisively, as soon as your sweetheart shows up, you'll be sniffing around like an old dog again and reveling in the joy.

Let's return once more to X and Q: they felt in their innermost beings that biting, tripping, and slapping each other was the actualization of joy—and this makes some sense, but it is far from the whole story. If these two vulgar, insignificant people could grasp the profundity in the clouds, then who are we elites? Weren't our years of research all for nothing? I said they made a little sense, because these people are very good at piracy. They aren't qualified to participate, but they try to get secret information from every meeting in the dark room. When they have the opportunity, they use it. In this way, they actually unconsciously achieve a little bit. But since our elites haven't yet grasped the recipe for joy in sex, and are still exploring tenaciously, these two nobodies had nothing to plagiarize. Could it be that scuffling, biting, tripping, and pulling out five hundred strands of hair is the whole recipe for joy? Doesn't this belittle us? Is the scientific research that we do day and night so simple? These two shouldn't be too self-confident: The day will come when we will publicly announce the results of our research. Sooner or later, it will come. Dear ones, let's just wait! Of course, before the results of the scientific research come out, we must keep them confidential. I shouldn't reveal too much at this point. Yet, I can divulge a little of the results of my personal experiments. I'm not unscrupulous, and I dare not boast that I have already grasped the whole secret of this joy in sex. I agree with X and Q that biting and tripping are constituent elements. They are essential first steps. As first steps, they aren't anything wonderful. We can almost posit that everyone can do these things, although in various ways. My little sister—when attempting to get hold of joy—bites her beloved's scalp. She could gnaw out a hollow in the scalp if she didn't do it right. A decent person shouldn't have anything to hide. I will confess to everyone how I almost reached the brink of sexual joy (that highest level). And also how I suffered defeat.

One day, I sat at the window, staring at the clouds, immersed for a long time in a poetic vision. At that moment, I felt very close to that kind of joy, as if I could almost touch it with my hand. A voice said to me, why not go for a walk—go for a walk, there's profundity in it. I jumped to my feet and looked for my wife—my antagonist in sex. Just then she was cutting a hole in the seat of my trousers. She wanted my ass to show when I went out walking. I roared at her, "Go for a walk! Go for a walk!" Then we did go for a walk, as sprightly as immortals. We were both incredibly turned on. When we lay on the bank of the river, it seemed we were about to reach a stage such as we had never experienced before. We were laughing and doing all kinds of things in a careless way.

If it weren't for those damn ants, we would have walked ahead of all the elites and become the most notable scholars, with the most solid achievements and the most profound theoretical foundation. The first place the ants attacked was our private parts: this was a calamity we couldn't have expected. It was over for us. We'd prepared for five hours, walked about ten miles, and were just a half-step from success when suddenly—ants!! Just because of these damn ants, my wife didn't want to be with me. She scolded me wildly, saying that my walk was "plagiarized" from Madam X, and also that the little I had learned was "only skin-deep," that I was "truly disgusting" and would "never be successful." If she hadn't been in the park and caught up with me by mistake—this guy with no prospects—she would long ago have "reached the highest level." With her arms thrust out, she declared: "Joy in sex is my own affair. Why do I need a good-for-nothing like you? Hey! Walk! You fraud! Ass! You've walked my legs off, and what scenery have you discovered? Don't involve me in this again, or you'll be very sorry. I mean it."

Did this so-called high stage consist of no more than walks and ostentatious displays? Was what we cared about most realized in this, and from now on we'd be happy forever? Hey, dear ones, this can't be right. This is nothing more than a lengthy preparatory period. The true, substantial thing, the joy per se, is something very serious: who knows when it will do me in. I understand this all too well. Therefore, why should I take that decisive step? Why? The reason is that I can't find the right partner. My wife and I did go for a walk, and rolled around on the beach, endlessly chasing each other in a certain mood, as if advancing swiftly toward the highest objective. We were both overjoyed, filled with self-confidence. Was it possible that the ants emerged on the scene for no reason? Could outside factors interfere so much in our future? Ha, this was merely a hoax. There might have been ants, and there might not have been ants. It depends on your will. If you think they're there, they are. If you don't pay attention to them, they don't exist. So the sticking point of the problem lies with my wife. She always believed that joy was her affair alone and definitely didn't want to share the joy with me. Not a bit. As for my experiencing this high stage, she was simply a bystander. She said she'd "never feel this." What's more, she also said this was trumped up, "plagiarized," that she'd "rather die than share joy with me." The reason she patiently walked ten miles with me was merely "to see what stupid trick I'd play" and then jeer at me later. She also said that she had never guessed that I was such "horseshit." Those flowery motions were like acrobatic shows. If she wanted to watch a show, she'd be better off spending twenty cents at the theatre. What did these naked acrobatics amount to?

Now, dear ones, do you understand the significance of the ants? Even if you could visualize the joy perfectly, without a partner it would still end in tragedy. My heart is bleeding! There's too much despair, solitude, and loneliness! Too much!! If you think you want to pursue high-level "spare-time recreation," and if you think you want to climb to the peak of joy, defeat awaits you, shock awaits you, and you stand in a deserted field. The sun lengthens your shadow, and lengthens it some more. Under your feet, there's no road you can take. One slight move and you'll lose your balance. Or you'll fall into the grip of a malevolent being, and thus, the damn ants appear.

When you set out, you and your companion are holding hands. You walk on a long riverbank, your heart overflowing with lofty passion. You think everything is going according to plan. You feel you have a good grasp of it. And you feel you've become somebody. You don't realize that you have overlooked one thing, an important matter related to the future. This is none other than my damn wife (when did she bore her way into my life? How did this bitch swindle my trust?). She fully manipulated my purity and my idealism. She masterminded this in secret. She planned to pull off a major hoax. She walked on with me and actually blushed. It seemed that she was even more stimulated than I was, and she kept sighing, "Ah, I truly like you! Ah, I truly like you!" She did this in such a way that I thought she would turn reckless. How could I have guessed that she was feigning? I had already lived by myself so many years in solitude and loneliness, and now all at once I felt I had a soulmate! Didn't I find this most welcome? I was patient, planning to walk the whole ten miles and bring my pursuit of my ideals to completion. My wife couldn't hold back any longer, and in desperation she said I was steely and unfeeling and didn't satisfy her demands. I advised her patiently that this ten-mile walk was the lowest stage and that a higher enjoyment awaited us. If we didn't finish the ten miles, if we didn't let our emotions ferment completely (this was a little like qigong), and if we entered into this hastily, we would regret it in the future. Suppose that all our preparation was merely for that one minute of intercourse that had no feeling at all—wouldn't that be purposely making things difficult for ourselves? We could do that at home. We certainly didn't have to do it so mysteriously.

The more I said, the more spirited my wife became. Just when we were about to reach the place that was our objective, she jumped up and threw me to the ground. She said she wanted to experience this herself. She didn't want me to seize the initiative. At this, my joy was ruined. I lost self-control. I performed the damned one-minute thing as if dead. The color drained from my face, and I was sweating all over. I couldn't believe what had just happened to me! Women: what the hell are they? Where do they get such great strength? Why hadn't I figured out ahead of time all that was going to happen and prepared for it? Why did I give her my trust from the bottom of my heart? Friends, I curse those one-minute quickies. I wish to become an ascetic forever. I will. Only through this will I have any hope, because I've already become a joke, I've already been nearly destroyed.

After the incident of the ten miles, someone behind me was actually furtively happy, wanting to see me make a spectacle of myself. My wife and her confederates privately judged me to be "a kiss-ass," who kissed Madam X's ass, a public enemy of the entire Five Spice Street community. Some days when I was dizzy in the morning and didn't get up, they also crowded into my room, squatted at the foot of the bed, and declared that they needed to observe me and see "what acrobatics I performed under the covers." I didn't dare move. Unluckily, bedbugs also joined in the fun. All I could do was clench my teeth. Had I really been brought down? No. I had to turn my bad luck into momentum and struggle to demonstrate my existence to the world. On the third day after I had completely lost faith in the morals of these times, I began to pull myself together. I climbed to the roof of our thatched cottage and sat there cross-legged. I worked on summarizing all the lessons I'd learned in my lifetime. This included a new description of the high stage of sexual joy. I sat up there quietly, facing the firmament. Below were all the busy living things. I felt truly detached. I could hardly hear the sounds of the world. My thinking progressed steadily toward a high philosophical level. Days went by—both sunny days and rainy days. I'd become fossilized on the roof of the thatched cottage, or I had become a white-haired, omniscient old philosopher. I merged into the great universe and embraced the whole world. Humankind became adorable, even though their ways of having sexual intercourse were so absurd.

One day, in a gentle mood, while immersed in abstract thought and with a slight smile on my face, I felt unbearable pain in the soles of my feet. I almost fainted. My thoughts were interrupted. I heard loud shouting from below. With my wife in the lead, a group of people were jabbing me with sharpened bamboo poles. They were shouting, "Bring this pile of horseshit down from the roof." They also said, "The smelly fart from the roof has gotten into the cooking pot." The fart "was the smell of the public enemy of Five Spice Street's people." Their shouting grew louder and louder. It was impossible to defend against their assault. My neck, chest, and ass were hit several times. My blood streamed down. Seeing this, my wife and her followers were so frightened they threw the bamboo poles away and ran off. I heard them talking to each other and disclaiming responsibility. The disturbance had ended, and once more philosophical thoughts occupied my mind. I felt that I had become steadier than ever. A gigantic consciousness of self-confidence was obscurely nascent. Who was I? What was my mission? Why was I sitting alone on the roof while people all over the world were playing out the drama of life below me? After forty-nine days, or maybe sixty-four days (I had long since lost any sense of time), I finally came down from the roof, bringing with me a crystal-clear mind. When I walked into the dark room, all the elites present were filled with deep esteem: they shook with anxiety at each step I took.

Dear ones, probably you think I'm going to launch into a tirade or the summary of my thoughts on the roof of the thatched cottage? Hadn't a torrential argument already accumulated in my mind? Wasn't my incomparable eloquence already mature? I swept grim eyes over all the people in our community and then slowly sat down. The hoped-for event didn't occur. Having seen me on the roof, who would dare speak nonsense, or recklessly spread generalities about experiences they had not had in order to temporarily satisfy their vanity? So all of them were waiting, looking with children's eyes at my lips. They didn't dare miss anything. I said just one thing, "This is a tragic time. Higher sexual joy can exist only in our illusions." With that, I raised my eyebrows, sat cross-legged, and once more became the fossil on the roof. The room was silent. Everyone's head drooped. The last rays of twilight fell. Night would soon descend, and the cold wind poured in from the broken window: the atmosphere in the meeting room was icy. What I'd already said summed up everything, and I didn't say another word during the meeting.

Who else but the old philosopher who had spent forty-nine or sixty-four days cross-legged on the roof could have uttered these words?

Their impact was overwhelming. Their aloofness and worldly pessimism would have convinced any intellectual regardless of his experience. After the meeting broke up in silence, I can assure you that the intellectuals were no longer concerned with Madam X and Mr. Q. The little slights were all low level. This was not what we needed. "That day" will eventually come. The tide of history can't be stopped. On a foggy morning, holding hands and shoulder to shoulder, we will sit by the street and sing a song: *"That day* is still far away. Everyone should wait quietly. In the silence comes the song of the lark. Life is this weighty. We moan in the midst of torment. Ah, we moan . . ." I'm also the writer of this philosophical song, now popular on our Five Spice Street. Even people like my wife are inspired by it. Once, at midnight, she suddenly rushed into the garden and belted it out. Then she started slapping herself.

Ever since I wrote the song, no one had paid attention to X and Q. Because of my curiosity and fantasies, I observed them but discovered that their little tricks were of no use to theoretical research. From the time I climbed up to the roof of the thatched cottage, I uncompromisingly expunged those two people from my research. I began considering the mutuality of elevation and popularization. X and Q still had a great influence on the crowds (though curling their lips, everyone secretly watched every move they made). But if I put the issue on the table or publicly debated it, I'd get caught in a dogfight, so all of my research would become obsolete. This would be a gross misstep, not in accord with my status. Dear ones, don't worry: I didn't engage in that nonsense. I squatted as steadily as Mt. Tai on the roof of the thatched cottage and considered a counter-measure—the popular song, whose profound pessimism would influence the crowds. I knew this wouldn't be very useful, for while on the roof, I had given up all conceit. But I was determined to do it this way because I wanted to break the monopoly of X and Q in the realm of consciousness. As soon as I put this plan into effect, the elites would tacitly understand, and their understanding would turn around the consciousness of Five Spice Street.

Of course, this isn't to say that they possessed consciousness or that I became optimistic. Definitely not. My pessimism had long since penetrated to the marrow of my bones. The crowd's consciousness should rather be said to be like a plastic plaything. You melt it into whatever shape you want. From the bottom of my heart, I believed they had no true consciousness except for what was shaped by the elites, and the elites' inspiration came from my enlightenment. I sensed obscurely the possibility of future high-level sexual joy and communicated it to the elites through an ordinary popular song. After the elites acknowledged this (there is a qualitative difference between acknowledgment and comprehension; no one could comprehend my abstract consciousness, because it was divine will), they indoctrinated our beloved ordinary folk with it as if force-feeding ducks. Then the beloved folk would begin strolling on the main street like drunks, belting out these high-level lyrics of mine. It may have looked like blasphemy or a farce to an outsider, but what else could we do?

This is life. I had achieved my goal. Who cares how? The fact is that X and Q's influence had already been swept away. What they did in the granary was purely low-level. The people had already unwittingly recognized another high-level format. They didn't know what it actually was or what they should feel about it, but still they recognized it. Some people might still be confused, some might be weeping sadly, some might be dreaming, some might be filled with enmity. Still, they recognized it. In any case, I am the winner.

The writer has already made it clear above that the first speaker was supported by the vast majority of the elites, and controlled public opinion on Five Spice Street. The women who supported the second speaker merely pretended to be crazy and made a terrific fuss for a while. It was over soon. It had no effect: it was no more than a "tempest in a teapot." It seemed that one day, all of them chopped boards at their doors and unanimously threatened to make black-boards from them, but after they'd chopped for a while, they all threw the axes down and went into the public toilet and began discussing the movement. They talked exultantly. They believed that as soon as the blackboards came into use, they could hold their heads high. They wouldn't put up with being deceived any longer. Some of them even decided to sleep that night in separate beds from their husbands, to starve "these old dogs." But as soon as they emerged from the toilet, they forgot about the blackboards. They left the axes on the ground and went around visiting, talking animatedly, as if from now on they would break from the old days and their new, high-level life would begin. "Madam X is a piece of shit, though she did enlighten us in some ways." They all agreed on this. But as for action, they took none. That night, they took care of their men as always. Driven by guilt, some were even more humble and wished to hold their men all through the night. The next morning, their eyes not yet fully open, the men discovered those planks of wood and axes. Before they had time to ask anything, the women began cursing loudly, saying that thieves had come in the night. "They were going to pound the doors and windows down and come in and pilfer." Luckily, it was discovered in time, and they threw down the axes and took off. "Too contemptible!" they shouted. "They wanted to wreck our happy family life. If I hadn't discovered this in time, wouldn't they have also murdered us?"

The writer was impartial: he could only record this awkward, embarrassing incident. We couldn't understand why women had this bad habit of making a great start and then not following through. Beloved readers, I don't intend to deprecate our lovable women of Five Spice Street (I don't have to mention that there were many pretty, voluptuous ones among them). Perhaps it's only a tiny flaw. Anyway, who's perfect? And so our comments on the second speaker had better end here.

The third speaker is truly lonely (C). But his powerful eloquence, his philosophical theorizing, and his well-known communication with God actually cowed all the elites into submission. There was a time when the majority agreed with him. In several rounds of debate, he almost beat out the first speaker. But just as he was about to triumph, history played another trick on us. Madam X jumped out from the dark granary whose location we didn't know, and announced to every passerby: she wanted to establish a "normalized" relationship with her beloved! This lightning bolt so shook the elites that their eyes flashed with red and green sparks. Those supporting the first speaker immediately assembled and hooted: "What is a woman? Ah? Look, this is the beginning of retaliation! The krait has crept out of the cave! What civil war are we still fighting? We're on the verge of calamity!"

Really, it was this damn Dr. C whose third opinion actually fostered Madam X's wicked bluster. He had sat on the roof for forty-nine or sixty-four days: did this mean that he must have talked with the gods or the heavens? Can it be proven? Only his wife verified what he had done, but she didn't verify any communication between him and the gods, or that he had reached any high-level sexual joy. Rather, she verified that while he was on the roof, he had farted several times because of indigestion, and these farts had gone into her cooking pot. After Madam X had tugged at every passerby and announced her intention, all the elites suddenly became crazy and cursed Dr. C fiercely, temporarily forgetting their upbringing and manners. They said it was this politician (that's what they called C) who had put forward some dirty advocacy of high-level sexual joy and also had come up with some sort of popular song, thus abetting Madam X in her arrogance and caprice. In the past, these two publicly unknown cockroaches (for the moment, that's how they decided to refer to X and Q) had never had this kind of courage. Because of C's agitation, all of Five Spice Street's ordinary people would become immodest and restless, just waiting to see. Immoral things would occur. If things turned out like this, how could we elites face society and how could we continue to hold the fucking meetings? Thinking of these questions with bitter hatred, the elites felt regret for the first time. When C climbed up to the roof like a centipede, no one had predicted this outcome. Everyone had watched with admiration from their small windows, as if entrusting him with all their responsibilities and obligations, and waited to enjoy the harvest he would bring. As he looked up at the firmament (in fact, he was calculating), we gasped unanimously in admiration, hoping that he would redeem our world, and redeem our souls as well. We also foolishly sang the popular song he used to trick us! What kind of "popular song" was it? It's too shameful to hum even one word of it now. We really wished we could hide in a closet and not come out! Just think, even the elites behaved disgracefully. It was nauseating to remember. And what about the ordinary people? What about X and Q?

The time for firm measures has arrived, dear ones! We mustn't hesitate any longer. We have to correct our position and take Mr. A's viewpoint as our motto. Let's learn it thoroughly. The meetings will continue. Everyone must gouge his selfishness from the deepest part of his soul, put the filthy thing on the table, and dissect it with a scalpel. There is a kernel in Dr. A's lecture—his point about the masculine spirit. The reform he mentioned is significant; unlike just taking photographs, it contains a truly qualitative change. If we realize this change, we'll reach a new realm. Our bodies will grow strong muscles, our mustaches will be thick and dark, our voices deep and stentorian. Our gestures will be vigorous and convincing. With such photographs on our walls, the world will change into a man's world filled with masculine activities.

We elites have made mistakes. We have decided to correct our weaknesses. To start we can use a back thrust, or it's also all right to say that we will turn our guns backwards and shoot. We'll aim at Dr. C. Having stripped off his mask, we see the original. How can he be considered a major scholar or a philosopher? Someone carefully identified him and remembered that years ago he was a peddler selling quack medicine at the Five Spice Street intersection. Later, he changed his identity and bored his way into the ranks of our elites. Does this suggest that we're a bunch of fools who mixed up a peddler with a philosopher and social elites? Here, we must emphasize a little something: his "sudden change of identity" didn't occur overnight, but only after assiduous study—after exerting the strength of a peasant in a field of books. Lapping up information without digesting it, he finally reached the high level that he occupies today. At first everybody respected his erudition. He was very good at suiting his actions to circumstances and saying whatever people wanted to hear. Knowing we didn't like compliments, he might not compliment us. He just refined our thoughts. As soon as we stated our opinions, he immediately followed up with his, expounding reasonably, causing you to be delighted and to accept him as a comrade, as a most beloved friend and confidant. After many years of hard study, this damn medicine peddler changed and became erudite and multi-talented. If it hadn't been for this unfortunate incident, who would have remembered his origins? Hadn't he been on the same footing with us not long ago? One bad element among us had purposely praised him, wanting him to ascend so that he himself would skyrocket ahead! That bad element had also tried to climb to the roof of the thatched cottage and participate with C in the swindle of the dialogues with the gods. It was only because the rafters were rotten and couldn't support the weight of two people that he had to give up his plan. During those forty-nine or sixty-four days, he waited under the roof. If there was the slightest sound from above, even a fart, he would announce this to others and say that he was "the old philosopher's proud disciple" and that he "was almost united in one body with the old philosopher."

All the elites believed their greatest weakness was that they didn't learn enough from history; they suffered from amnesia. It was only eight years ago, or maybe twelve years ago, that this C had been a medicine peddler: how had we forgotten? While the tune he sang to peddle fake medicine was still in our ears, how could we forget and blindly worship him? It was as if we were purposely forgetting, or as if we considered his squalid background part of his glorious struggle. After recognizing this, the elites decided to have meetings in the dark room once every three days instead of once every five, and in urgent situations, once a day, in order to exchange views and summarize them in a timely fashion and to guard our homeland as tightly as an iron pail that "would not allow even a mosquito to fly in."

Okay. Let's look at how X implemented her "normalization"! Is normalization the same as legalization? First, we can dismiss this possibility, because the relationship between her and him definitely cannot be legalized. Never! So, how did she "normalize"? Did she jump out from that dark granary to the main road and have sex in broad daylight? Did she force her way into Old Meng's loft and live openly with an adulterer? Neither solution would work. We are "waiting"! This "waiting" isn't something we can easily deal with. X and Q had learned lessons from it in the past. We should consider X's pronouncement a kind of overstated exhibitionism. According to Dr. A's theory, a woman is simply a woman. How much difference could she make? She may have overcome Q (perhaps in fact Q overcame her), but that didn't mean that she could overcome all of our elites. She may perform her "normalization" in midair: she's certainly welcome to try; she just shouldn't make a clamor. C took her hen-like cackle as a stage of sexual joy. Fuck! We'd rather cut off our tongues than accept this. She might have taken advantage of C's foolishness and performed her joyful activities in dark places at first and then moved to the open street. Does that mean that we elites have to stand on the same side with her? Fuck! If she allied herself with C and put together a mighty battle array and then forced her way into Old Meng's loft, would our elites have to retreat to avoid a conflict, or would they flee at the sight of the oncoming force? Fuck! As we see it, there's something wrong with X's mind. She must think that she and Q had become invincible to dare to make such an uproar on the street. Otherwise, why did she previously have to hide? Otherwise, why was it that no one had located the granary, which so far existed only as a hypothesis? Analysis of her past behavior showed that X did have this weakness. She would become overconfident and intoxicated too soon, unaware that fierce battles awaited her. Really, now an excess of self-confidence would cause her defeat. Even if she were smarter than others and had the ability to plan and perform, this self-confidence—so distant from reality—would ruin everything she had imagined.

I ask you, if a person wasn't a lunatic and possessed common sense, would she have the guts to announce publicly that she wanted to "normalize" a relationship with an adulterous lover? Absurd! As a matter of boasting, it's probably okay, but she said it with an unusually serious and frightening expression to passersby who had nothing to do with it! I hate it, hate it, hate it! Let her go to the North Pole to normalize her relationship! Let her go to some doghouse to normalize her relationship! Just don't do it on our Five Spice Street. We don't approve of this kind of "normalization." Sooner or later we would expunge this man and this woman's existence from the stenographer's historical records and never mention their "normalization" again. If C is right and her mind is normal, wouldn't all our elites, as well as ordinary people, be lunatics? This C was the source of evil: he ruined everything With his above-average petty trick, he had almost reversed the wheels of history. Luckily we had the insight to refute his argument swiftly. What a great danger we averted! But for this, these three might have forced themselves into Old Meng's loft when no one was watching and made it their beachhead. It would have been a thorn in the flesh of the people of Five Spice Street and would have remained an iron reality! Then the stenographer would have had to record this damn thing in his notebook! The optimists might think that even if the plot were realized, it would have been only temporary: in the end, they would have been swept into the dustbin of history. This is wrong. What is most frightening? A latent virus. For example, C had been lying low for eight years or maybe twelve and eventually created this major uproar. After eight or twelve years, what kind of unbearable situation would result from these three viruses lying low in Old Meng's loft? Friends, you must never be off guard, you must never be careless when seriously discussing theoretical questions. Let us continue to be acutely aware of reality. Let us strictly prevent viruses from invading! This time, X unscrupulously announced that she would "normalize." Next time, life-and-death warfare may befall us! In general, though, there won't be any warfare, because she will completely fall apart: how is she qualified to battle with us? Ha!

7

HOW TO WRAP UP ALL THE ISSUES LEFT HANGING

Having brought the story to this point, the writer has left innumerable issues hanging. The story cannot end here. Everyone on Five Spice Street knows it's not over. So the writer must do his best to clarify the mess piece by piece. It has no beginning ("The Beginning" is merely an assumption), and has no ending, either. If earth and sun collide, the story may end but will no doubt begin again on another planet. The writer's task is like boring into the maze of a gigantic anthill, but he cannot shirk it. He knows through experience that only the methods of abstract art, used in diagramming each aspect of the maze, will enable him to lead readers to grasp the "general idea," even if they can't find their way through the specifics. This is the fascination of art. Though it can't be fathomed, it has supreme influence. Only the heartless and coarse have nothing to do with art.

The First Diagram of the Maze

Does Madam X really exist? Why does she exist on Five Spice Street? It seems too late to raise this question. Could we have described such a complex historical episode, duping vast numbers of readers, if it turned out to be nothing but trumped-up nonsense? Would we do this just for fun? It isn't so simple, beloved readers. We are all mutually dependent. The lesson taught me that you are closer to me than my parents, and more important, too. I would never be flippant with any of you. My objective is only to kindle doubts and criticisms, to purify our ideological dimension. After the writer's investigation, which has undergone scrupulous examination, and after compiling various opinions, he decided that the following questions were worth consideration.

First of all, this Madam X was no genius. Aside from her work in the snack shop and her deceptive sorcery, she had no special skill. On our Five Spice Street, very few geniuses (for example, the writer and the widow) were truly aloof. It appears that Madam X is really a lonely person; indeed, she's even lonelier than the writer or the widow. She kept secrets not only from her husband but also from her lover Mr. Q. Everything she did resembled an improvisational act. Had she ever revealed any of her innermost feelings? Absolutely not, not even a hint. Only geniuses are mighty. And the mightiest are the loneliest. X is neither a genius nor is she mighty, yet she is inscrutably lonely. What on earth is she? Perhaps this person does not exist at all. Is it possible that she is merely a figment of our imagination, an expression of our collective consciousness?

Just this morning, however, the writer saw her selling beans on Five Spice Street! She was tying an apron around herself. Her hands were rough. Aside from the expression in her eyes, which were still unusually empty, she was no different from anyone else. Hardly a genius, she wasn't even part of the elite (she had never been close to our intellectuals; instead, she seemed to stay as far away as possible). The writer had once seen Mr. Q suggest timidly that he perhaps belonged to the elite stratum; all at once, she flushed. "Hunh," she said, "luckily, I can't read. It is a great advantage." Mr. Q's face turned red. Where had this weirdo come from? How could she reside on Five Spice Street?

It seemed that we had to investigate this from another angle. We couldn't keep focusing on X herself but had to return to our own concepts, carefully straighten them out and test them, and learn where the defects lay so that the mistakes could be corrected. Of course, we couldn't do this without aesthetic awareness. Aesthetic awareness was always the wellspring of our creation.

The writer started his work by analyzing the concept of loneliness: what essential difference was there between Madam X's loneliness and the loneliness of real geniuses? The loneliness of geniuses was a thing that surpassed reality and surpassed space and time. One was born with it. No one could imitate it. This type of rare person is usually sitting on a deserted mountaintop or the roof of a thatched cottage (like C; of course C wasn't a genius—he merely imitated one remarkably well) while engaging in conversation with the gods. His body gives off golden rays. Ordinary mortals like us cannot hear that dialogue. He is a static sage or a fossil. Only the highly cultured who rid themselves of selfish ideas can sometimes recognize him when they look up. He doesn't always sit on a mountaintop or the roof of a thatched cottage to maintain his solitude. He also has an uncommon warmth and attentiveness for humankind. His solitude consists in always walking in the vanguard of history, and humankind doesn't understand him in time. When he comes down from the mountain-top or the roof of the thatched cottage, he becomes one of us: there's no way to tell him apart. He participates in ordinary affairs and perseveres in guiding others. He transmits the macrocosmic and microcosmic worlds he has seen from the mountaintop or the roof of the thatched cottage and leads everyone to propel the wheels of history forward. In his lifetime, the writer has met one or two such sages. It's easy for the same types to recognize each other.

What is Madam X's solitude? The writer considered this exhaustively and concluded it was a wholly morbid thing. Her solitude resulted from obstinacy. A person who neither converses with the gods nor possesses education and who practices that sort of common trade isn't elevated above the crowds. Her haughtiness and disdain arise from inner weakness and manifest her struggle to achieve selfish ends. This morbidity is as follows: against all reason, she is able to make her eyes "retire" so that they no longer "see any people." She can actually grow a plate of armor over her whole body so that "nothing can penetrate it" and "she doesn't feel any outside attack." Her way of interacting with ordinary people is bizarre: she calls them by random names. Even more annoying: she fakes the loneliness of geniuses in order to delude everyone! Who's interested in the solitude of an ice cave? If she died in that cave, no one would know or be alarmed. The ice would seal the cave for years and no one would notice! Her loneliness is part and parcel of her own madness; it has nothing to do with ordinary people. She had definitely better not try to identify it with the loneliness of our geniuses. While we accepted Madam X's impersonal existence on Five Spice Street, some confused people sometimes forgot that she was just a sick, inferior person. They were mistaken about some of her odd behavior. They got excited about it and raised X's image, forming a dense fog around her. Outsiders who didn't know the whole story would think Madam X was some kind of genius. Only because of this did people question whether Madam X was real, and why she existed on Five Spice Street. This question grew bigger by the day and branched out. It became mysterious and inexplicable. If pursued to the end, this train of thought would exhaust anyone to death—no matter how erudite. The writer's conclusion was: Madam X's loneliness was essential to her individual psychosis and wasn't at all worth investigating.

Next, we want to speak of Madam X's special work. It might seem that Madam X is actually engaged in the special work she calls "dispelling boredom." This work isn't at all clear. You'd never succeed in investigating it, and if you tried, you'd become a laughing-stock. One or two guys with evil intentions would love to see the writer try this. They would say: let's see what kind of silly explanation you can come up with for this stubborn historical problem. Stenographers and artists are annoying gossips. Let's hope they bungle everything they write. The more plagued and haggard they are, the better. We wish all the stenographers and artists in this world would die! Readers! You cannot imagine the risks of a writer's work. How often the writer struggles to survive the dangerous shoals and the swift current.

Did this damn problem stump the writer? Would the writer drown silently if he didn't pull back from the difficulties? Those of you with ulterior motives, please be patient: the main show hasn't started yet! The writer wants to avoid answering this question directly and will pull the threads really long—until they lead him to

Madam X's distant and obscure youth. Let us join material from X's sister with the writer's imaginative power into a picture of Madam X's shadowy youth. That very thin little girl, with wild fiery eyes, hopped around all day long and yapped like a puppy. Her fingernails were long and sharp, and she had never been able to "pick up" things easily; rather, when she saw things, she "clawed" at them. She clawed countless holes in the colorful shirt she wore. Except for her silly little sister, she considered everyone around her enemies. She played games of murder incessantly. She was merciless and ruthless (the time she threw her mother's spectacles proves this). Even if she suffered a thrashing (her parents, at their wits' end, did this once or twice), it didn't occur to her to repent; rather she came up with countless "new tricks" for revenge. After this devilish child grew up and left home, she discovered that in this world, her childhood tricks would not work. If she persisted, she risked destruction. She didn't change her essential self, but she wasn't a blockhead, either. On certain occasions, she was very flexible! As the years rolled on, her murderous psychology did not diminish but actually grew by the day! But she understood very well that this world didn't offer an opportunity to express it. If she couldn't control this instinct, she would die.

My beloved readers! Friends! Having read to this point, you've certainly guessed the truth, haven't you? Flexible and with small intelligence, Madam X chose our Five Spice Street to fulfill her childhood dreams. She had investigated Five Spice Street and learned that the people were nice, warm, honest, and magnanimous. She concluded that no matter what kind of disturbance she made, she would incur no punishment. And so, not long after settling down here, she bought those evil props—mirrors and a microscope. She smiled slightly when she played with those things, and her motions were terribly exaggerated. She "celebrated" the beginning of this "work" with her husband and son and then closed the door and ignored others. It's said that one day, holding her precious son on her lap, she taught him how to look through the microscope with one eye, and he did this for more than half an hour. Then the two of them rolled happily around on the bed. They said they'd seen "the most interesting stuff in the world." She also said that she would "give" her son all she had lost when she was a child.

The situation immediately became unmanageable. The woman spent every day inside, leading her "double life." In the daytime, she spent the whole day with her head buried in her small trade. When the people of Five Spice Street passed by her shop, they would be blinded, absorbed in observing her eyesight, her neck, and so forth. No one sensed that, when they turned around and left, she stared fiercely with hawk-like eyes at their receding backs. (One time, the writer suddenly turned back and met her eyes. The writer grew dizzy as a result and had to lie down for three days. He is still suffering from the effects.) So you see the sacrifice artistic work requires. It's not something those hooligans can understand. In the public toilet, they labeled the writer a "fame-fisher." The murderous scene flashed from her innermost being. We had never seen that kind of murder without lethal weapon or blood. People became aware of it only through the writer's analysis, which explained profound things in a simple manner. Maybe instead of being actually "aware," they could only "understand it in a general way."

There was no so-called "double life" at all: it was a smoke bomb she had set off herself. Everything she did—running a small business (that was her device for staring at people's backs), closing the door (that was her device for analyzing the terrain and choosing her battlefield), looking in the mirrors at night, and engaging in adultery with Mr. Q (to reinforce her plot by adding a conspirator)—in fact, all of these were one thing. Even her sleeping at night was a ploy to conserve strength and store up energy. Otherwise, how could she behave with such spirit in her murderous activity? No one took better care of herself than she did. Someone might object: so what about those teenagers? Was it possible that they, too, were taking part in her murderous activity? At one point, they raced to her house every night and sat there seriously without moving. Not all of them longed to be killed by her or thought it would be a great pleasure. The writer once more must stretch the threads out very far—to the time before Madam X and her family came to Five Spice Street.

Back then, no one knew of Madam X's existence, and her murderous plan was still hidden in her mind; she hadn't yet taken any action. After entering Five Spice Street in disguise and implementing a lot of on-the-spot reconnaissance, she framed her plan. Then she embarked on carrying it out. The teenagers were her first targets. After consideration she decided to employ means whose effects would resemble smoking dope. The fad-loving teenagers were very happy. They went every night in high spirits. Some even proclaimed that they could "adopt this method to become well known." How could they prevent Madam X from injecting them with poisons? Although sometimes they hated her and stole her shoes, and so forth, in general they were innocent, infantile children wholly in X's clutches.

Did Madam X's unusual powers and murderous activity create a great tragedy? Excuse me, here the writer must speak only of the facts and real situation. The real situation was: except for her colleague's son, who had indeed been affected, she hadn't harmed anyone else's physical or mental health at all. Because of the climate on our Five Spice Street, people who were already living here possessed a kind of immunity. Madam X overlooked this in her reconnaissance. With this immunity, we could be marinated in poisonous juices for years and still retain good health. As for the colleague's son, he was poisoned because of a serious childhood disease that destroyed his immunity. Madam X jumped for joy because of this *one* success. Her precious husband's foolish chatter made people laugh their heads off. He told everyone about her "great power," "mighty as an A-bomb." Madam X called this success "an unexpected harvest" (she didn't intend to affect anyone; as she claimed, she had long since completely "forgotten" everyone around her). "It didn't occur to me that there would still be one left for me!" She was enraptured. "This is really a nice, nervy child! Maybe he too will create miracles."

We will get "more of a general idea" if we examine the incident of the colleague's son more carefully. This son was the colleague's own flesh and blood. And from the day he was born, he had the same immunity as other children on our Five Spice Street. Later, he unfortunately contracted a serious disease and lost this protection. But this isn't the same as affirming that he must necessarily have become the person he is now. Ahead of him a bright broad road was rolling out. With the guidance of elders, he could have averted disaster and disease and grown up to be one in a thousand. One summer at dusk, he was mesmerized by a strange shout, and following it, he walked into Madam X's home. There, he stayed woodenly for two hours and went crazy. Suddenly all his mother's painstaking efforts in bringing him up turned to nothing. Madam X's plot was an "acetabulum" that sucked him in so tightly he couldn't get away. When his mother asked about this frightening "acetabulum" and tried to help him detach himself, he flew into a rage. He denounced his mother's good intentions as "murder" and said he would "rather die" than change back! Terrible! Was Madam X really not aware of the havoc she caused? Did she think only of her own inner tranquility when she did her damnable work at night? Who would buy this bullshit?

If a person wanted to remain aloof from worldly affairs in order to cultivate herself, she wouldn't do such things. Madam X flaunted her dynamism; she expressed fake inhospitality; her activity achieved impersonal effects (although very small); and she was utterly determined: everything substantiated our established view. Could a person who had secretly cultivated murderous intentions since childhood become detached, expunge those intentions, and blindly start attending to her inner tranquility so as to become a saint? Is it possible that she simply ignored the youthful, tender bodies of those teenagers swaying before her eyes instead of pouncing and biting them? If she had really ignored them and become detached, she should have sat on the roof of a thatched cottage or on a mountaintop and communed with the gods. On the contrary, she was surrounded by crowds all day, and only at night did she fuss with broken mirrors or create dubious miracles. Yet she dared talk of detachment!

Now, as soon as X talks of detachment, we "turn pale." Our "turning pale" doesn't mean that we look terrified. Our "turning pale" is rather like "having a stern countenance." By this we show that we have completely seen through her deception. Everyone was watching her! Her detachment = murder. Probing it this way, we "completely grasped the general idea." If we consider this from the standpoint of murder, Madam X not only hadn't "forgotten" the people around her, she was on the alert all the time. Her movements were full of tempting traps aimed at her quarry. (Too bad only one had fallen for the bait.) What else was she relying on? She claimed that her eyes had "retired." This was also a crafty trick. (Otherwise, why bother making an official announcement?) Nobody knew that in the back of her head, she had grown a third eye. This eye was even more formidable. Though it didn't penetrate everything, it "was like a sharp sword." With this mystical eye hidden in her hair, she saw everything in the world: she had her finger on everyone's pulse. Our naïve, simple people saw only the two eyes that she had "set" on her face. Many swallowed what she said, and thought that she really had begun to be detached. Someone even talked of her detachment and a genius's aloofness in the same breath! X manipulated the gullibility of ordinary people and talked self-importantly about her philosophy of "detachment." She said that her detachment was higher than that of geniuses, and more profound. At any time and any place, she could "divide herself in two." If she didn't will it, the "two would become one again." She didn't have to climb up to the roof of a thatched cottage or to a mountaintop in order to commune with the gods. She could do this whenever she wished. And she boasted that her dialogue would be loftier than that of the geniuses, as though she had already surpassed them.

She also had some blasphemous abuse for geniuses: "They exaggerate the facts and put on airs. People live in such a weary way that most became exhausted a long time ago: how would anyone still have the strength to climb up to the roof of a thatched cottage or up to a mountaintop? Most die before they grow up. Just think how fragile people are: how is it possible to be a genius? Luckily, I haven't been bothered by such thoughts. I have no interest in being a genius. Long ago, my body grew a protective armor-plated layer. I can never again be thin-skinned and quick to anger as geniuses are. I am callous to almost everything. This has made it possible for me to protect my inner serenity and remain as happy as a clown. There are no geniuses today. There are just some people who, from inner fragility or terror, use this word to fool others. They think if they flaunt it, they'll become detached and won't be responsible for anything. The word hangs on their tongues all day long. Every time they run into someone, they boast that they'll soon be qualified to talk with the gods, blah, blah, blah. I don't sympathize with them at all: they look for trouble. Every idle genius should take a job and live the life of an ordinary person, working hard for daily necessities, and then, in his spare time, he can do his so-called genius work, which is nothing so wonderful."

Everyone could see she was saying this in order to vent her jealousy. She was well aware she wasn't good enough to be considered a genius, and she begrudged anyone who was fortunate enough to be one. Over time, she perfected this rationalization When she got on the subject, she tried to show she was confident and knew everything. She would look upward and show the whites of her eyes to express her "aloofness." Who among her listeners knew that in fact her third eye was hard at work? She cared deeply about other people's assessment of her! If someone had discovered her "third eye" and pointed out that her "aloofness" was a fraud, she would probably have fainted! On Five Spice Street we all knew: whenever someone expressed contempt for a certain thing, that thing was what he or she secretly desired. Madam X was talking like this, yet there was not a moment when she didn't look forward to being recognized as on an equal footing with the geniuses. She disguised her ambition well, but why else would she attack geniuses? She knew that no one on our street had ever judged the handful of geniuses who stood high above ordinary people. They were our leaders, our guides, the idols we venerated. Madam X knew this: she knew that only by blaspheming geniuses could she get people to pay attention to her and set her in their ranks. Unwittingly, people would talk of her and the geniuses in the same breath. This was precisely what she desired. She was overjoyed and declared that "turning the world upside down" gave her the greatest happiness.

We might as well say that this declaration was one component of her murderous nighttime activity. It also showed her stupidity. If she wanted to be a genius, she needed to be down-to-earth and endure humiliation and thereby gain the people's trust. She could never achieve her objective by being so blindly self-indulgent and using such crooked ways. Who had ever seen a misfit succeed? Just think of how much castigation and censure the writer had endured to reach the position he holds today, and yet the people still haven't publicly recognized him as a genius (the writer knew that this was because they were exceedingly prudent; in fact, they had long ago tacitly recognized him. The writer understood this). Madam X was a different case. She did nothing (just think about the writer's difficult interviews!). She "had nothing to do with people." She just hid out in her little room, engaging in magic. How could she expect to be recognized as a "genius"? Isn't she insane? She even attempted to alter the definition, declaring that the common practice of geniuses (climbing up on a thatched cottage or a hill) was "merely an artificial pose," and that they "didn't have to be that serious," blah, blah, blah. Wasn't she implying that we had to accept her redefinition of genius? Of course, she also said that there were no geniuses today, that they were already a thing of the past. She had only one goal: "to turn the world upside down." And from this, she reaped unfair gains. We can say for sure: Madam X was definitely unable to do anything like climb to the roof of a thatched cottage or climb to a mountaintop. She suspected that the gods would punish her—whether by lightning or by accidental death. She ridiculed things she couldn't do, saying it wasn't that she couldn't do them, but that they weren't worth doing, thinking that this would elevate her over others.

She told her sister: "As for taking great pains to imitate a genius, it would be better for me to sell a few more pounds of peanuts! That benefit would be real. . . ." When the people crowded together below the thatched cottage to listen to the genius's words, she deliberately lowered her head and looked down and went about her work at the snack shop. When someone questioned her, she affected surprise and said that she had never paid attention to public life. Her inner life was so rich and happy that she saw no reason to pay attention to external matters. She "angrily brushed off" the visitor's hand (the visitor had tried to take her to the thatched hut, saying that this was the closest route to the elites). She chided the visitor for "interfering in her individual freedom" and said that she "would never take part in such foolish, deceptive nonsense!" She wouldn't waste her energy on this kind of "pointless thing at the cost of selling one less ounce of peanuts." She had precisely allocated her energy, and this system "couldn't be altered." Ruining her system was the same as "robbing" her. She stared at the visitor with her third eye for a long time and concluded that he "was a dust rag." Then she bent her head and weighed peanuts, paying no more attention to him. Completely unaware of this, the visitor wanted to argue, but Madam X's husband hit him with a broom handle and threw him out of the shop. "This dust rag was in the wrong place, and that bothered you. I threw it into the garbage," he said in a leisurely tone.

Now, let's return to the diagram of the maze. We have followed the thread to where Madam X surveyed the territory, settled on Five Spice Street as a new base, and harmed people with a soft knife. To substantiate this, the writer compared and contrasted her activity with that of geniuses, providing readers with almost "a complete general understanding." The writer's work went on smoothly and was about to succeed, but he didn't guess the new problems he would encounter. The writer's research suffered a major setback when Madam X gave up her nighttime activities and scurried to the street to proclaim her desire to "normalize" her relationship with the adulterous lover. The result was that people objected to the characterization of her nighttime activities as "murderous." Someone even joked, "Nighttime activities? That's purely her personal bagatelle!" People turned their gazes completely from her nighttime activities to the "adultery."

Okay. The writer dropped his research for the moment and followed the gaze of the crowd to Madam X's new transformation. What was normalization? From the standpoint of the law and of tradition, normalization of male and female relationships = monogamy. Since Madam X already had a husband and hadn't yet divorced him, how could she normalize her relationship with the adulterous lover? Even if she had said she wanted to "leave" her present husband, that was not at all the same as going through a legal divorce, and there was not the slightest evidence that she intended to go through this procedure. It was said that she "abhorred" this kind of procedure "from the bottom of her heart." Since she wasn't going through this procedure and was also wildly involved in adultery, what significance did her normalization have? Did she plan to live with Q for the rest of her life? If we look back for a moment, we will remember that Madam X had been a wanton woman who "never turned down the men who showed up," "the more the better," and sometimes she even "took the initiative." Later, she hooked this Mr. Q, and still later, she announced that she "was deeply in love with him." But she had overstated it: "I don't give the time of day to any counterfeits (other men)." It seemed that she would divorce and marry Q, and that she would promptly give up her evil ways and return to becoming a virtuous wife and mother. We have to point out that all through her illicit affair, Madam X had never mentioned "marriage." Conceivably, she abhors this procedure, too. So we'd better have no illusions or try to bring her into our moral compass. She'd exposed her nature since childhood ("grabbed" everything in sight). Now, in her thirties, how moral could she be? Just think about it! She won't get married, and she won't bother to get a legal divorce. In other words, she would do whatever she wished—be with anyone she likes, have sex with anyone she wants. This is what she meant by normalization!

There was nothing new at all. Wasn't "sexual liberation" about just this? Yet, Madam X didn't seem to be at all about "liberation."

She really scared people with her seriousness. She thought stubbornly: first, she had to normalize the illicit affair with Q by "leaving" her husband (although she didn't put this into effect, because Q wasn't taken in). Second, she didn't have to marry Q legally as long as she carried on the adultery "in a fair way." That was normalization. Third, she didn't necessarily "have eyes for only one person." While having an affair with one person, if another attracted her, she'd happily "shift" right away. (From the beginning, Q could not accept this and often objected. This was one reason they broke up.) At this point, perhaps the readers can't refrain from shouting: "Isn't this the old trick of beggars wrapped in hemp and riding in oxcarts? Those people have lice!" X had called a spade a spade and said that she "liked" those beggars with lice. Transposing the concepts of civility and barbarism, she told Q: "Compared with those people, we are barbarians!" Anything that met her needs, she called civility; and anything that stood in her way was barbaric. We can imagine that her future civility was a world of disorder and convulsion. All along, her evil intention was to actualize her ideal blueprint on our Five Spice Street. My dear readers, the new transformation in Madam X isn't the least bit new! As for her normalization, never mind our elites and ordinary people—even her adulterous lover Q was extremely repulsed by it. That normalization was her invention; it could exist only in her crazy mind. It would be best if she just kept this idea in her brain. Otherwise, she would discover how difficult it was to take even a tiny step. What was new about it? Was it "new" to wear hemp sandals, ride in an oxcart, and be dressed in rags? If she wanted to do it, so what? This had nothing to do with us. But then she wanted to pull Q in and even announced her filthy idea on the street (a certain person calculated that fifty-eight people were contaminated by her. Luckily, Old Meng bore her a grudge because she wanted to occupy his loft, and, with the help of Madam X's husband's good friend's wife, fired a pellet from his slingshot and injured Madam X's leg. Only this put an end to X's villainy). Was some other meaning hidden in this stubborn will and perseverance? We should have been on the alert. In half a year she had broken up

Q's family, while making a big hullabaloo over not wanting at all to tie herself to Q through marriage. She would be satisfied with "normalization" (namely, wearing hemp sandals and riding in an oxcart).

It seemed she had ulterior motives. Everything Madam X did— her so-called adultery—had little to do with Q. It could have been Q, or Y—whoever. Hadn't she threatened to "create miracles out of thin air"? This was precisely what she meant by miracles! Some of our best minds were too conventional—they focused on her secret room and her microscope, assuming her "miracles" were created there. A slight shift in perspective would have puzzled them. Madam X used this as the opportunity to act speedily: she changed the place, the time, the methods, and objective and went to that dark, gloomy place to "create miracles"! She crowed over it: "This is way more brilliant than using the microscope!" (She said this to her sister.) She drew her curtains, making the room airtight to prevent anyone from hearing or seeing a thing. She told her husband to pretend to guard the door. If an outsider charged in, she confused him with dream talk. Even the writer almost fell for her trick, while ordinary people absolutely believed in her feint.

The writer still remembers that one person waited outside her window for three days and kept whisking with a broom at the black curtain Madam X called a "miracle." That person did this seriously and diligently. He asserted that he was doing "the most significant work." When he grew lightheaded from sleepiness, he pounded his temples with a stone so that his spirit would rebound! If he had known that no one was behind the curtain, and that Madam X was at the granary, location unknown—"creating a miracle" out of the male body and feeling extremely happy about her evil actualization —how disappointed he would have been! "All rivers lead to the sea." After tracing so many other people's routes, we still have to go back to our conclusion: creating miracles was one facet of murder. Madam X didn't care a whit about Q or Y. All she cared about was revenge. When certain people fell for her plot and waited beneath her window, she lit up with pleasure! Her announcement on the street was not motivated by how much charm Q held for her, but by her wish to "smash to smithereens" everything in this world.

According to her husband's good friend's disclosure, one day Madam X's son, Little Bao—doubtless under his mother's influence —overturned a blackboard on the ground and then swiftly fled back home. Madam X strove to conceal her obvious joy and with a straight face gave her son a dressing-down. This dressing-down was unique: "if that board fell over and hit you on your little head, you might die," "if other people discovered you did this, your parents would be fined or locked up in jail," "you're just a kid—you mustn't interfere in adult matters; it's better for you to hang out with other children—playing marbles, catching birds, and so forth—that's much more interesting for you," and so on and on. She didn't mention that his behavior was evil or stupid, because she knew very well that her son had been influenced by what he'd seen and heard at home. The same kind of murderous psychology was gradually coming into being in his little body. And because of this, she saw her son's future "gradually taking shape" (she said this to her husband, smiling as she did so, just like a loving mother).

Though only seven years old, it was already evident that he was replicating Madam X's childhood. He was even more audacious— "passionate" in Madam X's words—because he had never been disciplined at home. When his mother's adultery began, he was called a "whore's kid" by the other children. He didn't bat an eyelid, as if he hadn't understood. He inherited his mother's inane, dream-like expression, which enabled him to recover and rapturously return to his companions. This child's mold was already set at the age of seven; his whole body was soaked in toxins. Nothing could have shaken him. However much zealous adults tried to enlighten him (Madam X's husband's good friend exhausted nearly all his energy on this until, once, "the tip of his tongue was blistered"), he didn't change at all: "My mama, my papa, and even Uncle Q are all wonderful people." If you asked him why, he said, "Mama can see things in the sky in her mirror. At midnight, she can also fly. The peanuts that Papa fries are fragrant and crisp. No one can do this better than he does. Uncle Q can dribble a ball more than a thousand times in a row. I can do this only fifty-seven times." He had an inspiration and suggested to his mother: "Ask Uncle Q to move to our home. If the four of us lived together, wouldn't this be even more interesting?" These words were like a heavy slap in the husband's good friend's face, so much so that his face was partly purple and partly pale for a week.

When the incident ended, Madam X wrote her sister a long letter. The widow prudently tore it open and read it with other members of our elite. This letter proved that the writer's diagram of the maze was one hundred percent correct. She had never had eyes for either Q or Y. She was simply acting. In her letter, she professed she had mistaken Q for a peddler from far away wearing a baize overcoat, when in fact Q was an eccentric who had been born and reared here. But what she had looked forward to was a peddler from afar. Reason told her that this kind of person could exist only in a mirror. Although she was capable of creating miracles, she couldn't create a person out of thin air, so she had to find a stand-in from among the local weirdos. Every stand-in had some characteristic of her ideal peddler from afar, but she would never decide to "unite" with this stand-in. All she could do was continue looking and continue "changing direction." Each time she might experience that greatest joy. And for that, she could "ignore everything else." Even though she was now discredited in the eyes of others, she "didn't care." She had enough physical and spiritual strength "to start over again." If she had this kind of opportunity again, she "wouldn't let it go." Of course, she didn't intend to harm anyone. She hoped to be "on friendly terms with everyone." If she unwittingly hurt others (for example, she always felt very kindly toward Q's wife and couldn't figure out why she took this dead end. In X's view, Q's wife could definitely have found a much better way out), she was anguished but had no choice: everything she did was involuntary.

After tearing this letter open and reading it, the writer and the widow went to the snack shop on the corner and observed X closely for an entire day. They wanted to see how she would "start all over again," but their labor was futile: Madam X's eyes had once more become sightless. She could see the counter, the roasted nuts and seeds, and the marks on the steelyard (she wasn't off even a little), and so forth. But she couldn't see people. When she jostled against us, we felt flustered. It seemed she was still adhering to old principles and wanted to "meet by chance." "Waiting for the fish to rise to the bait" was written all over her face, and a lot of people on Five Spice Street wanted to be that "fish." They all nosed around Madam X's fishhook, and all of them suffered! Madam X didn't consider them fish at all, but only "dust rags." The writer assumed that if she did consider some Y or Z to be a big fish, her objective would not have changed. Her respectful expression as she weighed out peanuts and beans told you that her joy was extraordinary. Her pleasure was murder. Whoever took her bait was finished. In the beginning, that person may have thought it was a good thing (like Q—with "hot tears brimming in his eyes"—rapturously hurrying to the rendezvous at the intersection). Only later did Q discover that he was a big fish caught in a net. Either the fish died and the net was torn, or the carp jumped out and fell heavily to the ground—and was left deformed. Meanwhile, Madam X just sat by. Nothing made her sad. She had never been accustomed to sorrow or regret. As before, she sold peanuts and quickly forgot the incident. Later, if possible, she would secretly throw out her line and wait, full of hope, for the next fish. She confided to her sister that she was destined to reenact this procedure for a lifetime. Even if she were a "discolored pearl in old age," fish would still jump to her bait. "This world is very large," she said, and then immediately added, "But this large, deserted world wouldn't hold a peddler from afar. I'll wait a lifetime in vain."

Our diagram of the maze is finished to this point. People will want to shout, "We've done so much miscellaneous work—meetings in the dark room, doodling, pasting up posters, tailing her, and so forth. We've worked so long, and yet everything has been fruitless from the beginning: all along, X and Q were simply acting. Was X merely toying with the crowd? Is that what you mean? Or was it that you, the gloomy stenographer, came up with this sophistry to demonstrate your own damn literary talent? If you just want to promote yourself, be my guest. But you shouldn't turn the crowd into horseshit while making a hero out of a whore. What you did was too—"

Hold on, friends: the writer never said X had great talent, that she could make life into a stage and then put on a play or something.

The writer sought only to stress: X is a woman with neither conscience nor feelings. As for this fiasco, it had nothing to do with talent. She wasn't educated (she herself said she "didn't know even one character"—of course, this was a little exaggerated). She had never "given much thought" to anything she chanced upon. How could she have great talent? "Friends, don't worry: you didn't work in vain." There will come a day when "conditions are ripe." Everything will become clear. Our meetings in the dark room and our lofty methods of expression—all were unique: they embodied the wisdom of our ordinary people as well as our elite. These have practically and realistically been entered into our glorious history, which is on the writer's windowsill, its rays of light shooting in all directions. A thief who one night planned to steal this treasure unexpectedly couldn't open his eyes because of the rays of light. He took a hard fall—this audacious thief! In the writer's eyes, Madam X lived an unprofitable life. She couldn't actualize her plot. She was lonely, too, as a result of what she did. She didn't mix with anyone, nor did she have one friend in whom she could confide. Was this worthwhile? Would she keep fishing? After this she would probably catch fewer and fewer fish and in the end run out of patience!

The Second Diagram of the Maze

How can we predict Madam X's future direction? Our analyses reveal Madam X to be an insignificant, eccentric person. It seems we've verified that, as an entity, she exists on our Five Spice Street. But just when we were about to move on to blackboard work, the second problem flashed into the writer's mind. He shouted loudly: "Hold on!" And so everyone stopped what he was doing and stared at the writer with doubtful eyes. The writer began explaining: If this issue isn't resolved, all our previous efforts were in vain. The question is: If Madam X is an entity, she is destined to advance. And if so, then there must be a direction. How could we overlook this basic question?

This morning we all happened to pass by the snack shop on the corner and saw her and her husband offload peanuts and beans from a small vehicle and move them into the house. We stood to the side for a long time, each person inwardly verifying Madam X's existence. But was this all? Verifying her existence was like lifting a heavy load. We must carry this heavy load to the end. How could we turn our backs on the issue of her future and her outlook? She wasn't an old philosopher, nor could she change into a fossil like an old philosopher. So her possibilities for change were infinite. Consequently we must observe her forever, present our conclusions, and make predictions. Otherwise, we won't have thoroughly verified her existence. It was irresponsible. A living person was "doing things" right under our noses: how could we now and in the future pretend to be "aware of nothing"? These words startled the elites, who were intoxicated with their success. They once more summoned their courage, came together, and brainstormed intensely. We already knew that after going through that storm, Madam X had recovered her inner serenity, and now every day, she happily carried on her trade in peanuts and beans without a worry and hardened her heart "not to see anyone." She just looked at the weights on the steelyard and so forth. Had she thereby become enlightened? Had she remolded herself? Only infantile, ignorant young people would raise this kind of question. Our elites who knew the ways of the world and who had crossed swords with Madam X couldn't cling to such an illusion. As the proverb says: Despite apparent changes, a thing remains the same. No matter what face Madam X shows, she is always the same: Carrying on her illicit affair in the dark granary and selling peanuts on the corner were simply two aspects of her essential nature. If we think it through, we can see that selling peanuts was "a continuation of her illicit affair" or "preparation for a new illicit affair" or "an accumulation of energy for a volcanic eruption." Each characterization is apt. Didn't she whimsically reveal to her sister that she still had enough energy to start all over? In fact, she isn't there selling peanuts at all; she's adjusting her secretions and exercising her energy! She's looking for new quarry with her third eye!

Many of us used to go out of our way to be solicitous of her welfare. Some worked so hard at this that their families broke up (for example,

X's husband's good friend). We had high hopes. Though it was clear that Madam X wouldn't change, nor would we gain anything from it, we persisted in "sticking it out." This remarkable process revealed our rare value. Even the gods were moved by it (at one time, a genius had proven this by sitting on the roof of a thatched cottage). Some people not only didn't plan to gain any advantage but actually endured a kind of self-torture, which turned into a mania. How much willpower our people had! With people of this sort, it didn't matter whether Madam X's future direction was obscure or bright. We would "have nothing to worry about."

As to the future, there were both pessimistic and optimistic opinions. The pessimists thought: Madam X's desires would increase, and after a few years, she would possess certain power, and the community's control over her would weaken. They reached this conclusion not because of Madam X but because of certain people in our community who were really devil-raising viruses. These viruses would spread over time, and our undertaking would be destroyed by them.

Let's look back for a moment. After the X and Q incident began, a small number of people couldn't remain calm. They put aside their work and all day long strolled around Madam X's small house. They talked while enjoying their leisure: the center of their lives had undergone a historic shift. Now it was better—they no longer had to deal with common things like blackboards. They had been fed up with this work some time ago, and long since had wanted to give it up. They hadn't been born to do this kind of dull work. Their talents should have enabled them to do better things. This X and Q incident allowed them to display their talents: this was really a good opportunity bestowed by heaven. One by one, they quit their jobs, and if they weren't allowed to quit, they walked anyway. A glorious future tempted them! Missions that would suit their tastes and interests awaited them! They had to come to a decision. If they didn't take part in a battle with light packs, how could they accomplish anything? First, they had to cut off all escape routes: quitting their jobs was the first step. After that, they would be as agile as snakes and as keen as dogs.

However, according to the observers' report, after these persons quit their jobs, they didn't act as they had planned. They used the X and Q incident as the excuse to leave home, and after circling around X's small house a few times, they went into their blockhouse —the public toilet. They didn't discuss strategy. They just squatted for a long time telling ribald jokes and made obscene conversation for the whole day. They labeled this conversation: theoretical discussion. It was precisely this "theoretical discussion" that caused them, with bulging bloodshot eyes, to attack Madam X twice on a secluded street corner. Although they didn't accomplish their goal, they still disgraced the community. Their fake discussion caused certain people to desecrate our ancient, elegant language. Because of this, one or two of them replaced such traditional phrases as "spare-time recreation" and "connubial harmony" with such low-class slang as "screw" and "bang." These dirty words hung from their lips the whole day: they said them over and over again to show their virility and defy tradition. In fact it was amusing and showed their low self-esteem. Everyone who ran into them on the street was disgusted, as though he'd eaten maggots by accident.

They not only quit their own jobs but agitated, provoked, and sneered at those who didn't. They wanted to mess up our rank and file. Every day, others went to work and got off work on time: they sneered that they were "robots," "klutzes," and were "born with crucifixes." Those who worked hard "were dumb oxen," "losers," "had no prospects," blah, blah, blah. They even goaded a certain person into destroying his tools, saying that they wanted "to smash to smithereens this thousand-year-old ball and chain" and wanted to "struggle for freedom." Their so-called freedom was no more than to live calmly on other people's hard work while they themselves squatted in the toilet and drew filthy doodles and used unbearably dirty language to besmirch our ancient culture. Even this wasn't enough: they sang tragic songs about Madam X's future and said that Q himself was the reason her future was tragic! They resentfully lambasted Q, claiming he was "a dabbler," "not thorough," "a neuter," and so forth. As they cursed him, they walked grandly past X's window, where they fawned, made eyes at her, tapped on the lattice, and dropped slips of paper inside. Some even climbed in the window and stole mirrors or pasted love letters on the door. One parent hanged himself from a tree outside the door because his child had disgraced him this way.

After the pessimists expressed their opinions, they dispersed, and let the setting sun draw out their long, thin shadows. They were numb and didn't talk anymore. What could be said? The end of the world was coming. We could only close our eyes and wait.

On the opposite side: the great majority of the people took an optimistic attitude toward Madam X's future (this was also Five Spice Street's future). They thought Madam X was a unique eccentric who couldn't change, and though she deliberately opposed our people, someday she'd melt into our generous embrace and disappear. From the very beginning, this trend had become more and more obvious. Right. She was still selling peanuts at the intersection, but her existence and her position were less visible. While we were busy, we didn't even "pay any attention to her." Someone even "swept her from his field of vision with a wave of his hand." Especially in the winter, when snow covered the roofs and the street, X, curled up all alone in the cold, couldn't provoke any response, no matter what disturbance she caused. In this season, our people "fought a great war against the cold"; "our spirits as red as fire," we were "struggling grandly against nature." In such a time, who would pay any attention to Madam X's mosquito-like moaning? X's excuse was that the ordinary people "could not understand the profundity of her voice." Actually, we understood it all too well. Both the elite and the ordinary people had seen through her superficial tricks long ago and were quickly distracted from it. They felt "it wasn't worth further probing." Though still in the dark, she did everything to "attract people's attention"! We believe that someday she will have "used up" her energy and will never be able to "attract people's attention." We can imagine one or two curious guys going into her little room at dusk on a snowy day and bringing their ears close to her mouth. They listen carefully for hours, but what can they hear? Only monotonous, repetitive murmurs that don't come from the heart but from her abdomen—indistinct and intermittent. Perhaps the only sound comes from their own fantasies, so that finally they rush out, stamping their feet, cursing, and vowing never to give X the time of day again.

The question of whether Madam X would melt and dissolve was raised not only by herself but, mainly, through the insight of our elite. To change heaven and earth, all we had to do was turn aside our mysterious vision. One day, drinking tea under the eaves, we spoke of her as of an ancient barbarian. She had gradually vanished from our memories and our field of vision. Indeed, in our annals, there was only a brief note about her, a historical reference—written as a small footnote to our people's great achievements. As an individual, she is now so abstract and vague that the only thing left is a symbol (that is, X). Someday, even the symbol will disappear from conversation, and she will exist only in the brief note in the dusty annals of history. To later generations, that note will be a riddle that can never be solved. As always, the tide of history rolls to the east. So splendidly bright is the rising sun!

After imagining this pleasant vision, we didn't rest on our laurels but remained very cautious and adopted suitable countermeasures aimed at X's last struggles. Our vision told us she was about to dissolve, but this wasn't at all the same as her "having already been finished." So we had to redraw the diagram. We all acknowledged the ironclad fact of her existence and knew that she would still furiously show up. For example, the day before yesterday, she announced a premonition: a new person would take Q's place in her life. She waited in high spirits for this new person so as to "experience" sublime feelings again, to "purify herself" and "be even more exuberant," blah, blah, blah. It was clear that she intended to bob up like a cork again. None of us was afraid: we felt happy from the bottom of our hearts about her bobbing up like a cork. Wasn't this a good opportunity for us to unfurl our spirit again? We hid at home and made our preparations. We even chose the place for her. This time, it wasn't the granary, but a lonely valley. We would call it "love in the valley," a significant title. As for the man, we called him Mr. P. Ah, before our Madam X dissolved, there was still a long, hard row to hoe! Our hearts were kind and bountiful, and our minds sensible and far-sighted. If this were not so, how could we have systematically reached the point where "the clouds parted and the fog dispersed," and "a new vista appeared"?

Looking at it from a grand historical perspective, from the roof of the thatched cottage, we saw that this X had all along been mixed up with the rag-tag crowds and danced with a mask. She had been sneaky, sometimes hidden and sometimes visible. She was the kind of inferior person who was always in the majority. People who under-estimated the enemy thought that in "the blink of an eye," she would disappear no later than tomorrow or the day after. Opposed to this mistaken belief, our optimists thought that the future would be rosy and beautiful, yet the task arduous. Madam X certainly wouldn't vanish in "the blink of an eye" (though the day would eventually come). We had to watch her actions carefully, rapidly work out our hypothesis, and draw up a blueprint that would be more real than her real existence—as vivid as a movie. If she took one step, we had to take five and see what she would do. She came up with an idea the day before yesterday, and today we've figured out the place, the name, and everything! Even though "nervier" and more daring, she can't hold out much longer in the face of our collective will. She can only move quickly to announce that "the new experience is finished!" Then she'll lie in her small room and moan soundlessly. And if a certain person again approaches to listen closely, he'll hear no mel-ody. Conditions are ripe to end that mysterious "blink of an eye." Then everything in the world will be young forever, X will retreat from this earth, and the brief note about her in the annals of history will offer a new and different explanation. That explanation will turn into a riddle-like symbol. Years later, when our children and grand-children ask about this symbol, a white-bearded, tottering old man will tap the cover of the annals with a withered finger and tell them: "Shhh. This is the secret to success. Please study the diagram of the maze." Wow! The diagram of the maze is blossoming and resplendent. Following the diagram, a large group of children and grandchildren will climb to the roof of the thatched cottage and to the mountaintop. And the lonely forerunner that was the writer? They will eventually exhume his name.

8

THE RATIONALITY OF THE WIDOW'S HISTORICAL CONTRIBUTION AND STATUS

Throughout the story of our Five Spice Street, the widow has been a glittering presence, and we want to sum up her historical contributions and discuss her character.

Thus far, we have described only her external image and physique, as well as the aspects of her character that derive from them. Our impression seems to be: her special stature and essence are responsible for her important position on Five Spice Street. This "specialness," the source of her contributions, consists of her provocative sexual power, without which her contributions (rated almost as highly as those of the geniuses) would most likely have gone unnoticed by both the elite and the people. We need to correct this impression.

Our conclusion is just the opposite: her brilliant status on our Five Spice Street as a sort of heroine, the people's love and esteem, didn't result from her individuality but from her universality and typicality. To begin with, the widow's sexual power lasted into her old age, and it was precisely this that most characterized Five Spice Street. People on Five Spice Street were full of youthful spirit. On the whole street, you could hardly find a single impotent man or frigid woman. Everyone was a master of sexual techniques. Everyone was in high spirits about "spare-time recreation"—even old men of eighty and youngsters of thirteen. The people here are healthy, creative, and ambitious. Madam X called them "counterfeit," never imagining that in her quest to become prominent, people might become suspicious about her own sexuality.

An example can demonstrate that our people are not counterfeit (this kind of example can be found everywhere). Old Meng from the pharmacy, for instance, is eighty-three this year and is as dissolute as ever. Such an example is rare in both ancient and modern times. On the outside, Old Meng doesn't appear strong at all, but frail. Yet inside, his muscles are steel and his bones are iron; his vigor hasn't diminished one bit. Not only is he not afraid of shacking up with someone, but he can actually "satisfy" a young person and even make her "surrender"! This example alone should refute Madam X's charge. Naturally, to recover their youth, the people on our Five Spice Street use various elixirs that have been handed down for generations. Old Meng has benefited greatly from those medicines in his pharmacy, and so he stays young. Not long ago, he actually dumped the wife of Madam X's husband's good friend and picked up a sixteen-year-old nursemaid. All day long, that nursemaid stayed inside the loft and looked after the house for him. Her "face was like peach blossoms," and her skin was "creamy white"! As for Old Meng, his appearance made people think "the older, the stronger"! Among our people, this general characteristic was inherited, and it also benefited from the feng shui here. This feng shui not only gave us immunity but also boosted our ability to procreate and strengthened us by the day. Our numbers grew. The widow's sexual power was in inverse proportion to her ability to procreate. We'll deal with this later.

Madam X's vilification of the people on Five Spice Street isn't worth discussing. Sex on Five Spice Street was never a problem from ancient times to the present. Just look at our descendants: that will settle the argument. Abstinence is the only problem, not encouragement. All of us abide by the rules. We're cultured and refined and put into practice the civil "spare-time recreation." Any lechery or anything against the law is censured. (For example, Old Meng has been reproached: even if he could "satisfy" that girl, and even if some people secretly envied him, his behavior has been condemned by certain authorities. We hope he will "reform" and be legally married to her.)

Second, her whole life, the widow has repressed her sexual desire. She never had a carnal relationship with any man other than her husband: she became a model of propriety on Five Spice Street and influenced many young men and women (for example, Madam X's husband's good friend, the young coal worker, Madam X's female colleague, and also the writer and others). Because of this, spiritual friendships became customary on Five Spice Street: outsiders felt refreshed by the novel atmosphere. Yet we have to say that this wasn't the widow's invention. The old woman with the black felt hat and her older male cousin, and also lots of other people, demonstrate this psychology. The widow's contribution was in carrying forward and developing this character. Spiritual friendship was definitely higher than physiological function, and it is this that led humankind to mutual dependence and created history. Even in marriage, spiritual relationships can predominate; the writer has witnessed many examples of couples especially strongly united through their spiritual love, even to the point of ignoring physiological needs. They seldom indulged in "spare-time recreation"; indeed, some didn't indulge at all, but their feelings for one another were deeper and more sincere than those of other people. Such a union was the perfect model and could last forever, despite leaving no descendants.

The writer definitely isn't advocating this insipid ascetic life but hopes only that everyone will elevate spiritual love to the first position. Ever since experiencing waves of emotion, our young coal worker has greatly matured. He broke off his sexual relationship with Old Woman Jin and moved into the work shed of Madam X's husband's good friend. They became permanent neighbors. This was a priceless example of returning to the fold, even though he was not nearly as perfect as the widow, Madam X's husband's good friend, and the lonely old woman. He was a youngster, influenced by unhealthy thinking, who had made mistakes and matured relatively late. He had been controlled by Madam X over a long period and had indulged in the ways of the flesh. Old Woman Jin was even worse. But now the darkness had passed; they awakened and were thoroughly ashamed. Full of self-reproach, they made up their minds to begin anew and struggle against their evil lust. The day he moved, he was very happy. Old Woman Jin ran over, barefoot and with disheveled hair, to help him. She was as energetic as a young girl. Clenching her teeth, she carried a desk on her back and walked as though flying. She said, "I've been looking forward to this day for a long time." She also said, "When he was five, I figured he had prospects. After being tutored by me, he is getting better and better by the day." In order to celebrate the young coal worker's separate household and the beginning of his new life, everyone squeezed into the work shed and sang songs and—shoulder to shoulder, hand in hand—danced a circle dance. Unexpectedly gaining a companion in the same boat as he was, Madam X's husband's good friend wept and wailed. Then he laughed and told everyone: he didn't have to worry that there would be no one to continue his work. He had crawled inside a long, dark tunnel for years, but now he could see a ray of light!

After the young coal worker moved, the widow stayed five days and five nights at his work shed in order to teach by personal example as well as by instruction. She thought the youth was still thinking erratically, and that this mustn't be treated lightly. So she abandoned everything to help him. For five days and five nights, the two confided in each other non-stop. When they tired of talking, they slept back to back on the earthen ground (from this time on, the young coal worker slept on the ground) and continued talking in their dreams. They spoke about paradise. After five days and five nights, the young coal worker became a deep thinker. At every sentence the widow spoke, at every imperceptible sigh, he was moved to the marrow of his bones and quivered all over. He wept uncontrollably when she stroked his soft hair with her warm hand. "My previous life was like a nightmare," he confessed. "Ah, I wish I could be reborn, I wish I could start over!" The widow consoled him: In fact, he had indeed been reborn and had started over. There would still be a lot of time ahead. If he lived as if each day were a year, as she did, he would discover just how clear and rich, and how significant, his life would be. She was now so sublime she was qualified to commune with the gods. When she opened her eyes, she could see things in paradise, but she still wasn't satisfied. Her greatest joy was to continue remolding herself. She told the young coal worker that as an elder and a mentor, she had to understand all the details before she could suit the remedy to the sickness. If he and Madam X had had a carnal relationship, he should speak of it without omitting anything. If, however, his love was unrequited, he should reveal the details of his lewd thoughts. The more detailed, the better in curing him of his illness. She could understand even the filthiest things and wouldn't deride him. Rather, this was the first step to starting over. Not until he "got rid of the stale" could he "take in the fresh."

The young coal worker got up his nerve to reveal his private life. The first assumption was apparently unfounded, so he talked of the second. He confessed his unrequited love over a long period of muddle-headedness—the dirty images in his mind in which he was always the master, as naked as the day he was born, incomparably ugly, while Madam X was seen only in shadow from the rear. He described every move he might possibly make, confusing his fantasies about Madam X with his carnal experiences with Old Woman Jin. Not blinking an eye, she urged him to continue. She stroked his lower abdomen and lightly kissed his cheek as if comforting a baby. Whenever he dozed off, the widow mercilessly woke him. "You're still a long way from your new life!" she would say. And so he summoned energy and went on talking, and then dozed off again. Hard as nails, the widow woke him up again. His face gradually started tingling, his eyes bulged out in a scary way, and he started to drool. When he finally closed his eyes and fell sound asleep, the widow went to the kitchen, ladled out some water, and splashed it over him. "This is good. This is effective. Don't relax. Go on talking. It's your only way out!" she chided.

In the work shed facing the street, these two had become the vanguard of Five Spice Street. They weren't at all isolated from the outside world. One piece of information after another leaked out from the work shed, causing tidal waves among the people. They dreamed in their rundown homes, and a world of dreams hung over all of the ordinary people. It was the world in which they lived their daily lives. A little forgetful, a little absent-minded, they always

shoved "the matter" to the back of their minds. But now their enthusiasm for life was greatly elevated by these two vanguardists. Something that had happened not long before also substantiated this. Not
long ago, Madam X's husband's good friend announced that Madam
X's new lover, P, known only through hearsay, had already made
contact with the lady! With this news, the people who had begun to
relax were aroused again, and they felt they couldn't survive without
these two vanguardists, never mind that they lived in the work shed
and slept on stones. Finding other such selfless civil servants would
not be easy.

Approaching fifty, the widow now had an even more transcen-
dent demeanor. After acting as the young coal worker's mentor in
the work shed for five days and five nights, she donned her oversized
black robe to cover her generous curves. Walking soberly ahead on
the main road like a mass of black clouds, she commanded the
respect and admiration of the people on Five Spice Street. The
people no longer referred to the widow's past "sex appeal." Or if they
did, it had nothing to do with her present state; rather, they spoke of
the seductive person she used to be, like the "pretty girls under the
camellia trees." Wrapped in the black robe, she was even more
charming, in a way that excluded sexual desire, like the ocean, the
rainbow, the primeval forest, the distant stars all over the sky. It was
mysterious and serene, as pleasant as fresh air—healthy, solemn,
and graceful: it drew people from the ground to the clouds; it was as
magical as a meeting in paradise. Just one glance at her would turn
even a lusty, wild young guy into someone earnest and noble. Your
lust would turn into fuel for work, or the inspiration for art, or the
pursuit of ideals.

Third, the widow's penetrating vision (this manifested itself in
discussing sexual problems, in vindicating traditional standards of
taste, in sizing up our male compatriots, and so forth) precisely
represented our Five Spice Street's people's extraordinary talent.
Every one of us has eyes like a structurally complex microscope and
telescope. (Who needs the stuff Madam X played with?) We maintained our composure because we were so excellent. Otherwise, X's

puzzling sorcery and her preposterous behavior would have disturbed our social system. Instead, we advanced. Outsiders thought it inconceivable! Madam X talked a lot of nonsense, such as "no one here paid attention to his or her eyes," they "didn't look in mirrors," and so forth. Her superficial mind could not possibly comprehend our self-knowledge and ability to take the initiative. We were born with this ability, this vision. We had long since observed our physiological structure and its function. What good would come of racking our brains or playing with mirrors and other such things? Madam X's "narrow views" weren't worth refuting. The facts contradict her remarks: Madam X didn't discover something in the mirror (even though, time after time, she announced her discoveries); rather, our innate vision penetrated her and revealed her plain as day. Her deceit didn't help. We sat down quietly and solemnly under the eaves, and all our problems were "automatically solved."

The best demonstration of our vision was that we knew what happened in the granary. Did anyone investigate this mystery? Did anyone collect information about it? No. We seemed indifferent to it. Each of us was drowsy from our own worries, but when this case was discussed, we all seized hold of it as if it were our own experience. We couldn't tell you how, but we just knew we had "seen" everything, although each of us might have seen it differently. If necessary, we could have seen all the details before it even began! Only people with penetrating vision could so focus their thought. It also made us superior at analysis and logic. Outsiders would have been puzzled and confused by the granary incident. They might think about it for the better part of a day and still come up with nothing and then leave in disappointment. They would have seen nothing. Their heads would be empty of any image, of even a hypothesis. The people of Five Spice Street had only to assemble once in the dark room to solve this knotty problem. Without even moving their lips everyone understood.

So we can posit that the widow's vision wasn't hers alone: it wasn't any better than that of ordinary people. We appreciated her and admired her, not because of something special about her (for example, like X), but precisely because she represented the interests of the ordinary people. It was only because of this that we planned to consider her a genius in the future (this commitment would be cashed in only at the point of death, so she experienced the same kind of trials as the writer; before that, only the writer could identify her as a genius). Thinking of her is always associated with thinking of ourselves, and a tender feeling of attachment is born. The more we look at her beautiful eyes, the more familiar and warm we feel. Such eye contact always stimulates sublime ideas.

Madam X's gaze is different. It is the gaze of a stranger, blank and unnatural. It frightens you. You get goose bumps. It's difficult to make eye contact with her for more than five seconds. Even a quick glance will confuse and disorient you. Her gaze doesn't belong to any category known to us. Perhaps we can say that it doesn't fit into any category at all. It is simply her foolishness and represents only her abominable inclinations. Everyone abhors it. Even if she stares at your back, you stamp your feet in fury as if it were attempted murder (like murder with a soft knife—referred to above). Hadn't she already killed Q with "saffron light waves"? Who could guarantee the safety of P or Y, who would appear later? And who could guarantee that she wouldn't pass this power down to her son, Little Bao, so that this evil would continue? No one could guarantee any of this. Therefore, we could only adopt the strategy of using our own gaze to "exclude" her. She had no way to deal with this strategy. After we came up with this strategy, we decided that except for doing business with her, no one should linger in front of her shop, and if we had to buy things from her, we should also avoid eye contact. We were particularly tense. As soon as we entered the snack shop, we squatted and wished we could make ourselves small (everyone knew that either X's glance was level or else she looked up. She never looked down. That's why we chose this special posture). Or we would stand outside the door and reach inside to pay, take the purchase, and run off. Someone wore a long red gown and red spectacles when buying things at the snack shop because X particularly abhorred red and would ward off the red rays with her hand. How then could she see the person?

It's worth mentioning that one day, our beloved widow crossed swords with Madam X. The widow met Madam X's wanton eyes with her own pure, righteous gaze. In one bout, she "defeated" her. The next day, this news was posted in large characters on the blackboard. "It's no big deal," the widow said calmly with a slight smile. "If you confronted her gaze directly, you'd see that she was too weak to withstand even one blow. I have long since foreseen this. If you're interested, all of you can give it a try." No one did, however. Our widow's test was enough proof: and the widow epitomized everyone's ability. Anyhow, Madam X's gaze was too weak to withstand one attack. All of us had absolute confidence in ourselves.

Fourth, the widow's discernment, diligence, and calmness when facing danger also precisely represented the collective character of the people on Five Spice Street. These qualities enabled us to get through difficulties easily, to accommodate and even assimilate aliens from outer space like X and her family. Not only were we not assimilated by her, but we made them nourishment for our organism. How rare this is in human history!

For example, when the female colleague was clamoring to "break into the adultery scene," our people demonstrated admirable calmness. No one made a move. No one discussed it or argued about it: there was only a quiet, iron-like consistency. An atmosphere like this can't be achieved in a day or two. We can proudly state that only in this place of ours and with our people could Madam X develop freely and contentedly and give birth to such a heroic and romantic story. Even if she finally became one of us, the story moves people greatly (who wouldn't be moved by a history about themselves?). Anywhere else, she would certainly have been caught "with her pants down" or she would have been exterminated before the adultery ever had time to sprout. It's also possible that this adultery would have been endlessly repeated with the approbation of the people, and licentiousness would have swept through society.

Don't you see that only our Five Spice Street could offer X the ideal home? Her landing here was only superficially an accident. In fact, it was inevitable. Without Five Spice Street, X would not have existed, nor would the story about X. Five Spice Street was X's hothouse, her cradle, her mother (in the end, she would finally return to this mother's womb—and dissolve). It was only after X arrived that she became X. We molded her, we helped her fulfill her wishes. In the refraction of her sincere performance, our collective spirit was carried forward. All of this also profited from our drive to refine ourselves and achieve control over the environment. A mother can't casually abandon her child, even if that child is a rascal or a traitor. As soon as Madam X reached Five Spice Street, our people, although sniffing out her dissidence, behaved as usual and received her with open arms. All the people here are children of the great mother. She kindly takes care of all of her children. Our people had long since blended with this land into one organism. Preeminent individuals like the widow are constantly born here. They sit unmoving in the dark room facing the street, but their bright minds discern every movement in the outside world. There is no way to measure the usefulness of this highly developed ability. Now, never mind one X, even if there were ten Xs, we had well-thought-out plans and could deal with them. It would be no problem to welcome them. Previously, the widow's profound theory about sex had become a milestone in our history. Not only was she not out of step with the times, she had directed our progress over a long historical period. The creator of this theory was in the midst of a new breakthrough. Her ability wouldn't dry up, nor could she stay in the same place a long time. "She was always pushing forward." Her face shone with kindness. She became more like the Earth Mother by the day. She, who had no children, was the heavenly symbol of motherhood on our Five Spice Street. Everyone who ran into her was moved to call her "mother."

Someone recalled that before X had come to this street of ours, and before X and Q's adultery, our widow hadn't yet fully demonstrated her genius. Back then, Five Spice Street was really like a small, quiet island, and the people were as simple as ants. Was it because X came here that our lives were turned upside down? We should put it this way: it was because of X that our good character and our noble sentiments had the chance to be revealed. Indeed, Madam X was the person we had earnestly longed for. She had come to Five Spice Street, and not some other place, in response to our summons. "That was an unforgettable day. That morning, the earth was filled with large, beautiful chrysanthemums. . . ." We all loved this sentimental song. From that day on, we—these silent ants—loudly proclaimed our existence to the world. Each of us revealed his or her true self. How could we be ants? Ladies and gentlemen, you've seen our story. How will you answer? X will go on living here, and our performance will pause for a while because of Q's disappearance, but it is not the end. Perhaps it will never be concluded. A new show awaits us! Not long ago, we ran up against a little puzzle: that was one noon when we were sitting along the street. A sixteen-year-old said to everyone in a clear voice: "This X incident actually isn't one bit interesting." We immediately surrounded him and interrogated him: "Why?" He said he didn't know, but in any case it was thoroughly boring. All along, he had wanted to break away and go to the mountain to collect butterflies. He had already wasted a lot of his precious youth. He argued until his face turned purple as an eggplant. We asked how old he was. He said sixteen, "almost seventeen!" At first, the crowd was so angry no one could say anything. Then they appeared embarrassed, and then our widow came over. She stroked the youth's hair and just sighed and acted as if she were going to leave. Then she stopped suddenly again, sized up the youth, and asked, "Have you ever believed in anything? Have you ever pursued anything luminous?"

The youth stood in amazement. He looked at her blankly. Her voice gradually became tough and powerful: "What makes you qualified to talk of the *shockingly* big question of life's significance? Huh? Do you want to deny the spiritual achievement of your father's generation? From the day you began to understand things, you took it for granted that the world had always been like this, and you were coming into this world merely to enjoy it. You could never imagine that over a long period, your predecessors were crawling through a dark tunnel. They could see neither an exit nor any light.

Only by relying on our strong inner faith could we continue our struggle. We can say that it was in the midst of despair that we clung to hope. 'We went on undeterred by the dangers ahead.' 'We risked our lives in the struggle.' Only by doing so did we emerge in this world of today. Sometimes, we looked all around with wide-open eyes: everything was black, everything an impasse. Those days of extreme misery: you never experienced them at all. How dare you speak such nonsense as 'completely boring'? How dare you disdain your forefathers' courageous pursuit? Looking at a kid like you, we really keenly feel our oversight. Aside from having fun and being mouthy, what do you kids have in your heads? You're rude, you want to cast off everything your forebears struggled for so that you can be—as they say—aloof. But, honey, what do you have? What do you rely on to stand up straight in this world? Do you collect butterflies to escape and show off your rebellious spirit? Have our youths all turned into playboys with butterfly nets, roaming around on the mountains all day long? Ah, I really do not dare imagine this. If you have to go straight to hell, that's up to you. I just want to ask you: what makes you say things like this 'are completely boring'? Did you mean that we who have made this pursuit, we who have wholeheartedly headed toward the light, are all hollow, blind, 'completely boring' people? Just because you can't see the present world, do we have to let you crazy kids create a new world? All our lives, our generation has struggled! Every minute and every second, our lives have been busy and meaningful. We don't have time to think about whether something is interesting or uninteresting—questions that people with nothing better to do come up with. After the X incident emerged, we saw a little light at the end of the tunnel. Our hopes were kindled, we were pleasantly surprised, and we threw all of our energy into this struggle. We demonstrated unprecedented courage and resourcefulness. With our spiritual strength, we conquered the darkness of the outside world and walked on the road of light. We obtained a new lease on life. This kid: is he our Five Spice Street people's flesh and blood? He sits here and, without a care in the world, swings his *skinny* (of course, they're skinny!) legs and puts on airs. How could anyone believe him? I have to say: there's no such kid here. And he said nothing that had to do with our life. He just moved his mouth and joked with us—that's all. It's impossible to believe there was such nonsense and a kid who talked such nonsense. He lives on Five Spice Street; he's everyone's child. One noon, he joked with us. I think he will agree with this narration—right, honey?"

She held the child's hand, but the child turned bashful. It seemed that everyone saw him nod his head and then start whimpering. He hid his face in the widow's black robe. "This kind of child is still adorable."

The widow turned toward the crowd. "My research into this incident has gone deeper and deeper. We are rushing toward the torch in the midst of the dense fog."

9

THE VAGUE POSITIONS OF MR. Q AND MADAM X'S HUSBAND

By now, we "have a good general idea" of Madam X. We've drawn the diagram of the maze from her birthplace to the valley or hillside where she is destined to go in the future. Though phantasmagoric, she can't deviate much from the diagram.

However, she isn't our biggest problem. Rather, it's the two who stick to her like shadows—Q and her husband. After further thought, we realized that these two are even more shadowy than Madam X. They are mere shadows—X's shadows, two parasitic vines, parasites on X's large, rootless tree, colorless and shapeless. X brought them with her to Five Spice Street, and when X dies they will disappear. Of course, this is only a superficial impression, or perhaps the misconception they produced by getting mixed up with X. As individuals, they remain ordinary men. This is substantiated by Dr. A's argument about who took the offensive. The problem is that in our story, we haven't yet considered these two persons as individuals. All along we've looked at them as a trio—one person and two shadows, or a moth and two pupae. As long as the moth flies back and forth below the big tree, the other two can only be unmoving pupae forever. Their metamorphosis ends at this point.

All the men and women on Five Spice Street resented this analysis. We all wanted to draw our swords and help them. We need to differentiate: in general, most of those who wanted to draw their swords and help Q were beautiful, dissolute women who had desired him for a long time because Q was good-tempered and gentle.

But X was an obstacle, and they couldn't succeed. If they disposed of X, they were convinced they would get Q.

"A momentary slip," the lame woman said as she bent her head and sharpened the sword. "Our eyes met for twenty-five seconds. This allowed thousands of opportunities to change fate. Just because of a momentary slip, I lost it all. He left the dark room and strode ahead along the gray wall. That was death, not a new life. He was racing toward raw and bloody bones."

Over time a lot of other women forgot Q's weak points, forgot, too, that they'd been annoyed by him, and simply gave him their unstinting affection. They commented on what a handsome, feeling man he was, and how bewitching his physique before he got involved with that demon. The woman who had "encountered" Q at the foot of the stairs attested to this. "He's an endearing god," that beautiful woman said, taking a paring knife out of her pocket. The other women also took out knives.

Their enthusiasm was of course praiseworthy. Unfortunately, the effect of their actions was questionable. After his metamorphosis into a pupa, Q lies unmoving in the crack of a tree trunk—probably for his whole life—and can't make use of their "drawing swords to help him." Though he chose this lamentable final scene for himself, and later might regret it, there wasn't time to reconsider, for he had "gone crazy heading toward death." The childish, optimistic guy might say, "Spring is coming." But spring would never be his again. He was only a pupa, and in the spring, he would slowly dry up and atrophy and become merely an empty husk. He'd had so many hopes when he rushed toward X. He'd imagined changing, like her, into a colorful butterfly. But the ruthless laws of nature had changed him into an empty husk in the crack of a tree. What led him to this end?

We must seek the reasons from his own being.

From the age of eleven, a person developed a certain romantic notion and would always be a child who couldn't grow up because he had no way of expunging his inner dread. To begin with, he should have kept his childishness and lived a calm and quiet life with his dear wife, who also couldn't grow up. However, he fell into this demon X's wide-open, passionate net and began acting out all kinds of adult tricks. Inwardly, he also felt that his performance was awkward (for example, dribbling the basketball—he still blushed over this). In the eyes of bystanders, this was ridiculous, but how could he control himself? He'd gone crazy. He'd adored X so much he shed tears and all day long thought only of going into that granary. He wished to stay there forever. And then there was X: from her bragging, it seems she was also madly in love with Q. She was good at creating miracles, so why didn't she turn Q into a butterfly so the two of them could fly off into midair? "No," she said, denying her power. "I can just make curtains and toys. I can't create people." Alas! So our Q could only stay in the crack in the tree and become an empty husk! With bitter hatred, the women of Five Spice Street rammed their heads against the tree trunk. They did this until blood poured down: they cried their hearts out. One question kept bothering them until the last day of their lives. Since Q, this lovable man with beautiful eyes, wanted to become a real man, why wasn't he looking for them—Five Spice Street's beautiful women? Why was he racing after that skull and crossbones? In their warm embrace, he would certainly grow up fast, shuck off his childishness in a short time, and change into a brave, resolute, and bewitching man. They had already trained many heroes with their abundant creativity and strength! They had never publicized this but had quietly contributed their youth and energy to society. This selfless spirit made them fascinating and youthful all their lives, so even when they reached the old widow's age, they were still glowing with health and were as good, innocent, and graceful as young girls.

The most inexcusable thing was that having once encountered our widow who was going to be a genius, Q was blind as a bat and didn't size her up carefully. Later, he didn't even realize what caused his "lust to burst and glow with health." He forgot the effect of that one encounter and confusingly felt he owed his physiological change to X. This is exactly what people mean when they say, "Rotten wood cannot be carved." We may boldly imagine: if in that one encounter, Q had really seen the widow clearly from head to toe and rather than going to the granary had turned around and pursued our widow, then under the widow's guidance, he would have started the process of genuine evolution. In which case, how could he have ended up as an empty husk in the crack of a tree?

The widow's power to infect people was astonishing: everyone on Five Spice Street had experienced this repeatedly. Unfortunately, Mr. Q hadn't seen her clearly, and she remained humble and aloof. She had never forcefully projected herself, nor had she wanted to control people (on the other hand, when X saw men, she pounced like a hungry tiger and didn't hesitate to take advantage of their stupefaction to inject them with hallucinogens and perform cruel experiments on their bodies and then, when this was over, just kick them out. As she put it, "Each was going his own way"). She also had the kindly heart of a mother: she cared for the nation and for the people. She loved the people as if they were her children. All her influence was latent, invisible. Only people with pure hearts were permanently attracted, so in his confusion Q, whom X had injected with toxins throughout his body, lost his only opportunity to evolve and quickly sank into a deep pit. The widow's brief sideways glance made him "glow with health" for a few days, but he definitely wasn't aware of what this was all about. Nor did the widow bring more of her influence to bear on him (she had too much work to do, and it was too heavy a burden; she couldn't neglect everyone else in order to look after Q!). And so X—this demon—pulled him into a muddy pit. He divulged that in the process of seeking fun with X, he'd wanted several times to wash his hands of it and free himself from that unsportsmanlike position he was in (of course, this was because of the latent influence of the widow's brief glance), but that damn sorceress's witchcraft intoxicated him and made him crazy. So he went all out in trying to become a colorful butterfly like X.

"Even if I can't change into a colorful butterfly, I can appreciate the true meaning of being human," he clenched his teeth and said. "Anyhow, I'm bored with being a child. Just think about it: I've been like that for almost forty years!"

When the incident reached its crisis, Mr. Q's colleague stuck his head out of his blanket and gave his views: "A person makes himself out to be neither old nor young. It's really odd when someone your age dribbles a basketball or looks into mirrors. In the countryside, this sort of thing is called being 'bewitched,' and the consequence is usually serious. This guy believes wholeheartedly that he can be whatever he wants to be. How's that possible?" He sneezed several times from the dust stirred up on the other side of the room by Q, who was dribbling the basketball.

Many people were slinging mud, and many were making faces. Q's eyes were somewhere between seeing and not seeing, and his ears between hearing and not hearing. In fact, he saw everything and heard everything, but—filtered through his mind—the things that he saw and heard changed into grotesque colors and deafening noise that made him uneasy day and night. He frequently felt scared and coerced. It wasn't even possible for him to have the few seconds of quiet he wanted. His legs were constantly springing, and he lived that way, too. He couldn't stand this. He had worked hard at imitating X: he wanted to "achieve that highest degree of serenity." The result: fifteen seconds of quiet. That was when he and X were together and X led him into a certain fairyland where they stayed for fifteen seconds. After he returned, the situation grew worse. He jumped back and forth like a kangaroo and didn't go to bed for three days. His wife wept for three days and three nights and became even skinnier.

"That world has lured me in. Unfortunately, it doesn't belong to me." He summed things up dejectedly. He looked into the mirror and saw the wrinkles in his forehead and his absurdly stiff bearing. "I'm no more than a cockroach."

Though he reached this gloomy verdict, the next time X suggested they roam around in fairyland, he couldn't wait. Even more afraid he wouldn't be able to enter, he hugged her tightly around the waist so she couldn't abandon him. When someone asked what he had seen, he became blank and feverish, and his eyes brimmed with tears. He laughed idiotically and forgot to answer. It was this way every time. In such brief moments he could neither see nor hear and was completely happy.

Our Q was nearly forty years old and up to now had passed his time playing games. That laughing and joking romantic sentiment was the fundamental cause of his death. He wasn't killed by a wave, or by hallucinatory drugs, and certainly not by public opinion. He realized his romantic idealism by disappearing into the crack of a tree and becoming an empty husk. From the age of eleven, he had looked forward to this day. His romantic ideal coincided perfectly with X's murderous complex, and thus this series of incidents occurred. Earlier, we set forth X's murderous complex merely to explain this evil virus and not to stress her social potency. Up to now, she'd had only enough power to drag one child into the water. A metamorphosis such as Q had undergone had little to do with X's power. Things like waves and drugs all came from the imagination. His metamorphosis was caused by his inner elements. Of course, "combining two into one" with X was the key activator. As for the slow-witted Q, at first he owed being "reborn" (he wholeheartedly believed he was going to be reborn) to the waves in X's eyes. He had called X a sorceress and by frequently looking in the mirror had verified his rebirth. When he put his mirror in his pocket and walked proudly down the street, and when he looked at himself in the shop windows, who on Five Spice Street could keep from covering his mouth and giggling? Especially since he had been such a serious, timid, conservative guy, and except for lying under the melon rack and dreaming wildly, in all his forty years he had never done anything rebellious.

As soon as we thought of Q, a strange feeling surged up in our hearts, and we felt unsure of our footing. Really, what was good about him? The odd thing was that our beautiful women actually yearned for him. Some were desperate. One clamored: she didn't care whether he was strange or not, dependable or not, she was in love with him. He was the only man she could be friends with! Even if he was an empty husk in a crack in a tree, she still wanted to "draw swords and help him"! Women desperately ran to check on Q. An empty chaise longe stood under the melon rack at the entrance to the small house. They searched carefully a long time before discovering that Q had "dissolved" ahead of X. The women found a broken mirror under a rock behind the house and smiled at each other. Some guy with a vague expression and wrapped in a blanket walked over and told them that Q was sitting in his office working on statistics. "Those days after he went crazy were a nightmare for us," he said.

The beautiful woman from the foot of the stairs immediately offered her opinion: "Since he's returned to normal, his charm is gone. Before this incident, there was nothing so wonderful about him."

After some reflection, everyone felt this opinion was brilliant. Without X, how would they have known about Q? Wasn't it only when he entered Five Spice Street on a beautiful afternoon that he became adorable? They vied with each other in yearning for him. This was also a spiritual trust directly related to the incident. Now he had retreated, melted into the crowd, and become an ordinary person. He would no longer be the object of desire for Five Spice Street's beautiful women. Who would fall for an ordinary guy? Our women's love required self-sacrifice and a courageous spirit. Only an outlandish love would do. We weren't gray and solemn! We'd run over here with knives to wholeheartedly undergo baptism by fire. We were ready to "die for love." Who knew we were pouncing on thin air? This Q really was uninteresting. How difficult it was to realize our spiritual ideals! We regretted getting in so deep, regretted embracing unreasonable hopes. In reality, things that could make you happy were so rare! Sometimes the reality was precisely the opposite of what you'd imagined, and you met with blows that simply confused you. If we'd known earlier that Q merely wanted to be dissolute, that he didn't regard this "incident" as real and would draw back into his shell, we wouldn't have given him the time of day. Who would ever have known of this rundown, worm-eaten house!

Shaking with anger, they thought they had been greatly humiliated and duped. Following the lame woman (she recalled her breathtaking twenty-five seconds and realized that she and Q were absolutely irreconcilable; in fact, this goddamned Q was a hundred times worse than the young guy who robbed her of her virtue), they broke the window with stones and smashed the door. Then they barged into the house and broke every piece of furniture to smithereens. When they came out, they faced the open fields and laughed out loud to their hearts' content. Someone started singing a march. Finally, they left triumphantly. Our widow didn't participate, because she was enlightening a young person about his serious mistakes.

She summed up the incident later: "To be a man, one has to be consistent from beginning to end. One should mind one's manners, keep one's word, and be responsible. Throughout my life, I've most feared chameleon-like people. The worst thing that can happen to you is that a man makes you feel uncertain or changes overnight. How can a decent man hurt a woman's pride? That's a crime! We women sincerely want to trust men. We would always like the man we love to make us feel secure forever. Only then can we be vital and energetic. In general, when we women of Five Spice Street yearn for a certain man, we unhesitatingly endow him with these qualities and hope we can grow old with him in spirit. Such a situation develops naturally, and up to now our adorable men have not disappointed us. Regarding Mr. Q, our adorable women were candid, gullible, and absolutely unreserved. No one guessed that this puppet, this guy with a dubious background, would play such a trick on us. After kindling everyone's enthusiasm and dreams, he suddenly took off and cast us beautiful women aside to look at each other in hopeless despair. Who among us had ever been ridiculed like this? We were all fine ladies. I completely understand their smashing doors, windows, and furniture. I didn't think it at all barbaric."

After that, the women of Five Spice Street were despondent about men for a while. "I might become an ascetic. I can't take despondency and dejection anymore."

One after another, the women said, "By comparison, my husband is much more dependable. Although he's ordinary and dull and provides no spiritual satisfaction, he's solid and won't give me much trouble. For years, I've planned to do something to show him my appreciation. Tomorrow morning, I'll do it."

The next morning, each did something good in her home: some placed the photograph of herself and her husband in a gilt-edged frame and hung it in the most prominent place in the room, where previously photos of deceased ancestors or parents had hung; some took out the husband's best clothes and dressed him up and then took the day off so the two of them could stroll around on the street as if celebrating a holiday; while others deployed their best cooking skills and made wonderful lunches and invited guests to eat with them, with everyone drinking until intoxicated. Afterwards, they felt relaxed and shoved Q to the back of their minds. But the good mood didn't last past midnight.

In the still of the night, with the dim street lights flickering, women were inclined to feel romantic, but they could not awaken the husband in their arms. Thus, they returned their unbroken affection to the pre-metamorphosed Q and recalled the strong impression he had made the first day he came to Five Spice Street. They yearned for him so much they went limp and tears covered their faces. Why hadn't he sought them out that afternoon? He should have known that any one of them had already made up her mind to become one with him in spirit. And then how wonderful and how powerful he would have been. They cursed his detestable momentary slip. That slip had affected their whole future. That slip had changed the fate of all the women and of Q himself. But for that momentary slip, wouldn't the lame woman have thrown away her cane long ago and become a graceful lady? Wouldn't the widow have had one more success—one more follower? Wouldn't the old widow and the forty-eight-year-old good friend and others have regained youth in their later years and become even more ambitious? And Q himself: wouldn't he have become not only a real man but also one commended by society? Losing a good opportunity served this guy right. How many ways out had been offered to him! Suppose that he had wanted to keep his chastity and independence. Suppose he hadn't become so involved with Madam X. He'd still be all right as a man, and wouldn't have turned into a dead insect in the crack of a tree. And the women would have some consolation and something solid to cling to at midnight. They wouldn't have to fill the emptiness with memories or wistful dreams. Maybe they could also secretly hide his picture under the bed. When their husbands couldn't satisfy them, they could furtively look at it for spiritual support.

But now all the possibilities were gone: this guy Q had messed everything up. At midnight, the women were suffering unspeakably. Even the writer could not describe it. Without a new ideal object, they would never be satisfied. Public projects suffered because blackboard work was delayed by women whose insomnia made them sleep until noon. Other women wished only to please their husbands and for several days missed work in order to stroll around with them, thereby undermining our serious work ethic. Noticing what was going on, Dr. A—the brainpower of our community— closed his door and stayed home for several days, neither eating nor sleeping. Finally, he thought of a new project based on X's new lover, P, which soon put an end to this improper behavior.

Dr. A called his doctrine "empathy" and ran all over proclaiming it. He built up P's image to substitute for Q's disappearance, as well as to stimulate the women's hormones, so that once again they could feel self-confident and strong and be doubly enthusiastic about their life and work.

"Empathy is omnipotent," he proclaimed. "If a woman's child dies prematurely, she can rebound only by having another."

Dr. A had become an authority. From the night he had climbed to the mountaintop and talked with the gods, he had established himself as a genius surpassing both the writer and the widow. From then on, his voice rang out like a large bell. This was the voice Five Spice Street longed to hear. Everyone wanted his own eardrums to feel the impact of this voice, for it made each person indescribably happy. Q had shamefully vanished without the permission of our women, and we no longer wished to analyze him. With Dr. A's help, we shook off our affection and set up a new idol.

Now for Madam X's husband. From the previous description, we get this impression: This husband was impotent, a yes-man, and a sycophant. In the long years of living with Madam X, he had lost his gender and become a kind of eunuch. This was a confirmed fact before they came to Five Spice Street. Heaven only knows how Madam X contrived this situation and why her precious husband accepted it. But even this pitiful creature struggled to express himself and made his true feelings known to his good friend: he confided that he had his individual "hobby." But it turned out to be nothing more than hopscotch—hardly proving he wasn't impotent.

He had served as X's nursemaid from beginning to end. This was plain as day. Just look at what he did in the home: he was the gatekeeper, served as guard, hung the curtains, and purchased the microscope and mirrors. All were inexplicable. And he was so earnest about it. In what ways was he like a man? Despite his agony, he rarely poured out his feelings to others. Only once did he confide to X's younger sister that he "just wanted to escape to an uninhabited place and live quietly with X" because "there was so much dust on the streets, he could hardly breathe." Of course, this wish did not come true, nor would it. All he could do was keep it to himself.

The widow's profound view of sex suggested that this husband had been totally created by X. If he left X under the guidance of a suitable patron (the female colleague, for example), he might regain "a lot of sex drive," or at least recover his masculinity. What were the consequences of his androgyny? No woman on Five Spice Street was the least bit interested in him. We've mentioned this already but must add something about his temperament. He was not nearly as warm and feeling as Q. He was arrogant toward women and was also a tightwad and a snob. Shunning other women, he announced that all his feelings were reserved for X. Once the widow saw through his ruse, our women really despised him. Everyone knew he was a doll (we don't want to deny the facts or swear that black is white), but how could this help him? Was it any different from "rubbish coated in gold and jade"? Had he been plain-looking, at least that would have been easier on our eyes! Sometimes the Creator likes to oppose people. We had summed him up in the dark room but had no way to classify him. Finally, the female colleague shouted:

"To begin with, he couldn't be considered a person, so how

could you sort him out? Dear X and I have been intimate friends for more than ten years. I've never considered him a person, and definitely not a man. I've gone in and out of their home, and I've always taken him to be something like a curtain. How could a man not react to my feminine charms? This impression has been confirmed over more than ten years of friendship. I didn't try to attract him. In more than ten years, I've never even laid eyes on him. I still don't know what he looks like. I'm not like some people, pretending to be a genius while trying to seduce him. Others have flirted with him in broad daylight and shown him some flesh, but that didn't succeed, either."

The widow followed:

"This husband deserves the most sympathy. We have no way of learning how this man ended up in X's clutches before they settled down on our Five Spice Street. We know only that from the first day we saw him, he had already lost his sexuality. That woman strictly scrutinized his every move, so he developed a conditioned reflex: when he saw a woman, he ran away. As time passed, this developed into an abnormal, detestable psychology. He spent his life immersed in trivia. Only if X vanished before he did would he be able to hold his head up and recover his masculine image. Some nutty persons felt they were great just because they didn't try to seduce him. They're deluded and narrow-minded. They didn't know that on our Five Spice Street, no woman could really seduce him, simply because *he was not a man*. I've tried many times to illumine and awaken his masculine characteristics. But I was defeated each time. X completely destroyed his being, and I couldn't waste so much energy on just one person. Many people needed me and I let this matter slide. But because I had occasionally made these efforts, one or two crazy people on our Five Spice Street resented me. They couldn't conceive that I sacrificed myself to save others. On the contrary, they imagined I was seducing him, this person with no sexuality, this good-for-nothing. The world actually contained such fools! The people spreading this gossip exposed their inner world. If the female colleague hadn't been covetously eyeing this idol all day long, how could she have known that someone wanted to seduce him? This kind of thing was really very tricky! This snoop is also an undeveloped androgynous person, a person lacking female hormones. This kind of woman adores boys who can never grow up, and X's husband happens to be one of them. Once she fell in love with him, she would become unusually jealous and despotic. It just took another woman glancing at him (other than me with my lofty motive, who else would look at him?), and she was immediately enraged and went all out to fight with her imagined rival. Ladies and gentlemen, let me tell you: as I see it, both this man and this woman need my salvation. I know being underdeveloped isn't their fault, for all kinds of outside factors influence this. All along I've wanted only to sweep away that bad influence on their bodies and release their inner energy so that they could return to being a real man and a real woman. It's too bad one's ability is limited: I can't take care of everything while protecting myself from arrows aimed from all directions (this also wastes a major part of my energy). I've already done a lot of work, some of it successful and some not. I admit that I've failed with Madam X's husband. This is because I've always taken him too lightly, seldom giving him any attention. I never ever thought that this little amount of work would be labeled 'seduction,' although the person who said this also needs my help. She said this because of her hypoplasia, but still I have to dig deep for the roots of this kind of thought so that people in general will be educated. Why do these boys who can't grow up exist here? Who created them? You may say that it's X who created this kind of person. But in fact it isn't something she could do by herself. On our Five Spice Street, there are quite a few girls who—like X's husband—can't grow up, so those boys don't feel alone and don't feel that they're strange. They think the world and people are what they see with their eyes. It's this that finally makes it impossible for them to grow up. If he'd been attracted to me and had broken away from X's control, and if a certain resentful woman had restrained herself and let him remain under my good influence, would he still not have grown up? Anyhow, it's too late, absolutely too late. That pitiful boy and this mouthy girl are stuck midway. Like midgets, they will never fully grow up! Life jokes with people too much!"

The other women of course all took their leader's side in this debate. Their sensitive minds grasped that something was wrong and associated this with other things that had happened (such as the time they had gone to the police station and reported X's adultery). Annoyed that history seemed to be repeating itself, they began to pout.

Pretending to look for her handbag while hoping to make her escape, the female colleague anxiously stood up before all these pouting people. She stole to the door but was blocked by the wife of Madam X's brother-in-law's good friend—that muscular dark-skinned woman who shouted:

"Are you trying to fool us? What makes you say he's a curtain? There's something fishy here! A person, even if he has lost his sexual function, certainly is not a curtain! Your words are like a blow to my head! Every man, including this one, secretly adores me. I'm sympathetic toward them, just like my leader. Her description of the boy who couldn't grow up almost made me cry from pity. But your heart is as hard as a millstone. How could you compare a living boy struggling through a painful metamorphosis to a curtain! Your accusation makes us wonder what you're made of and how hard your heart is. We have observed you coldly all along. Ah, God, that the world still contains a woman as evil as you! Not until I heard the leader's analysis did I understand what you're after. All along, your actions have come from your hypoplasia. Your abnormal psychology makes you most interested in a pretty little boy whom you then turn into a cheap curtain. In fact, you want to sweep the crowd away and secretly monopolize him. I bet that if you had escaped just now, you would have immediately looked for him. You threw up a smoke-screen and then meant to take to your heels, thinking you were incredibly smart. You never imagined a prophet had seen through your deception and was waiting for you at the door. Are you flustered now? Listen to me: go back and wash your hands and lie down. Stop your wishful thinking, or you'll make an exhibition of yourself in public. There are rules for everything, and what will be, will be. Open your eyes and look at the people in this room. Who else is as obtrusive as you? You must be a little more careful. An artist here has taken responsibility for writing the history. The night that we were cooling off outside, he and I rushed together into the small dark room. After I had taught him some secrets, he became both delicate and humorous. You mustn't bring up some curtain in front of him. That's risky. Our artist now is almost at my level: with one glance, he can discern your inner world. My God, how hard it is to talk with you! In my whole life, I've never talked so long. You are really extraordinarily dim-witted."

The dark-skinned woman didn't let the female colleague pass. Gazing brightly at her, she blocked the door by spreading out her arms and legs.

"No, I've changed my mind," she said. "I definitely won't let you go home. I won't go home tonight, either. I'll guard this door until dawn. I feel that tonight is the key. I can't tolerate other people spreading rumors about a serious matter. Once the nonsense about the curtain starts spreading, my social status will decline disastrously."

After many meetings, Madam X's husband's role was still ambiguous. The writer had used the diagram of the maze to solve the problem of Madam X's image, but the diagram wasn't suited to this man, for a particular problem needs a particular method to solve it. We have to find the right key to open this door. Our Dr. A had employed "empathy" to solve the problem of Q. But the writer believed that he could not also solve the issue of X's husband. That was the responsibility of genius. After eliminating all other possibilities, the writer acted independently and called on X's little sister.

Here we want to explain that ever since X's sister and her lover eloped and then "settled it peacefully," X's sister had lived in a narrow loft with her present husband. The loft was close to the wharf that was used for transporting "night soil." Though every day they cooked in the midst of the odor of human excrement, it seemed this couple was actually happy. Through the window facing the wharf, you could often see them hugging and kissing. Occasionally, they also stuck their heads out the window and shouted something we couldn't make out.

The writer walked around the house several times without finding the staircase, so he stood on the wharf with his legs apart and waited. He waited about half an hour and then two startled faces were reflected on the window glass. The writer immediately began gesturing. The woman smiled a little and shrank back inside. Another ten minutes went by, and then she lowered a rope ladder from the window. The writer bravely clutched this ladder and clambered up.

"This is great," the woman said to the man. "The method we chose is secure. No one can climb up. Isn't that right, darling? This young guy is an artist."

"An artist?" The husband was surprised. "Excuse me, I must go to work."

He climbed to the window and lowered himself by the rope ladder. From the bottom, he shouted up, "Watch out for that damn guy!" Then, without turning his head, he disappeared.

"He's really adorable. Hey, please close the window. They're starting to pump excrement again. You want to ask me about my sister's husband, but I have nothing to say to you."

"Why? You're very close."

"That was before I moved here. Now I have forgotten everything from the past. I don't go out the whole day long. I can't remember anything. It drives me crazy to remember; it's scary. You don't have to be so concerned about him. As I see it, he has nothing to complain about. He's a stud: happiness is guaranteed for him. Of course, my husband is also a stud. You saw him just now. You can't imagine how happy we are living in this loft like two little birds. What's more, he—this precious man—also invented this rope ladder, and we then immediately blocked up the passage downstairs. Our life is like that of the immortals. What do you think of it? It's already been three months since I've gone out, and I don't plan to go out ever again. My sister is a warning to me. I am timid and weak. Luckily, my darling found this loft. If I were still down below, among all of you, it would be too frightening. Watch out!"

She leapt up, looked left and right for a few seconds, and quickly burrowed under the table and squatted there. "Please sit at the table, and I'll talk with you. You know, as long as we don't go out we're happy up here, but it doesn't mean we don't have worries. Some people are always climbing up to the roof and making trouble. The biggest problem living up here is using the toilet. You have to carry the chamber pot up and down, with the risk of being attacked on the way. You simply can't imagine this kind of trouble."

"I can." Showing consideration for her, the writer said, "I came to see you about your brother-in-law. Maybe you still remember—"

"How can I remember? You're forcing me to do what I just can't do. All I remember every day is burrowing under the table and the chamber pot. These things can't be neglected for one second. I've already told you, I'm not free of worry. I have to keep in mind these two things, even when I'm sleeping with my darling. A few days ago, just at that time, people threw blocks of iron at us from the roof. I was really annoyed. How can I remember anything else? Ever since we moved to this building, I've felt I've lost my memory. The table and the chamber pot are too important. There's no way to get away from them, and you have to concentrate on them. You don't want your home filled with excrement, right? Even less do you want your wife to be smashed to smithereens, right? A female friend from the past came to see me. I refused to see her. Where do I have extra energy to deal with this sort of thing? Although you've come up here today, that doesn't mean I can let my guard down. I can pay attention only to these two things. You can't tear me away from them. Please open the window and see if my darling has come back. Every day at work, he finds some time to come back and empty the chamber pot because I can't go out. If I go out, I'm attacked. You'd better not think he doesn't want to do this. He's happy to do it. We're a good pair. I like a family atmosphere, although in these conditions it seems impossible to have a child. In this respect, my sister and I diverge. I like being with one person to the end. I plan to be with my present husband until we grow old. Ha—the little bird has flown back!"

She rushed over, opened the window, and lowered the ladder.

Then she turned around and said to the writer, "You should leave. Isn't it strange that you're still here? He won't like you very much, I can see that."

That afternoon, the writer achieved nothing. As he was sitting, annoyed, at the curb, tapping his heels, a heavy hand pressed his shoulder. When he looked up, the writer saw his counterpart—the black-clad mother of the street.

"I've evaluated that incident all over again. You certainly didn't offend me. I can't overlook your strong points. There can't be many talents like you." She patted the writer's cheek and said contemplatively, "I greatly appreciate your genius in working hard to track this down. Just now, you've succeeded."

"What?"

"Your work is finished because that baby has already parted from Madam X. I saw this scene with my own eyes. Carrying his bag on his back, he vanished from Five Spice Street. And so in this way, the problem has been solved! When we write the history, we can write him out completely. Ah, it has saved us from so much unnecessary dissension! My mind is empty. I can't say what kind of feeling it is. From the day this baby arrived, I've been carrying a heavy burden on my back. Now, it's over. I should be happy. Why am I at loose ends? All of a sudden, I felt that while he was here, I had vitality and purpose. Then, I looked even younger—right? If he had come and said good-bye to me before he left, making a transition, maybe the situation would be somewhat different, but he just lifted his bag to his back and left: this was too callous! We've been used to his being here for some years now. Every time I organized an activity, I took him into account—even when I decided what clothes to wear. Whenever I made a speech—ah, those splendid speeches!—I always thought of him as my audience. It was only because I imagined this that I exerted myself particularly energetically. How could he have thought of leaving so cruelly? I still thought that he would at least come to my home and bid me farewell. Haven't we been good friends telepathically for a long time? All along, I thought there was a tacit understanding of friendship between him and me because everyone here has this kind of tacit understanding with me. I am the mother of the whole street. After X hooked another man, I just began waiting contentedly. I thought that on a stormy night, he would certainly come to my home. He had no other place to go, so he could come only to me. At a time like that, all his memories of me would be revived. He would see a plump and appealing image for the first time. He would immediately connect this beautiful image with this piteous woman in front of him who was covered in black mourning clothes. He would certainly recall every detail of her charm and appeal, and regret that he had let a great opportunity slip away. Inevitably, he would even conceive an evil thought, and in that instant he would change from a child into a man. This very moment, the woman in the black clothes looked up, and their two gazes fleetingly crossed: it was the exchange of a soulful gaze between two adults. Then the guy's beautiful head drooped. 'Why have I been so blind?' he asked bitterly.

"I would comfort him patiently and tell him there was still time for everything. His past mistakes were actually a good thing. He could change to be even stronger and more energetic; he could be indomitable. Without those thirty years of mistakes, there couldn't be this enlightened person of today. Every one of us has made mistakes. These mistakes become the motor for progress. I think that after this kind of misunderstanding, each of us sees the other's face clearly. The person I see is no longer a little boy but a charming man. This is very gratifying. The guidance I gave wasn't in vain. It had the desired effect. From this, you can also see that my feelings for him were virtuous. This defies certain people's dirty lies. Filled with confidence, I sat in the doorway waiting day after day. I was waiting for the time for our meeting, watching the young guy's expression become more cloudy and despairing by the day, watching the situation gradually become more favorable for me, watching certain people's conspiratorial performances. I saw everything. I foresaw everything. I just didn't guess that he would lift his bag to his back and take off. I didn't reckon that he would so resolutely end our friendship. Of course, I can also understand his drastic action: this was an unexpected result of the guidance I had given him. After being enlightened, he was ashamed and made up his mind that only by cutting himself off from the past could he adopt this drastic action. It might even be a good thing that he acted this way: it saved us a lot of trouble. Now we can simply write him out of the history with one brushstroke. Because now it is the same as if he had never existed on Five Spice Street. As for the time after he grew up, he went to another place to start over again: this had nothing to do with us. From the point of view of ordinary people, it is fair and reasonable to think this way, but I am a mother. Seeing a newborn infant leave me and go far away to an alien land is not easy to accept. I can tell you that when he disappeared at the end of the street, I even shed tears! He certainly could have stayed here. My door was wide open to him day and night. He could come to me whenever he wanted. Why couldn't this child think of this? Had a certain person's spiteful lies reached his ears, and so, to keep people he cared about from being hurt, he decided to sacrifice himself? By contrast, that person looked so filthy and ugly. When this child left, at one stroke he exposed the schemer's inner world. Under our august gaze, did she still have the courage to make her fallacious arguments? My dear stenographer, when I saw you just now and found that you and I are working for the same cause, I immediately felt more relaxed: I'm not the only one paying attention to this incident. Have you considered that this matter before us is ingenious? If you can record the subtle psychology I just described so brilliantly and eloquently, this will educate and enlighten everyone, and the schemer will be too ashamed to show her face. He certainly isn't gone forever: do you believe this? If a person falls into this kind of situation, even his own existence becomes problematic. Everyone forgets his name and just calls him by the awkward name 'X's husband.' It was difficult enough for him to stand up again at the spot where he fell, and he also faced other obstacles. He didn't have time to bare his heart to me and get my protection. So he became temporarily depressed and couldn't see a way out. In leaving, he was subjectively embracing a self-destructive resolve. Of course, in reality, it can't turn out this way. My latent influence on him must have determined his whole life. After he got a new life, he made a circuit outside, finally returning to his mother's side—the only friend he revered—to live out his life. My dear stenographer, after discussing all of this with you, my train of thought has gradually become clear. Isn't this an astonishing skill? Now I've become optimistic about X's husband's future. He's already been transformed from an awkward symbol into a person. After this, he will complete his travel in the outside world, and finally he will throw himself into my embrace. Twenty minutes ago, I had a heavy heart as I watched him leave me, and aged ten years all at once. You saw this yourself. But after only twenty minutes, I'm the same as ever. Now how do I look?"

The writer told her that she couldn't look better, that she could absolutely be called "a budding flower," but that she was even more gorgeous than "a budding flower." After experiencing her loveliness, no one would be satisfied with those young girls. She was really the epitome of perfection.

Only now did it occur to the writer that he had left his house early and until now had taken a twisting path. His objective definitely hadn't been the small loft next to the wharf—that was just an excuse, a feint. After the writer left that place, the gods had led him to his real destination. Now the problem was already solved. The solution was "to wipe out all the records about this man." This was wonderful! Too bad the writer hadn't brought his notebook. Otherwise, he would have been able to finish this major pioneering work right away. This was precisely a case of "great minds thinking alike" and "reaching the same goal by different routes." Today really was a memorable day. In essence, this major pioneering work was both merciful and humane. We constructed a home for a stranger, and the door to this home was wide open day and night to people traveling far from their own homes. This was so inspirational.

The widow made some additional comments to the writer: at daybreak, she had taken a pair of that man's shoes from the windowsill of X's home. Now she was keeping these cloth shoes, full of symbolic significance, in her drawer of memorabilia. This was also forceful evidence. If she met with an accident, the writer should remember this pair of shoes. He could use this fact to fight off the possible attack.

Now, the writer had finally finished dealing with the problem of these two vague persons. He doubtless felt greatly relieved. The writer got that pair of cloth shoes at the widow's home, and so the two of them uttered a sigh of relief in unison. This spelled the end of one section of our work. The widow sat down on a recliner in her doorway, her gaze slack and numb. She also seemed to have become much thinner. The writer secretly thought she was indeed getting old.

"Nothing matters." She suddenly gave a forced smile. "The wind is blowing in front of you, the road stretches out before your eyes. None of this means anything at all. I keep asking myself: what happened to me? I'm gorgeous, young, and pretty—so what? Even if I were as old as the woman wearing the little black felt hat, I would still look okay. But whenever I cast off my responsibility to society and come back home and sit in this small coffin-like room, I am caught up in frightening thoughts of death. Most recently, I've worried more and more about the future of human beings, and I've had more and more self-doubt. All along, I've been exhausted from carrying too heavy a burden on my back. Now I'm telling you the truth: just now, if that man hadn't been so ruthless, I would really have wanted to go far away with him and start over. This place of ours is really a little too closed. All at once, I've abandoned myself to despair."

She gave another forced smile. Her mood infected the writer, who had a sudden impulse: he thought he would go home and burn this precious historical record. Luckily, that impulse lasted only thirty-seven seconds. Luckily, after those thirty-seven seconds, another new question occupied our beloved friend's brain. Only then did we cast off our individual sentimentality.

10

HOW WE REVERSED THE NEGATIVE
AND ELECTED MADAM X OUR REPRESENTATIVE

Many people opposed electing Madam X the people's representative, arguing that no one could get used to seeing our former
antagonist on Five Spice Street in this high position. There was
nothing strange in this opposition because new ways of thinking are
always attacked, but after a few months, X entered the historical
records as the people's representative.

The reader must think this very odd. Common sense tells us there's
something fishy in this alien from outer space, this dissident, whose
murderous plot had been directed against the people, this abettor of
juvenile delinquency, this hooligan with corrupt morals all of a sudden
becoming the people's representative! People shuddered. But the new
idea was finally born, and survived with a tenacious life-force. The
change in thinking occurred silently and secretly. Today, when the
outside delegation came to make an on-the-spot investigation of orderly Five Spice Street, the residents boasted:

"The one who used to be Madam X has been elected our representative. This is worth bringing up, for it indicates a transition in
our history." Then someone pulled a delegate over to the side of the
street for a "talk." This enlightened person made the following significant remark:

"We acknowledged X's essence long ago: we were very familiar
with her conduct and never made a fuss about it. X's mistakes all
derive from her having no concept of time. She was completely
mixed up and ignored our present social system. She made a mess of

everything. If we hypothesize that she represents a society of the future, we discover that everything she did is something we had been longing to do. It's just that we weren't audacious enough to release our natural instincts. We weren't audacious enough to scoff at the rules. There was no need for such troublesome audacity. Only a lunatic would have had such nerve. Everybody is born with a destructive inclination. It's just that from birth, we fall under restrictions that turn our desires to the right path and make us well-bred people. X did nothing that we had not desired long ago. The difference is that we restrained our natural instincts. Only in a highly developed future society could we let ourselves go. That's how things are. Why did we usually feel that X's actions seemed so familiar? Why did we feel that our life and death were associated with her? After carefully considering all the facts, we found that she did everything we weren't audacious enough, as well-bred people, to do in our present society. No one wanted to deviate from the norms. No one wanted to be talked about behind his back. As for ability, we believe that any of us can do anything many times better than X can. X, however, gambled with her jokes and accomplished what others wouldn't. We could do it much better! Our talent and clear concept of time will one day allow us to begin the real performance. Today we elected X our representative, not because she is more talented than others, or because she actually represents us (we stress this again): her performance was actually very poor. The reason we elected her is that she was the first to act out the theme we will all perform in the future. We aren't jealous people. When a new form comes into being, even if infantile, flimsy, or immoral, we can all be reasonable and accept it, and live and let live until it dissolves in the process of evolution. In this, X was useful. No matter how she performed, we all wanted to elect her. This demonstrated our community's tolerant spirit. Dear delegates, what you're interested in today shouldn't be the content of Madam X's performances but the forms that lie outside her. These are our community's forms. The official performance hasn't yet begun. On the stage of the future society, we will shake the whole world." After all of them talked to the delegates about their own hopes, they all marched over to ask X to give a speech, since she had been recognized openly as the people's representative.

X was washing beans in her snack shop and perspiring heavily. The crowd stayed quietly outside as Dr. A and Ms. B went inside to deliver everyone's wishes. As the quick-tongued Ms. B helped X wash beans, she explained to her that there had been a major misunderstanding about her superb lecture in the past, and the people had done certain things that they shouldn't have done and had harmed her to a certain extent. It was simply a normal stage through which emerging social phenomena had to pass. She asked her to understand the people's behavior, because their original idea had been to protect her. She mustn't oppose the people because of this misunderstanding. Over a long period, the people had accepted some of her activities. They now thought of her as the "wave of the future." They hoped she wouldn't belittle this trust. The wave of the future belongs to the people. This was very glorious. Ms. B herself had already worked many years for the benefit of the people. She had offered up her entire youth and spared no effort in performing her duty. But she hadn't attained the status of X: she was still a nobody called Ms. B. Yet, X reaped rewards without deserving them. She did nothing. She only hopped up on a stone bench, said a few words, and then lay in her room for a month pretending to be hurt. And now all of a sudden she had gained such a high honor: not only was she the representative, but she was crowned with the "wave of the future" laurels, an honor she didn't deserve (just think of the nameless heroes on Five Spice Street who had done so much for the people). She had only bumped into the opportunity and gotten lucky.

During her previous reeducation, Ms. B had offended her, which was entirely in the public's best interests. That reeducation was absolutely correct. Without it, she wouldn't be a representative today, nor would she be the wave of the future. Not only shouldn't she bear a grudge against the women's reeducation movement, she should be grateful. These women had fought hard for the honor she received today. They had helped her greatly but received no advantages for themselves. This alone should spur her to make the speech, unless she has no conscience at all. Everyone had helped make the fire, yet she alone enjoyed its warmth. This was unfair, and anyone with a conscience would feel uneasy about it. All along she had acted only for herself, yet now honor and position had dropped upon her from heaven, making her a revolutionary hero. She must make up for this. Ms. B would have been very much ashamed had it had been she.

Ms. B discussed these principles as she washed the beans. She washed them so earnestly that Madam X was touched, and because she was touched she listened. Finally, she understood the woman's words and answered that she was very moved by being elected representative and receiving such a high honor. However, it would have been good if they had sought her out earlier. At one time, she had wanted the honor of being the representative and had wasted a lot of energy over it. If she had become the representative then, she would certainly have given countless profound speeches. Unfortunately, now it was too late. Time had rolled on, and she was middle-aged. Her heart was like dead ashes. Not only did she not want to be the representative, but it was difficult for her even to see people. For example, just now, if Ms. B hadn't helped her wash beans, she wouldn't have seen a man and a woman enter her shop, nor would she have heard what the woman said. Ever since she gave up the idea of being the representative, she had become deaf and blind. Why did they want a cripple like her? What use was it? If she were shoved up to the platform to make a speech, she would certainly fall down and make a spectacle of herself. No, she was definitely useless to them. They must have made a mistake and gotten everything mixed up. She—the representative? That was too funny. It could not happen. If they pushed her into it, she would bark like a dog on the platform and do somersaults.

As Madam X went to dry the beans in the sun, she crushed Dr. A's instep, and he let out a frightening scream.

"Why hasn't this man left yet? I can't see him at all," she said.

Now it was Dr. A's turn to talk. He leaned against the wall (for fear she would step on his feet again) and spoke with fervor and assurance. He talked of the sublime significance of representatives and of all the hope the residents of this street had invested in her. As a Ph.D. in the field of her kind of problem, he was clearer about this than anyone. "This is the highest honor." Please don't think she earned this honor because of her ability. Not at all. He could divulge a little of the inside story: it was he, acting on his own authority, who bestowed this honor on her. After he won the debate over who had taken the initiative, he acquired more authority every day. Everything he said became a decree. Ordinary people esteemed him: no matter what important thing occurred on Five Spice Street, when a ruling was needed, everyone said, "Let's get Dr. A." Without him, the people were lambs that had lost their way. Now, one word from him, one glance, determined the people's destiny. All day long, his head was filled with grave problems; it was nearly bursting with them. Recently, X's problem had become the core issue: with one sentence, he made her eminent. He did so because he was determined to reform her. She should know that a lot of people had worked hard their whole lives without getting this opportunity. Some even knelt before him and implored! He thought her behavior just now inconceivable. How could she not repay him for his kindness (he had never wished for repayment from those whom he had benefited; he was a person with lofty thoughts and didn't want cheap praise)? What's more, she'd even stepped on his foot and his toes were still numb. Her behavior made him wonder whether it had been a mistake to confer these laurels on her so lightly. Just think of all the good words he'd said about her to the delegation. How could he take them back? But he was committed to his original intention of cooperating with her. He asked Madam X to consider it carefully. She shouldn't be indiscreet. After all, she was still young and would live several more decades on Five Spice Street. As long as she lived here, she couldn't get away from his governance. If she was driven to offend him, her future would again be problematic. He would give her no further opportunities. Not only would she not be the representative, the people wouldn't even mention her name again. Many historians and artists on Five Spice Street were close friends who would die for him. He had to look over all their articles. If she rejected public opinion, who would concern himself with her innovations and unconventional behavior? She would never have a chance to appear in public again. If she recognized this now, he could still forgive her for stepping on his foot. He was a magnanimous, well-bred scholar. When others hurt him, he never much minded. He just hoped she would change her mind at once.

Madam X crossed her eyes, and didn't look at the two people who were standing against the wall. She busied herself in the room. After a little while, her new brother-in-law came in. She grabbed him and complained loudly:

"Two others came in just now. They'll seize any opportunity! Take a look outside for me. I suspect I'm surrounded."

A lot of people were outside, he told her, but it didn't matter. They weren't organized. Some were cracking melon seeds; others were climbing trees. Some were heading home. By noon, not a single person would remain; they didn't have much patience. If she didn't go out, they would soon forget their purpose. He whispered that two shady characters were leaning against the wall in the house. Did she want him to get rid of them?

"Ah, never mind!" she said. "Now I know you're hiding inside. I already said I'm not the least bit interested in being the representative. Why can't you give up? Hiding won't help you at all." She added that if they had nothing better to do, they could help with the work. She would greatly appreciate it.

She heard that one of the two was a Ph.D.; she didn't think much of Ph.D.'s. Selling peanuts was a lot better. A Ph.D. was just a boasting cheat. If conditions allowed, each Ph.D. should be sent to the snack shop to be reeducated and break the habit of lying. All her life she had hated them. If this Ph.D. became the representative— fine. But if one hid out in her home, she'd go nuts and might hit him. So speaking, she lifted a large steelyard. They were so frightened they ran away.

"All Ph.D.'s are traitors," she said to her brother-in-law. Then she blinked teasingly and said, "Is my sister still remembering to set up a household?"

Her brother-in-law answered that she was. He enjoyed it, but it was a lot of trouble to carry the chamber pot up and down every day. If they had a baby—hey, he didn't dare imagine.

"The smell of human excrement would surely damage the baby's brain. The environment is scary." He was a little dejected.

"Why don't you both come to my shop and help out here? Sitting in the loft all day will paralyze her legs. How can a person not move all day?"

"That won't work," he said. "She's already fallen apart. You can't imagine what her nerves are like now. She takes precautions day and night. We're both weak. Sorry."

"I want to teach her how to use the javelin."

"It's too late, dear sister. She spends the whole day squatting under the table because someone is making a disturbance on the roof. I want to engage a good doctor, but no one will climb our rope ladder. Whenever I suggest unblocking the staircase, she threatens to jump out the window."

The matter of Madam X's becoming the representative didn't end here. Everyone knew that one or two arguments wouldn't work, considering past events; and without being able to talk with her, there was nothing to do but go ahead with the election. The young coal worker and others loyal to her saw her sitting on the windowsill, truly both deaf and blind. They pleaded with her, but left in disappointment. Later, the election took place in the dark room. As expected, Madam X won. She got nearly all the votes. She officially became a representative. Only a few ambitious people who wanted to be representatives overestimated their abilities and voted against her. After their hopes were dashed, they hatched a plot, but a shout from Madam X's husband's good friend scared them so much that they scattered. Among them were Madam X's female colleague, Ms. B, and others. Only now did the people realize that Ms. B didn't really want Madam X to be the representative. Her objective in going to the snack shop was to wreck this possibility! She was the one responsible for Madam X's insistence on not being elected! Furious, Madam X's husband's good friend picked up a shovel: he wanted to split Ms. B's head "in half."

"So many people," he roared indignantly, "so many people have assembled here to see Madam X. Now they can't see even a shadow. Weren't all of my years of effort and all my hopes just for today? When I think of those hurtful past events, my heart aches. I thought that the hard days were over. Who knew there would be a day like this! I'm telling you: a person like you has no excuse to go on living. You not only slapped me, but you also smashed my friend the young coal worker's ideals. Look at him (he was picking his nose with a grieved expression). Ever since he became my neighbor, we've gone through so many trials and tribulations together! You—ugly crow! Go straight to hell!"

He had been holding the shovel high. Now he let his hand drop, and the shovel hit his instep. Grimacing, he jumped around the room five times. Then he turned happy again and clasped the young coal worker's shoulders:

"This is the last proof," he said. "My instep has cracked open and the bones are exposed. On this day when the esteemed lady appears in public, I will also soon have days of glory. I'm convinced she represents our future. I haven't wavered in this belief at all. I think this must be rooted in my subconscious. I am talented: isn't this clear? My friend! We are both talented. While others didn't understand, we've been struggling alone until today. Look at the big blister on the back of my head: this came from sleeping on flagstones. Who is Madam X? She's a model I have shaped—the well-known "wave of the future"! Few people were aware of my efforts, but it was only because of those efforts that the people were able to put into effect this grand election. Buddy, we need to start working at night and come up with a new project. Do you feel some pressure?"

The young coal worker confirmed that he "felt pressure in every part of his gut." He couldn't even pass gas. The most important thing was: Madam X had been absent without a reason, and this concealed innumerable dangerous portents. No, he wasn't the least bit intoxicated over today's election. He couldn't see anything worth being intoxicated over. He had long ago learned about X. More often than not, when everyone was intoxicated with her, she didn't notice it at all! At first, he had employed a lot of measures to attract her attention, but they were all ineffectual. One day, he ran into her on the street and greeted her. She just called him "a newcomer." Of course, not being intoxicated wasn't the same as wanting to abandon his efforts. The election process was half of what he wanted to do. But Madam X hadn't shown up, and so the other half hadn't yet been put into effect. If he couldn't get Madam X to appear at the meeting, then the whole thing was unfinished and anti-climactic.

The heavy responsibility of making the request of Madam X fell to the writer. "Because you're a stenographer and this matter is fit for a stenographer to deal with," everyone said solemnly. So the stenographer stayed at the snack shop from morning until evening and explained to Madam X the significance of being a representative. Now and then, he also broke in on what she was doing, so that she couldn't focus on her work, and forced her to turn her attention to him. Finally, the lady compromised and agreed to go to the meeting place with the writer. But she had one request—namely, that she would just do two somersaults on the platform and then come back. She "definitely wasn't going to waste time on this shit." She went, and the whole group stood up, filled with deep esteem. With one leap, she charged up to the platform. *Ping-pong, ping-pong*: she turned two somersaults and then rushed for the door and left. There was no trace of her. It was as if the crowd had awakened from a dream: they sighed with emotion, and one after another they said: "Marvelous! Super! What skill! It can't be done without years of practice!"

The writer had completed his historical mission. So now, X's husband's good friend and the young coal worker had nothing more to say. Although X didn't make a speech, the result could be ten times better than a speech! You have to know that Madam X was a celebrity now. The actions of celebrities of course were somehow unusual. Doing the somersaults was the embodiment of her unique style. "The wave of the future" should have this kind of show. Otherwise, how could it be called the wave of the future? Of course, now, except for intellectuals like the writer, it was hard for people to understand the significance of Madam X's somersaults. Some people put on a show for the enjoyment of audiences decades or centuries later. We encourage and welcome this kind of performance, as well. As long as the somersaults were skillful, we considered them a lofty art. On our Five Spice Street's cultural stage, now every kind of flower is really flourishing!

After Madam X left, everyone began singing and dancing festively. A large group of cameramen also arrived, and took a lot of manly-type photographs, both of people alone and of groups. Women were also in the pictures as foils. In the electric atmosphere, everyone elected a "grand king of beasts" (this was the men's leader). They were almost unanimous in choosing Dr. A. Everyone saw that, after the test of time, he was a real tough guy with some softness mixed in. He was always refined and courteous in dealing with women and never lost his temper or put on airs. He never mentioned his scholarship: how humble he was! How far-sighted! All right, Dr. A became the grand king of beasts. The photographers told him to mess up his hair and to let "intrepid rays of light shoot from his eyes." They took several shots and then told him to comb his hair neatly, rest his chin on both palms, and "look solemn." They took several more photos. Finally, they told him to turn a somersault for a photo, but he sternly turned them down.

He told everyone very plausibly: turning somersaults suits only artists and the wave of the future. How could someone like him—a serious philosopher—do this? That could hurt his image. It was not that he wasn't able to do it; in fact, he could do it a lot better than Madam X could. But this was what he had loved as a child a long time ago. Now he wasn't interested in pretending to be young. He had been growing his hair long because he was going to the mountain. Very soon, he would leave the dear people here. But he wouldn't forget everyone's earnest hopes. Rather, he would ponder everyone's hardships, and he would also come down from the mountain frequently and get together with them. He would help the people rid themselves of worries and resolve their difficulties. He asked everyone to preserve these photos. Looking at his photo was the same as looking at him. This way, he would live forever among them.

The photographers' arrival interrupted the meeting's agenda. Everyone crowded forward desperately, wanting to be photographed and get a picture to hang in his house. No one cared a bit about the meeting itself. They had come to the meeting only to be photographed—to embody their handsome manliness! They didn't want to lose this singular opportunity! Seeing this struggle, the writer was furious. Gasping for breath, Dr. A also crowded over. He sighed from the bottom of his heart and said to the writer: How difficult it is for ordinary people to appreciate art! He planned to write a book and make detailed notes about Madam X's two splendid somersaults. He asserted that this book would be unique. Of course, this book wouldn't be written for today's readers. It would be for readers hundreds of years from now.

"We can't abandon Madam X," Dr. A said. "We can't abandon any of the things that we don't understand now. History tells us: the things that can't be understood are usually the loftiest. I've known this a long time. It can't be wrong. For example, the two somersaults just now: I tape-recorded them. I always think things through thoroughly beforehand. Beginning tomorrow, I'll play this tape dozens of times a day until it becomes a conditioned reflex. Then I'll leap from feeling to reason. We made too many mistakes in the past. If everyone adopted my prudent attitude toward the wave of the future, the philistinism we've seen today would never appear."

After repeatedly saying, "Philistines," he went home to work on annotations. The room was still noisy. One photographer's face was black and blue from being shoved by the crowd. The writer couldn't continue watching. He also shouted, "Philistines," and went home.

After turning her somersaults, Madam X went back to the snack shop without paying the least attention to the commotion she had caused. As she worked, she was humming "The Lonesome Little Boat." Just as she dumped a basket of peanuts into a wooden barrel, she suddenly saw two bolts of lightning flash by, *kecha kecha*. This really frightened her. She set the basket down, jumped back, and asked fiercely, "Who is it?" Hiding outside the door were two photographers. Shrewdly, they didn't make a sound. Their faces were filled with the joy of adventurers as they waited for Madam X to lose her temper and jump out: they wanted to get two frontal shots. But after asking that question, Madam X seemed to have no thought of jumping out. They waited several hours without getting a chance to photograph that histrionic scene. As their legs were going numb, someone inside said, "My work is finished now. I can strike a pose, but you have to pay me for it."

With reverence and awe, the photographers nodded and immediately aimed their cameras. She had changed her costume: she had a belt tied at her waist, and she held a sword as she stood there. Her "bearing" was absolutely "heroic." She said humbly, "It's too bad I don't know how to play with this sword. I'll sit on it for a picture!"

The photographers thought this was ingenious and agreed. So she laid the sword under her butt. They didn't take just one photo but ten! Each was special. Although the expression was the same, because of the photographers' high level of skill, the more you looked at them, the more extraordinary they were. After a few days, Madam X wrote to the photographers asking to be paid. This startled the studio. Such a screwball! Others had brought her to the forefront, but it was as if they owed her something. Her tone was tough: she spoke of current financial difficulties and the work which had been delayed because of the photographs.

At first the photographers' eyes bulged, and then they began cheering because they remembered the fine outline that Dr. A had published in the newspaper. All their doubts were dispelled. It was reasonable for a wave of the future to act oddly: if her actions were commonplace, they wouldn't be worth the photographers' while to photograph her. Now it was clear that they hadn't been wrong: the odder her actions, the better, for this would have a direct impact on the studio's reputation. They would also contact the stenographer, who would make a special effort to write something that would describe her peculiar relationship with the studio. As for money, although they couldn't be completely satisfied with her request (this was at odds with the financial system), they decided to pass the hat, and each dug down to express his regards. They did this willingly. They all felt that they'd become part of the romance.

After electing Madam X as their representative, the people felt very excited. Now they loved congregating to talk about this. "Our Five Spice Street is really full of talent." Soon afterward, "innovative movements" began to appear spontaneously on Five Spice Street. One morning, a few young guys coincidentally showed up on the street with wool sweaters wrapped around their heads. That was really a novelty. From a distance, it was as if a large bundle had grown on top of their heads. Someone commented that it "was as if the neck were weighed down by heavy thoughts." They went back and forth several times on the street. The next day, more than half the people on Five Spice Street wound their sweaters around their heads. Most were young people. They were the nucleus of the new movement. Of course, the old philosopher Dr. A led the movement and in doing so discovered a fatal weakness: this weakness led to certain individuals' dissociating themselves from people in general. They unilaterally pursued odd and flighty styles and gathered in small groups of three or five, "as if they were rebels." They had given up winding sweaters around their heads and had begun talking day and night. When their talking reached a fever pitch, someone jumped to the window and "shouted and screamed," which made all the people on the street very nervous.

Enraptured, Dr. A observed these guys for a long time and finally discovered the sticking point. From the time this phenomenon began, it was clear that its creed was fuzzy. When we elected Madam X our representative, our heads were muddled by a certain blind emotion. We forgot that at present this lady still didn't share our objective. She was merely a symbol—a gleam of the dawn of the future. The reason we wanted to canonize her was certainly not to serve today, but to serve our descendants hundreds of years hence. So certain people's blind imitation of her style was absolutely unacceptable. To transplant her style into the context of present life would only create jokes. It was ridiculous.

Dr. A proposed several more discussion meetings. He told everyone clearly: what Madam X does and is today is not at all related to real life. It's an artificial performance. If we do not understand this, all the positive aspects of our canonization of her will be lost. Dr. A also said this kind of movement could proceed only under his leadership, for it needed a great spirit of risk-taking. If it wasn't done well, it would become "rebellion," and that was a capital crime. If he didn't watch everything strictly every minute and every second and "correct errors," all kinds of consequences were possible. He was a seasoned person with abundant experience. Ten years ago, he had gone through a similar movement. That movement, not having a leader like him, never developed and finally became a child's game of hide-and-seek. Now it pained him to think about it, because it represented the retrogression of human intelligence.

At this point, Dr. A remembered the heated dispute he'd had with other scholars over who had taken the initiative. He had mentioned that everyone should pay attention to the meaning of the word "symbol." "It's only a form, a matrix, an indeterminate matrix. There's nothing more fitting than our electing a woman to be the representative. In this, there are a lot of things worth thinking about."

As for Madam X's remaining a bystander in the election, Dr. A commented: "She understands her position. What else can a woman do? Especially a woman like Madam X, who has been scrutinized by the crowd. Being a representative is a mere form—an honor generously bestowed by everyone. She should cherish and esteem herself. Apart from improving her skill in turning somersaults, she should make no further changes. If she is overbearing, stops practicing, and lets her skills get rusty, she'll lose this honor. Honor isn't inexhaustible capital. If it isn't handled well, it becomes a burden!"

11

MADAM X'S STEPS ARE BUOYANT; ON BROAD FIVE SPICE STREET, SHE WALKS TOWARD TOMORROW

The writer has brought this complicated story close to its end. This morning, he met with Madam X, who had just been elected representative. The writer found but a slight wrinkle on her forehead, the mark of past years, yet it could be ignored. Madam X had not aged; she was still "hot." And the writer speculated that even Dr. A (more than ten years older) might wish to marry her if she gave up her celibacy and A's wife died. After all, he was still in good health and had an eminent position. Not to mention the young coal worker and her husband's good friend—if they wanted to marry, both of them would think of her first. This morning, the writer was a little indirect: after her husband left and the incident with Q was made public, did she intend to marry a handsome man of about the same age? After she served as representative, did she want to walk hand in hand toward a beautiful tomorrow with someone who could also be a career partner?

How did Madam X answer? She told the writer (looking left and right, afraid someone would overhear) that her greatest wish was that the people would "forget" her. This would give her the greatest happiness. She had been observed for so many years that she had come to understand that she was different from others. She wasn't a person but only the embodiment of desire. Because it could never be actualized, this kind of desire could only upset people. The greatest thing would be if everyone could do what Dr. A suggested and see her only as a symbol and with the passage of time forget her. The inconsistency lay precisely in that no one saw her as a symbol; they all had to see her as a person. They also kept making demands and giving her trouble. All at once, they wanted her to turn somersaults; all at once, they wanted her to be photographed (at this point, she expressed again her great indignation at the photographers for failing to pay her as they had promised); now, they also wanted to entice her to get married (she threw a glance at the writer). All of this made her station very nebulous: she was neither an ordinary person nor an abstract symbol; rather, she was swinging between the two. It was like being kicked back and forth like a ball. It seemed that she was destined to this fate: she couldn't become one of the ordinary people, nor could she become a symbol. It was damnable. However, he shouldn't imagine that she had no way to go on living. She still had "layers of armor-plate protection," so up to now had lived "better than people expected." It was not necessary for anyone to worry about her marriage. She "had her own plan" (she gave the writer a sweet smile that made the writer's heart skip a beat).

She said, "Yesterday, I had a fascinating date. You'll never find out this kind of thing. So don't waste your time." The writer felt enlightened, and asked if this was P.

"Or perhaps O. Anyhow, there'll always be someone."

"How can you be so fickle?" The writer was indignant. "You must know that it was only recently that we hypothesized there was a P. We haven't seen even his shadow. Now, great, there's also O. You're a representative: how can you get involved in such disgraceful things?"

The writer urged Madam X to focus on P because her status wasn't the same now. In everything, she now had to consider the effect on the people. How could the writer explain this to the people? Madam X couldn't take the writer's complaints and agreed to change the person she had met to P, but her attention wandered as she talked, and she also called him O or D, while the writer tirelessly insisted it was P.

"What business is it of yours?" she demanded, staring above the writer's head with great disgust, as though dead fish hung over him.

The writer said that it had nothing to do with him, but had to do with the destiny of all of the people on Five Spice Street. P was the idol hypothesized by all the people. How could she smash it or replace him? This wouldn't do. Even if she wanted to replace him, she had to give the people time to get used to it. She couldn't do it in one fell swoop, nor could she do this every day, replacing lovers as often as she pleased. People would get the wrong idea: they'd believe in nothing. People who have lost their faith are like trees chopped down at the roots. It wasn't right. It was dangerous. P had already become part of the crowd's social life: as soon as he was mentioned, everyone grew excited. They talked endlessly about him, hypothesizing and making plans. Even old men (for example, Old Meng) were not exceptions. His appearance kindled everyone's youthful spirit, so P was a good, objective entity independent of Madam X. Therefore, she should treat this entity reasonably and not look upon him as her private property, because he wasn't. He was the creation of all the people.

After the writer enumerated everything significant about P, he also told Madam X that she had become everyone's friend and soon she would have a lot of visitors. The writer estimated that almost the whole street (including the elites and even the geniuses) yearned to bare their hearts to her and establish even closer relationships. It was only past misunderstandings and estrangements that prevented them for the moment from coming to her home: they were all waiting for her to declare herself. As a first gesture toward the people, should she post an announcement or publish something in the blackboard newspaper? If she felt this didn't suit her, she could just open her doors and windows, place a vase on the windowsill, and sit there to show her inner transformation. Everyone would understand. She should know how magnanimous the people are. Hadn't she done a lot of "extremely improper" things, and had we acted too harshly? Seeing her with brand-new eyes, we not only overlooked her improprieties but connected them with the wave of the future! It was only because she'd taken the initiative to cast Q off that we hypothesized that there was a P. If she was still trysting with Q in the granary, if they were still "deeply attached," perhaps everyone would be "profoundly enlightened." She should realize that Five Spice Street was a rare, sweet place. The road was so wide! The architecture so ancient and solemn! Only in this miraculous place could her existence be so respected; only here could she freely and lightheartedly develop herself.

The writer finished speaking and noticed that Madam X was no longer in the house. He found her in the snack shop. He was about to repeat his suggestion that she open the door and put a vase on the windowsill when she suddenly complained: "Haven't they paid me what they owe me yet?"

"Who?"

"The fucking photographers! Who else? I won't be tricked again! Huh!" With that, she turned deaf and mute again. The writer could not revive her.

Soon after, another big event occurred in Madam X's life. The wall of her house that faced the street seemed on the brink of collapse from years of wind and rain. Madam X thought carefully for a morning and decided to apply to the community for repairs. She wasn't hopeful. It also contradicted her desire that the people "forget" her. Why then did she apply? Here, we will inform the reader that certain of Madam X's principles were not invariable; they might change several times a day. She thought of her application as if "watching a play," as if the wall on the brink of collapse didn't belong to her but to someone else. "Let's see how they deal with it," she gloated. Then she didn't think of it again. From that day on, she just locked the front door and went around to the back door to go in and out.

However, the community was excited by her application. Everyone recognized that this was the first time Madam X had taken the initiative to establish a relationship with the people! She had become one of us! Could a fish survive without water? Could a melon leave the vine? In the end, Madam X couldn't exist without the community. We had been absolutely correct in electing her our representative. If she had established a direct relationship with us earlier (for example, had she made an application the day she moved here), maybe she would have become the representative much earlier! Her strange principles had prevented her from doing so, and she had kept the people at arm's length. Actually, we had always considered her one of us, and all our former suspicions were dispelled when she submitted her application. Now people feel close to her, think of her as a family member, and warmly call her "our Madam X." As for the wall, the people thought it a pretext, an excuse to get close. The main thing was that her application was unprecedented! Dr. A urged the writer to make a big-character poster that very night: "Especially big news that is creating a stir on the whole street."

"That wall can last at least another fifty years," the widow said, her saliva flying. "It's almost 'indestructible.' Why did she make this application? She's always been vain and mischief-making, unable to be serious. But we still welcome this pose. This is no different from opening doors, placing a vase on the windowsill, and then sitting at the window. She always takes a roundabout way"

The young coal worker and the husband's good friend also put up articles on the blackboard newspaper. In their articles, which were as long as ten thousand characters (taking up more than ten blackboards), they told of their close relationship with this present representative. Their words moved people to tears. In the articles, they stated that they had contributed to Madam X's enlightenment and had almost "paid with their lives for today's beautiful scene." Look where they lived, look at what they ate: you'd have to be a stone not to be moved! They were down-to-earth, practical workers. In writing his tracts, even such a high-level theorist as Dr. A could not be without the fine materials they offered. They didn't want glory. They were willing to be invisible. This gave them even greater pleasure. Now, seeing the lady they loved and esteemed throw off her burden and stride forward buoyantly toward a beautiful tomorrow, how could they not feel relieved from the bottom of their hearts! They had been looking forward to this special day for a long time!

After the blackboard newspaper was published, they embraced

tightly and shed hot tears. They were now doubly devoted to Madam X for having thought up such a brilliant pretext. They hoped she would think up even more and write even more applications so they would be able to exert their ability and wisdom even more. "To apply for help when the wall is weathered but still far from collapse is romantic. To apply when it is on the brink of collapse is merely pragmatic."

But two weeks later, the people saw that wall of Madam X's home facing the street had become a heap of rubble. Luckily, Madam X had taken precautions and had moved all her valuables to a room in the back whose four walls were still very strong. They could "last at least another fifty years." She seemed happy. She told others, "I foresaw this a long time ago. I submitted the application in order to watch them contradict themselves."

After the collapse, she enjoyed a long period of quiet. The people on Five Spice Street were concerned about Madam X's thoughts, of course, for they were directly related to everyone's destiny. But they hesitated about whether to rebuild her house. Was this necessary? Would they be pampering her too much? Would this make her haughty? Would she forfeit her small achievement? They had to think carefully because their reaction would affect the future. Thus, they pretended to be ignorant of the problem of the house. The people said they hadn't seen the application or hadn't gotten a good look at it. "That isn't our responsibility. Our Ph.D. can take care of everything. We hear that he has an original idea about this problem." The people remained concerned about Madam X, but no one visited her. If you wanted to find her, you had to go around the rubble to her room. But then she might latch on to you and suggest you work as a coolie—and that wouldn't be great. To make a little effort was okay, but we couldn't wreck principles. In addition, we're all extremely busy. The best thing is just to think about Madam X. We don't have to go to her door every day and disturb her. Later, they'll substitute a code—"T"—for the house problem. "The T problem," they would say. "Dr. A will take care of it."

Madam X gained experience: sometimes, to achieve oblivion,

you have to be noticed. Then people will start leaving you alone. She experienced this several times and gained spiritual pleasure from it. Later, she made use of this experience. It's said that "it all succeeded." No matter what Madam X's intention, submitting the application made it clear that she was on normal terms with everyone. Whenever an outside delegation arrived, we pointed to Madam X's application as evidence that on our Five Spice Street impossible things became realities.

Madam X submitted five applications in a row. In addition to the one to repair her house, the others were: (1) a request for financial aid; (2) a request to relieve her of civic activities (the reason was that she had too many callers; receiving them was the same as taking part in civic activities); (3) a request to renovate the front of her shop (it was already old, and the red-painted sign was dingy); and (4) a request to provide her with a quiet environment (because she wanted to concentrate on studying the wave of the future, she didn't want anyone to enter her house). We looked upon her applications as symbolic. Each time she submitted an application, everyone felt inexpressibly gratified, warm, and magnanimous.

An explanation was attached to each application, and they were framed and hung below pictures of our elite citizens in the meeting hall. We hoped that Madam X would continue to write applications. What more could she desire than such an understanding and receptive community? She was terribly fortunate. From her first day on Five Spice Street, she must have decided not to move even an inch from this place that could satisfy all her desires. After quietly gaining advantages, and fearing jealousy, she wrote applications to express her firm relationship with the people. We needn't pay much attention to the contents of her applications (she herself didn't seem to care, for she hadn't once come by to insist on any of them). Though half her house collapsed, didn't she still live there comfortably? If she had received material help, she might have ceased her spiritual pursuits. We wisely ignored her requests, enabling her to redouble her efforts and achieve even more.

Madam X lived in that small, shabby, half-collapsed house. She reminded people to pay attention to her applications so that she could remain isolated from the crowds. She became as proficient in writing applications as she had been in using microscopes. She also called them *creations*. Initially, she began each document with distinctively large characters to indicate what she was applying for. Thus, we knew the contents of her application. But once her applications became "creations," no one could understand them. They were full of disconnected, broken words and phrases. They were repetitive and excessively long. Luckily, nobody walked into the trap. Why would we want to understand those absolutely meaningless things? It was simple: almost every day, Madam X submitted applications; she had finally realized that she'd made the mistake of isolating herself. This was advantageous to us: we welcomed it. Sometimes, she wanted to complain a little, and put these complaints into her applications. This was all right. In any case, nobody would read them. We certainly didn't read her applications, so how could we use old impressions to judge a person? Maybe there actually weren't any complaints in her applications. Maybe they were filled with praise? Why not? From the position she had achieved (without expending the slightest effort), from the caring the people felt for her, she certainly could have written some praise: this should have been the wellspring of her inspiration. We wished she would come up with even more witty remarks and even odder ways of organizing her words to write her praise. We would preserve what she wrote for our descendants decades and centuries hence.

As a result of our encouragement, Madam X wrote even more applications, a new one almost every day. So as not to sway her, and to heed her request that others not bother her, we didn't go to her home to pick up her applications but sent someone to her shop to pretend to buy beans. She tacitly understood: she would wrap the beans in the application sheets and give them to the person. The writer confirmed that she deeply appreciated the profound consideration of the community. Once when buying beans, the writer (this time, as it happened, he went himself) saw that Madam X's "eyes were watering." After receiving her applications, the people couldn't help but sigh again and again: Madam X was terrific! Using the applications as bean wrappers was a splendid idea! A "post-future" creation! Even more wonderful was her carefree attitude—she actually was carefree as she wrapped beans with the application sheets! Our Five Spice Street had characters; all of us had become characters!

The more applications she wrote, the more ardent she became. She wrote not only on paper but also on the whitewashed wall of the small half-house. Dr. A's gaze pierced her wall like a knife and found it dotted with tadpole-like little characters. It seemed that X didn't abstain from her nighttime activities. She frequently told her patrons: "Last night, I had insomnia and wrote until dawn." Her tone was as casual as if she had said, "I sold another ten pounds of peanuts." Once she linked writing applications and selling peanuts, her private life no longer interested us. Her half-collapsed house also kept visitors away. Even such an enthusiastic person as her husband's good friend didn't have the guts to go into the dangerous house to "steal a look at her ID card" (even though X herself had asserted that "she could live there at least five more years").

The writer bet that even if Madam X now wrote her applications with chalk all over the walls of everyone's home, people would still ignore her, because: (1) no one would walk into her trap to try to figure out what she had written; and (2) this was monotonous and dull, absolutely different from her earlier sexual exploits. Who had the patience to watch her doodling with chalk? Just let her draw. I wouldn't pay the slightest attention. Even if it's valuable for research, let posterity deal with it. Our responsibility is only to provide her with space, protect her work, and leave it for future generations. Since her works haven't yet been evaluated, she mustn't expect any privileges (she has already gained a lot from us!). Whether it's gold or brass, this is something our descendants must settle! Before this appraisal, we will continue to regard her, as always, as a peanut vendor, both friendly and mysterious. Imagine how we will introduce ourselves to the outside delegation. We'll describe the wave of the future—how it will flourish and develop here, how much deep philosophy it contained, and then we will suddenly say: "Our representative of the wave of the future is a peanut vendor!"

The delegation will be dumbfounded! How indescribably pleasant! Now, at last, we've thought it through and won't expend any more effort to drag her into the ranks of our elite citizens. We want her to be a peanut vendor forever. This is best for her and for us. But we also hope she won't consider herself simply a peanut vendor and let up on writing applications. We want her to go on writing applications. If she wants to be recognized posthumously, could she do any better than by writing applications? Her position will be secured only by the number of her applications. In this lies the value of her existence. When all is said and done, Madam X is full of petty tricks. Without any hints from us, she understands these principles and consciously goes about implementing them. And so we continued receiving applications from her (still in the form of wrappers). We were satisfied that she did not make her daily activities public. In this way, we had a kind of tacit agreement with her, the sort of agreement that exists between a fish and water.

One cloudy morning, Madam X walked to the suburbs and sat on the flagstone where she had spent the night a long time ago with some young guy. She picked up a coin from the flagstone. It had dropped out of his pocket that night. She recalled everything about that night, how it was that in the end they hadn't done anything. She laughed for no reason. She threw the coin with all her might into a distant thicket.

She didn't know that two of our Five Spice Street scouts were lying in wait! People had been uneasy about her going out so early, and we had to send people to follow her. If Madam X had run into something unexpected, our plan would have been wrecked; it would have been a disgrace. After seeing her on the flagstone, our scouts wondered if she was waiting for P. The two thought of P at the same time. He had made a deep impression on the people of Five Spice Street. If she was waiting for P, what the two scouts saw would be most fascinating. And so they were very excited. In order to satisfy the wishes of the people on Five Spice Street, they wanted to recite an invocation summoning the romantic P, whose whereabouts they didn't know. They waited and waited, but P didn't show up. Instead, they saw Madam X asleep on the flagstone (perhaps she was faking this).

Actually, Madam X was sleeping. To be sure, we can also say she wasn't, because her dream life was as clear as day. Her eyes were wide open, but she didn't see anything. She slept this way until dusk, then yawned, sat up, and headed back to Five Spice Street.

Our scouts saw her taking light steps, striding toward tomorrow, striding toward the beautiful wave of the future. They were suddenly moved. They sighed and said loudly, "From the perspective of the grand sweep of history, what has happened on our Five Spice Street is so heroic and romantic!"

Naturally, this marvelous scene quickly appeared in the writer's notebook. After a series of baptisms, everyone now acknowledges that Madam X is "inexpressibly wonderful." Even the widow does not disagree.

Of course, this "inexpressible" feeling is different for everyone.